HARD
JUSTICE

ANDY WISEMAN

Andy W

Acknowledgements

To Jo Spir for all her hard work in helping me produce this
book, and more importantly, her patience.

*For my good friends, Tony Hall and Jo Spir, and the belief and
encouragement they provided all those years ago.*

All characters and events in this publication are fictitious and
any resemblance to real persons, living or dead, is purely
coincidental.

ISBN: 978 1 916181 80 9

CHAPTER 1

Harry was finding it difficult to breathe. The arm wrapped around his throat was tight, strong, and unrelenting.

Harry's assailant had attacked him from behind, to hold him in a vice-like neck-lock, the crook of his elbow pressing hard against Harry's Adam's apple, his beer gut against Harry's lower back. Harry could feel hot breath on the side of his face, as his attacker made disparaging remarks about his advancing years and questionable parentage, while trying to squeeze the life out of him.

Harry sensed the approach of attacker number three, just before he entered his peripheral vision. He cursed himself for getting involved; for not minding his own business.

Harry had gone out for a couple of beers 'early doors' after what had been a busy and difficult day fitting kitchen units. Harry was not, by any means, a qualified or experienced tradesman; he generally achieved what he set out to do by dogged persistence and a grim determination not to be beaten - not to mention a considerable amount of cursing and swearing.

His local pub was the Kings Arms in Crouch End, North London, and five minutes' walk from his home. Harry liked the Kings Arms because it was a traditional pub with traditional clientele.To the younger crowd this meant boring, which is why they generally passed it by in favour of the more popular drinking places - another reason Harry liked the Kings Arms.

Still in his work clothes of jeans and tee-shirt, Harry had thrown on his old army surplus combat jacket to brave the November chill and walk to the pub. He didn't own a car; he either used public transport or walked. And he didn't mind the extreme weather either; in fact he quite enjoyed it.

The creak of un-oiled hinges on the heavy timber door noisily announced his entrance to the pub's few customers, the smell of coal and wood smoke welcoming him in as he approached the bar. He gave a curt nod of the head as a greeting to the Barman.

'Usual?' the Barman asked. Harry simply nodded in reply. The Barman picked up a clean pint glass and then angled it under the pump. 'You ok?' he asked, conversationally and without curiosity, as he pulled back on the hand pump: one, two long strokes, and then a short third to top-up the pint of bitter.

'Fine,' replied Harry, equally noncommittal, putting the few pence in change into a plastic charity box that sat upon the bar, before then adding, 'You should get that fixed down.' He indicated the charity box. 'Someone might nick-it.'

'Don't get that kind of clientele,' said the Barman.

Harry took his pint over to a table close to the open fire. The Kings Arms consisted of one large rectangular room, with the fireplace at the far end to the entrance door. A solid oak bar ran partway down the back wall, opposite to the mullioned windows that overlooked the London streets. The bare floorboards, tables, chairs and bench seats were scarred with the passage of time. The yellow staining of nicotine on the walls evidenced the pre-smoking ban.

Dusty plate racks supported porcelain figures, Toby jugs, and trophies showing success in darts competitions of long ago. Beer mats, horse brasses, and notes of foreign currency were pinned to the exposed ceiling beams.

Once seated, Harry checked out the other customers: two male London Underground workers standing at one end of the bar - probably having just finished their working shift - discussing the merits of the English game of cricket; at a table towards the other end of the bar, quietly playing dominoes was an elderly couple. The elderly lady, sensing she was being watched, glanced up to meet Harry's gaze with a kindly smile, before turning back to her dominoes. Harry returned her smile, conscious he'd been caught intruding on a quiet moment.

That was the total amount of the pub's custom.

He took a sip from his pint, opened up a copy of the *Evening Standard* newspaper, to then settle himself down for a relaxing couple of hours.

Harry Windsor - given name, Henry - was forty one years old. He was a lean six foot two inches tall, and broad in the shoulder. His dark hair was collar length, casually swept back, and beginning to grey at the temples. Harry's idea of unwinding after a busy day was a couple of pints in the pub - maybe more if it'd been a *very* busy day. He rarely interacted with the locals, other than a polite greeting when required. Another advantage of the Kings Arms was no one bothered you with inane banter - unless you wanted it. He'd always preferred his own company, the solitude of his own thoughts. The irony that he did this in a public place was not lost on him.

He didn't get his relaxing couple of hours, because the creak of door hinges had announced new arrivals.

A wall of sound preceded the group of five young people who entered, closely followed by a thick fog of aftershave and perfume: three guys who looked to be in their early twenties, and two young women, a blonde and a brunette who were probably in their late teens - though to Harry, they looked like they'd barely left school. It was a Saturday evening, and judging by the way they were dressed, they were on a big night out. The guys were wearing smart trousers, clean shiny shoes, and their best multi-coloured shirts - which of course were not tucked into their trousers; the girls were wearing... not a lot, as girls seemed to do those days: there was more flesh on show than cloth.

Harry then wondered when he'd turned into a grumpy old fart.

'Fuck me!' said the shortest of the three guys. 'It's like a fuckin' mausoleum in 'ere.' This got some laughs from his mates. 'All right, granddad?' asked 'Shorty', as they passed the elderly couple.

The Underground workers reluctantly and warily moved away from the bar, to give the new arrivals more space. Shorty winked at them, acknowledging their giving way. 'Mind the gap,' he said, 'the train now arriving at the bar is the lager express. All aboard, toot, toot.' He then mimed the pulling of a train chord, which his friends found highly amusing.

The Barman asked what they were drinking.

'Three lagers,' Shorty replied, before then turning to the two girls. 'What're you girls 'aving?' The girls surveyed the range of optics and the bottles in the chilled cabinet, clearly uncertain. 'Brandy and coke?' said Shorty, trying to be helpful, an arm around the waist of each girl.

Of the other two guys: the biggest of the three - and a bear of a man, with a shaven head - was closely examining the foreign currency pinned to the exposed beams; the third was taking a keen interest in the elderly couple's game of dominoes, a man of a similar build to Harry, with spiked gelled hair, a thick gold chain around his neck, and two or three gold bracelets on each wrist, which jangled as he pointed out the next move the elderly couple should play in their game of dominoes.

At the bar, Shorty continued to suggest drinks for the girls. 'I know what you'd like,' he said, as he squeezed their waists, 'a Harvey Wall Banger!..., Or... a Screwdriver!' he said, putting emphasis on the words 'banger' and 'screw'. 'No, no. Better still, a Muff Diver!'

'I don't think I've had one of those. What do they taste like?' asked the blonde.

Shorty licked his lips and assured her they tasted divine, while his hand reassuringly patted the thin cloth that covered her backside, which he then lifted to expose her bare buttocks. The blonde - who continued to study the row of optics in search of inspiration - seemed either not to notice, or care. Shorty then looked over to the Underground workers and gave them a conspiratorial wink of the eye. Their returned smiles were half-hearted.

He glanced in Harry's direction, also looking for approval. Harry looked him squarely and levelly in the eye, before returning his attention back to his newspaper. The youth smirked, thinking he'd won the 'staring-out-your-opponent competition', that so often seemed to determine the pecking order between males.

Harry knew and appreciated the value of posturing, and how it could determine if conflict was to happen. He'd looked away in embarrassment rather than fear. Looking at the exposed buttocks of a girl young enough to be his daughter - not that he had a daughter - was something he found uncomfortable.

Harry then wondered when he'd turned into a prude.

Raucous laughter drew Harry's attention back. 'Spike', had picked up a domino, and was stamping it down upon the table, shouting, 'Check-mate!' while the elderly couple were rigid with fear, intimidated by the youth's loutish behaviour.

Bored with playing dominoes, Spike then turned his attention to the elderly lady's handbag, snatching it up from the chair beside her. 'What 'ave we 'ere?' he said. 'What exactly *does* a lady keep in her 'andbag?' The elderly gentleman - unsure what to do but feeling an obligation to protect his wife - started to rise from his seat, while Spike's friends looked on, curious to see what would happen next. 'Sit down granddad, if you know what's good for you,' Spike told the old man.

The elderly gentleman didn't need to be told twice.

Harry looked across to the Barman - who was studiously polishing glasses - to catch his eye, and then raise questioning eyebrows, but the Barman quickly broke eye contact to continue his polishing.

Harry sighed heavily as he folded up his newspaper. *No respect.*

By this point, Spike had had a good rummage in the old lady's handbag, before plucking out her purse, and to then hold it aloft. 'Bingo!'

'Please,' the elderly woman said, holding out her hand.

Grinning, Spike quickly turned away from her to shield his next move, but as he did so, he bumped into six foot two inches of muscle and attitude standing right behind him.

'Put it back,' said Harry, to which a look of surprise and uncertainty crossed Spike's face. 'Put it back and apologise to the lady.'

Spike stared at Harry. He then looked across to his friends. All conversation had stopped: all eyes on Harry and Spike.

Spike just shrugged. 'Hey, man, just fooling. No 'arm meant,' he said, while grinning at Harry, who regarded him coldly. Spike again looked across to his friends for support, to see them grinning back at him. 'See, just fooling.'

Harry continued to hold Spike's gaze. Waiting. After an uneasy moment, Spike then turned around to the elderly couple, and placed the old lady's bag on the table in front of her. 'Sorry darlin',' he said, still grinning, and with no trace of sincerity or remorse.

From his position behind Spike, Harry saw him once again shoot a glance across to his mates, and when he saw the muscles in the youth's neck start to tense, he slowly and subtly eased his weight and balance to his back foot. A fraction of a second later, Spike spun around, his left arm and fist swinging towards Harry's face, but with his weight and balance now on his back foot, all Harry had to do was just simply duck.

The punch sailed harmlessly over his head.

The momentum of the swing had left Spike's body open and exposed. Seeing this, Harry then dipped his shoulder to deliver a powerful right jab to Spike's ribs, before quickly adjusting his balance in preparation for delivering a follow-up left hook, and bringing the fight to an end.

But Spike stayed down on one knee, holding his side, clearly in pain, and, for the moment, going nowhere.

That altercation had lasted only a matter of seconds, yet time seemed to have stood still. The onlookers' had not moved; had not spoken. The fight had finished with Harry having his back to the bar, and to Spike's friends, leaving him exposed: and he knew it.

That was when the 'Big Guy' launched himself on to Harry's back.

Harry was finding it difficult to breathe. The arm wrapped around his throat, was tight, strong, and unrelenting.

Big Guy was holding him in a vice-like neck-lock, the crook of his elbow pressing hard against Harry's Adam's apple, his beer gut against Harry's lower back. Harry could also feel hot breath on the side of his face, as his attacker made disparaging remarks about his advancing years and questionable parentage, while trying to squeeze the life out of him.

The two girls were screaming hysterically. The elderly couple were cowering in their seats. The Underground workers' faces showed their indecision about whether to get involved or not. The Barman stayed behind the safety of the bar, shouting for the fight to stop or he would phone the police.

Harry sensed the approach of Shorty, just before he entered his peripheral vision. He silently cursed himself for getting involved; for not minding his own business.

Shorty took a swing at the captured Harry, the punch catching him low on the cheek. Harry felt soft flesh make contact with hard teeth, closely followed by a metallic taste, the blow serving only to annoy him rather than inflict any serious damage. Shorty's lack of height meant he'd been unable to get any weight behind the punch. 'Hold him still,' said Shorty to Big Guy, as he prepared himself for a run-up at Harry.

As Shorty launched himself forward, Harry kicked out, his steel toe-capped safety boot connecting with Shorty's groin area. Shorty dropped to the ground, pole axed, screaming like a girl.

Taking advantage of this surprise turn of events - to everyone but Harry - Harry then planted both feet firmly on the ground and pushed hard, propelling himself and his captor backwards towards the oak bar. Big Guy hit the bar with a resounding crash, the small of his back taking the full impact. Harry heard the rattle and breaking of glass as he felt the vibration of the impact through Big Guy's body, yet the grip around his neck loosened only slightly.

Harry couldn't afford to lose momentum of attack, so he dipped his head forward, to then whip it back, his crown striking his attacker on the bridge of the nose. Without pausing, he did it again, feeling the bridge shatter. Then, raising a foot and using Big Guy's shin as a guide, Harry stamped the heel of his work boot hard down upon the arch of the man's leather brogue, to feel fragile bones give way. Big Guy screamed with pain, finally releasing his grip. As he did so, Harry drove his elbow backwards into soft flesh, aiming a few inches deeper than contact point, to maximise impact.

As his attacker slowly slid down the bar to the floor, Harry turned, poised to strike: fists clenched, body tense, adrenalin racing to deliver the killing blow. But the big man's eyes were glazed and unfocussed, his face a mask of blood and snot.

He hit the floor, body slumped. Unconscious.

Harry stepped away to study his attacker. Some might have said he looked a little disappointed.

But the fight was not yet over. While Shorty was still in the foetal position on the floor, whimpering in pain, and wondering if having sex would ever again be a possibility, Spike was back on his feet. And he was holding something.

A faint 'snick' sound was then heard.

Harry turned, to once again put his back to the bar, with even less room to manoeuvre. But the danger now lay in front. Spike had plenty of space and, in his hand, a flick knife. He was still hurting from Harry's blow, but now fancied his chances.

He grinned at Harry.

He then feinted a lunge with the knife. Harry leaned away from the blow. Spike feinted another lunge. And then another. Each time Harry swerved away, the bar top pressing against his back, Big Guy unconscious at his feet, restricting his movement. Harry knew Spike was testing him. That he was weighing-up his speed and agility and would soon strike, proper.

He also knew he had to end the fight. And end it soon.

Harry shifted his weight to his back foot, and then flicked out a sidekick towards Spike's surprised face, which he evaded by quickly leaning back, as Harry knew he would.

Harry had to get him off balance.

He aimed a roundhouse kick towards Spike's left side. Spike skipped to his right. But Harry didn't follow through with the kick. Instead - in anticipation - he swept his left arm across the bar, scooped up the heavy coin-filled charity box, to then bring it crashing against Spike's right temple.

Spike's legs gave way, and he also crumpled to the floor.

A hush had fallen.

The silence was broken by the chink of coins, as Harry replaced the charity box back on the bar. But not before glancing at the name on the box: Barnardos. The irony brought a smile to his face.

The two young girls were clinging to each other, rigid with fear, their faces frozen, wide eyed and open mouthed, tear streaked mascara staining their cheeks.

Kneeling down next to Spike, who was semi-conscious and trying to blink away the dizziness, Harry picked the flick knife up from the floor and inspected it. It was shiny and new. The handle was of bone, the blade keen. The weight felt good; balanced.

Aware of movement within his line of vision, Harry looked up to make eye contact with the elderly lady. He saw appreciation... yet also uncertainty and apprehension. For a brief moment he was looking into the eyes of another woman. A woman whom he'd held dear, and who'd loved him dearly also.

He blinked. The image was gone.

He looked back at Spike, who was now watching him carefully, fear in his eyes. He flinched as Harry reached out towards him, but it was only to pick up the elderly lady's bag that had fallen to the floor. Standing, he placed the bag back on the table in front of her. As she retrieved it, her fingers lightly and tenderly brushed the back of Harry's hand.

That intimate gesture left Harry feeling awkward and humbled.

He looked at the knife, wondering what to do with it. He retracted the blade, then placed it in his pocket. Nodding a courteous farewell to the Barman, Harry then collected his jacket and newspaper and drained his glass, before sauntering out into the chilly November evening.

CHAPTER 2

At exactly seven o'clock in the morning, Harry awoke. He didn't need to set an alarm clock. Every morning, for a fraction of a second and before he was fully awake, he still thought he could hear the banging of the warder's fist upon the cell door.

Swinging his long legs out of bed, he sat for a moment to collect his thoughts. Harry wasn't a morning person - not before caffeine, anyway.

Harry's bedroom was sparsely furnished: a matt black metal framed bed, a double freestanding wardrobe of Jacobean mahogany with bedside cabinets to match, and - other than the beige cord carpeting and cream painted walls - that was it. There was nothing else. No pictures, wall hangings, mirrors, knick-knacks or clutter of any kind.

He headed towards the en-suite bathroom which was equally spartan: a spacious walk-in shower, white ceramic toilet and basin, black ceramic floor and wall tile finish, a mirror above the basin, a wall-fixed glass holder containing a single toothbrush and toothpaste, and a bottle of shampoo and a bar of soap in the shower. Harry didn't like clutter. "A cluttered room is a cluttered mind", his mother used to say - his foster mother. Harry had read somewhere that there was a name for this particular style, and it was called 'minimalist'. *Yeah, whatever.* While cleaning his teeth, he was careful to avoid the inside of his cheek where it'd been cut during his fight in the pub, two days ago. A gentle probing with his tongue confirmed it was still a little sore. He inspected his face. Shorty's punch had caused some bruising, which was now turning a yellowy black colour. It was of no consequence. 'I've had worse,' he said to himself.

Once showered and dressed in clean blue jeans and a tee-shirt, he collected the mail from the front door mail basket, taking time to sift through and separate his morning newspaper and mail, from that of his two tenants', upstairs. Their mail he placed on a small table in the hallway.

In the kitchen of his own ground floor flat, he turned a radio to a low volume, before then putting the kettle on. Harry's kitchen, like his bedroom and bathroom, was also new: light oak finished units with black granite worktops, brushed aluminium oven, hob and extractor; all offset with grey slate flooring. There were very few items on the worktops. It looked unused.

With a mug of tea, he took a seat at the kitchen table, to look out through double French doors to a small, high walled courtyard garden. The garden was simple and elegant in its layout, with a variety of evergreen shrubs and tall grasses surrounded by a gravel base. This was an easy to maintain garden, which was just as well, because gardening was still an enigma to Harry. He made a mental note on his to do list to read more about gardening. The garden was one of his favourite places. In one corner was a timber bench, where - out of sight of overlooking windows - he would spend many an hour just thinking, while listening to the wind whisper through the long grasses. He never felt alone in that garden. Sometimes he would talk to his mother, tell her about his day, how he was getting on with the building work to the house; how much he missed her. These conversations would be held in hushed tones, because Harry always felt a little awkward talking about feelings - *and* because he didn't want his tenants or neighbours to by-chance overhear him. They would probably think he was mad, sitting outside in all weathers, talking to a woman who'd died a few years ago, and whose ashes were buried under a large mock Greek urn that stood near the timber bench. Harry still couldn't decide if the urn was a bit OTT, and that maybe something a little more subtle might be more appropriate for a woman as genteel as his mother: a true lady.

Having partly drunk his tea and starting to feel a little more alert, he decided to tackle the morning's post. As per usual, junk mail seemed to be the bulk. The only two items of any interest were a gas bill - which wasn't too expensive - and a letter from the bank - which was.

This was the letter Harry had been expecting. Dreading. Harry's house was previously owned by his mother. On her death it had been willed to Harry and his foster brother, Stephen. Their mother's passing, and the circumstances of it, had hit Harry hard, and it tormented him still. Wanting to keep some memory of his mother, and provide himself with an alternate form of employment, he'd paid Stephen for his share of the house, rather than sell it. But before he could do that, he had to draw up a business plan on how he proposed to cost and convert the large three storied Victorian house into self contained flats, and then present it to the bank for funding, which they'd granted. The problem was, Harry was behind schedule with the works. He'd completed three of the flats - one of which being his own ground floor flat - with two left to do.

Harry wasn't a qualified tradesman. Apart from some basic training on carpentry while he'd been inside, he was mostly self-taught, which - along with being a perfectionist - meant it took longer to complete a task. Which was why he was behind schedule, behind with his payments, and the bank wanted to speak to him. But with only the income from the two flats that were finished and tenanted, he was barely managing to cover his costs.

He pushed the letter away. It would have to wait. He would have to stall the bank. He had to finish flat number four. He just needed another couple of weeks. A new tenant would bring in a month's rent as deposit, and a month's rent in advance. He'd be over the worst by then. He flicked through a DIY manual on how to fit kitchens while he finished his tea. Once he had, he washed, dried, and then put the mug away. Then, while gazing out through the French doors at his garden, he pondered his next move. Today, he needed to order some building materials for delivery. Normally he would have paid with his debit card, but he felt sure the bank would have put a block on it until he'd cleared the arrears. Tomorrow was rent day for the two tenants he already had. Could he ask them for it today, he wondered? Would that be unreasonable? Their tenancy agreements clearly stated what day the rent was due, so they would be within their rights to say no. Harry wanted to do the right thing. To be reasonable and fair. He'd collected money on many occasions over the years, on behalf of a man who was now his ex-employer, and the methods he'd used had been far from reasonable and fair. But that was in the past.

"Going straight' isn't proving to be easy, mother,' he said, quietly.

Harry checked the time. Lucy, in flat three, was a veterinary nurse and would be leaving for work soon.

She answered the door after the second time of knocking.

'Hi, Harry.'

'Hi, Lucy,' replied Harry.

'Sorry I took so long,' she said, 'I was in the shower.'

'So I see,' said Harry. Lucy was wrapped in a large towel that barely reached down to the tops of her thighs, with a smaller towel wrapped around her head, turban style. 'Sorry to bother you, Lucy -'

'You can bother me anytime you like, Harry,' she said, interrupting. 'Even when I'm wet.' She grinned.

Harry smiled back.

Lucy was in her mid-twenties. She was five foot seven inches tall, and she was a redhead with a wicked sense of humour; a fiery temptress. Harry liked her. He liked her a lot. But, he'd told himself, it would not be a good idea to get involved with his tenants.

'Err, Lucy,' he began, not quite sure where to start, then opting for a lie, 'I'm probably going to be away most of tomorrow -'

'Oh. Are you going anywhere interesting?' she asked, again interrupting him.

'Well -'

'Because, I'm not working tomorrow, and if you wanted some company, I could come with you,' she said, while smiling broadly and adjusting her towel slowly enough to afford him a glimpse of cleavage.

She wasn't making it easy for him. In fact, she was purposely teasing him, so he gave her the stern look with the raised eyebrow, the one that said, *stop it young lady, I know what you're doing.* 'Would it be okay if I collected the rent today, instead of tomorrow?'

'Of course, I have it ready for you.' She turned and retreated into the flat, giving Harry a view of a rounded backside that was only just covered with towelling. She returned with a cheque. Cash would have been better under the present circumstances, but Harry knew where he could get it cashed - other than his bank.

'Oh, Harry. One of the doors on my bedroom cupboard is a bit loose. Would you mind looking at it some time?

'Sure, no problem,' he replied.

'It probably just wants screwing a bit tighter,' she said, flashing her green eyes at him. Harry smiled, waved the cheque to say thank you, and turned to leave. 'Don't forget, if you want some company tomorrow, just knock-me-up early,' she called after him, laughing as she closed the door to her flat.

Harry shook his head, 'Women!'

Old Mr Jackson, who was in flat two, was an ex soldier and an old friend of his mother's from her theatre days. Despite his age, Mr Jackson led a very active life, so Harry would have to take his chances as to whether or not he would be in. He knocked on the door. As much as Harry needed the money from his tenant - and "cash was king" with Mr Jackson - a tiny part of him hoped he wasn't in. Mr Jackson was a real gentleman; but a talker. Harry had heard more war stories than he could remember. He didn't mind the stories about his mother, though; about her life on and off the stage. This, if Harry were honest with himself, was probably the reason he'd let the flat to the old boy in the first place.

He heard the rattle of the key in the lock. 'Once more unto the breech, dear friends,' he said to himself.

'Custer!' said the old boy, as he opened the door. 'Damned fine General!' Obviously nothing wrong with his hearing, thought Harry. 'Come in, my boy, come in. Did I ever tell you about General Custer and how he and his men...'

The door closed behind Harry.

CHAPTER 3

The rush hour traffic was a nightmare, and the weather was foul - matched equally with Izzy's mood, which was becoming all the more stormy as she struggled to drive through the London traffic, using the powerful engine of her Saab to accelerate through gaps, braking hard and often, leaving a trail of blaring horns in her wake.

Isobelle Harker was a newspaper reporter who was on her way to interview a have-a-go-hero. In her opinion it was a non-story, but her editor had insisted she cover it.

It had all started yesterday, when she'd arrived at the office - slightly late.

'What fucking time do you call this?' said Geoff, her editor. 'It's half way through the fucking morning, for Christ's sake.'

Geoff was from Yorkshire, and didn't believe in mincing his words. Geoff didn't just call a "spade a spade", he called it a "fucking spade". He was a man in his late fifties, short, overweight, and fighting a losing battle with a comb-over hairstyle. His plain speaking was given out freely to anyone who pissed him off, and lately that was Izzy, who seemed to hold the monopoly on pissing-off Geoff.

After telling her not to bother taking her coat off, Geoff then thrust a piece of paper at her and told her to get down to the Kings Arms pub in Crouch End, to do a story on a have-a-go-hero who'd come to the rescue of an elderly couple.

'Isn't there anything a bit more... interesting?' she asked him. Then, realising, 'This is that grotty looking pub on the High Street,' she said. 'And it's probably full of losers.'

'No, it's small and quaint, and frequented by unusual characters,' Geoff replied, doing his best to suppress a torrent of plain speaking. 'Look at it as a feel-good story. A dark handsome stranger comes to the rescue of an elderly couple. He's a combination of Bruce Lee, Superman, and Don Quixote all rolled into one - and hospitalised three men. People love that kind of thing.'

'He sounds like a lunatic... And who the chuff is Don Quixote?'

'Oh, for the love of Christ,' said Geoff, before turning his attention back to what he'd been doing prior to Izzy's late arrival.

Izzy looked down at the piece of paper. 'Is this all the information we've got?' she asked. 'It doesn't give me a lot to go on.'

'You're an Investigative fucking Reporter. Fucking investigate,' said Geoff; plainly.

So that was what she did; went to the "quaint" little pub to investigate. 'Isobelle Harker, *North London Gazette*,' she said, introducing herself to the Barman, who was polishing glasses. After she told him why she was there, she then asked, 'How did the fight start?' The Barman just shrugged his shoulders. 'Are you saying you didn't see how the fight started?' The Barman pulled a face - which Izzy was unable to tell if meant yes or no - and continued to polish glasses. He obviously doesn't want to get involved, she thought. *This is going to be like pulling teeth.* 'Do you get a lot of trouble in here?' she asked. 'Because, surely it can't be good for business, especially if it becomes common knowledge.' The Barman paused in his cleaning of the glasses, her veiled threat clear to see. And just to drive the point home, she then added, 'And I wouldn't have thought the brewery would be too happy, either. Surely it's in everyone's interest that loutish behaviour is discouraged? The general public's, the brewery's... yours?'

At this, the Barman wearily put down his cloth and glass, to then lean forward on the bar. 'Three young lads and two young lassies came in,' he said. 'One of the lads got a bit... boisterous, you might say, with the old couple who are at that table over there.' He indicated by nodding his head in their direction. 'Then the tall fella got up and stopped it.'

'Why didn't you stop it?'

'There were three of them. Nasty pieces of work they were too, believe me. Doing this kind of job, you can tell.'

'Yet a complete stranger stepped in, who could have been seriously hurt.'

'That's the thing. He was just as dangerous. Took those three guys apart like it was a stroll in the park. Used some kind of Kung Fu boxing. The unsettling bit about the whole thing was that he hardly said a word. No screaming, or shouting threats, just told the kid to give the purse back and apologise. That's when the kid took a swing at the tall fella. End of story, as they say.'

'He asked him to apologise?' she asked, a little surprised.

'Yep.'

'Very civilised,' she then said, more to herself than anyone else. 'Who is he?'

'No idea.'

'Is he a local?'

'Depends what you call "a local". He comes in fairly regular.'

'Yet you don't know his name?'

'He's never told me, and I've never asked.'

'How am I supposed to find him?' she said, exasperated. 'My editor is expecting a story.'

'Not my problem, lady,' he replied, picking up his cloth and glass. 'You could try asking the police. They've been and taken statements, though I doubt they'll put much effort into it. It's not as though decent people got hurt.'

Not getting anywhere with the Barman, Izzy went over to the elderly couple to ask them their version of what had happened.

While playing dominoes, Ivy and Jim gave her a running commentary on how the trouble had started. How the "heroic young man" - they didn't know his name - had stepped in to stop the "young hoodlums" causing trouble. Jim told Izzy that the hoodlums didn't know how lucky they'd been. If he'd been a bit younger, he would've taken them outside and taught them some manners. Ivy told him to stop being so melodramatic, and that he probably would have put his back out, anyway.

Their description of their hero was as vague and varied as their estimation of his age. Izzy wondered if they were being deliberately obtuse to protect their saviour, or whether it was just their age.

Fortunately, just when she thought she'd come to a dead-end, the Barman recalled seeing the tall fella having breakfast in Ricardo's cafe on a couple of occasions.

This was where she was now heading. Hoping - if not praying - that the tall fella would be there, because she was loathe to go back to that obnoxious little Yorkshireman and give him the satisfaction of reprimanding her for not having a story.

Izzy had, on more than one occasion, visualised herself telling Geoff to stick his job up his fat backside, but since her father had reduced her allowance, she couldn't afford to. At least not until she'd found another job, or she proved them all wrong - her editor and her colleagues who she knew all thought of her as a spoilt-little-rich-bitch - that she could be a top reporter. She also knew her father and step-mother continually despaired of her, of the fact she would be thirty this year, was still not married, or had a successful career.

When she felt the hot sting of tears welling up, she attempted to blink them away, rather than risk smudging her mascara by wiping, but in doing so, she drifted close to the centre of the road. A loud crunching bang made her jerk and yelp with surprise, as her wing mirror hit the wing mirror of an oncoming car. 'Shit!' she said, glancing out the side window at the dangling wing mirror. 'Shit, shit, shitting, shit!' She quickly glanced in her rear view mirror to check on the other car. She could see it had braked to a stop, and that a man had jumped out and was gesturing in a less than friendly manner.

She carried on. She didn't have time to stop, and she certainly didn't relish a confrontation.

When she finally got to the cafe, she had to drive around the block a number of times, before a parking space on the opposite side of the road became available. Then, to add to her already stressful morning, she realised she didn't have any change for the parking meter, and as it was before nine o'clock, most of the shops were still closed. She toyed with the idea of going into Ricardo's cafe to get some change, but - rather than take her life in her hands by crossing the busy road more times than she had to - she decided against it. Besides, she told herself, the chances of a traffic warden being around at that time of the morning were slim, and the interview shouldn't take long; in fact, no time at all if the tall fella wasn't there.

As Izzy locked her car, she noticed she was parked outside a boutique. Maybe she would treat herself to some retail therapy later. In the meantime, she would have to make do with a cappuccino and a croissant.

As she approached the cafe, she was disappointed to see it was not of the modern European style, but a single frontage of Georgian window, with tired looking paintwork, and half-height net curtains that shielded the customers from the outside world. It's a tea room, she thought, as she opened the door and stepped inside. As she did so, her sight, hearing, and sense of smell were attacked.

It was probably the level of noise that struck her first; the boom of male voices, shouting and laughing over the constant hum of chatter and rattling crockery. The second thing to assault her senses was the smell; fried food and old cooking oil hung heavy in the air, which, along with the under-lying smell of body odour, threatened to make her gag. In a moment of panic - and to avoid throwing-up - she found herself desperately trying to decide whether it would be better to breathe through her nose, or through her mouth. She wouldn't recall which action she took - and nor did she vomit - because what met her eyes distracted her from thinking about it.

The cafe was half full of men. Of workmen. Dirty workmen, wearing dirty work boots, and dirty work clothes. Some of which, despite the time of year, did not seem to cover all extremities. The tops of buttocks where exposed, as were portions of gut, hanging over straining belt buckles, peeking out from under tee-shirts that appeared to have shrunk in the wash. She found her memory drifting back to the images of pork belly she'd seen on display at the butcher's counter in her local supermarket.

'Oi, darlin',' came a shout, 'shut the door will ya. My sausage is getting all cold and shrivelled.' This was followed by raucous laughter and comments about not wanting a shrivelled sausage.

Izzy couldn't decide what to do. Go into the cafe and close her only means of escape, or to flee, out into the fresh purifying London air.

She took a deep breath, and chose the former. With her cheeks burning to the point of self combustion, and aware that while she was still standing she was the focus of attention, she quickly scanned the cafe for her intended target. Along with a very vague description, she'd been told that the man she was looking for had been wearing what appeared to be an old army surplus combat jacket.

She spotted a man sitting alone, reading a newspaper. He wasn't wearing a jacket, but she could see a fading bruise on his face.

Taking a chance, she approached his table. 'Do you mind if I sit here?' she asked the man. He glanced up at her, then away, to survey the rest of the cafe, taking in the occupied tables and the few unoccupied tables that remained, making it clear he was wondering why she needed to sit at his table, rather than at an empty one. He looked back at her, studied her for a moment, and then returned to his newspaper.

Taking his lack of response for a reluctant yes, she plucked a paper serviette from a holder on the table, and - still feeling the centre of attention - quickly dusted-off the red faux leather bench seat of spilled salt and pepper - *and God knows what else!* She then quickly sat, bumping knees with the man as she did so. Feeling her cheeks again redden, she mumbled an apology. At least she could confirm he was tall, she found herself thinking. Once seated, she then wiped an area of the table in front of her, sensing, rather than seeing, the look of disapproval from the man opposite.

Izzy glanced around, looking for someone to serve her. A less-than-young, bleach-blonde Waitress approached with a heaped plate of disgusting looking fried food. 'Excuse me,' she said to the Waitress. 'Can you get me a cappuccino, please?'

'You order at the counter,' the Waitress replied, with a jerk of her head towards the other end of the cafe, as she placed the plate of food in front of the man sitting opposite.

The last thing Izzy wanted to do was to again draw attention to herself by going to the counter, but she could hardly sit there with nothing to eat or drink.

Taking a breath, she slid out from the bench seat, again bumping the man's knees, and again mumbling an apology. Staring straight ahead, she then made her way towards the counter.

'Yes, luv?' asked the burly guy behind the counter.

'Cappuccino, please,' she replied.

'Don't do frothy coffee.'

'Sorry?'

'Cappuccino. Don't do it. This ain't the Ritz, darlin'. It's regular, or tea.'

Izzy looked at the stubbled face leering back at her. The man's huge stomach was covered by a food stained apron. Some of the stains looked to be a few days old. She noticed he had egg yolk in the corner of his mouth. 'Regular is fine,' she said. She decided to pass on the croissant. Big hairy hands poured 'coffee' into a chipped mug and then pushed it towards her. She paid, and then retreated back to her seat.

As she passed the man sitting at her table, she glanced over his shoulder to the space on the seat next to him. She saw a folded coat. It was green, but whether it was a combat jacket, she couldn't be sure. She placed her coffee on the table, and slid onto the bench seat, taking care not to again bump knees. The man's newspaper was now laid on the table, and he was reading it while eating his breakfast. He appeared to be doing the crossword.

Izzy still didn't know if this was the man she was looking for. Yes, he resembled the vague description she'd been given, and yes, he had some bruising on his face where the "have-a-go-hero" had been punched, and yes, he was having a rather large cholesterol laden breakfast in Ricardo's cafe. But that hardly narrowed it down. The population of London was what, eight million or so?

She raised the mug of coffee to her lips, taking care to avoid the chipped parts, and took a sip - it tasted as good as it looked. As she tentatively sipped, she studied the man opposite her. She guessed he was in his late thirties, maybe early forties. He had a 'strong' face; handsome in a rugged sort of way; not like the pretty-boy-faced Hollywood actors that seemed to be popular - though Izzy felt his hair was a bit too long. *So, yesterday.* Unlike most of his fellow diners, he was both clean and cleanly dressed, making her wonder what exactly he did for a living. She noticed his finger nails were clean. She hated men with dirty fingers nails; the thought made her shudder. She didn't think he went to the lengths of a manicure, but he obviously made an effort with his appearance. His arms and shoulders were strong and toned beneath his close fitting tee-shirt, the pink colour of a first-aid plaster peeking from below the sleeve; until she realised it was not a plaster, but a nicotine patch. She was pleased to see he ate in a polite manner; in that he chewed his food with his mouth closed, and didn't gulp his drink of tea with a mouth full of food, only to then carry on eating. She watched him pick up a pen to fill-in the crossword. She mused as to which tabloid newspaper he was reading.

She decided he seemed quite civilised for a manual worker, if that was what he was. 'Food looks good,' she said to him, because she couldn't think of anything else to say.

The man looked up from his newspaper, paused, and then said, 'Do you like fried food?'

Izzy was caught off-guard by the question. She hated fried food: the look of it, the smell of it. She was surprised the muesli she'd had for breakfast had not as yet reappeared. 'Some,' she said, knowing she looked and sounded unconvincing.

He stared back at her.

She looked away, feigning interest in the decor of the cafe.

Harry was intrigued by the woman sitting opposite him. He estimated she was in her late twenties, and about five foot eight in height. She was stylishly dressed in trousers and a jacket that did not look cheap, and she had an accent that suggested a good education as well as background. Her hair was blonde, straight, and shoulder length with a casual parting, which - when she wasn't sweeping it back from her forehead by running her fingers through it in that affected way that women sometimes do - she would periodically tuck back behind one ear or the other. This lady has probably never had a fry-up in her life, he thought - and is *definitely* out of her comfort zone.

He watched her as she furtively looked around the cafe, studying its customers. She was doing a good job of hiding her emotions, but she was still revealing enough to show a thought process that swung from fascination to disgust, and then back again. He noticed she was wearing a large engagement ring, with which she absentmindedly fiddled as she studied the other diners, making Harry curious about the strength of her relationship.

Izzy's mind had wandered from her purpose for being there at the cafe, and she knew it had. She just couldn't help it; the way her mind seemed to lose focus sometimes and just drift off, leaving her really frustrated - not to mention everybody else she came into contact with. Izzy had been thinking about Jonathan, her fiancé. Watching the men in the cafe had set off a train of thought. She'd been comparing them to Jonathan. Of course, there *was* no comparison really, she told herself. Jonathan was everything they weren't: educated, refined *and* successful. But then she found herself thinking about his lesser points. How materialistic he was; how vain he could be; and how he was always sucking-up to her father. She wondered how her parents would react if she took a hairy-arsed builder home to meet them. The thought struck her as so bizarre and so funny, that a short, sharp, bark of a laugh, escaped her lips before she was able to smother it with her hand.

Harry smiled to himself, as he watched the young woman's observations end with a surprised yelp. Conscious she'd just become the focus of attention again, Izzy sneaked a glance at the man sitting opposite her. He was still studying his newspaper. Was he smiling, she asked herself? She could see a softening around his eyes, and what appeared to be the slight tug of a smile at the corners of his mouth. She wondered what was so damned funny. Then, getting a little annoyed and before she could stop herself, she said, 'That's quite a bruise you've got there. Been in a fight?'

The man looked up, smile fading, eyes narrowed.

Izzy felt her annoyance - and with it her bravery - suddenly desert her. The man bore no facial expression: not of anger, happiness, or indifference. Yet his eyes, which were of a light grey, seemed to look deep inside her: assessing her; judging her; touching her very soul, almost. For the first time in her young life, she felt vulnerable: afraid. Then - literally - in the blink of an eye, she saw what she thought was an amused twinkle.

She stared, opened mouthed.

'Another?' asked the man.

She stared dumbly back at him.

'Coffee,' he said, indicating her mug.

Realising, she shook her head.

He went to the counter for a refill.

Izzy was trying to make sense of what had just happened; why she was feeling confused. Why had she felt afraid - *he looked you in the eye, that's all* - and so... *excited?* This new thought brought more confusion. But she didn't get chance to dwell on it, because the man had returned and taken his seat opposite.

He leaned back and studied her.

She returned his gaze, attempting composure - if for no other reason than she didn't know where else to look.

'What do you want?' he asked her.

'I don't know what you mean,' she replied.

'You didn't come here for Rick's gourmet food and high class coffee.'

'I was just passing,'

'Just passing?' he said, surprise in his voice.

'Yes. I was walking past, and I thought I would have a coffee.'

The man smiled slightly, and then said, 'You're not 'Old Bill', then?'

'"Old Bill"?'

'Police.'

'Oh, no. I'm not the police.'

'Well, you're not good enough to be a reporter, so are you from the bank?' he asked, only to then see on her face, the same flare of annoyance he'd seen earlier. 'Which paper? Which newspaper do you work for?'

Izzy felt stung by his words; yet also curious by his remark about the bank. '*The North London Gazette,*' she replied, automatically.

'Isn't that a weekly paper?'

'It has lots of good stories.'

The man raised his eyebrows.

'Quality stories - feel good stories,' she added.

Harry continued to gaze at her impassively, happy to watch her confusion and discomfort.

Izzy could feel her annoyance levels rising. The man was toying with her, and he seemed to be enjoying it. 'Were you involved in a fight in the Kings Arms pub in Crouch End, last Saturday night?' she asked, slapping the palm of her hand upon the table top and surprising herself at how loud it sounded.

The man's response was to suddenly lean forward, placing both elbows on the table, while still cradling his mug of tea in both hands. Izzy, surprised by the movement, instinctively leaned back.

The man took a sip of his tea, eyes still fixed on Izzy.

'Off the record,' she said.

'Do reporters really say that?' asked Harry.

'What's your name?'

He took another sip of his tea.

'Is it Bruce? Or Don?'

He frowned.

'Doesn't matter,' she said. 'Were you in the Kings Arms?'

He sipped while studying her over the rim of his mug.

'Well?'

'Maybe,' he finally replied.

'Were you involved in a fight?' she asked him again.

Again, he said, 'Maybe.'

'You do know that all three of those kids had to go to A&E,' she told him. 'And, it's debatable if one of them will ever be able to father children.'

This raised a smile from Harry.

'Do you not have a conscience, or any guilt over what you did?'

This brought a scowl to Harry's face. He put his mug down a little too hard, and a little too quickly, spilling some of its contents.

Izzy flinched.

'Firstly,' he said, 'they weren't kids. Secondly, if someone pulls a knife on me, they get what they deserve.'

'A knife!'

'A flick knife. Very sharp.'

'Nobody said anything about a knife,' she said. 'Neither the Barman or the old couple mentioned a knife.'

'Did you ask the question?'

'Well... no. But surely -'

'How long have you been a reporter?'

'Investigative reporter,' she replied.

Harry flicked a glance towards the ceiling before then saying, 'How long have you been an *Investigative* reporter?'

'Why wouldn't they mention a knife?' she asked, genuinely surprised.

'Sometimes, people don't like to get too involved because... they're afraid.'

'Of what?' she said, trying to understand.

'Consequences,' he replied, simply. 'Besides, it's probably for the best. If the Old Bill knew there'd been a knife, they would probably take more of an interest in the case.'

'Looking for you, you mean?'

Izzy saw the man's eyes move from hers, to a point just over her shoulder.

'You're about to get a ticket.'

'A ticket?'

'The gold coloured Saab convertible you arrived in when you were "just passing", is about to get a parking ticket,' he replied, with a big lazy grin.

'Shit and bugger!' said Izzy, as she leapt from her seat, hurtling towards the door.

Harry watched with amusement - and with some concern - as the young woman scurried across the dangerously busy road to remonstrate with the traffic warden. His grin broadened as he watched her waving her arms around wildly, in an attempt to sway the decision of the warden into not giving her a ticket. He couldn't hear anything of the conversation between the feisty young female reporter and the traffic warden, only the muted roar of the London traffic. He felt like he was watching an old silent movie, like Buster Keaton or Harold Lloyd. For a brief moment, Harry actually found himself feeling sorry for the warden, but the warden seemed totally unfazed by the reporter's histrionics. As he slapped a ticket onto the young woman's windscreen, she gave one more frenetic wave of the arms, followed by a small leap into the air of frustration. Spontaneous laughter erupted around the cafe, from the customers who'd also been watching. Harry found himself laughing along with them.

When he finally managed to stop, he had to wipe tears from the corners of his eyes, while marvelling at how a good laugh could clear away worry and despondency so easily and quickly.

Izzy was fuming. The broken wing mirror wasn't going to be cheap to fix, and now she had a parking ticket; not to mention she still didn't have her story yet, and her deadline was fast approaching, she thought, as she stomped back across the road to finish her interview with the less than communicative Captain Caveman.

As she entered the cafe once again, she got a round of applause, which - as she headed back to her table - she chose to acknowledge with her middle finger pointing skyward.

She came to an abrupt halt.

I don't believe this, she thought, as she looked across to the empty table where she'd been sitting only moments before. *He's gone.* 'Where's the man who was sitting here?' she asked the Waitress, who was clearing the table.

'Harry? Gone, luv,' she replied, without taking her attention away from her task.

'I can see that, *sister*,' said Izzy, 'but *where* has he gone?'

The Waitress straightened up and gave Izzy a well practised look of world-weary contempt, before walking away.

'Well, at least tell me his full name,' she called after the retreating Waitress.

Feeling utterly defeated and deflated, she collapsed onto the still-warm bench seat recently vacated by the man called Harry. She slouched across the table, forehead resting on her arms, and idly wondered if it was too early to drink wine. She noticed the Waitress had not cleared the man's newspaper, along with his cutlery and crockery. Maybe it belongs to the cafe, she thought, and not the man himself.

If there was one reporter's trait that Izzy did have, it was that of being curious. At a glance, she noticed he had completed the crossword. She unfolded the paper and turned to the front page, to be mildly surprised to see it was one of the more 'highbrow' broadsheets. *Maybe he isn't such a Neanderthal.* It was just at that moment when Izzy thought there might be a God, after all. There, in the top right hand corner of the newspaper, written in pen, was an address - and it certainly wasn't the address of the cafe she was sitting in.

'Hallelujah,' she said out loud, not caring who heard, as she scooped up the newspaper and headed for the door.

CHAPTER 4

He watched as his driver hammered his fist loudly against the locked door of the snooker club. He wondered why he was there. What it was he'd done to be summoned at that late hour.

Minutes passed.

The lock was turned, the door opened, and a wary face peered out. It looked at the driver, then at him, then back to the driver, before giving a twitch of the head.

They entered.

His shift had barely finished when the driver had turned up to collect him, sent by their employer: the Boss. Not told why or where they were going. Still wearing his work clothes of nightclub doorman: black suit, white shirt, black tie. Hair closely cropped to his skull. Black overcoat and black leather gloves to ward off the night's winter chill.

He followed the driver through the dimly lit snooker hall. The room was hot and stuffy, filled with cigarette smoke. There was murmured conversation, occasional outbursts of laughter, and coarse language. Dark shadows were gathered around a dimly lit bar in the far corner of the room. A jukebox could be heard playing. Ghostly figures moved around and amongst the tables, physiques and features looming suddenly into sharp contrast under snooker table spotlights. The features of hard men. Dangerous men. Men to be feared. Gangsters, villains, and a few off-duty Old Bill.

The Doorman recognised a few of the faces.

As he passed, comment was made. Laughter followed. He heard a voice, but not the comment. Saw a shape, but not the face. He walked on. Followed the driver.

He entered a large room that smelled of stale alcohol. Crates and barrels were stacked: the cellar room.

Elegantly dressed and perched on the edge of a beer barrel, legs crossed, hands clasped around his knee, sat the Boss. Standing next to him was a man he didn't recognise. He was similar in stature and age to the Doorman. He had a maniacal look in his eye. He shifted from foot to foot. Agitated. Full of nervous energy. Excited. Eager.

A few feet away, sat a third man. Young, strong, and heavily tattooed. He was also agitated. But with fear and apprehension.

All three turned as the Doorman and the driver entered. The driver stayed by the door. The Doorman approached the Boss, who greeted him by his given name. The Doorman responded by calling him 'Sir'. His employer explained why he had been brought. His employer had a problem, and he felt sure the Doorman was the man to resolve it for him.

The problem was the heavily tattooed man.

He'd been caught doing 'some business' outside his 'manor'. On the Boss's manor. And without permission. That was showing disrespect. Dishonour. And that could not be allowed. He had to be taught the error of his ways.

The man with the maniacal stare took a step forward, holding out his hand. His smile was cruel and twisted. His eyes mocking. He dropped an object into the Doorman's gloved palm, gave him a wink, then stepped back.

As the Doorman approached, the tattooed man quickly stood. Legs braced, shoulders back, chest out. Expectant. Fists clenching and unclenching. Jaw set. Expression fierce and defiant. Ready.

Their eyes met. Faces searched. Judging, weighing-up, deciding.

The Doorman opened his palm. Studied the object that lay there. His thumb pressed a button on the narrow handle. A faint 'snick' was heard, as six inches of spring-loaded steel shot out, breaking the hushed silence. A blade dulled by time, its edge keen, and covered with the microscopic scratches of regular honing.

He looked back at the tattooed man, whose expression was now less fierce and less defiant. He weighed-up what he was about to do. What was expected of him. He then asked of himself:

How do I feel?
Do I care?
No!
Do I care that I don't care?
Why should I care?

The Doorman knows he's at a turning point. He knows he's about to be judged by his next action. He knows he's being tested - initiated.

Over his shoulder, he hears the soft yet persuasive voice of the Boss. Encouraging. Asking to make him proud. Justifying the guilty man's punishment in that his business had been selling drugs to children.

He again looked into the eyes of the tattooed man. Defiance had been replaced by realisation. The need for survival. Fight or flight.

He tells himself he doesn't care.

Is there a reason for him to care?

Life was not fair. That was a fact. It was every man for himself.

He weighed-up what he had to do.

He retracted the blade on the knife and slipped it into his overcoat pocket, to then withdraw a dulled brass metal object which he slipped over the fingers of his gloved hand.

He taught the tattooed man a lesson.

The Boss looked on with interest and with curiosity. Silent.

The man with the maniacal stare. Disappointed.

The driver. Bored.

When he'd finished, the soft voice thanked him. Then dismissed him.

The driver left. He followed.

Back through the hall, past the tables, low conversation and enquiring eyes. The jukebox was playing a song that sounded familiar.

A comment was made. Derisive laughter followed.

His stride slowed.

From out of the dark, head and shoulders loomed into spotlight view. Palm flat on table edge, fingers forming a bridge for the tip of the cue. Polished wood handle caressing stubbled chin. Gaze focused on the table's contents, lining-up for a shot.

Lips moved to utter yet another insulting comment. More derisory laughter. Gaze momentarily lifted to look out into the surrounding darkness, mocking eyes, locking onto intended target.

The Doorman.

A sneer crossed the face, before returning its attention back to the table.

The Doorman recognised the man. A gangster from another manor. A right hard bastard. Rumour had it he usually carried a shooter.

This time he heard the insult. Didn't understand it though. A leery comment about who his natural father was. Made no difference. A piss-take was a piss-take. End of story. Disrespect had been shown.

An expectant hush had fallen around the table.

He remembered it was a Rolling Stones song, 'Sympathy for the Devil'.

A faint 'snick' sound was then heard, immediately followed by the soft thud of metal being embedded into cloth and wood, followed a heartbeat later by the cry of agonised pain.

He told the gangster he should've 'played safe' and gone for the blue, before casually and confidently walking-on towards the exit, with a swagger that belied his youth.

In the car park, the driver got back into the car. The Doorman paused for a moment before doubling over and retching, acrid bile burning his throat as he vomited. He wiped his mouth, regained his composure, then climbed back into the car.

The driver told him he'd get used to it.

A new order had begun. The Doorman had now become the 'Enforcer', setting the tone for what was to come: money, cars, women, violence and self-respect, all in equal measure.

And tomorrow would be the Enforcer's nineteenth birthday...

CHAPTER 5

Patrick was in the hallway of his large detached home in Hampstead, searching through an antique bureau, and becoming increasingly annoyed by the fruitless results of his search, until the sound of someone knocking at his front door caused him to pause for a moment, before then continuing.

Minutes passed.

More knocking. This time louder, drawing his attention to the door and its adjacent window, where two large shadows were attempting to peer through the closed vertical blinds.

He watched as the door handle turned. Locked.

The shadows eventually moved away.

The mobile phone in Patrick's back pocket started to softly ring. Removing it, he then frowned, perplexed, as he looked at the caller display, indecision on his face. He chose not to answer, but to turn it off and replace it back into his pocket. As he resumed his search, he heard the sound of a car engine start up and then drive away, fading into the distance.

'Who was at the door?' asked his wife, Maggie, as she came down the stairs.

'Nobody,' said Patrick, without looking up.

'"Nobody", makes that much noise knocking, you thick paddy.'

'It was the Jehovah Witnesses.'

'Well, why didn't you say that,' she said, going over to where he was standing. 'What are you looking for?' she asked, leaning in to see.

'Mind your business and watch your mouth, woman,' he said.

'Suit yourself,' she replied, turning away. 'I'm going to Mollie's. I'll be back later.'

'Fine.'

Maggie picked up her coat and bag, and went out the front door.

Patrick eventually found what he was looking for: two Yale keys tied together with a bit of string, which he put into his shirt top pocket. He then moved on to the next drawer, but as he did so, Maggie burst back in through the front door.

'It's gone! The BMW has gone!'

Patrick continued searching.

'Patrick. The car has been stolen! Phone the police!'

'In a minute, woman. Can't you see I'm busy,' he said, over his shoulder.

'What do you mean, in a minute? It's been stolen for Christ's sake,' she shouted at him.

Patrick spun around. 'Look, if it's gone, it's gone. Another few minutes won't make any difference,' he said, his face flushed.

Maggie took a step backwards. 'How am I supposed to get into town, then?'

'Take the Range Rover, it's parked out the back.'

'I don't like driving that thing, it's too big.'

'Then walk. I really don't give a fuck!' he said, raising his voice.

'Can't you run me in?'

'I'm busy,' he answered, turning back to his search.

'Doing what?'

'I'm going for breakfast.'

With an exasperated groan, Maggie snatched up the keys to the Range Rover, reminded him to phone the police and the car leasing company, and then strode through to the rear of the house, slamming doors as she went.

Patrick pulled out a bundle of papers. Sifting through them, he then selected a small single item. After studying it for a few seconds - which brought a smile to his face - he placed it in his pocket along with the keys. After casting a glance at the front door, he picked up a copy of the *North London Gazette,* from off the bureau, to then also go through to the rear of the house. He crossed a large garden, quietly slipped through a gate to an access road at the rear of the property, to then walk down to the main road and hail a taxi cab.

Patrick got a coffee from the counter, before then going over to the table and sliding his big frame onto the red faux leather bench seat. 'Morning,' he said.

Harry looked up at the big ruddy faced man sitting opposite him, then glanced around the half empty cafe, before returning his attention to his breakfast and newspaper.

'Nice day,' said the big man.

Harry did not look up, he merely grunted to acknowledge the man had spoken. Two thoughts popped into Harry's head: one, it was anything but a nice day - it was pissing-it-down; two, he must find a cafe where he could have his breakfast in peace.

'My name's Patrick,' said the big man.

This time Harry didn't even bother to grunt.

'And you must be Harry Windsor,' said Patrick.

Harry's head snapped up to fix the big man with a stare.

Patrick now had Harry's full attention.

Harry's gaze wandered over the big Irishman. He took in the ruddy complexion and the thread veined nose that indicated a love of strong spirits - probably Irish whiskey - the thinning hair, the cruel eyes, and the faint aroma of stale tobacco and aftershave, before gently placing his knife and fork onto his plate, to then sit back, palms flat to the table.

Patrick took a sip of coffee and grimaced.

Harry smiled inwardly before saying, 'And how would you know that, Patrick?'

'I hear you're the sort of man that helps people,' said Patrick, getting straight to the point. 'And I need help.'

Seeing a look of puzzlement cross Harry's face, he pulled a newspaper from his jacket pocket, laid it on the table, and after smoothing it flat, pushed it towards Harry.

Looking down, Harry saw it was a copy of the *North London Gazette*. His attention was drawn to a large article decrying the cut in funding for a community sports centre. Below that article was a smaller one titled: *'Have-a-go-hero foils knife-wielding thugs'*. With anger building inside him, Harry skimmed through the story, ending with the name of the reporter: *Isobelle Harker*.

'Fuck!' said Harry, still staring at the newspaper.

'You're obviously a man of principles and morals,' said Patrick, indicating the article.

'You couldn't be further from the truth,' replied Harry, looking up at Patrick, anger in his eyes.

Tension hung heavy in the air. Patrick took another sip of his coffee, the coffee mug lost in the cradle of his big hands. 'Coffee tastes good,' he said, simply. He looked back at Harry. 'I need help.' He then said, 'I need your help... to find my daughter. She's missing.'

'The coffee's shit.' Harry was annoyed. He was annoyed with Isobelle Harker for printing the story. He was annoyed with the man sitting opposite for intruding on his privacy, and he was annoyed with himself for the question he was about to ask and where it might lead. 'What do you mean by missing? Lost? Runaway?'

'Missing. Gone. We haven't heard from her in over a week, which is unusual.'

'You need to go to the police.'

Patrick shook his head. 'No, can't do that.'

'Why not?'

'Because my wife doesn't yet know she's missing.' Patrick could see Harry looked sceptical. 'My wife is under the impression that Mollie, our daughter, has gone to stay with a girlfriend who's helping her get over a recent split with her latest boyfriend,' he added.

'Where... or from who,' asked Harry, 'did your wife get that impression?'

Patrick hesitated, before then saying, 'From me.'

Harry didn't comment. He waited. Patiently.

'We had an argument - me and Mollie,' said Patrick, uncomfortably. 'I struck her... gave her a bit of a slap. We haven't seen or heard from her since.'

Harry had a very low opinion of men who physically abused women and who had no respect for family. 'You need to tell your wife,' he said, disgusted.

'My marriage is shaky as it is,' replied Patrick, 'and this would finish it. I'm sure Mollie's fine. That nothing bad has happened to her, and she's only doing this to punish me. She's always been independent and strong willed. Done her own thing. But she's always kept in touch. Her mother's getting suspicious. I need to find my daughter, and quickly.'

Harry studied the man. He could see, and sense, a physical and mental strength that bordered on bullying arrogance and which no doubt served him well in dealing with life's ups and downs, but Harry could also sense a genuine fear in the man; of what, he couldn't be sure.

Reaching into his shirt top pocket, Patrick withdrew its contents, which he then placed onto the table, before sliding across to Harry. 'I'll pay you five thousand to find her,' said Patrick.

Harry looked into Patrick's eyes, and knew he was serious. After a moment's hesitation, he picked up his knife and fork to finish his breakfast.

Patrick coughed to clear his throat. He shifted uncomfortably on the hard bench seat, trying to suppress his anger and impatience; he was used to getting his own way. 'Ten thousand and not a penny more,' said Patrick. 'Take it or leave it.'

'I'll leave it,' replied Harry, between a mouthful of bacon and egg, while studying the crossword.

'Damn you!' said Patrick, slamming a clenched fist down onto the table, rattling crockery, spilling tea and coffee, and sending out a thunderclap of noise around the cafe, which was instantly followed by a hushed silence.

The suddenness and volume of Patrick's outburst had taken Harry by surprise, making him flinch like a frightened rabbit. But the feeling of fear was only brief, instantly replaced by anger; anger at having his time interrupted, and anger at feeling and - more importantly - showing fear.

A dark look crossed Harry's face as he stared at the cause of those feelings.

Patrick knew he'd gone too far. He rested his forearms on the table, his shoulders slumped, head down.

Angry and tense, Harry watched and waited for Patrick's next move. Seeing the big man's body shaking, and anticipating the possibility of Patrick suddenly lashing out, Harry was again taken by surprise when he realised the big Irishman was crying. Huge spasms wracked the man's body, made all the more violent by his trying to suppress them.

Harry was now feeling embarrassed. He was embarrassed because of the attention this scene was attracting, and he was feeling embarrassed for the man sitting opposite. He was at a total loss as what to do, or what to say.

'I'm sorry,' said Patrick, once he'd managed to compose himself. Then, his voice cracking with emotion, 'Please, help me find my baby girl,' he said, searching Harry's face for a sign of compassion, acknowledgement, agreement.

Seeing none, he slowly dragged himself to his feet, and left.

Harry watched the big man shuffle out of the door. He looked down at his half eaten breakfast, no longer feeling hungry. He pushed his plate aside. Patrick's heartfelt plea had touched a place deep inside Harry. A place that had been touched only once in recent years, and that was at the loss of his mother.

The cafe Waitress arrived to clear the table. 'I can't wait to see who's going to join you for breakfast tomorrow,' she said, as she mopped up the spillage.

Harry scowled at her, and then told her to fuck off, as he tried to shake the gloomy thoughts and feelings that threatened to overwhelm him. He looked down at the objects Patrick had left on the table: two Yale keys and a business card with the name, *Patrick Dolan, Property Developer*. The third item was a small photograph of a dark haired young woman who appeared to be in her late teens or early twenties. He didn't touch the objects. Instead, he picked up the *North London Gazette* to read Isobelle Harker's report in full.

Harry noted the elderly couple from the pub had asked Isobelle not to print their names. He also noted with curiosity that she had used Harry's forename only. It was not that she had only printed his forename Harry found curious, but that Patrick had *known* Harry's *surname*.

CHAPTER 6

Izzy was sitting on her sofa, in her flat in Camden, sipping a large glass of chilled wine, often enough and deep enough to suggest she still hadn't got over Jonathan standing her up.

They'd arranged to meet up after work, at a bistro in Soho in the West End, they hadn't seen each other for five days, due to one or the other being busy. Despite turning up fifteen minutes late - which was early for Izzy, punctuality not being one of her strong points - Jonathan still hadn't yet arrived, so she'd taken a table near the window and in sight of the entrance. Two large glasses of white wine, five attempts to call Jonathan's mobile, and fifty minutes later, Izzy had had enough, and left to go home. It was three hours after that before she finally managed to contact Jonathan, who was in a bar in the West End with a group of his rugby mates, all of whom, judging by the background noise, were clearly drunk. Jonathan claimed he'd called her and left a message to say he would be late, but when she never returned his call, he'd assumed she was either working on a "big story", or she was in one of her 'moods', so he'd gone to meet his friends. When he suggested coming around to her flat, she'd told him not to bother.

If Izzy had had lots of friends, she would have made alternative arrangements. Sadly, she didn't. London was a big city, crammed with millions of people, yet it could also be a lonely city. So, to cheer herself up, she had a long soak in a steaming hot bath, filled with aromatic oils, while sipping a glass of chilled white wine and listening to some 'atmospheric' music; the sound of waves gently breaking on the seashore, accompanied by the sound of pan pipes. It was hardly cutting edge classical, but she liked it. When she started to fall asleep, spilling wine into the bath water, she knew it was time to get out. After wrapping her lobster-pink body in an old-but-familiar bathrobe, and putting on oversized slippers that were shaped like an elephant's head, she shuffled into the kitchen to put a 'convenience' meal into the microwave oven, before then flopping onto the sofa with a fresh glass of wine, to relax. Moments later, though, she was having a hot flush, so she loosened the belt to her bathrobe, and, grasping the lapels of the robe, fanned herself in an attempt to cool down.

It was at this point when she heard the knock at the door to her flat.

Placing her wine to one side, she struggled off the sofa; a little too quickly, because she suddenly felt faint. For a moment she stood, shakily, trying to focus, wondering if she was going to fall over. *A bit more cold water, next time,* she thought.

As she headed down the hallway to the front door, she silently cursed the old man on the ground floor for once again not properly closing the outer door; and she cursed Jonathan for ignoring her orders not to come around to her flat.

The sound of knocking came again.

'Yes, yes,' she said, as she threw open the front door and prepared herself to glare into Jonathan's eyes, only to find herself looking at an Adam's apple. She looked up, instead, into the eyes of Harry Windsor.

'Hi,' he said, handing her a bottle of red wine and breezing past, heading down the hallway towards her lounge.

'Come in, why don't you,' she said to his retreating back. *And I prefer white.*

Closing the door, she hurried after him, fussing with her hair as she went. 'What do you want?' she asked. Then, realising, 'How did you find me? Did someone at the office tell you where I live? Because if they did -'

'Friend-of-a-friend, sort of thing,' replied Harry.

'You've got friends?' responded Izzy.

'World's full of surprises,' he said, now standing in the middle of her lounge, looking at an ornate fireplace above which hung a very large mirror.

Izzy entered the room to then stand protectively in front of the fireplace; still clutching the bottle of wine. 'Why are you here?' she asked, looking up at him and realising just how tall he was.

'I was... just passing,' he replied with a smile. 'Are you on your own?'

Izzy suddenly realised, to her horror, that her robe was still slightly open, making her conscious of her nakedness beneath, and leaving her feeling slightly vulnerable. 'My fiancée is coming round for dinner, soon,' she replied, pulling her robe closed and tightening the belt one-handed. 'Very soon, in fact.'

'Are you feeling sick?' Harry asked her.

'Sick? Why? What makes you say that?'

'You're very pink, and you appear to have a fever.'

'Oh. I see. No, I've just had a bath.' As soon as the words left her mouth, she felt she'd just confirmed to the man standing before her that she *was* naked beneath her robe, leaving her feeling even more vulnerable. 'I really don't think it's a good idea you being here... now... at this moment. I mean, I hardly know you.'

'There are a lot of people in North London who now know me a lot better, thanks to you.'

'Is that what this is about?'

'What do you think?'

'I didn't print your full name. Nobody will know it's you,' she said. 'There must be hundreds of Harrys in North London. Even if the police did find you, you were defending yourself. They don't jail people for self-defence.'

'The law doesn't work like that. I approached them. I struck the first blow.'

'Even so, I'm sure they wouldn't convict you on that - especially as it's your first offence.' When Harry didn't reply, 'It is your first offence, isn't it?' she asked, a little worried.

'Nice flat,' said Harry, looking around the room.

Izzy's mind was now running riot, conjuring up all types of scenarios and ill deeds this man may have committed, increasing her feeling of vulnerability and the desperate need to have people around her - even Jonathan. 'Look, how about I buy you a drink in the pub across the road, to say sorry,' she said, desperate to get him out of her flat. 'I'll just get dressed,' she quickly added, hurrying from the room, not waiting for an answer.

While she dressed, Harry looked around. The book case held a variety of books, classical and modern - only some of which appeared to have been read. Also CDs: a few old favourites like Sinatra and Ella Fitzgerald, a lot of main stream pop, and a few new bands Harry had never heard of. There were a number of 'artistically hip' prints, hanging on the pastel coloured walls. Harry wasn't sure if 'artistically hip' was the correct description for that particular type of art, but what he did know was they weren't Constable or Picasso. Candles and silk scarfs adorned the room. Very girly, he thought.

He poked his head into the kitchen. The units were white Shaker, with Beech Block worktops; a style that didn't fit with the young woman's 'girl-about-town' image. Harry presumed the units were there before she was. Even so, she'd decorated it in much the same way she had the lounge, making it homely. A ping drew his attention to the microwave, which contained a 'ready-meal' for one.

Izzy was pulling on her fashionably-tight, blue jeans, as fast as humanly possible, which did not seem fast enough to her, having to resort to flopping backwards onto her bed, and then writhing her hips and legs. Her haste was such, that she had her jeans half way up before she realised she'd forgotten to put underwear on. After pondering this dilemma for a microsecond, she continued pulling at her jeans, while wondering what people would think, should she be involved in an accident, taken to A&E, only for it to be discovered she wasn't wearing any knickers. Feeling a sense of risqué liberation, she then surprised herself by abandoning her bra, also, pulling on a flimsy tight white tee-shirt covered only by a Burberry jacket.

Mascara and lipstick were cursory, and applied in record breaking time.

Harry gave the bathroom the quick once-over. There were still traces of steam from Izzy's bathing, along with casually discarded underwear. There were two toothbrushes in a glass, and a man's wet-shaving kit; but little else to suggest two people occupied the flat.

Izzy ran a brush through her hair, before bursting out of the bedroom and into the lounge at a speed that she hoped suggested a matter-of-fact eagerness rather than frantic panic.

She found Harry admiring her CD collection.

As they crossed the road to the pub opposite, Izzy asked Harry where he'd parked his car, because it was a 'residents' parking area only', and he might get a ticket. He told her he didn't own a car, he'd caught the bus. Izzy thought for a moment before saying he would've had to make two changes to get from his place to her's. Where exactly was he "passing" to?

It was Harry's turn to be surprised. 'How do you know where I live?'

'Your address was on your newspaper.'

'Ah,' said Harry, realising. 'And my name?'

'Electoral Register via Land Registry,' she replied, simply.

'Oh,' said Harry, not realising.

'So?' she asked again.

In reply, Harry asked about her dinner plans with her fiancée.

They were both pleased to arrive at the pub.

The pub was very busy, so while Harry went to find them a table, Izzy went to the bar. By the time the barman had pulled Harry's pint of Guinness, she'd almost finished her large glass of white wine. Torn between appearing to be a greedy lush, by having another before she'd even had chance to sit down, or nursing what remained, she said to herself, 'Fuck it, you only live once - unless of course you're a Hindu... or is it a Buddhist?' This made her giggle. She wondered if it was not wearing underwear that made her more adventurous.

Harry watched Izzy as she finally returned to their table. He watched the way she wore her emotions. Anxious one moment, girlish glee the next. He struggled to suppress a smile.

Izzy looked up at Harry's steady gaze, and didn't feel so giggly any more. After another large sip of Dutch courage, she then apologised for any trouble she may have caused. She hadn't meant any harm. She explained to Harry how she had desperately wanted to prove she could get the story. 'My editor doesn't have much faith in me. And I think the owner of the newspaper is of the same opinion too,' she told him.

'Why would the owner take so much interest in one individual employee?' Harry asked.

'The owner just happens to be my father.'

'Ah, I see,' replied Harry, who could see she was getting maudlin. 'How long have you been a reporter?'

'Almost a year. There was a position for a junior reporter, which I and numerous others were interviewed for, and I got it. I'm under no illusion it was down to my father, rather than the best person for the job. Geoff - my editor - said as much the day I started.'

'Do you enjoy it?' asked Harry.

Izzy merely shrugged her shoulders, gazing into her now empty glass. 'I'm not very good at things. I flunked college. My younger brother is a professor of psychology. My father is very proud of him.'

Against his better judgment, Harry went and got another round of drinks in.

Placing a small glass of wine in front of her, he said, 'Sometimes it can take a while before you find what you're good at. The important thing is to keep looking. It'll turn up. You never know, reporting could be it.'

Izzy looked at him quizzically, squinting slightly to focus. 'Have you found what you're good at?'

Harry inclined his head slightly, indicating: maybe yes, maybe no.

Izzy frowned, scrunching up her face in deep concentration. 'What exactly *do* you do?'

'There you go,' said Harry, grinning, 'thinking just like a reporter.'

She theatrically wagged her finger at him, saying, 'Oh, no you don't. I've noticed you are very good at sidestepping questions.'

Harry gave her a slight smile of acknowledgement.

Izzy raised her eyebrows; waiting.

'I'm turning my house into self-contained flats. The rent should give me a reasonable income.'

'Not very exciting,' responded Izzy. Then, realising, 'Oh, God! Fuck! Sorry!' she said, slapping both hands over her mouth and almost knocking her wine glass over, which Harry quickly caught. 'I didn't mean it to sound like that. I just thought you probably did something more... interesting... if you know what I mean...'

'Unexciting is fine with me,' said Harry. 'I don't do "exciting" anymore.'

For a while, they sipped their drinks. Harry casting his gaze about the pub, checking out the other drinkers, Izzy examining the bottom of her glass with great intent.

Looking up at Harry, she said, 'Do you have any family?'

'A foster brother, Stephen,' he replied, after a brief pause.

'Are you close?'

Harry gave a short, bitter laugh. 'Once.'

'Not anymore?'

'No,' he said, '...difference of opinions.'

'Mother? Father?' she asked.

'Mother died a few years ago.'

'And your father?'

Harry didn't answer.

'Is he dead too?'

'Not... that I'm aware of.'

'Oh.'

Harry studied the young woman opposite him. Despite her bravado and her airs and graces, she was, at heart, naive and innocent, which Harry found quite endearing. She was also slightly drunk. 'Are you planning on printing this?'

'God, no! Of course not!' she said, with genuine horror.

Harry believed her - and Harry didn't usually believe many people.

'I've never met my father, so I don't know who he is. Whether he's alive or dead. I know nothing about him.'

'Didn't your mother tell you anything about him?' she asked. 'Nothing at all?'

It was now Harry's turn to examine the bottom of his glass.

'Your mother must have told you something about him,' she said, gently pressing him.

'My mother... my foster mother, Lillian, didn't have anything to tell - was able to tell. My biological mother died giving birth to me.'

'That's awful.'

Harry shrugged. 'That's life - if you'll pardon the bad pun. Can't change anything.'

'So,' she said, 'the brother you mentioned -'

'Foster brother. No blood relative.'

Izzy was unsure what to say next. She wasn't always comfortable with long silences. Especially with strangers. She always felt the need to say something. She glanced at Harry, who was sipping his drink and looking around the pub, totally comfortable with himself and his surroundings. She, on the other hand, was not feeling so at ease; she was having difficulty in focusing, and she felt a little nauseous. She blinked a number of times. She had to concentrate on something; take her mind off feeling unwell. 'What was your first offence for?' she said, quickly, before she changed her mind.

Harry's head snapped around, his expression hard.

Izzy felt herself cringe; her focus quickly returning.

After taking a long swallow from his pint, and placing the empty glass on the table, Harry looked her in the eye.

Izzy realised she was holding her breath.

'Dealing drugs,' he said.

'Not murder... or rape, then?' she said, sounding and feeling relieved.

'Not charged with, no,' he replied.

Izzy looked at him sharply; totally focused.

'Joking,' said Harry, grinning broadly.

She told him he didn't strike her as a drugs dealer. Not that she was really sure what a drugs dealer looked like, other than the characters on television.

'I wasn't a drugs dealer. I was jailed for a crime I didn't commit.'

'You didn't deal drugs?'

'No.'

'They put you in jail and you were innocent?'

'I didn't say I was innocent. I just didn't deal drugs.'

'You're a criminal?'

'Was.'

'What did you do?' she asked, wide eyed. 'Crime, I mean. What sort of crime did you do?'

'I used to work for a man who needed things doing.'

'What kind of things?'

'The kind of things nobody else would do - or could be trusted to do.'

'What things?'

'It's better you don't know.'

'Who's the man you used to work for?'

'His name is Mr Solomon. He's also known by some, as "The Jew" -'

'Because he's Jewish?'

'Amazingly, yes,' said Harry, with a raised eyebrow. 'But not to his face. If it's illegal, he's involved in it: prostitution, loan sharking, money laundering and gambling, to name but a few. He's the kind of man that would stoop to anything.' Izzy saw Harry pause. 'Except drugs. He never got involved with drugs.'

'He sounds an unsavoury character,' she said.

'On the surface, he's a refined and charming gentleman in his seventies. An accountant by trade. And he does run a legitimate property business. If you were to meet him, you would never guess he was a major criminal. Or that once he gets his hooks into you, he never lets go.'

'Yet, he let you go?'

Harry gave a small nod as he checked his watch. 'We have a mutual understanding.'

'Which is?' asked Izzy.

'He doesn't interfere with my new life, and I won't kill him.'

Izzy searched Harry's face for humour. But found none. 'Have you ever -'

'I have to go,' he said, standing to put his jacket on. 'Thanks for the drink.'

Izzy again apologised for the story she'd published, reassuring him it would soon be forgotten, and probably wouldn't attract too much attention anyway.

Harry told her about Patrick and his daughter, Mollie.

'What are you going to do?' she asked.

'I don't know,' he replied, as he zipped up his jacket.

'Hey,' she exclaimed excitedly, 'I can help you find her. I am an investigative reporter, after all,' she said, knocking over her empty glass. 'Oh, bollocks...'

'Again, thanks for the drink. I really did enjoy it.'

Izzy then watched Harry leave.

'New boyfriend?' said a voice, startling Izzy from her daydream. James, the barman - who was supposed to be collecting glasses - flopped into Harry's recently vacated seat. 'Hm, still warm.'

'Not my type,' said Izzy.

'Still with Jonathan, then?' said James. 'He hasn't come out yet?' James - who was gay and made no secret of it - often teased Izzy about Jonathan's sexuality.

'No!' she said. Then, realising the implication, 'I mean, no, he's not gay,' she added.

'Suit yourself,' said James, letting it drop. 'So who is he?'

'He's a guy I recently wrote a piece about.'

'The guy in the pub fight?' he said. 'That's Dirty Harry?'

'Dirty Harry?'

'That's what people have been calling him,' replied James.

Izzy pondered this, realising she'd missed an opportunity to make the story bigger. 'OK, genius,' she said, 'what is my type?

'Harry is your type. Mean, moody, and deliciously dangerous,' said James, with dramatic flair.

'But why would someone like *him* be my type?'

'Because it would take someone like *him* to keep a stroppy minx like *you* in line,' he replied.

Maybe it was due to drink, but Izzy wasn't offended by this theory. Raising her hand, she then gave him the finger. 'I think I'd better go home,' she said, rising unsteadily to her feet. 'I feel a bit squiffy - and I've only had a couple.'

'And the rest, darling. And the rest,' said James.

CHAPTER 7

After a pleasant, but unexpected, turn of events, Harry was finally back at home, reclining in a worn yet comfortable Chesterfield armchair. Cupped in the palm of one hand, was a glass tumbler of Scotch whisky with a single ice cube, in his other, a book. His eyes were closed. Cole Porter - one of his mother's old vinyl records - was softly playing in the background, accompanied by the rhythmic tick of a grandfather clock, and the hiss and crackle of an open fire. It hadn't been long since he'd left Isobelle Harker, and he was feeling the need to unwind.

He opened his eyes to take in his surroundings. He was in his study, the only room he hadn't altered. It was almost wall-to-wall with bookcases containing classic and modern literature - most of which he'd read, old trophies for golf - his foster brother's, and old trophies for boxing - his. The remaining wall space was covered with posters advertising stage shows, photos of Lillian performing on stage or with actors past and present, and family photos of Lillian, Harry and his foster brother in their earlier years. Antique furniture and an old upright piano filled the rest of the room. It was very much the way it had been when his mother had passed away. Some would say - if they dared - it was a shrine.

Harry's gaze was drawn to the flames of the fire. He found the way they flickered and danced mesmerising. He briefly mused whether there actually were smokeless zones in London, and if he was in one. Not that he gave a shit. Harry had never been one to follow the rules. After all, what could they do to him? Fine him? Put him in jail... again? This thought brought a smile to his face. He was feeling mellow from the whisky and the warmth of the fire. He leaned his head back and let the memories wash over him, back to the first day he'd arrived at this house.

Accompanied - or had it been escorted? - by a stern faced social worker, a twelve year old Henry Windsor arrived outside the door of his new home. But not before he'd been washed, had his hair neatly combed, and put on his best pair of shorts and a necktie that felt like it was strangling him.

When the front door opened, they were greeted by a tall elegant lady with a bright beaming smile. Acknowledging the social worker with a courteous nod, she then looked down at Harry. 'You must be Henry Windsor,' she said, smiling and holding out her hand. 'I'm very pleased to meet you, Henry. Welcome to your new home.'

Harry risked a quick glance over his shoulder at the social worker who was blocking any route of escape. In return, the social worker fixed Harry with a firm and meaningful stare. Having received a clip across the back of the head not five minutes previously for being cheeky, Harry turned back to the elegant lady and limply shook her hand. 'Harry,' he said, scowling.

'My name is Lillian,' the elegant lady replied, 'and this is Stephen,' she said, indicating a boy who was standing behind her, a head taller than Harry, with a scowl on his baby face equal to that of Harry's.

After cake and tea in china cups, and the social worker having left, Lillian took Harry up to his room, where he placed the small holdall that contained his few belongings onto his new bed. He didn't bother to unpack, he wasn't planning on staying long. He never stayed anywhere long. That night, Harry ran away from his new home. The following day he was returned by the police. A few days later he ran away again, and again he was returned by the police.

Over the following six months, he ran away half a dozen times. Each time he was returned, Lillian would ask him to go to his room while she made tea for the police officers, which they would drink in the parlour. Lillian would thank them for their patience, while explaining about Harry's difficult childhood. Once the officers had left, Harry would then be invited down for dinner, and nothing more would be said.

The last time Harry ran away was after his foster brother had seen him smoking and grassed him up to Lillian. Lillian's response had been to light one of her own cigarettes, hand it to Harry, and tell him to "enjoy", while she explained the dangers of smoking. When Harry pointed out that Lillian smoked, Lillian informed him it was legal for her to smoke, and besides, it was too late for a woman of her age, yet not for a young man like Henry, who had his whole life ahead of him.

Harry hung his head in shame.

Later that afternoon, Harry once more packed his few possessions into his holdall. He then sought out his foster brother, and promptly broke his nose with a right jab punch. However, any hopes of him making a clean getaway out through the front door were dashed when Lillian, on hearing cries of pain, stepped out from the study and into the hallway. Taking in the now familiar holdall and the look of grim determination on Harry's face, Lillian asked him if he was running away again, to which Harry didn't respond.

'Are you not happy living here, Henry?' she asked. Harry just shuffled from one foot to the other, inspected the black and white chess board patterned tiled floor, and pondered that deep and meaningful question.

Of course Harry knew what happy meant; it was the opposite of sad. While happy wasn't an emotion he'd been overly familiar with in his young life, sad was an emotion he was all *too* familiar with.

Harry settled on a shrug of the shoulders in answer to Lillian's question.

'Why do you want to leave us?' Lillian asked. 'Do you not like being part of a family?'

Harry really wanted to answer Lillian. He really wanted to tell her he wasn't used to people being nice to him, treating him with kindness, that he found it confusing.

But he didn't.

With sadness in her eyes, Lillian wrapped her arms around Harry's skinny little body, and pulled him into a warm embrace. Harry didn't return the hug. He stood ramrod straight, arms down by his sides, confused, trying to remember if he'd ever been hugged before. His eyes then started to sting, he could feel a lump in his throat, and he was finding it difficult to swallow.

He realised, with horror, he was on the verge of crying.

After Lillian had released him from her embrace, she then turned away to pick something up from the surface of the small table usually reserved for deliveries of mail, newspapers, and door keys. Turning back to Harry, she pressed a Yale-type key into the palm of his hand, placed a kiss on his forehead, and then told him she loved him as if he were her own son, and that he would always have a home there should he want it. 'You should allow yourself to be happy, Henry,' she said, before returning to the study.

After a couple of very long minutes had passed, Harry heard the piano being softly played. He let himself out through the front door, and walked down the garden path to the front gate, still able to feel Lillian's warm wet kiss. It occurred to him he probably had lipstick on his forehead, yet he made no attempt to wipe it off. He paused at the gate to look back at the house, at his home, to hear the faint sound of music - accompanied by the girlish sobbing of his foster brother.

He grinned as he closed the gate.

A few hours later found him sitting alone on a children's playground swing, as dusk fell. Being in a North London park at night held no fears for Harry, he was afraid of nothing; he was a fighter, had to be, being small for his age he'd often suffered at the hands of bullies during his time in care homes. But on the streets of London, he'd learned to fight - and to win.

Now though, he was thinking.

Lillian was in the study, teaching Harry's foster brother how to play the piano, when she heard the faint rattle of a key in the front door lock. A few moments later, Harry sauntered into the room, heading for the chair next to the fire, pausing only briefly to choose a book from the bookcase. Aware Lillian and his foster brother were watching him, he simply said, 'Looks like rain,' as if by way of an explanation. After hopping up onto the big chair, and with his legs to short to reach the floor, he opened up the book and began to quietly read.

Lillian silently watched, before turning back to the piano.

From that point, Harry allowed himself to be happy - or at least he tried to. Like Harry, Stephen had been orphaned, and had spent time in care homes and with foster families. Neither boy found it easy to 'play', to do what would otherwise come naturally to other boys of their age, but over the following few years, they did at times manage to forget the horrors of their past, and play with abandoned joy, racing around the big house, laughter bouncing off the walls.

Lillian's home was always a busy home. There was always something going on. Whenever Lillian's fellow actors visited the house to read through their lines for their new and up and coming stage production, Harry and his foster brother would often be given bit parts: conscripted soldiers or Legionnaires with full battle dress of table cloth cloak and sweeping brush sword. When Lillian wasn't working in the theatre, she'd give singing or acting lessons to young hopefuls.

All these talented and creative people brought vibrancy to Lillian's home - to Harry's home.

Harry opened his eyes and took a sip of whisky. Fond memories. His gaze settled on a wall-hung certificate his foster brother had been awarded for something-or-other, sending his thoughts along a different path.

Due to the instability of Harry's home life, his schooling had always been somewhat erratic, and thus, had produced one of the more shameful moments of his young life. Shameful in that it was the first time his actions had made Lillian cry. Something of which he was not proud; still to this day there remained an element of guilt.

Harry hated going to school. He hated the rigid rules for behaviour and time keeping, and being told what he could and could not do. He was constantly bullied, which often resulted in a fight, for which he would then be disciplined with detention after school hours or corporal punishment. Harry always preferred the latter, because it was over within a matter of minutes, and the pain didn't bother him too much.

But one day, Harry went too far.

Two of his classmates - who were sitting behind him - were whispering taunts to him about Lillian being a "thespian", or was it a "lesbian"? The teacher, who noticed that Harry wasn't paying attention, dragged him out of his seat and up to the front of the class, where he had to suffer the admonishment and ridicule of the teacher, much to the amusement of the rest of the class.

As Harry returned to his seat, the two boys again whispered taunts, but as they did so, Harry felt a sudden hot searing pain at the back of his eyes, as anger, rage and frustration shot through his brain. Picking up a newly sharpened pencil from his desk-top, he then stabbed it into the shoulder of one of the boys, feeling the pencil point burst through the thick fabric of the boy's school blazer, to bury itself into the soft flesh of his armpit.

The other boy, who'd got his hinged, desk-top lid vertically open, could only look-on in frozen surprise as Harry, with all his might, slammed the desk-top lid closed, breaking most, if not all of the boy's fingers that rested on the lip of the desk.

The Headmaster himself accompanied Harry home to personally deliver the news to Lillian; that Harry's conduct was not acceptable within his school, and to expel him was the only option. Any possibility of a reprieve was soon dashed when it also became apparent that the articulately written letters explaining Harry's often frequent absences had not been written by Lillian. After the Headmaster had left, Harry was sent to his room, where he was able to hear the sound of gentle crying, coming from below.

Some hours later, found Harry in the street outside his house, idly kicking a football against a wall, feeling thoroughly dejected and the lowest-of-the-low at having made Lillian cry. He hadn't seen Lillian all afternoon. The door to the study, which was usually open, had been firmly closed to uninvited guests. Harry thought he'd heard hushed tones, suggesting Lillian had been talking to someone on the phone, but he couldn't be sure.

Out in the street, Harry looked on as a large majestic car pulled up to the kerb; a vintage Bentley. The driver had got out to open the rear door, for an elderly gentleman to then emerge. He was well dressed in a three piece tweed suit, with a crisp white shirt and necktie. In his hand he carried a silver tipped cane.

The elderly gentleman paused at the gate to Harry's home, before then looking over at Harry, to study him for a few moments. Harry didn't know why, but he found the old man's level gaze and calm demeanour unsettling.

'Would you like to wash my car?' the elderly gentleman asked, in a quiet, well spoken voice.

'Sorry?' replied a bewildered Harry.

'My car. Would you like to wash it for me?' he said, pointing the tip of his cane towards his car. 'I'll pay you for your trouble.'

Harry looked at the car. It was spotlessly clean. It was also beautiful, in immaculate condition, and no doubt worth a lot of money. If he were to accidentally scratch it... He shuddered at the thought.

'Five pounds,' the elderly gentleman said.

Harry just gawped. Five pounds was about three months worth of pocket money for doing chores around the house.

The elderly gentleman then turned and headed up the garden path to Lillian's front door. 'Be careful not to scratch it,' he called over his shoulder.

This was Harry's first meeting with Mr Solomon, the man also known as "The Jew". It would not be his last.

Harry never returned to school. Through Mr Solomon, he had regular employment. His first job had been at the tender age of fifteen, working as a general labourer on a building site. It was gruelling work, but he enjoyed it. His older work mates would push him to his physical limits, but Harry would not give them the satisfaction of giving in. He would work to the point of exhaustion, often only managing to shower and eat the evening meal that Lillian cooked for him, before then collapsing into a deep sleep. By the time Harry had turned seventeen, he'd grown five inches taller, and gained almost a stone in muscle weight. By eighteen he was a trusted and valued doorman at one of Mr Solomon's nightclubs. It was a big responsibility for one so young, but none of Harry's nightclub colleagues questioned or challenged it, because it was obvious Harry was favoured by Mr Solomon. But also because Harry was a hardened street fighter, and could easily hold his own against most men.

As Harry grew older, Mr Solomon gave him more responsibility. Mr Solomon owned a lot of property, private and commercial. When rent was outstanding, Harry would be sent to collect it. The more responsibility Harry was given, the more he was paid, and Harry liked having money.

Harry realised his train of thought had strayed from the memories of boyhood, to the dark activities of early adulthood. He wondered how he could have been so naive or arrogant. Or was it a case of both? What he did know, was he'd done very little good in his life - other than help himself.

On the arm of the Chesterfield lay the business card he'd been given by Patrick, Mollie's father. He drained the remainder of the whisky, placed the glass down, and reached for the card.

CHAPTER 8

Harry's mood was as black and as sombre as the London sky. He had been striding along the Maida Vale Road, heading towards Mollie's flat in Kilburn, when the heavens had opened up. It was a further few hundred yards before he found the sanctuary of a shop doorway which had space enough for him, along with the few other pedestrians already seeking shelter there. Harry was wearing his trusty combat jacket, which was ideal in cold weather, but acted like blotting paper in rainfall. He could feel rainwater soaking through to his tee-shirt, which, coupled with the water trickling down the back of his neck, only served to darken his mood.

In a matter of minutes though, the downpour had ceased as dramatically as it had started, and the dark clouds had passed, allowing the sun to shine through, raising steam from the pavements.

As Harry stepped from the doorway, he found himself once again questioning the wisdom of searching for this missing girl. After all, she meant nothing to him.

He turned into Mollie's street. Each side of the road was lined with three storey houses. As Harry approached Mollie's building, he noticed how tired the facade looked, and that there was a 'for sale' sign attached to the black wrought iron railings, though the sign didn't indicate which flat was for sale. A flight of concrete steps led up to the main entrance door, where a figure now stood, jabbing a finger at a button on the intercom. The figure, which had its back to Harry, was wearing blue jeans and a black hooded top, with the hood up. Harry guessed it was a young male, approximate height of five-ten.

As Harry mounted the steps, the hooded figure turned and skipped down, bumping Harry's arm as he passed, face averted, muttering to himself. Harry watched him shuffle off down the street. He wondered at the lack of manners in today's youth.

There were four buttons on the intercom. Presumably four flats. He decided to press the button to Mollie's flat - just in case. It would be impolite to just walk in, unannounced. He pressed the button, long and hard. No response. From his pocket he produced the two keys given to him by Patrick. Selecting the larger of the two, he inserted it into the five lever security lock, turned the key, and then entered.

The lobby resembled a lot of converted old properties in London. Dimly lit, yet bright enough to reveal faded decor: a dado rail below which the wallpaper bulged from salt damaged plaster, confirming the musty smell of rising damp, and an uneven ceramic tiled floor led to an open staircase. Across the lobby was a numbered door to the ground-floor flat. Like Harry's home, there was a small bureau where mail could be placed for the tenants' to collect at their convenience, and on which there were at least half a dozen items.

Harry was flicking through these when he sensed he was no longer alone; he was being watched. He turned to face the door of the flat across from where he was standing. He saw a shadow of movement below the bottom of the door and the tiled lobby floor, followed by the faint sound of a creaking floorboard from within. He lifted his gaze and stared squarely at the spyhole in the centre of the door. A moment later the shadow moved away, followed by another faint creak.

Harry returned his attention back to sorting through the mail, checking the names. None for Mollie. The faint creak, again caught his attention, to be then closely followed by the click of a latch being turned.

He slowly turned back to the closed door, only now it was slightly ajar, and the small wizened face of an elderly woman - not much higher than the dado rail - peered quizzically out at him. He gave her one of his brighter smiles. She treated him to a frosty glare, before abruptly closing the door. I must be losing my touch, he thought, as he made his way up the stairs.

Harry opened the front door to Mollie's flat and stepped into a small lobby, off which there were three doors. The first led to a small bathroom, the second to a medium sized bedroom - both windowless - and the third to a reasonably spacious lounge that had windows overlooking the street and a small kitchenette at one end. There was a faint smell of stale air.

Harry looked around. The lounge was simply decorated and sparsely furnished. The walls were of a magnolia colour, and the bare floorboards had been sanded and varnished; a sofa and an armchair that had seen better days had brightly coloured throws to give them some life; a small table with two mismatching chairs sat against one wall; and a poster showing a long haired and bare chested rock guitarist in full swing, was fixed to another wall. Harry, who was a keen music fan, recognised neither the face nor the name that was printed along the bottom. *Must be getting old.*

The small kitchenette was equally sparse in its worktop utensils. Cheap containers identifying tea, coffee, and sugar were neatly lined up, along with an electric kettle, microwave and toaster.

The flat was generally neat and tidy, but Harry's overall impression was... here he paused in his thinking, looking for the right word... tired! That was the word; much like the rest of the building. He was mildly surprised. If Mollie's father, Patrick, was as wealthy as he'd implied, why wasn't that wealth reflected in the quality of his daughter's flat? Maybe he didn't believe in spoiling his children.

More questions than answers.

Where to start?

Standing in the middle of the room, dripping rainwater onto the floor boards, Harry was feeling a little out of his comfort zone. Finding people wasn't his forte - it was more the opposite.

He took off his wet coat and hung it over the back of a chair. He decided to make a start with the small table, upon which was a desktop computer, some writing materials, and a stack of books on Art & Design, borrowed from the library of the college that Mollie attended and almost a week overdue. There was also a small pile of unopened mail, the postal dates varied but recent. Either Mollie didn't bother opening her mail, or someone else had brought it up to her flat.

A cheap looking telephone answering machine was also on the table, the digital display indicating six messages. Harry thought it unusual that someone of Mollie's age had an answering machine. He thought the younger generation were too into their mobile phones - texting and tweeting - to bother with an old fashioned answering machine - and just what the fuck was 'tweeting', anyway, he mused, as he pressed the play button.

The first caller identified herself as Mollie's mother, asking Mollie to call her back. The following three calls were disconnected once the answer machine message kicked-in.

The fifth message was the voice of a man shouting the single word, "bitch!", before then disconnecting, the volume so loud, and the anger so intense, that Harry recoiled in surprise. The sixth message was the mother again, asking - almost begging - Mollie to call her back. There was no mistaking the edge of desperation in the mother's voice. Harry wondered who the angry male might be: Patrick, Mollie's father? By his own admission, he'd struck his daughter. The one word and the manner it was delivered, didn't really give any indication of an accent; regional or foreign. He studied the machine intently, unsure. It didn't appear to be able to display the caller's number, or when the message was left. He watched the digital display cease to flash, to then return to the number six.

On the wall above the small table was one of those clip-art picture frames, which held a montage of photos. Most of the photos featured Mollie and people of her own age, probably friends and other students from the college, and most of which seemed to have been taken in pubs and clubs, portraying scenes of revelry. There was one photo of Mollie giving another girl a full-on, girl-on-girl, French kiss. He wondered whether it was staged for the camera, or whether Mollie was bi-sexual. Either way, Harry again found himself wondering about the mindset of today's youth.

He moved into the small kitchen area, which consisted of two double base units - in one of which was the sink - and two double wall units. The oven and hob were housed in an adjacent single base unit. It was tidy and clean, but definitely past its sell-by date. In the cupboards, he found dried pasta, tinned tomatoes, rice, dried pulses and Tofu. Just about everything Harry didn't eat - and no baked beans. Didn't all students eat baked beans? While this may have been one student stereotype that Mollie didn't fit, she certainly fitted the stereotype of enjoying alcohol, judging by the number of empty wine bottles that were dotted around the room and now served as candle holders. The opened packet of Marlboro cigarettes and the king size packet of cigarette papers - with pieces torn off - that Harry found at the back of the cupboard brought a wry smile to his face.

An inspection of the fridge confirmed more alcohol, an opened carton of orange juice, some Brie, and a Cling-filmed bowl of cooked pasta; the smell and colour of which suggested it - like the kitchen - was out of date.

Harry moved onto the remaining two rooms. In the bedroom was a king sized brass bedstead covered with a brightly coloured throw, on which was sewn hundreds, if not thousands, of beads, sequins, and tiny mirrors. It was a beautiful piece of cloth, most certainly made in Asia, and no doubt, hand sewn. Brightly coloured silk-type scarves were also draped and looped on and through the bedstead. The bed was without doubt the centre piece of the room. At the other end of the spectrum was a free-standing double wardrobe and an overly large mirrored dressing table, both of which looked like they may have come from a Swedish furniture store. Items of clothing hung from the wardrobe handles, bulkier items were perched on the top. The mirrored dressing table was adorned like the bed, with scarves, necklaces, and items of jewellery. The top of the dresser was, and this was a word Harry knew the fairer sex would not agree with, *strewn* with items of makeup. He shook his head. Like most men, he'd never been able to understand a woman's need for such a vast array of cosmetics. There were enough brushes, powders and paints to stock the local DIY store.

On the wall above the dresser was a large portrait of a reclining nude, and it was clearly an original. It was painted in garish colours - probably what was referred to as abstract art - and didn't resemble real life, or hold any titillation. The face had a familiar look, though. From his back pocket, Harry withdrew the photo of Mollie. Even allowing for the dramatic style of brushwork, there was a strong resemblance. He leaned in close. Mollie had signed the corner of the painting, and it was dated the previous year. Harry studied the artwork for a few more seconds before turning away, idly wondering if the girl was as big breasted in real life.

Above the bed was a cloth wall hanging, not much smaller than the bed's throw. This too, though made of thinner cotton, was similar in its bright colours and sequins. Harry stared at it for a moment. Something wasn't quite right. Other than the fact it wasn't level - it was only *slightly* askew - it looked ok; but it was enough to offend his sense of precision and warrant a closer look. Harry's eye was drawn to the top corners of the cloth, where it was pinned to the plasterboard wall with large drawing pins. That was when he realised what it was that had been bothering him, yet had been unable to put his finger on. In the wall, around the top corners of the cloth, were numerous tiny holes. Harry moved towards the cloth, gripped a lower corner, and raised it to look behind. 'Well, well,' he said to himself. He gave the cloth a sharp tug. It fell down, revealing a very large mirror fixed to the wall. As Harry looked into it, he realised it was perfectly in-line with the mirrored dresser on the opposite wall. Judging by the many additional pin holes in the plastered wall, Mollie certainly got plenty of use out of the mirror.

He then turned his attention to the wardrobe. It was full. Some of the labels had names even Harry had heard of, so they were probably not cheap. Even though the rails where filled from end-to-end, there were some large gaps, and if the missing clothes were anything like the remaining ones on either side, they didn't seem suitable for the British climate at that time of the year.

He moved on to the draws of the dresser. The top drawer was full of knickers, the second of bras, and like the wardrobe, a large clump was missing from each, suggesting packing had been done in haste. Harry's experience of women - which was vast and plentiful - was that a woman would always pack a selection of underwear; some for everyday and some for 'special occasions'. The third and last drawer, revealed a mixture of items: stockings and suspenders, PVC underwear, sex toys, pornographic magazines and DVDs;

even a bullwhip. Harry was beginning to think his experienced opinion of women was a little outdated.

Pulling over the dresser stool, he used it to stand on and inspect the top of the wardrobe. Like most free-standing wardrobes, it was a haven for dumped and abandoned items: shoe boxes, little-used handbags, a rucksack, and a large suitcase were just a few. There was also a square of empty space, defined by the lack of dust, to suggest the absence of an overnight bag or a small suitcase.

Harry decided it was time for a brew, and some thinking.

Back in the kitchen, he boiled the kettle, and pre-warmed a mug by rinsing it with a little hot water, before then putting in a teabag and filling it. Having already noted the age of the milk, he opted to have his tea black. Placing the mug on an out of date television magazine which sat on top of a dust-filmed coffee table, he then slumped onto the sofa and stretched out his legs, resting his heels on the edge of the coffee table.

He gazed around the room, trying to imagine Mollie living there, seeking inspiration. To one side was a small wood framed bookcase made of the ever increasingly popular Indian wood. On top was what looked to Harry to be an MP3 Docking Station - Harry had only just started using CDs - and in it was what looked to be an MP3 Player, which struck him as a little odd. To Harry, people appeared as slavishly attached to their MP3 players as they did their mobile phones, so it seemed odd that Mollie didn't have hers with her.

As he sipped his tea, he brooded over the missing girl's whereabouts. The more he thought about it, the more he thought she'd simply gone away, abroad maybe; 'Done-a-runner', if you like. If she had, she'd probably done it to piss off her father. And having met the man, he couldn't really blame her.

Harry was unsure whether he should be getting involved in family disputes, and whether five grand was worth the aggravation. Aggravation he didn't need. He wondered if he were to prove to Patrick that his daughter was alive and well, yet not reveal her whereabouts, whether that would placate him enough to stump up the five grand. What Harry was sure about, was that he was out of his depth. There was no doubt in Harry's mind that this would "end in tears", as his mother used to say.

Once his mug was empty, and his brain equally so of inspiration, he decided he'd better make a move.

CHAPTER 9

The Doorman's official job title was now 'Head of Security', looking after the Boss's nightclubs. Unofficially, it was 'Enforcer', solving the Boss's problems. Of which, so far, there had been few.

Today, at the Boss's request, he was driving his employer and mentor to visit his ailing mother. Unusual. In that he'd been asked, and not the Boss's regular driver. The Head of Security was wearing a tailored suit, driving his own car. A sports car. An XJS. The Boss had cast an appreciative eye around the car. He'd also commented on the young man's suit, the cut of the cloth, that he'd taken his advice and gone to his own tailor. The Boss could see the young man growing in confidence.

He was pleased.

During the journey, the Boss gave directions and made small talk. He also intimated he had something to ask of his Head of Security. They would discuss it later.

The young man wondered why. Why he was favoured. Was he favoured? What was it the Boss wanted? Everybody wanted something, didn't they? That had always been his experience from as far back as he could remember.

In the car park, the Head of Security looked through his windscreen at a modern building. A private hospital. Discreet signs indicated direction and department.

Authoritarian... institutional.

The young man shifted uncomfortably in his seat, fingers tapping nervously on the steering wheel.

The Boss assured him it would be okay. He asked the young man to walk with him.

They walked along quiet, antiseptic corridors, the long elegant fingers of the older man gently touching the elbow of the younger. Guiding him.

Outside the door to a private room, the young man hesitated, prepared to stand watch outside, until the Boss's grip tightened, leaving no doubt.

In the bed lay a frail and wizened old woman, made more diminutive by the large hospital bed. A woman who was awake, yet the tired eyes that stared up at the ceiling seemed unaware of all around her.

A nurse sat by her bedside, keeping vigil.

A long hushed conversation between the Boss and the nurse followed. It did not appear favourable.

The young man stood to the rear of the room, and looked on.

The Boss turned to the woman in the bed. To his mother. He inquired after her health. She stared at the ceiling. He took her hand in his. She blinked, her head turned, a trickle of saliva ran from the corner of her mouth. Her son took a paper tissue and dabbed it away.

The Head of Security adjusted his tie, then his shirt cuffs. Nervous. Wanted to protest. Didn't think he should be there. Didn't feel comfortable. Again, wondered at the favouritism shown to him.

His employer called him over, introducing him to his mother as the young man he'd told her about, drawing a curious glance from the young man. The Head of Security shook woman's bony hand, uncomfortable at being in a personal family situation.

Suddenly, the old woman seemed very much awake, and very much aware. Her grip was strong. Recognition gleamed in her eyes, wild and intense. The Head of Security stepped back, alarmed.

The Boss smiled, knowingly, before turning to soothe the old woman, and straighten her bed sheets.

The young man quietly stepped from the room. Breathing hard, he loosened his tie, wiped his sheen covered forehead with the back of his hand.

The Boss rested a hand on his employee's shoulder, as he led him back through the long, yet empty corridors, and to the main entrance. He told the young man how his mother was not the woman she once was, but she seemed to like him, trusted him. He told the young man how you should be able to trust in family... despite what may have happened in the past. He emphasised the importance of family. How their set-up, the gang, were family.

The young man reflected on how the Boss had become a father figure. A man who had helped him, given him the break he needed. He didn't mind. He felt good about it. He felt secure, finally happy, at ease with the matriarch and patriarch figures in his life.

They reached the main entrance to then step outside. The Head of Security was relieved to be outdoors. He offered the Boss a cigarette. The two men quietly smoked, alone with their own thoughts, until the Boss spoke. He asked his young Enforcer to do an important job for him, one which was vital to his future, his freedom. Therein the young man's future.

A court case was pending, where the Boss was to be tried for a number of crimes. An informant in the police force had told him the whole case rested on the testimony of a key witness. A man who had turned Queen's evidence. A man who had once been an employee, and a member of the gang. A Man who had been nicked, banged-to-rights, for the brutal murder of a male prostitute, but had then made a deal. Turned on his own kind, to save his own skin. Turned grass. Become the lowest of the low. A Snitch.

The young man watched his Boss getting angry. He'd never seen the Boss angry before. The Boss said the man had no honour! Had been disloyal! Had betrayed a trust! He said trust was hard to come by. People to trust were few. He looked at the young man, to then say he'd made mistakes in the past about trust.

The Boss made it clear the problem had to be dealt with. Had to go away. Didn't matter how, just gone.

The young man, feeling loyalty, didn't want to say no.

The Boss laid on the guilt, so the young man couldn't say no.

The Boss passed his young Enforcer, an automatic handgun, telling him he might need it, and that he shouldn't take the Snitch's unusual sexual peccadilloes as a weakness.

The young man looked at the gun, unsure. Said he could take care of himself. The Boss did not doubt it, but the Snitch - who'd also been the young man's predecessor - was not a man to play by the rules. The gun was for back up only.

Talking of which...

CHAPTER 10

Bang! bang! bang!

There was a pause, then the pounding noise continued.

Bang! bang! bang!

It pounded incessantly into Izzy's brain, refusing to stop. She couldn't work out where it was coming from; and everything was black, she couldn't see *anything*.

She blinked rapidly. Nothing changed. She was blind!

She also felt uncomfortably hot, and was finding it difficult to breathe, as she became aware of a weight bearing down on her, leaving her feeling trapped; entombed.

The banging noise persisted. She started to panic. She threw up her arms in desperation, feeling the weight upon her, shift. A searing bright light hit her full in the face, forcing her to throw her hands up protectively. She gulped in fresh air as the banging noise suddenly doubled in volume.

As her eyes adjusted, she found herself looking through metal bars, at a familiar sight of tree tops and blue sky. For a few seconds her brain struggled to make the connection, while the banging noise continued to hammer away to such intensity, she thought she would scream.

Managing to wriggle out from under the overbearing weight of her duvet, she then shot out an arm to the bedside cabinet, to grab the mobile phone that was on the brink of pushing her into insanity. 'Hello,' she said, her voice unsteady.

'Isobelle?' came a voice.

Izzy opened her mouth, only for nothing but a rasping sound to come out.

'Isobelle? Is that you?' came the voice again, even louder.

She instinctively jerked her head away from the phone, but in doing so, caused a pain to shoot through her skull. She groaned aloud.

'Isobelle!' shouted her editor.

'Stop shouting,' said Izzy.

'Shouting? What are you talking about?' he replied. 'How are you getting on with the church story?'

'Church story?' said Izzy, trying to massage some life back into her face.

'Saint Aidens,' replied her editor. 'The one mentioned in the Doomsday book. The one you're supposed to be writing a story about, for Christ's sake! The one I want on my desk in time to go-to-press.'

Izzy groaned.

'Please tell me you've made a start on it?' screamed her editor. At least it seemed like screaming to Izzy. Then again, the drop of a pin would probably sound like a nuclear warhead going off. She came to the conclusion she had a hangover, but couldn't recall how or where it came about.

'Can't Jerry do the story?' she asked.

'No. He's covering the 'drugs in schools' story. You still need more experience in general reporting. You need to learn your trade, cut your teeth, before you cover the bigger stories. That's how it was done in my day, and while I'm still the editor here, that's how it will always be done.' He then proceeded to tell Izzy, at length, how it had been done in the old days, stories she was already familiar with, almost word-for-word.

She laid the phone down, rested her forehead in the crook of her arm, and groaned yet again. God, she felt rough. She could feel a headache building, and worse yet, she was feeling queasy.

She breathed slowly and deeply, trying to quell the urge to throw-up. She needed a distraction from the thought of projectile vomiting across the room and over her new and recently laid bedroom carpet.

She picked up the phone. 'Ed,' she said, cutting him off in mid-flow.

'What?'

'I'm on it, okay. I'm meeting the vicar and his wife, later,' she lied.

'Oh, right,' replied her editor, the wind taken out of his sails. 'Well, remember you'll be representing this paper, so be polite. And mind your Ps & Qs, no swearing,' he added.

'Don't worry, Ed. I will justify the money my father spent on my privileged education, and your well placed faith in me as a cutting-edge reporter,' she replied.

'Are you being sarcastic?' he asked.

'Moi? Me? No, perish the thought.'

'You sound funny. Odd,' he said. 'Are you all right?'

Izzy caught sight of herself in the tall dressing mirror in the corner of the room, and what she saw was a shock of wild blonde hair and a pasty face peering out from under a duvet tent. Not a pretty sight.

'Where are you? And what exactly are you doing?'

'I'm undercover,' she replied. 'I've got a lead.'

When he started to ask more questions, Izzy cut him short, saying she'd just spotted someone and she had to go, disconnecting before he could reply.

A short while later found her sitting at her small kitchen table with a cup of fresh steaming coffee in her hands, gazing out of the second-floor window at her neighbours' gardens below.It was a bright autumnal day. There were a few leaves left on the trees, but the majority were on the ground. She marvelled at the variety of rich colours. It looked like it had rained earlier. It was now almost midday.

As she sipped her coffee, she wondered what she'd done the previous evening. Had she gone out? Had she met anyone? Along with an empty bottle of white wine here on the kitchen table, there was also an empty bottle of red. Had she drunk both of them herself? She usually preferred white over red, but would drink it if there was nothing else. She couldn't remember having had any red in the flat.

She checked the diary in her BlackBerry for last night. It said she was meeting Jonathan straight after work. Had she met him? She couldn't remember doing so. Had Jonathan come round to her flat? She didn't know. The flat door was locked, bolted and the chain was on, so if anyone had visited, she must have locked up afterwards.

Feeling restless, she wandered around the flat, eating dried toast. As she entered the lounge, she stopped dead in her tracks. *What was that smell?*

It was the smell of food. The smell of stale food. And not just any food. *Meat!*

On her coffee table was an open Styrofoam carton, the type you get from a fast-food take-away place, and in it was what looked like half an eaten kebab. With her hand over her mouth, she leaned in for a closer look. It was a Donner kebab. Fat laden minced lamb... with chilli sauce... *and* garlic sauce... *and* chopped gherkin... *gross!*

'Oh, God,' she said, aloud, 'I think I'm going to throw-up.'

Izzy had been a vegetarian most of her adult life, and found the thought of eating meat - particularly red meat - repulsive. *How in God's name can anyone eat cooked flesh?*

She backed away from the kebab. Who had been here? Who had left half a stinking kebab in her lounge? Had Jonathan come over, after all? Had she simply forgotten he'd been there? Maybe she was just trying to convince herself he had been there, because the alternative was too gross to contemplate: *she* had eaten the kebab. She had got drunk, and then gone out and bought a kebab. A Donner kebab at that. With both chilli *and* garlic sauce!

She instinctively started to run her tongue around her teeth, searching for particles of meat as evidence of her lapse, and then smacking her lips for any residual taste of kebab. She was wondering if the procedure to analyse stomach content was complex and lengthy, when her probing tongue found something between her molars. Alarm bells started to go off. The logical part of her brain told her it was probably a piece of toast. The emotional part of her brain told her it was a piece of rotting flesh. It was then, Izzy realised with horror, that if she did want to have the contents of her stomach analyzed, it wasn't likely to be as lengthy or as complex as she'd first thought, because it was heading back up her gullet at a fast rate of knots.

Her eyes desperately searched the room.

A large ornate floor vase - which held artistically arranged dried grasses and twigs, only seconds before - had now become an emergency receptacle for what turned out to be coffee and undigested toast. No kebab.

In the bathroom, she vigorously brushed her teeth, to remove all and any trace of foodstuff - fresh or regurgitated. While doing so, she viewed herself in the mirror, taking in the bloodshot eyes, the smudged makeup, and a hairstyle probably last seen in a low-budget zombie horror movie. She pondered on how low she'd fallen.

Turning the shower on to a high temperature, she then stripped off and stepped in, under the powerful jet of hot water, gasping at the heat and force as it beat against her fragile body. She endured it for a few masochistic minutes, before reducing the temperature and reaching for the shampoo. As she showered, she desperately tried to recollect the events of the previous evening. She didn't like not knowing, not being in control. It made her feel vulnerable.

She was having maddeningly fleeting images which seemed to hover between her conscious and subconscious mind, just out of reach. Were they were actual memories or dreams? She couldn't be sure. But slave traders seemed to have some relevance... or was it bondage? Yes, that was it, it was bondage! She'd had a dream about a tall dark stranger - and whose face she couldn't quite make out - who'd stripped her naked, tied her up, and, despite her begging and pleading with him not to, was about to ravish and roughly take her against her will, when... what? What had happened next? Damn, her mind had gone blank. Who was the tall dark stranger? She tried to search out the scrap of memory so badly, it increased her headache, overriding the painkillers she'd taken earlier.

Then, all of a sudden, the elusive scrap broke free from her subconscious to her conscious. The face of the man - who'd been about to defile her, to do unspeakable things to her, things she couldn't comprehend, didn't want to comprehend - loomed towards her in a maddening rush, his identity about to be revealed. It was... it was... Oh-me-God... Harry! It was Harry and he was about to take her against her will!

Before she had chance to come to terms with that thought, another scrap of memory was released. 'OH-ME-GOD!' she said, yet again.

Harry had been here last night.

Here, in her flat.

Was it Harry who'd eaten the kebab?

A new thought occurred to her. What if she hadn't been dreaming, and that she had had sex; and with Harry? She might have done, she thought. Could have done, considering the amount of wine she appeared to have drunk - though she couldn't recall seeing any rope lying around the flat. She then found herself idly wondering that if they had had sex, had it been any good? Had *she* been any good?

Izzy's vivid imagination was beginning to run away with her, until - realising she was soaping her breasts in a caressing manner - she turned the water temperature to icy cold, dampening her sexual urges, and gasping at the sudden change in temperature.

CHAPTER 11

Harry exited Mollie's building to the cacophony that was London traffic: car horns blaring, engines revving, brakes squealing. The sky was blue and the sun was shining brightly. Other than a few small puddles and a damp patch between his shoulder blades, the recent rain shower was a distant memory. Harry was heading for the nearest Tube station. On the way, he took in the various local cultures, represented by the wonderful smells coming from the variety of cafes and restaurants, the shops and the wares they sold, and the street vendors. This is what he loved about Old London Town: its diversity.

Along the way, he would periodically go into a shop, show Mollie's photograph, and ask if she'd been seen recently. Most didn't recognise Mollie. A few said she looked familiar, but couldn't be sure. Some simply weren't interested. London was a big city full of strangers.

Harry reached the Tube station without finding anyone who'd recognised Mollie, and could say for certain they'd seen her recently. Next door to the station was an open-all-hours convenience store. He watched a flood of people exit the Tube station from a recently arrived train, and then head-off in all directions for their individual destinations, with a large number of them going into the convenience store. Harry followed. It was obviously a popular stop-off store for people using the station; particularly the homeward-bound rush-hour commuters, who didn't have the time or energy to go out of their way to any of the big supermarkets. He figured this was probably a store that Mollie might have used while travelling to and from her flat, maybe for cigarettes.

An elderly Asian couple - probably husband and wife - operated the two cash registers with ease, used to the wave-after-wave of demanding commuters. Harry waited for a lull at the counter, before approaching and showing them Mollie's photo. The couple viewed Harry with suspicion, asking him if he was the police, and was the girl in trouble. He'd already been asked this question previously, and at first, hadn't replied in a manner that had put the questioner at ease. Harry had never been much of a talker; he was the original Mr Monosyllabic - and because of that, it'd made them wary of answering. But, by this point, he had an answer on the tip of his tongue, should he need it. He told the Asian couple a part truth, that Mollie had had a slight disagreement with her parents, hadn't contacted them recently, and they were worried. This seemed to placate the couple. They studied the photograph and debated in their native tongue. They didn't seem sure. He then asked them if the girl had ever bought cigarettes. This seemed to prompt a memory. The man confirmed Mollie had bought Marlboro. He emphasized this by taking a packet from the shelf behind him, and waving it in the air. Then, still grinning, he plucked a king size packet of cigarette papers from the shelf, and waved that too, giving Harry a knowing wink of the eye. Unfortunately, that was all they were able to tell him. They hadn't seen Mollie for a week or more, and had no idea of her whereabouts.

Harry's next stop was to be the art college Mollie attended. Question was, how to get there? If he took the Tube, it was only a few stops, and straight through. If he took the bus, he would have to change. After a moment's hesitation, he headed towards the Tube entrance, telling himself it would be quicker, and that everything would be all right.

Joining a growing queue of travellers at the automatic barriers, he shuffled along, swiped his travel card, and then passed through the opened gate and towards the escalator which would take him down into the bowels of the earth. He could hear the sound of trains, coming from below, arriving and departing, closely followed by a blast of displaced warm air that would wash over the travellers.

Harry was being swept along amongst a sea of bodies and towards the platforms. He was struggling to breathe. It was hot, and there wasn't enough fresh air. A train hurtled out of the tunnel, braking hard to finally come to a stop. The doors opened, and the passengers who alighted were immediately swallowed up by the mass of bodies waiting to board.

Harry felt himself being pressed forward towards the open doors. Despite the heat, he felt himself breaking out into a cold sweat. His eyesight was blurred, and he was having difficulty in focusing. He was starting to panic.

He turned, forcing his way - none too gently - back through the crowd and to the rear of the platform, where he pressed his back against the cool tiled wall, fighting for breath. Once the train had pulled away, and the platform was almost deserted, he then hurriedly made his way towards the exit. He took the escalator two steps at a time, heading up towards fresh air, sunlight, and open space - and good old London buses.

When Harry walked into the main lobby of Mollie's college, the place was buzzing with youthful chatter and animated exuberance. He looked around, finding it hard to believe that most of the kids were in their late teens; they looked like they should still be in junior school. He was also surprised to see the college employed private security guards.

He made his way to the college library.

Unlike the lobby, the library was a haven of serenity, where students sat quietly, studying books and computers.

He approached a service desk. Behind it was a woman who appeared to be in her mid-fifties, not too tall in height, and, what could be called, broad in the hips. Her thick hair was more grey than dark, and cut short. She wore dark grey trousers with a navy blue pullover, and wire rimmed glasses. 'I've brought these back,' said Harry, dropping two of Mollie's library books onto the countertop.

'Good for you,' replied the Librarian, without looking up from her computer screen.

Harry stood waiting. He hadn't been in a library since he was a kid. Did they still stamp books in and out? Or was it all somehow computerised. He wasn't sure.

The Librarian finally reached over for the books. She started to type. 'These are out of date,' she said, as a matter of fact.

'Yes, I -'

'There'll be a fine to pay,' she said, interrupting.

Harry reached into his pocket for some loose change. 'That's okay. I don't mind paying -'

'And you're not Mollie Dolan, are you?' said the Librarian, as she looked up at Harry over the top of her glasses.

'How very perceptive of you,' he replied, smiling, struggling to suppress the sarcasm in his voice.

The Librarian's very bushy eyebrows knitted together in a frown. 'Boyfriend?' she asked.

'Please,' replied Harry, 'I'm old enough to be her father. I prefer my women a little more... mature.' With that, he gave her one of his best smiles.

'It wouldn't matter a jot to that one,' she said, impervious to Harry's charm. 'So, who are you?' she asked, raising her voice slightly.

Aware that people in close proximity were starting to take notice of his protracted conversation with the Librarian, Harry replied, 'A fellow student,' then instantly regretted it as the Librarian raised a bushy eyebrow. 'A mature student,' he added, as if in explanation.

The Librarian raised the other eyebrow. 'Is that what you call it,' she replied. 'There's mature, and there's old.'

Harry scowled; annoyed. This wasn't going as planned. His intention had been to ask a few simple questions. He looked at the Librarian, mentally weighing up how much effort it would require to drag her over to his side of the desk to answer some simple questions. Thing was, he didn't believe in violence against women - and she probably wasn't worth the hernia, anyway.

'Look,' said Harry, 'I just wanted to ask -'

'Ten pounds, please,' said the Librarian.

'What?'

'Ten pounds is the cost of the fine.'

'You've got to be fuckin' joking, me.'

'I don't joke,' she replied, 'and there's no need for profanity.'

Harry hesitated, wondering whether to continue or to leave it. He didn't like being ripped-off. Across the room, he spotted a security guard strolling. He dropped a ten pound note onto the desk, turned, and then walked away. He didn't need the aggravation. Seeing a sign for the cafeteria, he headed in that direction for a well earned brew, and maybe a few questions answered.

The cafeteria was busy. Harry went from table to table, showing Mollie's photo to the seated students, at which - as Harry loomed over them - they would quickly glance, before then shaking their heads and looking away.

Harry realised he wasn't getting anywhere; the students were either more interested in their food, or they felt intimidated.

He tried a different approach. Walking through to a lounge area where there were sofas, armchairs, and a bank of vending machines, he got a cup of tea from one of the machines, and then chose a chair close by to settle down in.

As students passed or used the machines, Harry would show the photograph and ask if they'd seen her. Some said they knew Mollie; some said they knew of her. But none seemed to know her well, and none had seen her recently.

Harry was beginning to feel he was wasting his time, until a boy and a girl approached the machines. Harry studied them. Both were dressed in black with hair colour to match. The girl had a large number of facial piercings that Harry found morbidly fascinating; the boy had only a nose ring and bottom lip pierced - but where he lacked piercings, he certainly made up for with facial spots. Harry concluded that these must be what are known as 'Goths'.

'Seen enough?' said the girl to Harry, when she noticed him staring at her.

Harry showed them Mollie's photo, and asked if they'd seen her recently. The girl just shrugged her shoulders while looking Harry over, weighing him up; the boy just grinned, inanely.

Harry asked the question again.

'Might have,' the girl replied.

The boy just sniggered.

'Well?' asked Harry, getting impatient.

The girl confirmed they'd gone to some of the same lectures; occasionally sat together. 'Are we friends?' she replied, in answer to another question. 'Yeah, right. Anyway, what's it got to do with you?'

'Yeah,' said the boy, speaking for the first time, 'who are you? Her dad?'

'A family friend.'

'Yeah, well,' said the girl, 'you look and act like her. All attitude. High-and-mighty.'

Harry, who wasn't known for his patience, unfolded himself from the armchair, to stand to his full height, forcing the boy and girl to take a step backwards, giggles and grins quickly disappearing. 'You're right about one thing,' said Harry. 'I've got more attitude than you've got pimples and piercings. So, stop fuckin' me around, and tell me if you've seen her.'

They both vigorously shook their heads, and meekly replied that they hadn't seen Mollie for almost a week. They did however, give him the names of some of the bars where she liked to hang out.

CHAPTER 12

Feeling slightly more human for having had a shower, Izzy was once again sitting at her kitchen table. Now wearing a pair of baggy jogging bottoms, one of Jonathan's old rugby shirts, and with her damp hair pulled back into a small pony tail, she was on her second coffee of the day.

On the table in front of her was her laptop computer, open and ready for the purpose of researching Saint Aiden's church for the article her editor had asked her to write. But she was bored. She found her attention constantly drawn to looking out of the window, daydreaming. She was dreaming of working for a proper newspaper, when the ringing of her mobile interrupted her thoughts. The caller display said 'Daddy'.

'Hello, Daddy.'

'Hello, Sweetheart,' replied her father. 'How are you?'

'I'm fine. You?'

Izzy and her father made small talk. They rarely discussed work and the *North London Gazette* outside of the office. Not that Izzy's father was often in the office. He was very much a hands-off proprietor. He preferred to leave the day-to-day running of the paper to his editor. He was also very much aware his daughter wasn't happy with her job, and that she felt she should be in a better position. For that he blamed himself, for spoiling his daughter and giving in to her demands.

'Are you ok?' asked her father. 'You don't sound too good.'

'It's just a head cold,' Izzy lied.

'Why don't you come round for Sunday lunch,' suggested her father. 'Bring Jonathan with you. Your mother would love to see you.'

'Stepmother, Daddy. And me and Jonathan are having... err... a bit of a break.' *Though I've yet to tell Jonathan!*

'Oh,' said her father. 'Well, you're still welcome, of course. Give it some thought, yes?'

'I will. Thank you. Love you.'

'Love you too, Sweetheart,' said her father, disconnecting.

Izzy knew her father wasn't big on talking about emotions. Probably just as well, she thought, sighing, as she turned to look out the window.

She found her thoughts turning to Jonathan. They'd been seeing each other for almost three years, engaged for the last two, yet neither of them seemed to want to push the relationship any further on. *Maybe we're both afraid of total commitment.*

Izzy decided to push all thoughts of Jonathan out of her head before she got herself emotionally wound-up, but in doing so, she then found her thoughts straying to Harry, and before she could stop herself, the thoughts she'd had in the shower. She felt herself flush with embarrassment, which annoyed her. She was a grown woman for Christ's sake, why should she feel embarrassed about such thoughts in her own home?

To distract herself, she moved her finger across the mousepad of her laptop, to bring the blank screen springing back to life, and the page she'd been viewing - which had absolutely nothing to do with Saint Aiden's church. Just before her father had called - on the spur of the moment and out of curiosity - she'd typed 'Harry Windsor' into Google's search engine. Unsurprisingly, most entries had been about Prince Harry of the British Royal Family. She'd then tried typing the name, 'Henry Windsor'. She knew Harry's given name was Henry, from when she'd searched for him on the Register of Electors. Again, most of the entries had been for Prince Harry; though there had been a few other Royals from the past (Dukes and Barons), and also one or two notables from the world of science and medicine: but no gangsters.

'Facebook!' she said, loudly, to no one other than herself. 'Gottcha, Harry Windsor. *Everyone's* on Facebook.' She first typed Harry, and then Henry, into the Facebook search engine. There were plenty of people called Harry and Henry Windsor, just not her Harry... that sounded weird, she thought. *Her Harry.*

Izzy rested her elbows on the table, cupped her face in her hands, and stared at her computer screen. She told herself she shouldn't be surprised. Harry wasn't a Facebook-kind-of-guy... more of a mugshot-book-kind-of-guy. She laughed out loud at her own joke, and then winced as her headache reminded her she had a hangover.

She then tried a different approach. She Googled 'gangster'. There were hundreds of entries. Some about gangster films, some about popular music with gangsters as the theme - generally rap music - and then there were the articles from newspapers and books on organised crime: this was the trail she started to follow.

Eventually, after three hours of trawling through hundreds of articles, she found what she was looking for: an old article on organised crime in London reported the collapse of the criminal trial of a man called Henry Solomon, an antique dealer who was on trial for allegedly masterminding a string of robberies, money laundering, and a variety of other crimes. The trial had collapsed after the key witness had mysteriously disappeared.

There was a photograph of Henry Solomon descending the court steps to a waiting car. The photograph was small and grainy, but Izzy could clearly see he was elegantly dressed in a three piece suit with a cravat, and that he carried a walking cane. *Dapper* was probably the word to describe him, she thought.

She peered closer. In the background, a few feet behind Solomon, was another man. He was also smartly dressed, had a closely shaved haircut, and came across as having an unmistakeable air of confidence about him. He was turned away from the camera, in profile, but she was sure it was Harry, the faithful lieutenant.

CHAPTER 13

It was late afternoon and Harry was in a bar opposite Mollie's college, its close proximity making it a popular choice with the students. In his lap was an open copy of the *Evening Standard* newspaper. On the table in front of him was a pint of ale and a whisky chaser: it'd been that kind of a day. His head was still buzzing from conversations he'd had, and questions he'd asked. He'd spent most of the day showing Mollie's photograph to anyone who was prepared to listen. Along with local shopkeepers and traders, he'd asked students and college staff. In fact, he'd asked enough people to cause enough concern, that he was asked to leave the college premises by the security staff.

Unable to concentrate on his newspaper, Harry was now people watching. The alcohol had started to take effect. He could feel the warm glow of the whisky spreading throughout his body, his racing mind beginning to slow. He was idly staring into space, enjoying the moment, when he became vaguely aware someone was approaching him.

Two young women stood before him: a rake-thin peroxide Blonde, and a dumpy Brunette. 'Are you the guy looking for Mollie Dolan?' asked the Brunette.

Harry was wondering how they knew to ask him, until he saw the spotty faced Goth at the bar, looking over towards them. 'Do you know where she is?' he asked.

'Are you the police? Is she in trouble again?' asked the Blonde.

Her comment made Harry pause for thought before answering. 'No, I'm not the police. Mollie's father hasn't heard from her. He's concerned.'

'Yeah, right,' said the Brunette. 'The only thing he's concerned about is his wallet.'

'Are you friends of hers?' asked Harry.

'We hang out together sometimes,' replied the Blonde.

'So, you any idea where she is?' Harry asked again.

Both girls just shrugged their shoulders. 'Mollie's her own woman,' said the Brunette. 'She's probably shacked up with her new smackhead of a boyfriend, having a drug fuelled shag-a-thon.' This made both of the girls giggle.

Harry realised he hadn't seriously considered a boyfriend being the reason for the girl's disappearance. He recalled Patrick using a boyfriend as an excuse for Mollie's mother's benefit, so Harry had assumed there wasn't a boyfriend. 'Do you know who he is? Is he a student?' he asked them.

'No way,' replied the Blonde. 'Mollie likes her men rough and ready, with a low IQ. She likes to be in charge, if you know what I mean,' she said, winking at Harry.

They turned to leave, giggling, until the Brunette stopped and turned back to Harry. 'You do know she's gone missing before, don't you?' They then turned and walked away, arm-in-arm, cackling loudly.

'Bollocks!' said Harry. He drained what was left of his pint, knocked back the whisky, and then scooped up his newspaper and headed for the door. He decided he would find a decent boozer on the way home, have a proper drink, and sod the consequences.

CHAPTER 14

It was early, and it was cold. Sal knew it was cold because he could feel it in his aging bones, and if he needed any conformation, all he had to do was breathe out, to see the vapour of his breath hang in the air. He briskly rubbed his hands together as he made his way from one portable gas heater to another. Out of the four heaters placed around the huge room that was Sal's Boxing Academy, he only lit two: every penny counts. Besides, he told himself, you can't mould kids into hardened fighters by pampering them.

Francisco Salvatori - Sal, for short - was a born and bred Italian. He'd moved to London in his late teens, to follow his childhood sweetheart and her family. It hadn't been long after the swinging sixties, and London - in contrast to his small Italian home village - turned out to be a young man's dream. The childhood sweetheart was soon forgotten.

After drifting through a number of dead-end jobs, he'd taken his hobby of amateur boxing professional and made it a career. But because he'd come late to the sport, and because he cut easily, he never managed to get into the big league, where the serious money was. But that was then, this was now. Sal still loved the sport, and what he enjoyed now was teaching the young kids, watching them learn the discipline of boxing which would serve them in later life. Some of them even went on to become professional boxers - though they usually moved on to a bigger and better gym when that happened, and who could blame them?

Sal's gym was in a rundown part of Kings Cross, and the building, like Sal, had seen better days. He leased the first-floor of what had once been a two storey warehouse building; the ground-floor now split into three units: a mechanic's body-shop, a mini-cab company, and self-storage. Unlike the ground-floor, the first-floor was mainly one large room, running from end-to-end, with one entire wall filled with old and ill fitting metal framed windows, through which, in the depths of winter, icy draughts would whistle, turning the place into an icebox, and forcing Sal to take a blowtorch to the frozen water pipes for the toilets and showers to work -

not that any of the kids would use the showers in the winter. In the summer, it was like a greenhouse. The roof was of slate, where holes would frequently appear, allowing in inclement weather and nesting pigeons. On occasion, Sal would have to venture up into the attic space, past pile-upon-pile of pigeon droppings, to block-up a hole and prevent any further water finding its way through to the gym below. Over the years, Sal had often asked the letting agent if the owner would consider selling the building. Every time he'd asked, they'd said no, the owner wouldn't sell; nor would they tell him who the owner was. He'd taught young kids to box there for almost thirty years; it was like a second home - though his present wife would argue it was his first, because he spent seven days a week there.

Sal moved around the gym, straightening the floor mats, putting away the free weights that had been carelessly left out from the previous day, checking the punch bags were securely fixed, and then vacuumed the floor of the full sized boxing ring that stood at the far end of the room: Sal's end of the room.

A few of the kids were drifting in - anyone under fifty was a kid to Sal. He saw the Windsor kid going through some stretching routines with one of the kick-boxing coaches, who he sub-let part of his gym to. It wasn't, in his opinion, proper boxing, but it helped pay the rent, and sometimes he would spot a genuine talent who he would then lure away from what he called "girly boxing" to teach them real boxing. Harry Windsor had been a genuine talent, but sadly had lacked the discipline. He'd been more interested in fast cars, fast women, and making a fast buck, as the Americans would say.

Sal stood and watched for a while, as the kick-boxing coach took Harry through some stances, getting him to sharpen up his movement. Front kick; side kick; roundhouse kick: kick, kick, kick.

Sal shook his head, mumbling, 'Girly boxing!' He had to give Harry his due, though: he was fast. *Very* fast. 'Hey, kid?' said Sal, calling over to Harry in his cockney-Italian accent. 'When you finished playing footsie with Jackie-fuckin'-Chan, maybe you come over here and let an old man show you how to fight proper, eh?'

Harry briefly glanced over, before turning back to the kick-boxing coach, who was busy giving Sal, the finger.

Half an hour later, Harry went over to Sal. 'Okay, old man. Show me what you've got.'

'We'll do some bag-work, first,' replied Sal. 'Using your hands, eh? Proper boxing. Get you loosened up. Give you a fighting chance before I beat the crap out of you.'

Harry put his bag gloves on, then adopted the boxer's stance: one foot slightly behind the other, shoulders hunched, elbows tucked in, gloves up, and with Sal using his bodyweight to brace the punch bag from behind while giving direction, he then proceeded to pound the bag.

'Left jab. Left jab,' instructed Sal. 'Right hook. And again.' Sal put Harry through his paces, pushing him harder and harder. 'Keep your elbows in, you flapping like a fuckin' bloody chicken!' said Sal, making loud clucking noises.

Harry could feel himself getting angry, but directed the anger towards the punch bag. Sweat was pouring from his body. He blinked rapidly as it ran into his eyes, making them sting, and difficult to focus on the bag. 'Hey, kid,' said Sal, 'you're sweating like a pig, and you smell of cheap fuckin' whisky.'

'It... wasn't... fucking... cheap,' replied Harry, in between punches, each striking the bag harder than the last, and forcing Sal to hang on to keep his balance.

'I thought you'd put all that behind you, eh?'

'Fuck off, Sal. You're not my mother,' replied Harry, as he landed a hard left jab. Then, dipping his shoulder to put maximum body weight behind the punch, he slammed a right upper cut into the bag, catching Sal by surprise, and putting him onto his backside.

Harry stepped back, breathing hard.

'No, kid,' said Sal, looking up from where he'd landed, 'I'm not your mother... She was a fine lady.'

They looked at each other for a moment, before Harry stepped forward to stretch out a gloved hand, and haul Sal to his feet.

'Get some water,' said Sal. 'Take a break.'

Harry pulled off his gloves, stripped off his tee-shirt, and then grabbed a towel and a bottle of water from his bag. He took a long pull on the refreshingly chilled water, then towelled the sweat from his face and upper body.

'Haven't seen you in a while,' said Sal. 'Where you been?'

'Still working on the flats,' replied Harry.

'How's it going?'

Harry shrugged. 'It's going - just. Money's a bit tight.'

'Hey kid. I know how hard you worked on that house. No one knows more than me. If I had the money, it'd be yours, you know that, but I'm barely covering my overheads, as it is,' said Sal, waving his arms around, indicating the gym. 'And the fuckin' rent's going up again next fuckin' month!'

Harry commiserated with Sal, before then telling him about Patrick's offer to find his daughter.

'Five fuckin' grand?' said Sal. 'You gotta be fuckin' joking me. You said yes, No?'

Harry merely shrugged. 'The girl's a tearaway. Doesn't get on with her father. Probably disappeared just to piss him off. It's a wild goose chase.'

'Are you fuckin' crazy? It's five grand for a few days work, for fuck's sake!'

'It's a family affair, Sal. None of my business.'

'I'll do it then,' said Sal. 'Just like that other great Italian.' When Harry frowned, 'Columbo, the detective,' Sal then added.

'I always thought of you as a Clouseau, type of character,' replied Harry, grinning.

'You cheeky fuck,' said Sal, throwing a headguard in Harry's direction. 'Put that on and get in the ring, so I can kick your shit.'

With both men now in the boxing ring and wearing protective headgear, they danced around the canvas, sparring with each other, blocking and trading punches, using enough force for the other man to feel the blow, but not enough to do any serious damage. While Harry had the advantage of height and reach, Sal - despite his age - had experience on his side. He would avoid a jab, or a hook, by coming-in under his opponent's swing, to then deliver a punch to the ribs, stomach, or an uppercut to the chin.

'Who is this Patrick?' asked Sal, as he caught Harry with a left. 'One of your 'old friends'?'

'No, he's not one of my "old friends", as you like to call them.'

'So why did he come to you, eh, Mr Clever Shit?' So Harry told Sal about the newspaper article and Isobelle Harker. 'Is she pretty?' asked Sal, grinning broadly as Harry threw a left hook, and which he avoided by dipping his head, followed by his shoulder, and then delivering two quick jabs to Harry's ribs. Sal heard and felt Harry's breath blow past his ear. He could see Harry thinking about the question as if for the first time. 'Bloody hell, kid. If you gotta think about it, she must be a fuckin' dog,' he said, as he skipped backwards out of Harry's reach.

As Harry moved around the ring, he found himself thinking about his first meeting with Isobelle, in the greasy spoon cafe. He'd looked her over; of course he had, as any red bloodied male would have done. Yes, she was pretty and attractive, but he hadn't really taken any notice, had he? His second meeting with Isobelle had been at her flat. Why had he gone to her flat? His reasoning had been to give her a bollocking for putting his name in the local newspaper, yet, as she'd quite rightly pointed out - and of which he had been aware before setting out for her flat - she hadn't printed his surname. Some of his "old friends", knowing he lived in the area, might have given some thought to the possibility of a connection - as might some of the older coppers who still worked the area - but hardly conclusive. Then he remembered he'd taken a bottle of wine as a gift - not the action of someone who'd gone to deliver a bollocking.

'Hey, kid,' said Sal, interrupting Harry's thoughts, 'you're not turning into a gay-boy, eh?' Then, just to wind Harry up further, 'What you need is a good woman with child bearing hips. You gonna have to get fuckin' married sometime, kid. This Isobelle, does she have child bearing hips?' he said, laughing, as he bobbed and weaved away from Harry's punches.

'You're a fine one to talk,' replied Harry. 'How many times you been married? Seven? Eight?'

'Hey, you cheeky fuck,' said Sal. 'Six. Six times only.'

'Tell me, old man, what is it they see in you?' Harry asked, grinning. 'It can't be your good looks, because you're one of the ugliest fuckers I've ever met.'

'Hey,' replied Sal, trying to look offended. 'They love my cooking. I am Italian. I love women and food. Beautiful women. Beautiful food. My meatballs are to die for.'

As Izzy made her way up to the first-floor, via a rickety metal fire escape, she wondered two things: whether she'd got the right place, because the building looked derelict - though the guy at the mini-cab company on the ground-floor assured her she had - and whether it was safe, because it sure as hell didn't look it; there were weeds growing out of the brickwork for Christ's sake!

Inside the gym, she pulled her coat tightly around herself; it didn't seem any warmer inside than it was out. She looked around the large room. There were about a dozen men of varying ages, from their teens to their forties, all working-out in one form or another. The few who'd noticed her entrance seemed to double their efforts - boxing harder, quicker, and with more ferocity, lifting weights higher and faster, their torsos rippled in muscle and gleaming in beaded sweat.

Izzy's thoughts strayed to Jonathan. Since he'd injured his knee playing rugby, he'd put on quite a bit of weight, though not so much from lack of exercise, but from the amount of lager he consumed when meeting up with his rugby mates in the pub.

At the far end of the room, Izzy saw the boxing ring, in which were two men who appeared to be sparring - at least that was what Izzy thought it was called, but couldn't be totally sure. The taller, younger man, had his back to Izzy, and was in the crouched stance that boxers take. Izzy felt sure it was Harry.

Harry and Sal were still trading hard hitting blows, along with equally hard hitting insults. Harry's height, reach, and youth helped him to hold his own against the experience of the shorter and older man, and Harry was starting to get his second wind, the alcohol from the previous day and night's drinking now almost purged from his body, leaving his dulled reflexes sharper, his eye more focused. But Sal was aware of this and keeping his distance, bobbing and weaving, striking only when the opportunity presented itself.

Harry, seeing Sal's gaze flick briefly away and to the left of him, went for a quick jab, but Sal saw it coming, too nimble, too wily. Harry's glove slipped harmlessly over Sal's shoulder.

'Hey, kid,' said Sal, 'that little bambino, the reporter...'

'Isobelle.'

'Yeah, yeah. Isobelle. I bet she's a cute blonde with great cheek bones and freckles. Hey, kid?'

Harry was so surprised at the accuracy of Sal's description, he dropped his guard slightly. Seeing an opening, Sal moved in. But Harry was quick to raise his gloves, deflecting the punch.

'Something like that,' replied Harry. 'How did you know?'

'Heh, heh,' chuckled Sal, as he bobbed and weaved.

Again, Harry saw Sal's gaze flick to the left. This time he whipped in a right hook to Sal's temple, catching him off guard, and once again putting him on his backside. Harry skipped backwards, towards the ropes, grinning broadly.

Izzy approached the ring, fascinated, almost mesmerised. She'd never been a fan of boxing, never seen a fight other than a maybe few minutes on television. She thought it brutish, vulgar and violent. Izzy's sporting interests only stretched as far as lacrosse, which she hadn't done since school - and shopping. To Izzy, shopping for clothes wasn't a necessity or even an idle pleasure; it was a sport - an 'extreme sport' and sometimes a *blood* sport if anyone got in her way during the sales.

She watched Harry and the older man move around the ring with surprising grace, intermingled with bursts of raw power. She realised she actually found it quite appealing, alluring, even... sexually exciting.

She saw the older man go down. She saw Harry backpedal, arms loose at his sides, clearly enjoying his opponent's discomfort. She gazed up at Harry's half naked torso, took in the width of his muscled shoulders. Then, in surprised shock, she let out a gasp at what appeared to be scars across Harry's back, dozens of long thin red welts.

Harry quickly turned at the sound, to see Isobelle standing there and looking slightly self conscious. 'What are you doing here?' he said, a little more abruptly than he'd intended.

Izzy, who was now feeling *very* self conscious, and a little annoyed at Harry's tone, shrugged her shoulders and replied, 'I was just... passing.'

A wry smile tugged at the corner of Harry's mouth as he removed his gloves and head-guard. He quickly towelled his upper body and then pulled on his tee-shirt. 'How did you know I was here?' he asked, his tone a little softer.

'The old man who lives in your house... I think he said he was a colonel? Anyway, he said you would probably be here.'

'Corporal,' said Harry, leaning on the ropes to look down at Izzy.

'Sorry?' she replied.

'Mr Jackson was a corporal. He spins some great yarns.'

Izzy made a silent 'Oh,' with her mouth.

'Don't get me wrong,' continued Harry, 'there's probably a lot of truth in them. How long were you there for? Half an hour? An hour?'

Izzy shifted from one foot to the other as she said, 'Two hours, actually.'

Harry raised an eyebrow.

'He's a very interesting man,' she said. 'A *mature* man has so many more life experiences than a *younger* man,' she added, to which then followed the sound of a polite cough coming from behind Harry.

Half turning, Harry said, 'Talking of old... I'd like to introduce you to Francisco Salvatori. Sal to the *few* friends he's got, and owner of this fine establishment. Sal, this is Isobelle Harker. Isobelle, this is Sal.'

Sal went down on one knee, to then reach through the ropes for Izzy's hand. She reached up to shake his, only to have a kiss gallantly placed on the back of hers.

'Izzy,' said Izzy to Sal, blushing. 'Izzy to my friends.'

'You are a very pretty lady,' said Sal. 'You bring a ray of sunshine to an old man's heart.'

Harry groaned, loudly. 'Haven't you got anything to do, old man?' he asked, prodding Sal's backside with the toe of his training shoe. Sal stood, giving Izzy a big smile and a wink of the eye, Harry, he merely ignored, as he wandered over to the other side of the ring on the pretence of looking busy.

Sal's right, thought Harry, she is pretty and does have great cheek bones. 'So, why are you here, Isobelle?' he asked.

Izzy held his gaze for a few moments before answering, 'Izzy,' she said. Then, 'How's your search going for the girl? Mollie?'

'It's not,' Harry replied. She looked at him, waiting. He continued, 'It's a waste of time. A dead-end. It's going nowhere.'

'No clues? No leads?' asked Izzy.

'No,' replied Harry. 'No "clues", no "leads",' he said, raising his hands and then patronizingly wiggling his fingers in the air.

'Who have you seen? What have you done so far?' she wanted to know.

'I've searched her flat, I've spoken to her friends, and I've talked to local shopkeepers. It's a dead-end. A waste of time.'

'So you're just going to give up?'

'What I do know, is that she's struggling with her college course work, and she's fallen out with her father. She doesn't want to be found. She's probably shacked up with her boyfriend somewhere.'

'But you don't know that for certain,' she said.

'It's not the first time she's disappeared,' responded Harry, exasperation creeping into his voice.

'Oh,' replied Izzy, looking deflated. Then, 'But what if something really *has* happened to her, and she's in trouble? It's been what, almost two weeks since she disappeared?'

'Then it's up to her parents to report it to the police.'

'But they won't. Or seem reluctant to. You said so yourself, Harry. Even if they do have a poor relationship, what self respecting parent would not have their daughter's best interests at heart?' she asked.

'I don't know,' admitted Harry. 'Though there's something about the father that doesn't quite add up.'

Harry looked at Izzy, who said nothing, just gazed back at him, waiting. After a moment, he said, 'Ok, I'll search her flat again. Maybe I missed something,' he conceded. 'Maybe there are some "clues" or "leads", as you put it.'

'Do you want any help?' she offered, eagerly.

'I'll manage,' he replied, straightening up from the ropes.

A disgruntled Izzy realised the conversation was over, as Harry scooped up his gloves and head-guard from the canvas.

'Hey,' she said to Harry, 'would you like to have Sunday lunch this coming weekend?'

'Sunday lunch...' replied Harry. 'Who with?'

'With me, dopey. Who else.'

Sunday lunch, thought Harry. *Why the hell does she want to have Sunday lunch? Is she asking me out on a date? Do people have dates over Sunday lunch?*

A thought occurred to Izzy. *Oh-me-God, he probably thinks I'm asking him out on a date!* 'You'll be able to tell me if you find anything in the girl's flat,' she quickly added. Then, because she couldn't think of anything else to say, and because Harry was staring dumbly back at her, she said, 'Do you like kebab?'

'Kebab?' repeated Harry, looking more dumbfounded. *Christ, this girl's weird!* 'No.'

'Oh,' replied Izzy.

Harry thought she sounded disappointed. 'Not for Sunday lunch,' he said. 'Maybe after a few beers.'

'Really?' she said, brightening slightly.

'Ah, the great British Sunday roast,' said Sal, who had quietly wandered back over to where Harry was standing. 'Roast beef, crispy roast potatoes, Yorkshire pudding. The family around the table. The grandchildren, the great-grandchildren... ah, bellisimo. Wonderful.'

'Must be a big table,' muttered Harry.

'You enjoy a family get-together, Mr Salvatori?' asked Izzy.

'Sal, please call me Sal. Of course, I am Italian. I like to cook and I like to

fu -' Sal was distracted from finishing his sentence, by a well thrown boxing glove bouncing off the top of his head. 'What?' he said, arms askance.

'You'll have to excuse me,' said Harry to Izzy, turning to leave, 'I have to go take a shower.'

'Need anyone to hold your towel for you?' said Izzy, grinning broadly.

Harry stopped in his tracks, as did Sal, both men staring at Izzy in surprise.

Izzy stared back, realising her flippant remark hadn't quite come across as she'd intended - in fact, she'd sounded like a common tart. She felt her face begin to heat up. 'I'll, err, pick you up on Sunday,' she said to Harry, as she took a step backwards. 'Mid-day.' With that, she turned and fled.

'Hey, kid,' said Sal, playfully jabbing Harry in the ribs, 'she likes you. She fancies you. Eh? You can tell.'

Harry merely gave Sal a look, before returning his gaze to a very embarrassed Izzy, as she hastened out of the door. 'She's certainly a strange one,' replied Harry.

'I said it before, kid. You ain't getting any younger. Did you check out those child bearing hips? You need to give her some of that cockney-boy charm you used to be famous for when you were younger, and still could get-it-up. Impregnate her, make lots of bambinos, and be happy.' Harry merely grunted, still watching the door, deep in thought. 'Ah,' said Sal, 'if only I were younger...'

Harry glanced at Sal. Then, throwing an arm across the older man's shoulders, he looped a forearm around his neck, in a mock stranglehold, and said, 'Since when did that ever stop you, you randy old fucker!'

CHAPTER 15

Harry entered Mollie's flat once again, but not before pressing the intercom button on the outer door, just in case; and not before knocking on the door of the ground-floor flat to ask the reclusive, yet beady-eyed old woman if she'd seen Mollie recently. He took the shake of the wizened old face through the crack of the open door - prior to it being slammed firmly shut in his face - as a definite no.

Inside the flat, nothing appeared to have changed. Surfaces were still coated in a light film of dust, and the stack of mail remained unopened. And what had also not changed in the last twenty four hours was Harry, again at a loss as to where to start.

So he started in the bedroom. He looked amongst the bedding, under the pillows, in the pillows, and under the mattress. He searched pockets of clothing, jewellery boxes, drawers and make-up bags. The bathroom cabinet revealed little more than another extensive array of cosmetics, toiletries and cleaning products. On the spur-of-the-moment, he even checked inside the toilet cistern, for no other reason than he'd seen it done in a film. In the kitchen, the search continued: tea caddy, coffee jar, tops of wall cupboards, even the freezer compartment got checked, which didn't reveal much, other than a few vegetarian sausages. Sofa seat cushions were lifted, CD rack given a close inspection, out-of-date television magazine scrutinized.

The effort of the search, and the stuffiness of the room, had Harry breaking out into a sweat. He took off his jacket, and draped it on the back of the chair in front of the small table. Hands on hips, he scanned the table top: books, writing materials and computer. He studied the blank screen of the computer, wondering if it was likely to be of any help. He wondered how you switched it on. Should he phone Izzy and ask her? He had her business card in his pocket. He reached into his pocket for his mobile phone, but instead of phoning Izzy, he skimmed through recently made phone calls, stopping at Mollie's mobile number, to then press the green button.

Since Harry's search had begun, he'd texted and called Mollie's mobile phone on a number of occasions, but received no response to either. He waited. The dialling tone started. Something wasn't right. The dialling tone seemed excessively loud. It almost seemed as though the ringing was in the same room as he was.

He looked around, trying to focus, to narrow down from where it came. He moved towards the sofa. He'd already checked under and behind cushions. The sound seemed to be coming from behind the sofa itself. Harry pulled it forward, away from the wall. On the floor behind the sofa was a bag. A medium sized black leather bag with a drawstring top. A ladies bag. Harry could imagine Mollie placing it on the back edge of the sofa, as a handy spot to leave it. It must have fallen down the gap between the sofa and the wall.

He picked it up, untied the drawstring, and then reached inside to pull out a ringing mobile phone. He looked at the caller display, and saw his own number, just before the phone stopped ringing and went to voicemail. Unlike Harry's less-than-new mobile phone, this one was a new touch-screen type. And like the computer, he had absolutely no idea how it worked.

Back at the table, Harry searched the remainder of the bag's contents. He pulled out a small leather wallet, inside which were credit and debit cards, shop store loyalty cards, a library card, some loose change, and twenty five pounds in notes. In a side pocket of the bag, were a handful of bank statements, untidily jammed in. He also found a set of car keys. Another handful brought out an A5 sized diary, and a foil strip of what Harry assumed was birth control pills. Replacing the foil strip, he turned his attention to the diary, opening it up at today's date, to then start flicking back through the pages, going back almost two weeks before he found an item. It consisted of a few lines of neatly written text, explaining Mollie's feelings on that particular day.

Skipping through the page-a-day diary, it became apparent Mollie only used the diary to record her feelings, and not for day-to-day appointments. The entries were few, and random. Days would pass without an entry, and then there would be a spell of consecutive entries. Sometimes they consisted of a few lines, sometimes a whole page. The writing varied in its neatness and clarity, often cryptic. Names were rarely used: "He did this", "he did that". Someone called "Maggie", who appeared to have a "drink problem", and with whom Mollie often argued, was also occasionally mentioned.

Harry noted the time of day was written in the margins. The longer, more rambling entries were often late at night, suggesting to Harry that Mollie may have been under the influence of something at the time. As he read further, it became apparent the girl's life was not a happy one. In fact, for one so young, it appeared tragic.

Harry was sitting at the table - the diary now closed - having difficulty in comprehending what he'd just read. The cryptic style of writing did not make the understanding of the entries any easier, but even if he'd managed to grasp only a bit of what Mollie had been through - endured - then the enormity of what he'd just read was deeply disturbing.

Whatever Harry's thoughts and concerns might have been, they immediately disappeared when he heard the frenetic rattle of keys in the door to the flat.

He leapt to his feet, scooping up the bag, the diary, and then his coat which he draped over his arm, hiding both bag and diary; his legs slightly splayed and his body tensed, in anticipation of what is about to burst through the door. The time period between the violent rattling of the keys in the lock, to the aggressive slamming shut of the door, suggested to Harry his unexpected visitor knew he was there, and was looking for confrontation; and he was prepared to wager good money on the old lady on the ground-floor being the snitch.

The door to the lounge was flung open, and a woman strode in, stopping abruptly when she almost collided with Harry. She stepped back, then looked Harry directly in the eye. 'Who the fuck are you?' she said.

So much for social niceties thought Harry, as he stared back at her. He saw a tall slim woman of about five foot ten, dark haired, mid forties. She was wearing a tight mini-dress that accentuated her long legs and cleavage, with a short leather jacket over the top, and a large number of gold bangles on each arm, with gold dangling earrings to match.

What he also saw, was a woman who was very angry.

He watched as she leaned across to place a brown envelope on the stack of mail - *well, that's one question answered* - seeming a little unsteady as she did so, having to rest her fingertips on the table edge to compose herself.

'Are you the prick who's turned my daughter against me?' she asked, jabbing a finger in Harry's direction. 'Are you the new boyfriend?'

Ah, thought Harry, Mollie's mother. He should have realised. The familiarity of the voice was, of course, the voice he'd heard only yesterday, on Mollie's answering machine. Harry could see that Mollie's dark and sultry looks had been inherited from her mother. 'Well? Talk to me for fuck's sake. Don't just stand there fuckin' staring at me. Where - is - my - fuckin' - daughter?' she screamed at Harry, spittle flying, fists clenched. The woman's accent was south of London, broad cockney, and Harry was sure there was a lilt of Irish in there. He was also sure there was a slight slurring in her speech.

Maggie.

She took a step forward; clenched fists, raised. She hesitated, wanting to strike out and vent her anger.

Harry stood his ground, waiting for the blow, no intention of striking back, no intention other than to fend off the blows. No intention of hitting a woman.

The blows never came.

'Tell me, please!' she said, as she slumped onto the chair Harry had just vacated.

He thought quickly. What to tell this woman? If he said he was the boyfriend, then the conversation was only going to get worse; there would be demanding questions to which he had no answers. If he said he wasn't the boyfriend, she would probably want to know what he was doing there in her daughter's flat. He couldn't tell this woman the real reason, because she wasn't aware of the argument her husband had had with their daughter, and that he'd given her "a bit-of-a-slap". As much as Harry despised men who beat up women, he wasn't prepared to get any deeper into their family issues than he already was.

'It's Maggie, isn't it?' said Harry. Mollie's mother nodded, brusquely wiping away her tears, and smearing mascara across her face, not thinking to question how Harry knew her name. 'Maggie, I don't know where your daughter is, and that's the honest truth.' Harry didn't know what else to say to the woman. He'd always found it difficult when it came to handling emotional situations. He tentatively touched her shoulder, in what he hoped was a gesture of reassurance, before walking out of the flat, and quietly closing the door on the sobs of grief that were coming from within. On the stairwell landing, he leaned his back up against the wall, head tilted back, to let out a long sigh. He found himself thinking he could kill for a cigarette.

CHAPTER 16

The noise from the blast of the shotgun, reverberated off the bank's walls and high Victorian ceiling, intermingling with the screams of human voices.

The smell of gunpowder was strong in Steve's nose, and - along with the painful ringing in his ears - he could feel an acrid taste at the back of his throat. The barrel of the shotgun was hot to the touch as he gripped it tightly, struggling to wrest it from the hands of the masked bank robber.

As they fought, Steve looked into the eyes of the masked man; they were wide and white with fear and with anger. For a moment, for a fraction of a second, Steve thought he saw - or sensed - familiarity.

The man was tall and powerfully built, and Steve could feel his own strength failing; he watched the barrel of the shotgun swinging upwards and towards him.

The gun went off for a second time. Again the roar of the blast bounced off the walls, and again the screams of the bank's customers and staff rang out. Steve felt a blast of hot air blow past his face, just before the masked gunman gave a final jerk on the now empty shotgun, pulling Steve off balance and towards him, whipping his head forward as he did so, to then head-butt Steve across the bridge of his nose. Steve felt his legs give way, collapsing to the floor as the gunman fled. The last thing Steve remembered as blackness crept over him, was the pretty blonde cashier cradling his head, telling him he was a hero; his hero.

The next thing Steve was aware of was that he was in a bed - what seemed to be a hospital bed - and that the bed was surrounded by people. Photographs were being taken, cameras were flashing. The Mayor of London was also there, and he was saying something to Steve, something about how proud the people of London were of his courage and actions, that he was an upstanding citizen. The Mayor wanted to give him an award for bravery. But something didn't seem right. The Mayor was Ken Livingstone. A number of years and successive Mayors' had passed since Ken Livingstone was Mayor, hadn't they? Was he suffering from concussion? Had he travelled back in time? His confused thoughts were then interrupted by the hospital fire alarm going off. Everyone in the room looked at each other, all thinking the same thing. Was it a drill? The alarm continued. Suddenly everyone was panicking and screaming, and running around in circles, pulling at their hair. All except the Mayor of London, who was now Boris Johnson, and who was smiling benignly down at Steve as the alarm continued to ring, getting louder and louder.

The shrill beep of the early morning alarm clock, wrenched Steve from his slumbers and back to reality.

Naked, and with eyes and head heavy from sleep, he stumbled through to his en-suite bathroom and into a hot Power Shower, to emerge ten minutes later, considerably more awake than when he'd gone in. Teeth cleaned and freshly shaven, he applied some moisturiser to his face. He believed in looking after himself. *The body is a temple, etc.* He studied his reflection. His boyish looks and stylishly cut dark hair belied his thirty eight years of age. His soft features made him almost pretty. He turned heads, both male and female. What he considered his only flaw was the bump on the bridge of his nose where it had been broken - twice, and by the same person. This train of thought then led him back to his dream. Weird, he thought.

Ablutions finished, he picked up a small cloth and then wiped around the basin and taps, leaving them as clean as when he'd started. Bare foot and naked, he headed back into the bedroom, enjoying the feel of the thick, lush carpet under his feet. He picked up a television remote control, and a forty six inch wall mounted TV screen sprang into life, showing the early morning BBC news. An adjacent door to the bathroom led him into a large walk-in wardrobe, where double rails on either side of the room showed rows of suits, shirts, trousers and jackets. From a drawer of underwear - all the same brand and colour of black - he took out and then put on, a pair of boxers and socks, followed by a starched and pressed cornflower blue shirt, which he first removed from the dry cleaner's protective cover.

Steve loved his three storey Georgian terraced house in affluent Hampstead. As he dressed, he reflected on how he'd come to acquire it: he'd bought the repossessed four-bedroomed property at auction, and for a fraction of its market value. Now fully renovated, it was worth a small fortune. The decision to use half of the adjacent double bedroom to create an en-suite bathroom and walk-in wardrobe was, in his humble opinion, inspired. While the remaining adjacent bedroom was now a large single - and presently his home gymnasium - it was still a four-bedroomed house, its value not just holding, but increasing. The two remaining bedrooms were kept as guest rooms for visiting friends - the few that he had.

He smiled at his own foresight and astute business acumen, as he chose a black, narrow pinstriped, three piece suit, a highly polished pair of heavy black brogues, and a primrose yellow silk tie, to finish off his ensemble.

Downstairs he collected a copy of the Financial Times from his front door letter box, strolled into the kitchen - where the television was already on and showing the BBC News - and switched on his Combi coffee machine, opting for an espresso.

Breakfast was a bowl of natural bran flakes, to which he added - because it looked and tasted suspiciously like cardboard without - a handful of dried fruit and freshly sliced banana, before liberally dousing it with skimmed milk.

As he ate his breakfast and sipped his coffee, he skimmed through his newspaper, checking the stocks and shares while half listening to the television news, until his ears pricked with interest at the name of a senior Metropolitan police officer who was being interviewed, vehemently denying allegations of fraud and corruption within the Metropolitan Police Force. A snort of derision escaped Steve's lips.

Breakfast over, he then placed his newspaper into his briefcase, along with his iPad and mobile phone. Before leaving for work, he checked the security locks on all ground floor windows and rear door, checked the CCTV was on, and then set the sophisticated alarm system. Closing his front gate, he cast a glance at his top-of-the-range Mercedes-Benz sports car, parked roadside, before striding out for the fifteen minute walk towards the Finchley Road train station.

Armed with a double Latte from the deli next door to the train station, Steve caught the six thirty five for a ten minute journey to Willesden Green. As the train gently rattled along, he sipped his coffee, and pondered what to do over his upcoming long weekend: go to the West End and see a show, or maybe catch a movie? Not quite the same on your own, though, he thought. Maybe he would call into his local pub, see who was about, watch some football on the big screen TV, though pubs weren't really Steve's 'thing', and he wasn't much of a drinker, either. Half a lager shandy would usually last him most of the night, and he certainly wasn't into football; he'd rather watch golf or tennis, neither of which was on that weekend. He didn't even have the option of working; overtime had been reduced to the bare minimum due to budget cuts, and because he'd taken very little leave-time, he was also having to take Monday off to use some of it up. 'Use it or lose it' was the department's policy. He would probably end up doing what he did most weekends: gardening, housework, and watching DVDs with a take-away meal, he thought, glumly.

Steve's place of work was a modern building. He walked through the main entrance and into a lobby area, to then nod a greeting to the uniformed man sitting at the reception desk. 'Morning, Sarge,' said Steve.

'Morning, Constable,' replied the Desk Sergeant, barely raising his eyes from the *Sporting Life* newspaper spread out in front of him.

Steve's office was 'open plan', one large room with about two dozen work desks and, as usual at that particular time of the morning, all empty. His desk was across the far side of the room, stuck in the corner. A fact not lost on Steve. The desk - like his house - was spartan and functional: a desktop computer, keyboard, telephone and a nameplate.

Placing his coffee and briefcase on his desk, he removed half a dozen paper case files from the briefcase before placing it on the floor. After hanging his jacket over the back of his chair, he sat down and turned his computer on.

While he waited for it to boot-up, he straightened his keyboard and untangled the chord to his telephone. The office cleaner never left things the way he liked. The nameplate - D.C. Stephen Marshall - wasn't quite parallel to the back edge of the desk. As he straightened it, he idly wondered what the record was for the oldest Detective Constable in service. He contemplated - and not for the first time - on his lack of career success. Would he ever make D.S.? Detective Sergeant? Probably not, for what he suspected could be a number of possible reasons: envy because of where he lived and because he drove an expensive car - which was the reason he no longer used it for work, opting to use one of the pool cars instead - or the suspicion he was a bent copper? It could be one or both of them. More likely though, it was because of his D.I., his commanding officer. In polite terms it could be referred to as a personality clash, in less than polite terms it could be because his D.I. was a wanker, and that he'd got it in for Steve - and Steve *hated* swearing. He glanced at the case files on his desk. No amount of accepting or volunteering for the dead-end cases, the crappy jobs nobody else wanted - runaways, prostitutes getting beaten up by their punters, car theft etc - or working long hours was ever going to change that.

At ten minutes to eight, Steve checked his watch, before then deciding to get a coffee to take into the eight o'clock briefing. His intention had been to get a cappuccino from the deli, two doors down from the police station, but as he headed towards the exit, he spotted two of his colleagues talking at the hot drinks vending machine. He veered towards them.

On most days, Steve would not be seen dead using one of these machines; the selection was limited, and the quality and taste was on a par with industrial cleaning fluid. But today, he couldn't be bothered to make the effort to go to the deli, and besides, he hadn't spoken to anyone for at least an hour.

As he approached, he heard them talking about going out with a few of the other officers for a "Ruby" - a curry. 'Hi, Guys,' said Steve. His colleagues nodded acknowledgment, stepping to one side to allow him access to the machine. 'Did you Guys see the footie last night?' he asked over his shoulder, as he rummaged for some change. 'Cracking match by all accounts. Didn't get chance to see it, myself.' he reached down for his coffee, grimacing at its colour. 'The pundits' reckoned Spurs could go all the way to the final. What do you guys think?' he said, as he turned, only to find his colleagues had gone. 'Guess it's going to be a DVD and a take-away, then,' he muttered to himself.

CHAPTER 17

At eleven thirty five on Sunday morning, Izzy pressed the doorbell for the ground-floor flat, long and hard, a smile tugging at the corners of her mouth. After a few moments, the door was thrown open to reveal Harry: pencil tucked behind an ear, a battery operated power drill in his hand, wearing jeans, tee-shirt, a fine covering of sawdust, and a heavy frown upon his face.

'Morning,' said Izzy. 'My, my, is that a power drill in your hand, Harry Windsor? Or are you just pleased to see me?'

Harry's gaze took in a smartly dressed Izzy, wearing sharply cut beige trousers, and a white cotton blouse. 'You're early,' he said.

'My finely tuned reporter's instinct is telling me you're not a morning person, Harry,' said Izzy, eyebrows raised.

'You'd better come in,' replied Harry, turning.

Izzy followed Harry into the hallway, past the stairs leading to the upper floors, and through to his flat. She glanced through open doorways as he led her through to the kitchen at the rear.

'Wow! Nice kitchen,' said Izzy, running her fingers along the shiny black granite worktops and highly polished stainless steel appliances. 'It looks like it's unused,' she added.

'That's because it's not,' he replied. 'Used, that is. At least not much. I prefer to eat out.'

'Kitchens excite me,' she said.

Harry paused in the filling of the kettle, and gave Izzy a quizzical look. *Weird.* 'Coffee?' he asked. Izzy nodded, making herself comfortable at the kitchen table. From a wall cupboard, Harry got out a clean mug, into which he then put a spoon of instant coffee. 'Milk's in the fridge,' he said, indicating with a nod of his head. 'I'm going to take a shower.' He started to head towards the kitchen door, but stopped, remembering. 'Oh, yeah.' From a kitchen drawer he extracted Mollie's bag, and put it on the table in front of Izzy. 'See what your finely tuned reporter's instinct makes of that.' He then walked away.

Izzy glanced into the bag, and then at the retreating figure of Harry. 'Why do you disappear off to the shower whenever I call to see you?' she called after him. 'Do I make you feel dirty?' she added, with a grin.

Harry carried on walking.

As soon as Izzy heard the sound of running water, she was on her feet and wandering around the flat, looking into rooms, cupboards, and drawers, as any good investigative reporter would - or so she told herself. She saved the bedroom until last, conscious of the fact that Harry was in the en-suite bathroom. Naked.

She was looking through the contents of Mollie's bag, when Harry walked in. She studied him closely, peering at him.

'What?' said Harry, under her scrutiny.

'Haven't you got a shirt?...With a collar?... And *ironed?*'

Harry looked down. 'This tee-shirt is clean,' he replied. '*And* ironed.' He looked up to see eyebrows arched, lips pursed, and a steady look staring back at him. He sighed heavily, turned, and headed back to the bedroom.

On his return, Izzy was staring out through the French doors. 'This really is a lovely view,' she said, before turning to look at Harry. A frown of annoyance started to form on Harry's brow as he saw Izzy's eyes drop. 'I don't think the blue jeans really go.'

'Where-the-fuck,' asked Harry, arms wide, palms upwards, 'are we having Sunday lunch? The fuckin' Ritz?'

'It's a surprise. And there's no need to swear,' replied Izzy, turning her attention back to the view through the French doors.

Ten minutes later, Harry was wearing a smart pair of Chinos and they were out in the street, standing next to Izzy's car. 'I'll drive,' said Harry. Izzy's eyebrows shot up. 'If you don't mind,' he added, seeing the look. 'I don't make a good passenger.' He shrugged apologetically. 'And I could do with the practice.' Izzy, not looking the least bit convinced, threw him the keys anyway. When Harry noticed the broken wing mirror that had been duct taped back into position with all the finesse of a five year old wrapping a Christmas present, he said, 'What happened to the mirror?'

Izzy shrugged indifferently. 'You know how it is in London,' she said, as they climbed into the car.

Harry turned the ignition, and felt the rumble of the Saab's engine.

Izzy glanced across at him as she buckled her seat belt, a look of concern crossing her face. 'Have you flown one of these before?' she asked, referring to the Saab's power and aviation link.

Harry grinned broadly. 'Where to, your ladyship?' he asked, as he quickly pulled away from the kerb.

Izzy told him to head towards Chertsey. Harry's only comment at the distance of their destination was to say it was a nice day for a drive. Izzy assumed he would take the simplest route: the North Circular around to the M4, out to the M25, and then down to Chertsey, but Harry surprised her by cutting through Central London towards South West London, passing Richmond upon Thames, and then onto Chertsey. It was clear he knew his way around London; Izzy found herself seeing parts of the city she didn't know even existed. She soon relaxed back into her seat; Harry knew how to handle a car, lack of practice or not.

'Where did you learn to drive so expertly?' she asked.

Harry merely shrugged. 'Part of the job,' he replied.

She flicked him a glance, but he was straight faced and had his eye on the road. *"Part of the job"! What did he mean, "Part of the job"?* Recalling Harry's checkered past, Izzy wondered if he meant a 'bank job'. *Was he the 'get-away driver'?* Izzy was trying to decide whether to ask him or not, when he spoke.

'What did you make of the contents of Mollie's bag?

'Well...' said Izzy, searching for the right words. 'Its odd... Odd in the fact that all the day-to-day things a woman needs were in there. Everything. Meaning, why hasn't she got the bag with her? Money, birth control pills, phone... credit cards! What girl leaves home without her credit cards? Also, her bank statements show there have been no transactions of any kind for almost two weeks.' Harry nodded in agreement. 'And the regular monthly payment into her account stopped some weeks before that,' she added.

'I didn't see that,' said Harry, briefly taking his eyes off the road to glance at Izzy.

'You said she was a student?' Harry nodded. 'At a guess, I'd say they were payments from her parents for rent and bills and stuff. But why would they stop? She hasn't finished her course, has she?

'No,' said Harry, shaking his head. Then, after a pause, 'Did you read the diary?' A shadow passed across Izzy's face. She nodded her head. 'And?' prompted Harry.

'It reads like she was being... abused... Sexually abused. She writes how "he" likes to call her "daddy's little girl" when they are having sex, and how he likes to beat her...' Izzy shook her head in disgust. 'She never mentions his name. It's always "he". I thought it was her father - and maybe it is - yet I also got the impression there was more than one "he", and that maybe... just maybe... she likes it, sometimes.' Harry threw her a sharp glance. 'I don't know,' said Izzy, shrugging her shoulders. 'Call it woman's intuition - or barking up the wrong tree.'

The rest of the journey was spent in silence, both of them with their own thoughts.

As they approached Chertsey, Harry asked for directions, so Izzy directed him through leafy suburbs, to eventually arrive at a large set of imposing gates and a long sweeping drive up to what looked like a small mansion.

'Bloody hell! What is this place?' asked Harry, as they slowly cruised up the driveway towards the house. 'A hotel?'

'No. It's my father's home.'

'What?' replied Harry, braking sharply, forcing Izzy's body forward against the seat belt. 'You're taking me to meet your mother and father?'

'Stepmother and father,' she corrected.

Harry stared at her.

'Don't worry, Harry, I'm not going to ask you to marry me. My father has been badgering me to visit, so I thought I would 'kill two birds with one stone', as they say.'

Harry looked back towards the imposing period house, shook his head, then put the car into gear and drove-on towards the main entrance.

Harry and Izzy were met by a butler, who opened the huge solid timber front door just as they reached the top of the stone steps. Izzy warmly greeted the butler - who was called Stanley - by calling him Stan. As they entered into a large entrance hall, Harry took in the scene: a wide staircase led-off the hallway to the upper-floors, the walls were covered in a dark timber panelling, and this in turn was covered with paintings, carvings, and other such fine items of artwork; a few antique dressers stood against the panelled walls, and on top of them were more antiques, while the flooring was old marble mosaic, which echoed footsteps - as it did now, drawing Harry's attention to the couple that approached.

They were greeted by a distinguished gentleman who Harry put to be in his early sixties, and who was smartly dressed in what was undoubtedly a tailored suit, with shirt and tie. Accompanying him was by an attractive woman who Harry figured to be late forties, and who carried herself in what might be termed as a 'woman of breeding'. She wore an electric-blue wrap-over cocktail dress, which was tied at the waist, and finished just above the knee. She clearly looked after herself as the dress showed by the way it hugged the curves of her figure.

Harry was feeling a little 'underdressed'.

Izzy embraced the distinguished gentleman. 'Hello, Daddy.'

'Hello, Sweetheart,' replied her father.

'Barbara,' said Izzy, coolly, to the attractive woman.

'Isobelle,' replied Barbara, equally as cool.

'Daddy, I'd like you to meet a friend of mine. This is Harry Windsor.'

'Hello, Harry. Phillip Harker,' said Izzy's father, shaking Harry's hand firmly while looking into his eyes.

Harry could see that Izzy's father was a confident and successful man who was now weighing-up Izzy's new - and Harry guessed probably unexpected - friend.

'Mr Harker,' replied Harry, politely.

'Barbara-Anne,' said the well-spoken Barbara, taking Harry's hand, and flashing him an expensively maintained smile. 'With an 'e',' she then added, holding on to Harry's hand longer than was politely required.

'Pleased to meet you, Barbara-Anne - with an ''e'',' responded Harry, with an even bigger smile.

'Izzy didn't mention she was bringing a friend,' said her father.

'No, she didn't,' replied Harry, flicking a glance at Izzy.

'Shall we eat?' said Izzy, hooking her arm through her father's, to then lead him off, and bring a halt to any further questions. Harry and Barbara-Anne duly followed.

Sunday lunch was a subdued three course affair, interspersed with brief and polite conversation. Harry thoroughly enjoyed the Roast Beef, which was slightly pink in the middle, came with an array of vegetables, and was served by Stanley. Izzy, being a vegetarian, only ate the vegetables. Barbara-Anne apologized profusely - though not with a great deal of sincerity, thought Harry - for forgetting that fact. Izzy smiled back tightly, saying it was no problem at all, and that Barbara shouldn't worry her pretty little head - with even less sincerity.

After the meal had been consumed, and a reasonable amount of fine wine had been drunk - mainly by Barbara-Anne - they retired to the lounge for coffee.

'Harry...' said Barbara-Anne, to no one in particular. 'Isn't that short for Henry?' Barbara-Anne - who was sticking with the wine - was reclining in a large wing backed chair, the lower half of her wrap-over dress having parted completely, to show her long and elegantly crossed legs while somehow still managing to maintain some modesty - a state of which she was either completely unaware, or didn't care about. Philip Harker also seemed unaware, but a quick study of his eyes showed he was embarrassed and chose to pretend it wasn't happening. Harry could see that Izzy, on the other hand, was doing her best - badly - to hide her contempt for Barbara-Anne's behaviour.

'A bit like royalty,' Barbara-Anne continued. 'Are you a prince, Harry?'

'Far from it, Mrs Harker,' replied Harry, with an easy smile.

'What sort of education did you have, Harry?' asked Izzy's father.

'Daddy...' said Izzy, knowing where the conversation was leading.

'The usual,' Harry replied.

'The usual?'

'Daddy, I'm sure Harry -'

'Ah, you mean as in grammar school, then on to university. A university education is good grounding for a young person,' said Phillip Harker, casting a glance at his daughter. 'I've always encouraged my children to go the route of an institutionally educated career, explained to them that if they didn't, they could end up like many of the 'unfortunates' on the streets - unemployed and dependant on drink and drugs.'

Harry could see Phillip Harker was warming to his topic. He could also see that Izzy was looking more and more uncomfortable. Barbara-Anne indicated for Stanley to top-up her glass. 'I can certainly confirm I've had an institutionalised education.'

Phillip Harker frowned at Harry's phrasing.

Izzy froze.

Barbara-Anne sipped her wine.

'May I ask which one?' Phillip Harker enquired.

With a big lazy grin, Harry then said, 'Pentonville.'

'I don't think I've heard of a university called Pentonville before. Where is it?'

'Caledonian Road, North London,' replied Harry.

'Caledonian Road... I don't think...' Phillip Harker struggled to place a university on the Caledonian Road.

Izzy looked across at Harry, concern and excitement flicking back and forth across her face.

'The only institution I can recall on the Caledonian Road, is H.M.P. Pentonville...' Phillip Harker finally said, as he looked up at Harry.

Harry smiled back, benignly.

Phillip Harker visibly paled, as realisation dawned.

Izzy's hands flew to her face - though more to hide the grin, than from shock.

Barbara-Anne choked on her wine. 'You're a convict?' she said, in a strangled voice.

'Was,' replied Harry.

'What was your crime?' asked Phillip Harker, sounding a little worried. 'And how long were you jailed for?' he added, as an afterthought.

'Possession of Class B drugs. Cannabis. I was given three years - but I was innocent.'

A snort of derision came from Barbara-Anne. 'Yeah, right,' she said, dabbing at some spilt wine on her dress, 'all the cons say that.'

Izzy leaned forward; while curious at Barbara-Anne's turn of phrase, she also wanted to hear the details that Harry had been reluctant to reveal in their previous meetings. 'Three years seems quite a long time for possession of Cannabis,' said Izzy.

''Mitigating circumstances',' replied Harry.

'Such as?' said Phillip Harker.

''Assault on a police officer in the execution of his duty'.'

'I suppose you were innocent of that, too?' said Barbara-Anne.

'No, I was guilty of that. Two police officers were sent to arrest me. I head-butted one, breaking his nose, the other, I hit with a left hook, breaking his jaw,' replied Harry, amusement in his eyes.

No one spoke. Everyone stared at Harry - even Stanley, who had paused in the act of refilling Barbara-Anne's glass. 'But that was then, this is now. I'm a reformed character. And I'd like to say how much I've enjoyed having Sunday lunch with you,' continued Harry, smiling broadly at each in turn. He then turned to Stanley, 'Any chance of something a little stronger, Stan? A whisky with a little ice, maybe?'

As Stanley left the room, Phillip turned to his daughter, and in hushed tones, made idle chit-chat about the *Gazette*. Harry looked across to Barbara-Anne, to find her staring at him intently.

'Where do you hail from, Mrs Harker?' he asked.

'Kensington. Why?'

'Hmm,' said Harry, frowning deeply, 'it's just that I could swear there was the slightest trace of an East End accent in your voice,' he said, smiling. 'Are you an East End girl?'

'Good grief, certainly not!' responded Barbara-Anne.

'Are you sure? Accents fascinate me. I can usually place an accent within a few miles of its origin, and I would've said you were from the Stepney area. But that can't be right. You're too refined to have come from an area like Stepney. I must've got it wrong.'

'I sometimes do charitable work on behalf of the W.I., in parts of the East End, maybe that's it,' she replied, taking a large gulp of wine and forcing herself to return Harry's steady gaze. Harry gave her a wink, then muttered an 'excuse me', and went in search of a bathroom.

CHAPTER 18

The journey back into London was a subdued one. Izzy, who was driving, was thinking about her Father's comment about Harry being a "rough diamond", yet an "interesting man". She'd hoped to shock her parents, by turning up with Harry rather than Jonathan, but, she realised, the more she saw of Harry Windsor, the less she seemed to know about him: he was an enigma.

'You ok?' asked Harry, breaking into her thoughts. When she nodded in reply, he said, with a smile, 'Did you invite me to your father's house for the shock value?'

She glanced at him sharply. *Christ, don't tell me he's a bloody mind reader as well!* 'My mother seems to like you,' she said, in reply.

'Stepmother,' he corrected.

'What*ever*,' she replied.

'You don't get on with her, do you?'

'She's a money grabbing bitch, who only wants my father for what he's worth, rather than who he is.'

'Where did your father meet her?'

Izzy frowned. 'You know, I'm not sure. It may have been at his club, Hadleigh House in Richmond. Why?'

'Just wondered.'

'Do you know something I don't?' she asked him.

'I know that no amount of pronouncing your 'aitches', can hide an upbringing,' he replied. 'What happened to your birth mother?'

'She died of cancer when I was young.'

'I'm sorry to hear that,' he said, meaning it.

Izzy shrugged. 'I don't really remember much about her. All I've got left are photographs.'

'It's something, I suppose.'

They drove-on in silence for the next few miles, before Izzy asked Harry what he knew about Mollie's father, Patrick. In answer, Harry took Patrick's business card from his pocket, and said, 'No more than what's printed on this card.' He then told her he'd telephoned Patrick Dolan a number of times and left messages, but had no response. 'Something doesn't feel right about this... this whole thing,' he said, shaking his head.

Izzy glanced at the card that Harry was holding. '"Dolan Developments". That name sounds familiar. I'm sure the *Gazette* has covered a story on them. I think - and I could be wrong - they're on the verge of bankruptcy.'

Harry just shook his head. Somehow he wasn't surprised. Izzy then suggested they call in at the offices of Dolan Developments while on the way back to Crouch End, until Harry pointed out it was a Sunday, and the chances of someone being there would be slim - even more so if they were going bankrupt. Not one to be deterred, Izzy's next suggestion was that they go to Patrick's house.

'We don't know where he lives,' said Harry.

Izzy pulled over and parked. She then took out her iPhone and started to tap on the screen. 'Register of Electors!' she announced. 'I'll search the Electoral Role, through the internet, for a Patrick Dolan.'

'Don't you need to plug that into in a phone socket or something?' asked Harry.

Izzy gave him a withering look. 'Remind me Harry, what century were you born in?'

Harry merely grunted, and continued to watch her tap the screen. Then, 'What if there's more than one Patrick Dolan?' he said. 'Or is that a daft question too?'

'No, that's a good question. In fact, I would be very surprised if there was not more than one Patrick Dolan. There are probably hundreds.'

Harry looked at her, waiting. 'Okay genius, enlighten me.'

'His business address is in Kilburn, right?' Harry nodded. 'So, chances are his home address is not far away.' When Harry didn't look convinced, Izzy ploughed on. 'Patrick is Irish, yes?' Again, Harry nodded. 'Kilburn and neighbouring Willesden both have strong Irish communities so, logically, he may want to stay near his own kind - so to speak.' Izzy could see Harry was getting bored. 'Plus, plus...' she said, waving her iPhone at him to emphasise her point, '...Mollie goes to Camden Art College which is only a stone's throw away...' Harry rolled his eyes. '...and, listen. As a property developer, he's bound to have a big house, reflecting his vocation and love of property. So chances are, he lives on the borders of Willesden, Kilburn and Hampstead, which should narrow things down a bit,' she said, jabbing Harry with the phone to drive home her point.

'Bit tenuous,' muttered Harry.

'Aagh!' said Izzy, in frustration. 'This is the internet, Harry, not a bloody crystal ball!'

She returned to tapping on the screen, hunched over in concentration. Harry watched her. Her blonde hair kept falling down over her face. When it did, she would tuck it back behind her ear.

Noticing something, Harry leaned in a little closer, to peer at her. Izzy, sensing she was under scrutiny, froze, her eyes flicking up to catch Harry staring intently at her.

'Did you know,' he said, 'you stick your tongue out when you concentrate?'

The tongue shot back in, the eyes dropped, and Izzy went back to tapping. Harry sat back, smiling.

'GOT IT!' said Izzy, loudly enough to make Harry jump, and his smile slip. 'Patrick Sean Dolan, lives in Hampstead,' she told him, beaming.

'Okay, Lois Lane, I'm impressed.'

'Who?'

Harry groaned.

'Just kidding. Of course I know who Lois Lane is,' she said, grinning, as she started the car and pulled away.

Izzy parked across the road. She and Harry both stared out at the large modern detached house. There were no vehicles parked on the drive, and the blinds were closed. It looked deserted. 'Drive around the block,' said Harry. Izzy looked at him questioningly. 'Please,' he added.

Ten minutes later, after circling the block twice, and then dropping Harry off at the end of a lane - and with no instruction other than to go and knock on the front door - Izzy approached Patrick Dolan's house, lifted the heavy brass door knocker, and knocked loudly. Receiving no answer, she tried again. After what seemed an age, and still no sign of Harry, she wondered what to do next. Should she drive around to where she'd dropped Harry off, to see if she could find him? She decided to knock once more - if for no other reason than because she couldn't make a decision.

She was reaching for the door knocker when the door suddenly opened, making her jump back. There stood Harry. He indicated with a nod of his head for her to enter. As she followed him through to the rear of the house, he explained how he'd caught Patrick trying 'to-do-a-runner', out through the back gate that led onto a lane.

Izzy walked into what she thought must be the biggest kitchen diner in the world: moulded pine doors, marble style Formica worktops, red quarry tile flooring, and flower patterned curtains. Very homey. Shame it was a pigsty. Dirty pots and pans littered the worktops, and the sink was also full to the brim.

In the middle of it all, sitting at a large kitchen table - also strewn with dirty pots and remnants of food - was a man that Izzy took to be Patrick Dolan. Patrick was slumped forward, his large forearms resting on the edge the table, chin resting on his chest, clearly worse for wear. He was dishevelled; his eyes bloodshot; his face florid; the smell of stale alcohol strong. An almost-empty bottle of Irish whiskey was on the table in front of him.

Izzy could also clearly see a livid red mark on Patrick's cheek. She looked questioningly at Harry, who merely shrugged and said, 'I had to give him a-bit-of-a-slap.' Izzy noted that Patrick was a big man, as big, as if not bigger than, Harry.

She pulled up a chair to sit next to Patrick. Harry stood with arms folded, leaning back against the worktop, watching. 'Hello, Mr Dolan. My name is Isobelle Harker.' Patrick Dolan did not respond. 'I work for the *North London Gazette.*' Still no response. 'I wrote the piece on Harry.' Izzy saw Patrick's eyes briefly flicker in recognition. He lifted his head agonisingly slowly, and then turned his tired and worn face to look at Izzy, who smiled back reassuringly, before then gently asking Patrick what was going on. Slowly but surely, between incoherent rambling, Patrick told them about how his business was going into liquidation, how his leased car had been taken back, and how he'd re-mortgaged the house without telling his wife, and because he was behind with the payments, the bank was going to repossess their home. Through tears, he told them that when his wife had found out about the repossession, she'd walked out on him.

'That seems a little harsh,' said Izzy to Patrick, trying ease his unhappiness.

Harry looked on intently, and with mixed feelings. The annoyance he'd originally felt for the Irishman was slowly turning into anger, and yet he was fascinated by the amount of tenderness being shown to the man by Izzy, the spoilt-little-rich-girl.

'I took a risk... I gambled...' sobbed Patrick, 'with everything... all of it... everyone...'

'Dolan!' said Harry, taking a step forward, no longer able to contain himself, 'What about my money, the five grand you owe me? How exactly are you planning on paying me?'

Patrick slowly shook his head in bewilderment, his palms upwards, before they dropped back into his lap in resignation. 'Gone. It's all gone,' he mumbled. 'There's nothing left... no one left...'

Izzy glared at Harry. 'I thought you'd agreed to be paid on results only,' she pointed out to Harry. 'And at this moment in time, you haven't exactly achieved much, have you Harry?'

Harry turned away in anger. He went back to leaning against the worktop.

Izzy continued to glare at Harry for his lack of tact. 'Patrick,' she said, turning back, 'tell us about Mollie. Tell us what's happened to your daughter, Mollie.' Patrick lifted his head. He stared blankly into Izzy's face. Izzy saw his eyes once again start to well up with tears, as his thought process struggled with the alcohol that was numbing his brain, to remember his daughter. His eyes took on a faraway look, before his face then slowly crumpled, appearing to collapse inwards. Huge sobs of grief erupted from him, wracking his body, his broad shoulders shaking with the effort. He tried to speak, but was unable. Izzy placed a hand on his forearm, gently stroking it to reassure him, before then asking, 'Why did you go to Harry, for help?' Between sobs and gasps for breath, Patrick managed to tell them he'd borrowed money to pay off some of his debts. Izzy frowned, 'But what does that have to do with Harry?' she asked. Patrick then told her how he'd read about Harry in the newspaper. He tried to explain - none too clearly - how the interest on the money he'd borrowed kept going up and up, and that he didn't have it, wasn't able to pay it back. They said that if he didn't pay up, they would take everything that belonged to him. *Everything* that was dear to him. 'Patrick,' said Izzy, gripping his arm, 'who's "they", Patrick?'

Patrick inclined his head in Harry's direction, and then said, 'His kind.'

Izzy shook her head, not understanding what Patrick meant. '"His kind"?' she repeated.

Patrick nodded. 'His friends.'

Izzy shot a look at Harry, who shook his head, equally mystified.

'The Jew,' added Patrick.

All of a sudden, it seemed as though time was standing still for Harry. Nobody moved. Not a sound was made. Harry's past came rushing back at express speed.

Izzy looked back at Harry, who appeared frozen to the spot, his body all tensed up, as he stared fixedly at the back of Patrick's head, all trace of anger now gone. If a pin was dropped, it would sound like a bomb going off. She blinked hard, but the tableau remained. She quickly thought back to what had just been said. "The Jew", Patrick had said. *Why did that sound familiar?* That was when she remembered the conversation she and Harry had had in the pub a few days ago. Wasn't Harry's ex-employer also known by that name? Could it be the same man?

'Patrick,' said Izzy, shaking his arm to get his full attention, 'tell me about the Jew.'

Patrick explained how he'd been put in touch with a man named Solomon - also known as the Jew - who'd agreed to loan him eighty thousand pounds while he completed a deal on one of his properties. Unfortunately, the housing market had worsened further, so Patrick was unable to sell. The interest on the loan was crippling, and Solomon wanted his money, so he'd sent a man to collect it. The man had told Patrick he would take everything he valued... everything he held dear.

'"Everything I hold dear",' repeated Izzy. 'He wasn't just talking about monetary value, was he Patrick?' Patrick shook his head. 'Mollie?' When Patrick didn't respond, Izzy asked again, 'Have they got Mollie, Patrick?' The big Irishman just shrugged his shoulders. 'Were you hoping Harry might know something about Mollie? Or would know where to look?' Patrick nodded.

Harry interjected, asking Patrick to tell him what the money collector looked like. Patrick's description, through his grief, was garbled and vague. 'Was he carrying a knife?' asked Harry. The look of fear on Patrick's face told Harry all he needed to know. 'Cutter!... Fuck!' said Harry, specks of spittle flying from his mouth.

At this point, Patrick broke down completely, saying over and over again how sorry he was, and how he'd been a lousy father and husband, his body shaking with convulsing sobs of grief and sorrow, mucus trickling from his nose.

Izzy's heart broke, as she looked on helplessly. When she glanced at Harry, she saw only disgust and contempt before he turned and walked away. In her pocket she found a clean paper tissue which she gave to Patrick, before then standing to get him a glass of water, though not before moving the whiskey bottle from within arm's reach.

Harry was staring out through the patio doors at the wide open space of garden when Izzy came up behind him. 'Do you know this man, Cutter?' she asked.

'Yes, I know him,' replied Harry, angrily.

'Is he a friend of yours?'

'If that dumb Irish fucker,' said Harry, jabbing a finger towards Patrick, 'had told me about Solomon and Cutter sooner, it might not have got to this stage.'

Izzy looked up at Harry, unsure what to say. Harry was seething; his eyes blazed with anger, his fists clenching and unclenching. This was a side of him she'd never seen; hadn't expected.

Then she realised. *Was Harry afraid? If so, of what?*

Harry took a deep breath. Tried to calm himself. 'Cutter's a fuckin' lunatic,' he said. 'A drug-taking-psycho. His name's Wayne Salter, not a name he likes or uses. He prefers to be called Cutter, because of his love of knives. As a young boy, he used to cut the limbs off stray cats'. He killed his first man at the age of twelve. He was part of a street gang who attempted to rob an Asian newsagent. It went wrong. The newsagent raised the alarm, so Cutter stabbed him through the heart. When the Old Bill finally turned up, all the gang had fled except Cutter, who was still stabbing the dead body of the newsagent. The police pathologist was unable to determine the number of stab wounds due the body being so badly damaged. Cutter was diagnosed psychotic, and detained 'at Her Majesty's pleasure', in a secure institution, from where he was released a few years later, after evaluation, good behaviour, and continuous medication. The latter he stopped taking the moment he was free.' Harry paused, before returning his gaze to the garden. 'Mr Solomon used to occasionally use him for the more... 'difficult' types of jobs.'

'How do you mean, "difficult"?' asked Izzy.

Harry turned back to Izzy, to look into her questioning eyes. 'Messy, would be a better word...' Izzy could clearly see the conflict within Harry. 'The jobs that I refused to do,' he said, finally.

CHAPTER 19

'PIG!' yelled Izzy, at the top of her voice. 'Bloody arrogant pig!' she added, as she slammed the palm of her hand against the steering wheel of her car, sounding the horn to vent her anger rather than to alert or berate fellow motorists.

Both Izzy and Harry had driven away from Patrick's house sullen and angry; but for different reasons. When Izzy had expressed to Harry her concern for Patrick in his present state, Harry had dismissed it in a less than complimentary manner, making the journey back to Harry's flat far from harmonious. On arrival Harry had told Izzy, in no uncertain terms, that was she to get any further involved, and that she was to forget about Patrick and Mollie completely; he would deal with it.

Izzy was now carving her way through the London traffic. To where, she did not know, and frankly did not care. She was angry. 'How... How...' Again, she slammed the palm of her hand against the steering wheel, as she struggled to articulate her feelings. 'I mean... dismissing me like that, after all I have done for him. The ungrateful... Aargh!' she exclaimed, again yelling at the top of her voice, oblivious to the alarmed looks she was drawing from the motorists parked alongside her at the traffic lights.

CHAPTER 20

Snick! Snick! Snick!

The Head of Security was driving his XJS, on the way to deal with the problem of the Snitch. To enforce the Boss's request.

Snick! Snick! Snick!

In the front passenger seat was the man with the maniacal stare. Excited. Eager. Boasting what he was going to do to the Snitch. Opening and closing his flick knife.

Snick! Snick! Snick!

The Head of Security wasn't happy. This was the Boss's idea of additional back-up. The man was clearly unhinged. He was probably psychotic or a heavy drug user - or both. Either way, he was a liability.

The Head of Security kept his own counsel and his eyes on the road. He could feel the gun tucked into his waistband in the small of his back. He pictured pressing it against Psycho's temple, and pulling the trigger.

As he drove, he thought about how to deal with the Snitch, and in such a manner that he no longer posed a problem to the Boss. There appeared to be only one solution, and it was a step he'd never had to take before - so far.

The Snitch lived in a tower block on an estate in Harlesden. The Head of Security pulled into what served as a car park, negotiating broken glass, litter, haphazardly strewn industrial sized Wheelie Bins, and the only other car in the car park, which was burnt out. He was reluctant to leave his car there, but a quick getaway might be needed.

They approached a battle weary looking building. Some windows were curtained, some boarded over, and some had gaping holes, surviving shards of glass desperately clinging to the edges. Getting through the heavy, black painted steel outer door, without trying to use the broken intercom didn't prove to be an issue. The door lock was missing.

The lobby contained a bank of wall fixed post boxes for the tenants' mail - every single door bent, twisted or ripped off; empty beer cans; more litter and broken glass; and the overpowering smell of urine.

The lift door was open, ceiling light flickering, dangling control panel held in place only by its electrical wiring. On the walls, spray-can graffiti depicted crude images of male genitalia, football teams, and a lack of grammatical education.

They took the stairs.

The Enforcer paused outside the door of the Snitch's flat, still uncertain, until Psycho pushed past to repeatedly slam the palm of his hand against the door.

Decision taken.

Seconds later, the door was opened by a young male: bare chested, wearing sweat pants only, and looking less than focused.

Not the snitch.

Without invitation or consultation, Psycho launched himself forward, pushing the young male backwards and into the first room off the dingy corridor.

The Enforcer strode down the hallway, throwing doors open, to reveal empty rooms, leaving a reverberating boom and the agonised cries of pain and punishment in his wake. He smelled the sweet and distinctive smell of cannabis.

Last door, ahead.

Adrenaline building, blood pumping, muscles taut. Tense, anticipating, conflict expected. Pace quickening, heart pounding, fists clenched. Pain to be expected, pain to be inflicted.

Last door, partly ajar.

The Enforcer threw it open, only for it to spring back at lightning speed, violently cannoning into his chest then forehead, before his skull was whiplashed backwards, the crown of his head crashing into the door casing, legs buckling, body sagging, hitting the floor.

Dazed and directionless, the Enforcer felt the onset of blackness, of floating, weightless. A feeling of comfort, of welcome sanctuary. A feeling of bliss.

But it was only to be momentary, prior to crashing into an unforgiving brick plastered wall, and harsh reality.

Strong hands roughly grabbed the Enforcer's jacket, before he was airborne once again, clearing a sofa and crashing into a huge widescreen TV, knocking it off its stand.

Eyes blurred with tears of pain, he shook his head to clear his vision, knowing he had only seconds before the next attack.

A shape loomed up before him. Tall, grotesquely muscular, and semi naked.

The Enforcer lashed out, before he was again thrown about the room. He bounced and crashed off walls and items of furniture, like a ricocheting squash ball. He couldn't believe the Snitch's strength, punches and kicks seeming to have no effect - probably high on Steroids and Speed, a deadly combination making an adrenalin pumped battering ram. He realised, painfully, that he'd got at least a couple of broken ribs. The gun - which he hadn't intended to use - had been lost amongst the wreckage.

The Enforcer landed on a glass topped dining table which shattered and collapsed under his weight. He lay amongst the debris of mangled chrome table legs, and thousands of tiny diamond-like glistening pieces of shattered safety glass. He spat blood.

So much for back-up.

Muted shouting and banging on the party-wall from the neighbouring tenants could be heard, prior to their music being turned up in an attempt to drown out the noise.

Screaming obscenities, the Snitch picked up a heavy chrome table leg and raised it above his head, preparing to bring it down with maximum force on the head of his prostrate victim.

With lightening speed and force, the Enforcer kicked out both his legs, his heels connecting with his attacker's kneecaps. He felt and heard the crunch of cartilage.

The Snitch howled with pain, before falling to his knees, only to again cry out on impact.

The Enforcer pushed himself backwards, extracting himself from broken furniture, feeling the tiny shards of glass embed themselves in the palms of his hands as he propelled himself across the floor and back towards the wall, speeding up when his attacker started to drag himself across the floor towards him, oblivious of pain and broken glass, bellowing like a wounded bull, anger and hatred etched across his face, intent on revenge and retribution.

As the Enforcer's back hit the wall, he wondered if this is how it would end - the nature of his passing. Never before had he felt so tired and defeated. Being beaten to death by a semi naked bodybuilder could be considered vaguely funny if it wasn't so final.

That was when he felt the shape of hard metal beneath him. The shape of hardened, pressed steel.

The nature of his passing? Maybe, but not today.

He raised the gun.

Hesitated.

Ear splitting, gun blast. Echoing, then fading.

The acrid smell of gunpowder.

The neighbour's music abruptly stopping.

Only the Enforcer's laboured breathing could be heard, no other noise came from within the flat.

The Enforcer entered the kitchen, battered, bruised and bleeding, gun hanging loosely in hand.

The young male was on the floor, sweat pants around his knees, not moving. Blood everywhere.

One less witness.

Psycho stood, knife in hand, adjusting his clothing. He grinned, his teeth stained by blood. But not of his own.

He winked at the Enforcer, declared he'd taught the 'fag', a lesson.

The Enforcer looked at him, despising him, before backhanding him and catching him by surprise just above and below his right eye, the hardened steel splitting the skin...

CHAPTER 21

The evening was drawing in. The leaden grey sky that had periodically released November rain showers throughout the day was now turning to a light- polluted hue of dark orange.

In the gloom of a black taxi cab sat Harry, alone with his thoughts. The partition between the driver and the rear of the cab was firmly closed. The cabbie didn't offer conversation, and Harry didn't invite any.

Harry was on his way to Golders Green, to meet his past; it could be said to confront it, and, if so, a confrontation it certainly would be. Harry was an angry man. He could feel the rage building within him. A rage possibly strong enough to kill.

He gazed out through the cab windows at London city life: the hustle and bustle. Even on a Sunday evening it was busy: clubbers, theatregoers, tourists.

CHAPTER 22

Izzy was parked on a quiet suburban street. For two reasons: one, she was lost - not that she was concerned, she could just turn on her Sat Nav; two: she needed to think. Her forefinger beat a rhythmic tattoo on the steering wheel, indicating she had calmed down to a point of being only slightly annoyed. He is so wrong, she thought. *He's going about it all wrong. Mollie will get hurt - he will probably get hurt!* She sighed heavily. 'He's a pig-headed fool,' she said, aloud to herself. 'The police are the only people who can sort this out.'

She made a decision. On the local police force, there was a Detective Constable who, through the *Gazette*, she'd had dealings with before, and who, she suspected, had a crush on her. She would give him a ring. 'I'll show you, Harry Windsor,' she said, as she dialled her mobile.

CHAPTER 23

The steady tick of a grandfather clock, the hiss and crackle of an open fire, and the faint scratch of fountain pen on paper, were the only sounds that could be heard in the large, yet dimly lit room. Had the room been fully lit, it would have revealed rare and valuable antiques, original works of art, hundreds of books, hand woven tapestries and rugs. Along with the beauty and textures of the room's contents, was the wonderful smell of beeswax, adding a sense of history. Other than the glow from the fire, the only light was an anglepoise desk lamp that sat upon an elegantly preserved Louis XIV writing desk, and which shone down upon the ledgers that the hunched figure of Henry Solomon was diligently and patiently filling in. A china cup, filled with Earl Grey tea - brought to him by his elderly housekeeper before she'd gone home - was close to hand, but now cold and long forgotten in his rapt attention to the ledgers.

Henry Solomon was a man of advancing years. No one really knew how old he was, many would guesstimate early seventies. They would be wrong. He was elegantly dressed in a tailored three piece suit with a shirt and cravat. His divested jacket was on a coat hanger on a nearby coat stand. What little hair he had left was greying and carefully swept back, and with his goatee beard and the gold wire rimmed glasses perched on the end of his long nose, people thought he looked like everyone's favourite kindly uncle. They would be wrong on that count, too.

As he worked his way down the columns of figures, his lips moved silently as he calculated the amount, the interest, and the due total. As a young man, he had trained as an accountant. He loved figures; numbers. He loved money. And there lay the problem. As an accountant, he felt he wasn't being paid enough; paid his worth. So he put his training to better use. To a more profitable use.

His advancing years were reflected in his outlook on life. He rejected outright the possibility of using a computer to record his business dealings. The traditional method of pen and paper was more than adequate. The touch and the smell of the paper, and the beauty of the italicised word written in ink, were something special, real, tangible, a link to a past being preferred to the present or the future.

As he reached the bottom of the page, he tallied up the overall total, his head nodding in satisfaction. This done, he gently blew upon the page to speed the drying of wet ink, feeling the lightest caress of air against his hand as he did so. Though strangely, he thought, there was a chill to it, making him pause in reflection for a moment, before reaching for the cup of Earl Grey, only to realise it had gone cold.

He glanced up, over the top of his glasses, to peer at the grandfather clock. 'My, my,' he said, softly, 'time does fly.' Then, in a stronger voice, 'Do you not agree, Henry, my dear boy?'

Harry stepped out from of the darkened doorway, and into the light. 'Hello, Mr Solomon, sir,' said Harry, in the same respectful manner he'd always shown to a man he'd known all his adult life. 'You really should keep your front door locked at this time of night. There are some untrustworthy people about. Even in a respectable neighbourhood as this,' he added.

'People around here know me. Know who I am. So I don't think that is likely to happen. Do you, Henry?'

'I guess not,' replied Harry.

'Besides,' said Solomon, leaning back in his chair, 'I have Samson there to protect me,' indicating the large, shaggy, German Shepherd dog that now sat obediently at Harry's feet, ears pricked and gaze steady upon Harry.

'That is how I knew it was you, Henry. There are very few people he trusts enough to allow into this house.'

'You've still got him, then,' said Harry, reaching down to affectionately stroke the dog's head.

Henry Solomon's craggy face softened, as he watched Harry greet the dog like an old friend, before the dog padded back to his spot in front of the fire.

'Yes. Though, like me, he's getting old. Not so agile as he used to be,' he said, easing his skinny frame from his chair to place the ledgers he'd been working on into a large metal safe that stood against a wall, its door open, key in the lock. Once locked away, he then poured two glasses of Scotch whisky, a single cube of ice in each.

'It's been a while, Henry. Lillian's... your mother's funeral,' said Solomon, as he handed Harry his drink and indicated a chair close to the fire.

Harry hesitated before sitting, filled with conflicting emotions, conscious of showing respect to the old man, and the need to conclude his business, to get it over and done with.

Solomon watched the young man opposite him as he, in turn, watched the dog settle itself before the fire. It was clear to the old man that this was a different Henry Windsor to the one he had known. The boy had always had a bit of a temper when pushed, but this was different. There was anger. Raw anger.

'I'm guessing this isn't a social call,' said Solomon, carefully.

Harry took a sip of his drink, before turning his gaze from the dog to the old man. 'Patrick Dolan,' he said, simply. Solomon inclined his head slightly, waiting. 'You lent him money.'

Solomon shrugged his shoulders, indifferently. 'I lend a lot of people money, Henry. As you well know.'

'You lent him eighty thousand pounds which he has been unable to pay back. You then instructed Cutter to collect the debt,' said Harry, watching the old man carefully. Solomon stared impassively back at Harry, who'd not failed to notice the amicable smile which had slipped a fraction, or the coldness that had crept into the old man's eyes.

Solomon reached for a small silver box on his desk. He opened it, revealing cigarettes, which he then offered to Harry, who shook his head, raising a quizzical eyebrow from the old man. Harry had not forgotten his former employer was a heavy smoker, the tips of his long bony fingers nicotine stained in evidence. He watched as the old man took his time lighting a cigarette.

Exhaling long and hard, he said, 'Tell me something, Henry. What is your interest in this?'

Harry paused for what seemed a very long time, before answering. He took a sip of his drink. He wasn't really sure what his interest was. What had started out as a simple task, for which he was getting paid, was no longer simple - and nor was he likely to be getting paid. Harry wasn't even sure why he was still involved. 'I have... an obligation,' he finally said.

The old man nodded thoughtfully, as if this explained everything. He reached down to stroke the sleeping dog's head, before turning his attention to the dying embers of the fire, and say, 'You of all people, Henry, know how these things work. I instructed Cutter to collect the debt. How he goes about that, I really don't care, as long as I get my investment back.'

'Dolan's teenage daughter has disappeared. And with all due respect, Mr Solomon, sir, that fuckin' lunatic you employ, has probably got something to do with it,' said Harry, leaning forward, body tense, voice tight. 'You know I never approved of you using Cutter. He's a liability. A liability that one day could lead back to you. He's one of the reasons I no longer work for you, Mr Solomon,' said Harry, finally sitting back.

The German Shepherd raised its head, sensing a charged atmosphere. The old man noticed this. He looked back at Harry, and again pondered the young man's anger. 'Cutter has his ways. His methods. We both know they are not... subtle. But that's why I use him, Henry. To do the jobs other people cannot do... or no longer want to do...'

Harry nodded. The old man's last few words were not lost on him. He knew what he was implying. 'Where can I find him?'

'That, I do not know,' replied Solomon. Then, seeing Harry's expression was one of doubt, 'I took your advice. When I want Cutter's services, I employ him through a third party, so there is no direct link back to me.'

'Who's the third party?'

'I'm sorry Henry, you know I cannot tell you that. Discretion is vital for my business, 'Honour amongst thieves', as they say.' Harry studied the old man's face as he stubbed out his cigarette, and immediately lit another. 'Needs must, my boy. Needs must.' Then, after sitting back and taking a sip of whisky, 'Times have changed. The world has changed. It's a far different place from when I was young - and for you too. With that change, crime has changed. Technology is one example. With the advancement of technology, comes the opportunity to abuse it. To profit from it. London is a multi-cultural city, as you well know, and since the government changed the immigration laws, even more so. And with that multi-cultural diversity, came a multi-cultural crime wave. Yardies, Triads, Eastern Europeans - the Russians in particular are a ruthless lot. There are far less pickings for old fashioned villains like us, Henry.' The old man paused in his musings, gazing thoughtfully into the fire, while the grandfather clock continued to tick reassuringly in the background. 'We have to move with the times. We have to adapt. If we don't, we become extinct.'

Harry found himself relaxing, the tension and anger ebbing away. Maybe it was the whisky. Maybe it was the warmth of the fire. Or maybe it was the eloquent and rich baritone of the old man's voice. This was how it used to be. He and the old man would occasionally spend an evening like this, talking: talking business, talking philosophy, talking life, the young Harry Windsor listening to the old man's worldly wisdom with rapt attention. He had never quite been able to explain the ease in which he found himself when in the company of this patriarchal man.

Harry's thoughts were abruptly brought back to the present when he heard his mother's name mentioned. The old man was talking about how he had first met Harry's foster mother, Lillian. He'd first seen her in a London fringe theatre production of a Chekhov play. He described how the young and beautiful actress had mesmerised the audience with her performance, receiving a standing ovation. How he'd followed her career.

This was all new to Harry. He'd never asked, never inquired as to what the connection was between Lillian and the old man. Other than the visit to Lillian's home after Harry's expulsion from school, the old man had rarely visited the property.

'She was a wonderful woman, Henry,' said Solomon. 'A dear, dear friend. I do miss her.' The fire crackled. 'It's funny,' he said, after a pause, 'we are such selfish creatures. We don't really appreciate what we have until it has gone.'

Harry found himself speculating on the nature of the old man's relationship with Lillian. She'd never spoken of Henry Solomon to Harry, other than telling him to be careful when he'd given her the news he was in the old man's employ.

'It was admirable how you nursed your mother in her last few months. And a shame your arrest for drug possession prevented you being there at the end.'

Harry felt a lump forming in his throat, as the memories of his mother's dying days resurfaced. Memories he'd done his best to bury. Lillian's final few months had been at home, bedbound, nursed by Harry and a team of carers before the incurable cancer finally took her. The carers, who came in daily, tended to her personal needs: food preparation - Lillian's weakened condition meant she could only manage soups or liquidised food - and the administration of painkilling drugs. Harry tended to her remaining needs: feeding her, and company. He would talk to her, read her stories - Shakespeare was her favourite - or play her favourite music, anything to take her mind off the pain and discomfort. He would sit by her bedside while she was awake, and he would sleep by her bedside while she slept. And it was there, for the first time, he stopped calling her Lillian, and called her mother, and where he was momentarily rewarded with a pain free smile. It was also there the police came to arrest him on drug charges. Harry had pleaded with them to be allowed to stay by his mother's bedside, but his pleas had been ignored. He had not gone quietly.

And it was there that Harry's anger had been conceived.

Solomon could see the torment on Harry's face, and could sense the anguish in his heart, and for the briefest of moments, he felt remorse. 'I've never feared death, Henry. Though I have to confess, of late, what I do fear, maybe, is the nature of my death. Being alone when it happens. Frail and alone with no family, no friends.' He paused. 'Your mother's passing was not a lonely one, Henry. She was not alone when she drew her last breath.'

Harry looked up at the old man, questioningly, the painful memories temporarily forgotten. Harry was in prison on remand and awaiting trial when his mother had passed away. He'd never enquired as to the manner of her passing, preferring the torment of ignorance rather than the confirmation his mother had been alone when she died.

'I was there when she died. I held her hand as she passed away.'

Harry stared back at the old man in shocked surprise. 'Was there any one else there?' he asked.

'If you mean your brother -'

'Foster brother,' said Harry, abruptly.

Solomon briefly paused, a strange look on his face that Harry could not read, before carrying on. 'No. Your... foster brother was not there.'

Harry tried to weigh this news against the recent years of tormented ignorance.

'Henry?'

Harry realised the old man had been talking, but he'd not heard what had been said. 'Sorry,' Harry replied.

'I was saying, come back. Come back and work for me. It would be like the old days. The good old days. We are stronger together than we are separately. I have ideas, Henry. Big ideas. We can take on the new crime. Become a dominating force.' The old man's eyes gleamed with excitement as he spoke, and as he became more animated, the years seem to fall away from him.

Harry shook his head. 'No,' he whispered. Then, more forcefully, 'No! I made a promise.'

'Henry, my dear boy -'

'Don't... please... Don't call me Henry. My mother is... was... the only person to call me Henry.'

The old man held up a placating hand. 'Of course, of course. Who more than a parent has the right to use the given name of their child? The mother has that right, of course... as does the father,' he then said, looking at Harry in earnest.

Harry frowned. *Where's the old man going with this? What's he implying?*

'I also made a promise once, too,' said the old man, continuing. 'A promise I never thought I was likely to keep.' He looked down, to then pick at an imaginary piece of lint on his trouser leg. He sighed heavily. 'Over the years, there have been many...' he paused, searching for the appropriate words, 'indiscretions,' he finally said, looking at Harry, weighing him up. 'Two of which, you could say, were... notable.' The old man's gaze, again dropped, to study his now empty glass, briefly wondering whether to get up and refill it, before then saying, 'Stephen, your... foster brother, was one of them. The other -'

'How do you mean?' interrupted Harry, irritation creeping into his voice, a frown crossing his brow. 'As in Old Bill? Him being a copper?'

'No, no,' replied the old man hastily, his attention still focused on his glass, clearly uncomfortable. 'I had a relationship with Stephen's mother,' he said, raising his eyes. Harry's frown deepened. 'Stephen was a result of that relationship.'

Harry was stunned.

'Stephen's mother was a casual drug user, but she eventually became an addict. She died of an overdose while he was still a baby. Social Services took him into care.'

'Stephen's your son?' said Harry, incredulously.

Solomon merely nodded.

'Does he know?'

The old man shook his head, gave a small embarrassed cough.

CHAPTER 24

It'd been close to midnight when Harry left the old man's house, though he had no recollection of doing so, or if he'd bid farewell, or of walking the few miles home. It wasn't until he had to unlock his front door that he realised he was still holding the whisky glass the old man had given him earlier in the evening.

Harry was now sitting alone in his study, the only source of light the amber glow of a streetlight through the blinds. There was no comforting warmth from the fire, no soothing sounds of Cole Porter. Harry's only company was a freshly cracked bottle of Scotch whisky, to ease his troubled mind. He put the bottle to his lips and took a long hard swallow, to then feel a trail of fire burn its way down his throat. It was going to be a long night of soul searching. He didn't know it yet, but he was going to search the very depth of his soul for answers.

It was late the next morning when Harry awoke, only to find he was lying face down on the study floor in his own vomit. Next to him lay the bottle of whisky. What little of its content Harry had not managed to consume was also on the floor. If Harry had found any answers last night, he couldn't remember what they were. What he did know was that he had a major hangover.

CHAPTER 25

The combination of twilight and the streetlights' first flickers of life went some way to masking Harry's visual sense of the eighteen inch deep pan pizza in its cardboard packaging, which rested against the car steering wheel. His sense of smell however, was less fortunate. Having not eaten since the Sunday lunch at Izzy's father's house the day before, he'd convinced himself a stodgy pizza of cheese and tomato, onion, peppers, pepperoni, salami and pineapple was comfort food that would give him strength. The anchovies, however - a spur of the moment decision - may not have been such a good idea.

He chewed slowly and carefully, taking frequent sips of bottled water, while trying to focus on watching the first-floor flat across the road for signs of life. Unfortunately, the lack of activity led to Harry's attention drifting. He had to concede his day had not started brightly. Waking up in your own vomit with the hangover from hell was bad enough, but finding flecks of blood in the vomit had caused him some concern. Harry could handle his drink - or so he believed - but he wondered whether he'd overdone it this time.

Once showered and dressed - he'd skipped the ritual of shaving as too much effort - he started his search for Cutter. Harry's first port of call had been to what he believed was Cutter's last known address, and, not surprisingly, from where he'd moved some time ago. Cutter had never been one to stay in the same place for long, always needing to be one step ahead of the law, or having to move due to complaints of antisocial behaviour from his neighbours. A visit to some of his old haunts of pubs, clubs, and eating places, also proved to be equally fruitless.

Footsore from walking the London streets, and still feeling like a bag of shite, he'd stopped at a burger van parked just off the High Street. The man bending over the encrusted hotplate was in his fifties, skinny, with thin lank hair tied back in a pony tail from a weasel-like face and a bad complexion; an unlit hand rolled cigarette dangled from the corner of his mouth. Harry watched the man 'expertly' move a pile of chopped onions, and what passed for a sausage, from one side of the hotplate to the other. Once they were neatly positioned, he looked up from his task, grinned a smile of rotting teeth, and then asked Harry what he wanted to eat. If Harry had been in two minds about whether he would be able to stomach any food, he was definitely now in one mind - and it was exalting the merits of vegetarianism. He considered a bottle of bland tasting spring water, that would no doubt go some way to rehydrating his alcohol ravaged body, but finally opted for a strong tea with four heaped sugars instead.

As the Weasel handed Harry his tea, he greeted him warmly, like a long lost friend. Harry returned a noncommittal greeting, unable to place if, or from where, he knew the man.

''Arry Windsor,' the Weasel said. 'The great 'Arry Windsor, eatin' at my establishment. It's an honour, 'Arry.'

'Do I know you?' Harry asked, wondering whether the man was taking-the-piss.

'You once threw me - a little roughly in my opinion - out of one of the Je... Mr Solomon's night clubs,' he replied, quickly correcting himself when he remembered Harry's loyalty to his employer had been legendary. 'How's life treating you these days, 'Arry? You don't look too chipper - if you don't mind me saying so.'

Harry just stared back, sipped at his tea, and then grimaced at the insipid taste that even four heaped sugars was unable to take away. 'Rumour has it,' the Weasel said, continuing, 'that since your stay at Her Majesty's pleasure, you no longer have 'business' dealings with Mr Solomon? Nice man, Mr Solomon. Got class. I occasionally do business with him myself,' he added, as he pushed the onions and the sausage from one side to the other.

It had started to rain. Harry - safe under the van's awning - turned to stare out at the passing London traffic. He watched the vehicles jockeying for position; bicycle couriers suicidally weaving in and out of an unforgiving stream of noise and excessive braking; beggars in doorways; Big Issue sellers; pedestrians rushing to their destinations, oblivious of everything and everyone.

'... it's completely changed. We're overrun,' said the Weasel.

'What?' replied an irritable Harry, having tuned out from what the man had been saying.

'Immigrants, 'Arry. Place is overrun with the fuckers. Especially the 'Eastern Europeans' as the popular press likes to call them. Nasty bastards. You sure you wouldn't like something to eat, 'Arry? I could do you a nice sausage and egg roll. I've got some organic eggs. Fresh from the chicken's arse. They're so fresh, they're still warm. Would you like that, 'Arry?'

'What I would like, you weasel-mouthed little fucker,' replied Harry, whose headache was getting worse by the minute, 'is for you to tell me where I can find Cutter. And don't give me any crap about not knowing who he is, because if you're familiar with me and Mr Solomon, you'll know Cutter,' said Harry.

The expression on the Weasel's face suggested he'd shit his pants. ''Arry, 'Arry,' he said, 'no need to get aggressive.'

The Weasel flinched when Harry suddenly stepped forward only to pour the remaining contents of his tea over the hotplate. As the Weasel's look of dismay dropped downwards, Harry's arm shot out and upwards, grabbing the man around the back of the head, before then pulling his face down towards the hotplate.

'Don't fuck with me, you little shit,' Harry told him.

Either the little shit didn't have an appetite for his own food, or he was concerned about losing his good looks, thought Harry, as the Weasel started to tell him how he might go about finding Cutter.

'I don't know where Cutter is. Honest to God, 'Arry!' he said. 'Tricky Dicky! Talk to Tricky Dicky! He should know. He supplies 'goods' for Cutter's sexual needs.'

Harry hadn't heard of Tricky Dicky, but the Weasel proved kind enough to tell him where he could be found. With reluctance, Harry released his grip.

The address for Tricky Dicky turned out to be a porn shop on the Willesden High Street, a double-fronted building that had once been a fine looking structure, its brick and stone facade now neglected and weather beaten, its windows covered with black painted sheets of timber to hide the vulgarity of its present trade.

An electronic buzzer sounded as Harry entered. The layout of the shop was no different to the majority of other porn shops: wall-to-wall shelving filled with magazines, DVDs, and sex toys of a wide variety. A single counter stood at one end of the shop, on which was a cash register and a tall stack of cardboard boxes, the latter of which a young kid was busily unpacking.

The kid looked to be in his late teens, maybe early twenties; wore baggy jeans, baggy tee-shirt, a mass of unkempt hair, and facial fuzz that presumably passed for a beard.

Harry stood for a moment, waiting. The kid continued to unpack. It was only then that Harry noticed the thin white wires snaking out from the kid's ears, disappearing beneath his tee-shirt. Probably one of those iPod things, he thought, as he called to the kid to attract his attention. With barely a glance in Harry's direction, the kid pointed to a door in the corner of the room, mumbled something about being expected, then returned to the boxes.

After a moment's hesitation, Harry decided to follow his instincts, rather than question what the kid had meant. He crossed to the corner of the room, pushed open the heavy door, then stepped into a long and dimly lit corridor that appeared to lead to the rear of the building, the fire door's automatic closer softly closing the door behind him as he did so. As he headed towards a door at the far end of the corridor, he noticed the wallpaper was peeling, and that there was a heavy smell of damp. He also noticed what seemed like a vibration coming from the walls and through the carpet beneath his feet, increasing in strength as he walked, and when he placed his hand upon the door handle, he felt the vibration growing stronger and then louder as he pulled at the heavy fire door, to then step into yet another dimly lit room and have his senses assaulted. The loud techno beat of the music battered his hearing, while his sense of smell detected that old and familiar smell of pubs and clubs of long ago before the smoking ban: the smell of stale and fresh nicotine, mingled in with alcohol and body odour.

The room was about forty feet by twenty; at the far end was a small stage, where twin strobe lights highlighted a young girl gyrating around a vertically fixed metal pole to the heavy techno beat. Silver high heels with a matching silver thong to cover her modesty was all she wore, her small breasts bouncing as she went through her dance routine, almost robotic. To Harry - despite the heavy make-up which belied her youth - she looked tired and underfed. Probably on drugs, he thought.

Once his eyes had adjusted to the low level of light, he took a look around the room. The contents were a collection of mismatched chairs and tables that looked like they'd been purchased from a charity shop, along with some threadbare sofas that stood against the walls, all facing away from Harry and towards the stage. Sitting together at a table close to the stage were two male punters drinking and smoking, their eyes transfixed on the girl, mentally salivating over her every movement, devouring her buttocks and breasts while willing her to remove the thin scrap of silver cloth.

Harry then noticed a third punter on a sofa further back, also intently watching the girl. It was hard to tell in the gloom, but he seemed to be twitching, until Harry realised it was more of a rhythmic body movement: he was masturbating.

A few feet away from where Harry stood was a crudely built, plywood sheeted drinks bar with a cheap Formica top. He crossed to the end of the bar, the carpet sticky underfoot. Other than the usual range of bottled mixer drinks and optics for strong spirits, there were half a dozen glass fronted fridges containing a variety of bottles and canned drinks; nothing on draught, indicating to Harry it didn't have a drinks license. That, and its covert location and the flouting of the smoke-free regulations, suggested it was an illegal drinking den.

A stocky looking guy was behind the bar, his back to Harry, reading a newspaper, unaware Harry was there.

Adjacent to the end of the bar was a closed door with a sign that said 'Private', and in the lock of which was a bunch of keys. Harry cast a glance back towards the barman, who continued to read his newspaper, before then turning the door handle and pushing open the door.

The windowless room was about ten feet square, but seemed smaller. A lot smaller. Claustrophobic, almost. Harry focused on the contents of the room. Almost everywhere he looked, cardboard boxes were stacked up. An office desk and chair stood in the middle of the room, the desk cluttered with sales receipts and invoices - also sex toys: dildos, a whip, and something the size and shape of a cricket bat, which appeared to be made of thick black leather with dozens of small pointed studs fixed to one side. Harry's sexual peccadilloes had always been a bit more 'traditional', so he made an educated guess the leather 'paddle', was an S&M thing. On the office chair sat an open cardboard box.

'...Well, he's not here yet, Lenny. You told me within the hour. Has he got my money?' said the man who was perched on the edge of a battered and stained chaise longue, while staring at a TV screen, mobile phone in one hand, and large cigar in the other.

The man was in his late fifties, early sixties, with a shock of white hair neatly swept back, well dressed in a jacket, trousers, and an opened-necked white shirt which helped to show off his perma-tan - probably gained from regular golfing trips to Marbella. This was the man known as Tricky Dicky, the 'Pedlar of Porn'.

Aware someone had entered by the increase in music volume coming from the bar, Tricky turned. On seeing Harry, he impatiently waved him towards the cardboard box on the office chair, before turning back to the TV. 'Lenny, I'm looking at it now, as we speak, and I gotta say, the quality is piss-poor. You assured me it was quality. There's better free stuff, on the internet for Christ's sakes. I mean, I can barely tell if the kid's been penetrated or not.' Harry turned his attention to the TV, where he saw a group of middle-aged men gang-banging a young boy and girl. 'Watching a couple of thirteen year old virgins being gang-banged should be good viewing, Lenny,' continued Tricky. 'Profitable viewing. I want to see it all. Screwing, sodomy, buggery. I want to see the pain on their faces. The blood and the spunk. It doesn't even get *me* hard, Lenny. Watching two dogs shagging in the street usually gets me hard. So if it doesn't get me hard, how can I sell it?' he said, loudly, while waving his cigar around to make his point. '...Whatever, Lenny. Whatever. He's here now. Just walked in. Do me a favour, and don't send me anymore crap,' Tricky shouted down the phone as he stood.

At first, Harry felt sickened to the depth of his stomach as he stared at the horrific images on the screen; until, that is, the rage started to build-up inside him. The quality may not have been up to the standard Tricky would have preferred, but it was clear enough to see that the young boy and girl were unwilling participants because you could see the pain on their faces, also the terror. This wasn't a gang-bang of consenting adults; it was gang-rape of children.

'Hey, delivery boy,' Tricky said to Harry, with a patronizingly fake smile on his face, 'if you want to watch it, you gotta pay for it. I'm not running a fuckin' charity here. Give me my money, and take that box of shite with you,' he said, again indicating the box on the chair. Harry looked at the box, then finally back at Tricky, who just stood waiting, smirking.

Tricky watched as Harry reached towards the cardboard box, only to see him pick up the leather studded paddle instead. Harry then wiped the smile from Tricky's face, the force knocking him off his feet, to collapse behind the desk. Harry followed, to then get down to the nitty-gritty of persuading Tricky to tell him where he could find Cutter.

A few minutes later, and slightly out of breath, Harry stepped from the room. He looked around. The barman was still engrossed in his newspaper and the punters were still engrossed with the anorexic pole dancer. The heavy techno beat continued. Harry then locked the door, removed the keys, and slipped away.

Tricky had told Harry what he wanted to know, relatively quickly, leaving Harry feeling cheated from being able to purge his anger on the vile pervert. So, as he left the room, he'd picked up Tricky's cigar lighter from his desk, and then set light to the cardboard box that had held the DVDs.

He walked half a dozen blocks before he dropped the keys into an open grated road drain. He didn't think it likely he would get caught for what he'd done. No one had really seen him to give an accurate description. The kid in the porn shop had barely looked at Harry when he'd arrived - or as he'd left, still ploughing his way through the mountainous stack of boxes. And Harry didn't think the local plod would bust a gut for a lowlife like Tricky.

The pizza was now long cold, and barely touched. Harry reached behind him to place the box on the rear seat. His vantage point was Mollie's car. After his visit to Tricky, Harry decided he needed some wheels. London buses were not always convenient, often requiring two or more changes to get from A to B. They were also, of course, subject to weight of traffic, and London was infamous for its congestion. Catching the tube would have been easier, but Harry's fear of confined spaces ruled that out. Having a car also gave him an inconspicuous vantage point from which to watch Cutter's flat. So, he'd caught a bus home to retrieve Mollie's bag, then caught another to Mollie's flat. Once there, he'd walked up and down Mollie's street, pressing the car's electronic key fob, until the hazard lights of a Volkswagen Golf Hatchback had flashed, unlocking the car. The fact that - technically - he was in a stolen car, and that Mollie's insurance policy probably didn't cover him, were merely inconvenient details to Harry. He didn't hold out much hope of seeing Mollie entering or leaving Cutter's flat, but it gave him time to think before he made a move.

Harry's hangover headache had eased to a dull roar, and he now only felt partially shit. He turned his mobile phone on. It beeped a number of times: text messages informing him he had missed phone calls, and all from Izzy. How the hell had she got his number, he wondered, he certainly didn't recall giving it to her. Harry gave his number out to hardly anyone - which was probably why he had few friends.

As he was deleting the text messages, the phone beeped again. Another text; and direct from Izzy. 'What the fuck!..'

said Harry, unable to believe what he was reading. *'Is that you in the Volkswagen Golf?'*

Harry's head jerked up, to look out through the windscreen. Movement drew his eye. Diagonally across the road, parked immediately below Cutter's flat, was a gold coloured Saab convertible. Izzy was getting out of it. She waved as she jogged across the road towards him.

Harry groaned. Two thoughts flashed through his mind: he'd obviously let his attention drift, because he hadn't seen Izzy turn up, and he wondered if he should quickly lock the doors.

Too late, the passenger side door was flung open, and Izzy threw herself into the front seat with enough youthful exuberance to rock the small car on its suspension, doing nothing to ease Harry's headache.

'Hello, Harry,' she said, brightly and with an impish grin. 'I was beginning to think you were avoiding me.' Harry merely grunted, before returning to stare across at Cutter's flat. Izzy couldn't determine whether it was a grunt of denial or conformation. 'I see you've borrowed Mollie's car for your stakeout,' she said, carrying on regardless.

Harry gave her a surprised glance. 'How did you know it was Mollie's car?'

'I simply applied my highly tuned investigative powers to analyse and deduct,' she said, straight faced. Harry raised a disbelieving eyebrow. 'I went to your house, and your dear Major Jackson -'

'Corporal,' said Harry, interrupting.

'Whatever,' said Izzy, with a shrug. 'Your Mr Jackson said he'd bumped into you as you were leaving home, and when he asked what you were up to, you said you were going to borrow a car to visit an old friend - very cryptic, Harry.'

'That doesn't explain how you knew which car it was,' replied Harry, making a mental note not to make passing conversation with old Mr Jackson.

'That's where my highly tuned investigative powers came into play,' she said, with dramatic flair. Harry stared back, deadpan. 'The small key ring attached to the car's electronic key fob. The back slides up, and printed inside is the car's make, model, and registration plate number. I saw it when you gave me the bag to look through. See, highly tuned.' She then added, 'But I'm sure you knew that already, because you obviously deduced the same.'

Harry flicked a glance at the key in the ignition, and the key ring dangling from it, to give another noncommittal grunt, before returning to his vigil.

'So which one is it? Which is Cutter's gaf?' she asked, peering through the windscreen.

Harry looked at her. 'Gaf?'

Turning back, she said, 'Isn't that what you Cockney geezers' call a flat?'

Something else had been niggling at the back of Harry's mind while Izzy had been rambling on. 'How did you know where Cutter lived?' he asked. Then, as Izzy opened her mouth to speak, 'And don't give me any bollocks about highly tuned investigative powers.'

She closed her mouth, pursed her lips, before then saying, 'I figured our Mr Cutter is not the sort of person to stay in one place long enough to be registered for council tax, or to be on the Register of Electors, yes?' Harry gave her a slow nod of the head. 'But wherever he stays, he's going to need gas and electric, yes?' Another slow nod of the head from Harry. 'I have a friend who works for a utility company. An ex-boyfriend, actually. We're still good friends,' she added, glancing at Harry. 'Anyway, I rang him and gave him Cutter's name.' Harry didn't look convinced. 'His real name, obviously - Wayne Salter. He could hardly register with a utility company under the name of Mr Cutter, the psycho cat killer, now could he?' Harry struggled to suppress a wry smile. 'You still haven't pointed out which one is Cutter's flat,' she then said.

'I thought you knew.'

'I do,' replied Izzy, craning to see through the side window and establish the number on the building next to them. 'It's number forty four B. I was too busy looking for a parking space at first, to check out the house numbers. If this one is twenty three, then forty four must be over there, just about...'

'Where the very visually bright, gold coloured Saab is parked,' finished Harry.

'Oh,' said Izzy, simply. 'Do you think he saw me?'

Harry was tempted to rub it in, but she sounded dejected, and he couldn't be arsed. 'I don't think he's at home.'

Izzy sat back, quiet. Thinking.

Harry heard her sniff a couple of times. He hoped she wasn't going to start crying.

She sniffed again. Then, 'What *is* that smell?' she asked, looking around the car. She spotted the pizza box on the back seat. 'Ooh, pizza!' She reached over and flipped open the box, then shrank back in horror. 'Oh-me-God! Don't tell me you actually eat this... this... stuff?'

'What's wrong with it?' asked Harry.

'Well... I mean...' Izzy struggled to articulate herself. '...What are *they*?' she asked, tentatively poking the pizza with a well manicured fingernail.

Harry irritably turned his head to briefly glance at the box. 'Anchovies.'

'Christ, Harry. This is a smorgasbord of 'surf and turf' with a token topping of fruit. It's a cholesterol killer! A colon crippler! A heart attack in a box! A -'

'Give it a rest, for fuck's sake.'

Suitably - yet reluctantly - rebuked, Izzy sat back, folded her arms, and pouted. *God, he's a sullen son-of-a-bitch. He gives a whole new perspective to 'mean and moody'.* She decided she was going to call him 'Mr Monosyllabic' from then on. It then occurred to her that she had never asked him if he was in a relationship. Was there a 'Mrs Monosyllabic'? Probably not - and she certainly wasn't going to give him the satisfaction of asking. She also decided she wouldn't mention she'd been trying to contact the police.

While they sat in silence, she secretly studied him. She was shocked to realise how rough he looked. Even in profile she could see that his eyes were bloodshot, and how tired and drawn he was. Other than the foul smelling pizza, there was another smell too, and that was the smell of stale alcohol. Izzy didn't need her highly tuned investigative powers to see that Harry had hit the bottle; the alcohol was oozing from the pores of his skin. And *what* was with the leather motorbike jacket that looked and smelled like it had lived in a garden shed for the last ten years?

Looking at Harry, she found herself thinking back to her dream of the other night, where the 'tall dark stranger' was going to have his wicked way with her, plunging her into the delights of sexual depravity. Had it been a dream? Had her 'Mr Darcy' finally come in to her life? Looking at Harry at that particular moment, she thought probably not. 'I presume Solomon told you where Cutter lived?' said Izzy.

'*Mr* Solomon didn't know. Or at least said he didn't know.'

'Would he lie to you?' Harry shrugged, continued to watch the flat. 'Did you catch up on old times?' she said, flippantly, instantly regretting it when she saw the expression on Harry's profile suddenly change. It wasn't exactly a dramatic change, Harry's facial expressions, she'd come to learn, were as economical as his conversation. She saw his eyes briefly drop down to the dashboard of the car, not looking at it, but far away, lost in thought, before again returning to stare across the road. Realising he wasn't going to say anything further, 'So who told you where Cutter lived?' she asked. Harry continued to stare out through the windscreen. 'I bet it involved pain, didn't it?' She saw another slight change of expression cross Harry's face. 'Ha! I knew it!' she said, loudly. She then proceeded to interrogate Harry as to his methods. Was it broken fingers? Kneecaps? Harry told her she watched too much television.

Harry felt thoroughly miserable. As well as feeling like a bag of shit, he was also very conscious that he looked and smelled like a bag of shit. He was sweating so heavily that *he* could smell it. He was worried what Izzy would think of him in his present state. But why was he worried? What was it about this young woman that both intrigued and attracted him, but also annoyed him?

They sat in silence for a while. It was after six in the evening, and now dark, the streetlights fully on. It was also lightly raining. They watched the hustle and bustle of the London commuters' heading home after a hard day at work:

the pedestrians stepping out with purpose, keen to be home and out of the rain; the nose-to-tail traffic at a more sedate pace, a moving river of light and rhythmic windscreen wipers.

So far, they had only seen one person come out of the building across the street, an unknown woman.

'Why are you still doing this, Harry?'

'How do you mean?' he said, turning to her.

'Why are you still trying to find the girl - Mollie?' Harry merely shrugged. 'After all,' she continued, 'it doesn't look like you're going to get paid. Wouldn't you be better off getting your flats finished?'

Harry ignored the question.

'The first time we met, you asked me if I was from the bank. I'm guessing you're financially stretched?'

Still Harry said nothing.

'I know what it's like to struggle. I get a Junior Reporter's salary, and my father recently cut my allowance,' she said.

Harry stared at her. *Allowance? Christ!*

After a while, he said, 'I guess it's the right thing to do... The girl, I mean,' he then added, to Izzy's quizzical look, before turning back to look out through the windscreen. 'I've never been big on doing the right thing,' he said, quietly, more to himself than to Izzy, as he flicked the wipers to clear the rain.

They watched the rain slowly build to again block their vision.

'What was it like in prison?' asked Izzy.

'Cramped,' replied Harry.

'It can't have been easy. I would have hated it. Did your family visit you?'

Harry shook his head. 'My mother died while I was on remand.'

'And your foster brother?'

After a moment's hesitation, 'No, he'd be the last person to want to visit.'

It was clear there was a lot of animosity on Harry's part, towards his foster brother, and Izzy was filled with curiosity as to what had happened to cause it. She wondered whether to simply ask Harry. She decided not to push it. Instead, 'You always refer to your *foster* brother, but not your *foster* mother.'

Harry shifted uncomfortably in his seat. He flicked the wipers again. He then craned forward. Someone had just gone in the main door to the building they were watching. Harry felt certain it was Cutter. After a moment, a light came on in the first-floor flat, shining through timber French doors that led onto a small balcony. No sign of Cutter.

'No doubt a psychologist would be able to explain the reason,' said Izzy, oblivious to Cutter's arrival. 'Family!' she added, with a shake of her head. Then, 'I don't think it's going to work out with Jonathan,' she said. 'We're two different people.'

Harry stared fixedly across at Cutter's flat. The light was still on, but as yet, still no sign of Cutter. Harry could feel his heart beating faster. His mouth was dry. He was sure it was Cutter he'd seen enter. Further up the street he saw the unknown woman returning. He had to make a move, and it had to be now.

'We just don't seem to have anything in common anymore. He doesn't take my views seriously. He doesn't seem to listen to me anymore. The problem is we are from different worlds.'

Harry twisted around in his seat to reach for the pizza box, and from the footwell behind Izzy's seat, he pulled out a full-faced motorcycle helmet. Izzy frowned on seeing this. Harry reached for the car door handle, paused, then turned back to Izzy and said, 'The problem lies in the fact that you, lady, don't *live* in the real world.' With that, he jumped out, slammed the door behind him, and jogged across the road, weaving his way through the traffic to the other side, leaving Izzy open mouthed and speechless. She watched as Harry skipped up the steps to the front door, holding the pizza box in one hand, while slipping the helmet on over his head with the other. The woman they'd seen earlier was at the door searching through her bag, presumably for door keys. She turned as Harry approached. Izzy saw Harry gesture with the pizza box, pointing upwards. She saw the woman nod, unlock the door, and then enter. Harry followed, closing the door.

After a few moments, a light came on in the ground-floor flat, which in turn drew her attention to the light in the flat above.

She realised she was still sitting with her mouth agape; stunned. 'How rude... How bloody rude!'

Harry made his way up the stairway to the first-floor. His plan - such as it was - was to surprise Cutter. Getting through Cutter's front door was his first big obstacle. Cutter was a seriously dangerous individual. Lightning fast with a knife, not afraid to use it, and with no regards to the unspoken laws of the street. Total surprise was Harry's biggest weapon.

In the thick leather jacket and helmet, Harry was sweating profusely. He could feel it running down his torso, sticking his shirt to his body, and soaking the waistband of his jeans. It trickled down his face, stinging his eyes. He blinked hard to clear his vision. He still felt like shit. And this was not a good time to feel like shit.

He reached the first-floor. Just the one door, with the letter 'B'.

He lifted the visor slightly to get some air. Would Cutter recognise him by his eyes, and what little of his face could be seen? He then recalled when he'd looked in the mirror, earlier that morning; he'd barely recognised himself.

He knocked on the door, and braced himself. He thought he heard a muffled shout come from within. He stared hard at the painted door, and the dull brass letter 'B'. He noted there was a spyhole.

No answer.

Harry rapped on the door again, longer and harder.

'Fuck sake!' came an angry reply approaching the door.

There was a pause - Harry sensed he was being watched through the spyhole - before he heard the latch being turned, and saw the door handle move. The door was violently thrown open to reveal Cutter. 'What the fuck do you want?' he asked, his eyes wild and menacing.

Cutter was a couple of inches shorter than Harry, but other than that, they were of a similar build. Cutter's hair was long and lank, down to his shoulders. He wore blue jeans, tee-shirt and cowboy boots. A bottle of lager hung loose in one hand.

Harry's gaze was drawn to the ugly, yet familiar scar, above and below Cutter's right eye. Story went he'd got it in a knife fight, his opponent's blade narrowly missing his eyeball, leaving a deep wound which, as the story goes, Cutter stitched up himself. Harry knew differently.

'Well?' said Cutter.

'Pizza,' mumbled Harry, lifting the box up for Cutter to see.

'I didn't order pizza, you fuckin' moron.' Then, almost in the same breath, 'What sort is it?'

As Harry started to lift the lid, he took a step forward. Cutter's gaze instinctively dropped down. Harry saw a look of confusion cross the scarred face when it saw the partially eaten pizza. Harry eased his weight onto his back leg, tensing the muscles. Ready.

'What the fuck...' said Cutter.

As his gaze came back up to look at Harry, Harry pushed the pizza box into Cutter's chest, who in turn automatically raised his hands to grasp the box. As he did so, Harry's whole upper body whipped forward at lightning speed, to then headbutt Cutter full in the face. Even through the thick motorcycle helmet, Harry heard and felt the crunch of cartilage as Cutter's nose was spread across his face, smearing blood across the helmet's visor.

From a young age, Harry had learnt that the secret for an effective headbutt was to put the weight and force of the whole upper body behind it, to maximise the damage to the opponent while minimising damage to oneself. The motorcycle helmet helped considerably, of course.

The force of Harry's attack threw Cutter backwards, crashing him into the wall of the hallway before he slumped into a heap on the floor. For a moment, Harry thought he might have killed him, but a groan confirmed he was still alive.

Harry pulled off the helmet, and stepped over Cutter. He had to be quick. He only had minutes before Cutter would start to come around. He quickly searched the flat, going from room to room. He really didn't expect to find Mollie, but was hoping for a sign she might have been there, confirming

Cutter had had a hand in her disappearance. Finding nothing, he returned to the hallway. 'Shit!' Cutter was gone. All that remained was a pool of blood, a crumpled pizza box, and a bottle of lager, leaking its contents onto the carpet. Harry whirled around, expecting an attack. Nothing. The only sign of Cutter was a trail of blood, leading off. Harry followed it into the lounge. There, he found Cutter, leaning against a large, solid marble fire surround, one hand gripping the mantelpiece for support, the other reaching for an ornamental samurai sword that was mounted on a wooden block; until it occurred to Harry that it might not be ornamental; it might be 'the real McCoy'. Either way, in Cutter's hands, it was a lethal weapon.

In three long strides, Harry reached Cutter, grabbed a handful of lank hair, and jerked him backwards, away from the sword, propelling him across the room, and crashing him into an armchair near the French doors.

Negotiating a solid looking timber chest that served as a coffee table, Harry approached Cutter. On the chest, he noticed a variety of small plastic bags. He recognised Cannabis Resin, some white powder which he assumed was Cocaine, and some brightly coloured pills - of what, Harry had absolutely no idea.

Cutter had dragged himself into a sitting position, knuckles white with effort, as he gripped the arms of the chair, breathing heavy and laboured, caused by the inability to breathe through his nose and the blood that was filling his throat, which he periodically spat out onto the floor, while blinking rapidly as he tried to focus on the man standing before him. Harry saw his eyes go wide in shock and recognition.

'Harry Windsor, you're a fuckin' wanker,' he screamed.

'Nice to see you too, Wayne,' said Harry, using Cutter's given name purely to piss-him-off further.

'What the fuck do you want?'

'The girl,' said Harry.

'What fuckin' girl?'

'Mollie Dolan.'

Cutter didn't answer. Just stared back at Harry.

'You know who I'm talking about,' continued Harry. 'The daughter of the big Irishman who owes Mr Solomon money.'

Cutter started to laugh, having decided to give up on feigning ignorance, just so that he could torment Harry. 'I thought you'd given up being the Jew's lap dog, Windsor,' he said, spitting more blood onto the floor.

Harry found himself wondering how difficult it would be to get the blood out of the carpet, which in turn reminded him he had to take his rug to the dry cleaners.

'So, you're looking for daddy's little girl, eh?' grinned Cutter. There was something about that sentence that struck a chord with Harry, but he couldn't quite put his finger on it. 'You won't find her,' said Cutter. 'I sold her.'

'What the fuck do you mean, you sold her?' said Harry, stunned.

'When it became obvious her old man didn't have the money he owed, I sold her to a gang of Eastern Europeans,' he grinned. 'A guy has to make a living somehow, and it would've been a shame to waste such a valuable asset - especially one as talented as she is.' Seeing Harry frown, he then said, 'She's a dirty little bitch who loves sex, and who likes it rough.'

Then Harry remembered: the diary. Mollie had mentioned that a man she'd had violent sex with, had referred to her as "daddy's little girl". It'd been Cutter. Harry had had suspicions her father had been sexually abusing her. He'd been wrong. He'd misjudged Patrick Dolan. Cutter had groomed the girl from the very start. If she wasn't a drug addict when she'd first met him, she certainly would be by now.

'Was it the Russians?' asked Harry.

'Russians, Albanians, Poles... fucked if I know, and fucked if I care.'

Harry looked up and over the head of the seated Cutter. He saw his own reflection in the darkened glass of the French doors. He sighed heavily. He wasn't going to get anything of use out of Cutter. Harry had known in his heart that this visit would be futile. He could beat Cutter to within an inch of his life, but he wouldn't tell Harry what he wanted to know.

Cutter was also a compulsive liar, so even if he did, Harry couldn't be sure how much would be true.

A sudden movement caught Harry's attention. He looked down in time to see Cutter pull a sheathed knife from his boot, whip the knife from its scabbard, and then lunge at Harry, all in the blink of an eye.

Harry quickly back-pedalled to get out of range and give himself some space, but he backed into the timber chest, stumbling, feeling himself teeter, his arms flailing desperately as he tried to regain his balance and avoid crashing to the floor, because if he did Cutter would be on him, and he would be finished.

Cutter's blood smeared maniacal face leered up in front of Harry as he slashed the knife across Harry's upper body. It was a big knife with a matt black handle, and a blade so shiny the overhead light danced off it as it rose and fell, momentarily captivating Harry.

Once, twice, three times, Harry felt the knife's impact.

He saw a look of consternation cross Cutter's face when he realised his slashing action wasn't penetrating the thick reinforced leather. This was the reason Harry was wearing the motorcycle jacket: to give him an element of protection from Cutter's knife skills - certainly not as a fashion statement.

Having managed to regain his balance, and avoid falling over the chest, Harry, who was still holding the motorcycle helmet in his left hand, now used it as a weapon, to swing it in an arc towards Cutter's head. But Cutter saw it coming, and skipped out of the way. But not before changing his knife action from slashing to stabbing.

At first, Harry thought he'd just been punched in the arm, seconds later, came the searing hot pain.

Cutter howled with laughter at the look of agony on Harry's face. Harry fought the urge to look down and check the damage. Taking his eyes off Cutter once was stupid; twice would be fatal.

Harry warily watched Cutter, who was balanced on the balls of his feet, legs braced, weaving the knife back and forth; hunched, poised, and ready to strike. Fully recovered. Fully composed.

Harry, on the other hand, was bleeding badly. He could feel the blood running down his arm, dripping from the ends of his fingertips. This carpet is going to be in hell of a mess, he thought.

As the blood slowly drained from Harry's body, so did his energy levels. He felt tired, so, so tired. He felt dead on his feet - and dead was exactly what he would be if he didn't end this, and end it soon.

'I've gotta say, Wayne, I'm surprised.'

'About what?' replied Cutter.

'Why a girl like Mollie, would be interested in a low-life scum like you.'

The leering grin on Cutter's face, disappeared in a flash.

'I'm guessing you spiked her drinks the first time you met her, and then you introduced her to drugs. Because there is no way an attractive woman like Mollie Dolan would want to have sex with a rancid little turd like you.'

Harry could see he'd hit the mark.

'We're not all God's gift to women, Harry. Some of us have to work at it. Use what means we have.'

'I'm guessing it was you who went to Mollie's flat and packed an overnight bag for her.'

'That was me. So what? A girl has to have clean underwear before going off on her hols to Albania, eh?'

Harry was trying to wind Cutter up, to get him angry enough to make a rash move. But he wasn't falling for it. 'Do you know how I found you, Wayne? I made a visit to your good friend, Tricky Dicky.'

'How is dear Richard?' asked Cutter, without the slightest trace of interest or sincerity.

'Toasty,' replied Harry, to which Cutter frowned. 'He was very talkative. Apart from telling me where you lived, he told me about your passion for young flesh. Both female and male.'

'We all got our vices, Harry. Our secret pleasures. And I know what you're trying to do. I know you're trying to wind-me-up to make a mistake. But it ain't going to happen,' he said, the knife weaving, mesmerisingly back and forth. 'There are skeletons in your closet too, Harry, whether you know it or not. And let's not forget your stay 'at Her Majesty's pleasure', for drug dealing.'

'That's common knowledge,' replied Harry, 'and I was innocent. I was fitted-up.'

'Correct on both counts, Harry. Correct!'

This time it was Harry's turn to frown. 'You know who framed me?'

Cutter grinned. 'The answer to that, matey, is closer to home than you think.'

'What the fuck is that supposed to mean?'

'Family secrets, Harry, family secrets,' taunted Cutter.

Harry's mind raced back to the conversation he'd had with the old man the day before. Had the old man told Cutter his secret?

'Did you know, Harry, your dear departed mother, Lillian, the lovely Lillian - I bet she was a 'looker' in her day, hey Harry? Did you know, the woman you adored and worshipped was friends with Solomon? That they were good friends? I mean *really* good friends?'

Anger sparked in Harry's eyes, his nostrils flared, and the muscles in his jaw clenched.

'Some people would say she was his mistress.'

Harry felt the rage sweep through him like a tsunami, washing away the fatigue and the pain.

'Personally,' said Cutter, grinning, knowing he'd hit the mark, 'I think she should be described for what she was - the Jew's whore!'

The words were barely out of his mouth when Harry threw the motorcycle helmet at him. Cutter raised his arms quickly enough to deflect the helmet, but in doing so, took his eyes off Harry. Harry launched himself forward, executing a skip-in side kick, his knee snapping up to waist height, before then shooting his leg out horizontally, his foot landing square in the centre of Cutter's chest. Two hundred pounds of muscle and momentum lifted Cutter off his feet, propelling him backwards, to crash through the French doors, and over the balcony to the street below.

Izzy's fingers drummed irritably on the armrest of the car door; her foot tapped a similar beat. Her gaze flicked from the surrounding commuter traffic, up to the light in the first-floor flat. From her position she was unable to see if anything was happening, so she waited. And she waited. Why was she waiting? She didn't know. What she did know, was that she was annoyed. *How dare Harry talk to her like that!*

'Sod this for a game of soldiers,' she said, yanking on the door handle and throwing open the door, almost taking-out a pedestrian as she did so. She stepped out of the car, briefly apologised to the pedestrian, and then weaved her way through the traffic towards her car, glancing up at the flat as she went. Still no sign of activity. She pulled her coat tighter against the rain and increasing wind. She was going home, she decided: home to a hot scented bath, and a large glass of chilled Pinot Grigio.

She paused in the middle of the road, waiting for a break in the traffic, before crossing the remaining short distance to her car. She was about to step out when she heard the unmistakeable sound of breaking glass. Her head jerked upwards in time to see a dark shape coming over the balcony of the first-floor flat. The shape hurtled towards the ground, only to hit the roof of a soft-top car with a resounding thump, the car's fabric covered metal structure then imploding under the body's weight, closely followed by the side windows exploding outwards.

A strangled scream of surprise escaped Izzy's mouth, which then turned into a scream of dismay when she realised the car in question was hers. Other than a protruding arm and leg, the body wasn't visible. She noted the wing mirror and duct tape were still in place.

She looked up. In the shattered doorway, framed by the bright light of the flat, stood a tall dark figure who appeared to be looking down to the street below. The strong backlight made it difficult to see his facial features, but she recognised Harry's posture. And, if she wasn't mistaken, he was smiling.

CHAPTER 26

It was early Tuesday morning, and Steve was back at work. He stared dejectedly at the pile of new case files that appeared to have been unceremoniously dumped on his desk for his attention.

His long weekend had turned out to be as uninspiring - though somewhat enjoyable - as he'd anticipated. He'd spent a large part of it in the garden, cleaned the house from top to bottom, and had even attempted some DIY - though with disastrous results. But by Monday evening, with the prospect of returning to work the following day, the good feeling had slowly disappeared, only to be replaced by a feeling of gloom, which had turned into despondency by the time he'd got up that morning. He briefly pondered the idea of asking his doctor to increase the strength of his medication, but then dismissed the idea almost immediately. That would not solve the root cause of his problem: he hated his job - Christ, he hated his life, if he were honest with himself.

On entering the station earlier, the Desk Sergeant had given him a handful of paper telephone messages, all from the same person - the female reporter for the *North London Gazette* - asking Steve to call her as a matter of urgency. Past experience of this reporter told him it was unlikely to be anything urgent, but more likely to require Steve's time and probably information. He put the slips to one side to deal with later. He turned his attention to the first three case files on his desk. All three had a Post-it note stuck to the front cover. One read, "Important!", the second, "Not so important!", and the third, "Don't-waste-too-much-bloody-time-on-this!!!". All care of his beloved D.I., and his truly amazing communication skills.

Before reading through the witness statements taken by the uniformed officers, he skimmed through the details on each individual cover sheet: a young woman had been reported missing by her mother - Steve noted she'd gone missing before; a "local businessman", who was known to the police for the type of "goods" that he sold, had died in a fire, and in what might have been suspicious circumstances; and a man had fallen from a first-floor balcony to the street below - also believed to be under suspicious circumstances. Steve peered at the name of the man who'd fallen from the balcony: Wayne Salter. He frowned, deep in thought. *Why was that name familiar?* Then he remembered, 'Cutter!' Wayne Salter, better known as Cutter, to his friends - if he had any - and enemies - of which he probably had many. Cutter was a psychotic killer who was - or had been - in the employ of a man called Henry Solomon.

Henry Solomon... That was a name Steve hadn't heard in a while.

CHAPTER 27

Harry awoke later than usual. He stared up at the bedroom ceiling, blinking away sleep. While the ceiling looked familiar, it wasn't *his* bedroom ceiling. He raised his head and looked around. *Of course.* He turned to look at his arm. It was neatly bandaged. He glanced beneath the bed clothes. He was naked. He laid his head back upon the pillow, and let his mind drift to previous night's events.

After watching Cutter's body disappear over the balcony and into the black of night, Harry had stepped towards the damaged doorway. There he lifted his face to momentarily to enjoy the cooling wind and rain that blew in, before dropping his gaze to the street below, where he saw the damaged car, on top of which lay Cutter, partially enveloped by the collapsed roof. Izzy's car. Concerned, he looked up, searching for her, to see her standing in the middle of the road, stock-still, hands raised towards her open mouth, her eyes wide, staring back at him in shock.

Harry returned his gaze to the wreckage of the car. He stared intently, looking for signs of movement, of life. He didn't think Cutter was dead, it would take more than that to kill Cutter, unfortunately; the car's soft-top had probably helped to break his fall. Harry then surveyed the damage that had been done to the car. It was certainly going to take more than a roll of duct tape to fix that, he mused, the thought bringing a smile to his face.

The sound of a distant siren told Harry it was time to leave. Exiting by a window at the rear of the flat, he climbed down a drainpipe to the garden below, scaled a wall into the street behind, then circled back around to Mollie's car, by which time the emergency services had turned up and, looked on by Izzy, were giving their full attention to Cutter, allowing Harry to quietly slip away.

Harry's saviour that night had been his tenant, Lucy, the veterinary nurse. Lucy had pleaded with Harry to go to hospital, but Harry had refused point-blank, in favour of someone he knew he could trust. He also knew hospitals logged the details of knife and gunshot victims, and with his past record, a run-in with the law was last thing he needed, and, he'd casually assured her, a hole in the arm was hardly life threatening - besides, he didn't like hospitals.

The knife had gone straight through the fleshy part of his arm, causing minimal damage. After Lucy had cleaned the wound of fragments of leather and lint, she then tenderly and neatly stitched it up with a sterilised embroidery needle and thread. Harry's anaesthetic was a large straight whisky, which he had at first refused, due to the previous night's excesses, but eventually accepted under Lucy's insistence.

As well as having a tender touch, Lucy also proved to be a good listener, which Harry figured was probably down to her caring nature; her love of animals. Without realising it, he found himself telling Lucy about his past, recent and long ago. He told her things he'd never told another human being, doing something he'd never ever done before: he opened up his heart.

It was in the early hours of the morning when Izzy had finally turned up at Harry's place. Harry was standing in the dark, at a partially opened first-floor window, enjoying a purloined cigarette, when he saw Izzy walk up the garden path to his front door. He watched her lift her head and sniff the air, her keen sense of smell detecting the cigarette. She glanced up towards the window, just before stepping into the open porch and disappearing from view. He imagined her pressing the doorbell to his ground-floor flat and, of course, getting no response. After a few moments had passed, Harry did then hear the faint sound of ringing as she turned her attention to old Mr Jackson's doorbell. She won't get any joy there either, he thought, Mr Jackson was away at an 'Old-Boys' reunion'. The ringing then suddenly became a lot louder, as she tried the third doorbell.

Persistent.

It was at this point that Harry heard the rustle of bed sheets. 'Who's that?' said a sleepy voice.

'Nobody, Lucy. Just kids, that's all.'

Harry watched Izzy throw another glance up to the open window, before stomping-off back up the garden path, his eyes following her while wondering what transport she was using to get about now that her convertible had been converted into scrap. He watched her get into a waiting taxi cab and leave.

It was only then that he realised something was bothering him. He realised he was feeling... uncomfortable? No... not uncomfortable... *guilty!* He wondered why he should feel guilty; it wasn't as though they were in a relationship. *Christ, Harry, you'll be developing a conscience next!*

CHAPTER 28

After signing out a pool car, Steve's first visit that morning was to the local hospital's A&E Department. He approached the nurses' station and flashed his warrant card. 'Morning,' he said to the Staff Nurse seated at the computer. 'I'm looking for a Wayne Salter.'

The nurse turned to her screen. She shook her head. 'There's no Wayne Salter logged on the system,' she replied. 'What were the circumstances of his coming in?'

'He was probably brought in by ambulance, last night.' Again, she shook her head. 'He "fell", onto a car roof,' Steve then added.

'Oh, him,' she said. '"Mr Cutter" was the name he gave us. Not the nicest of people.'

'That sounds like Wayne,' said Steve. 'What were the extent of his injuries?'

The Staff Nurse turned back to her computer screen. 'Mr Cutter/Salter had three broken back ribs, a fractured wrist, two broken fingers, cuts and bruises, and a very badly broken nose... which was curious, really.'

'In what way?'

'Well... when the paramedics brought him in, they said they'd found him on his back, and the injuries he sustained, apart from the broken nose, suggest that's how he landed,' said the nurse.

'I see your point. Where is he now? On one of the wards?'

'No,' she replied, 'he discharged himself as soon as he'd been treated - and good riddance too,' she added. Steve requested Cutter's address, and then turned to leave. 'Oh, by the way,' she said, suddenly remembering, 'you're not the first person this morning to be asking after him.'

'Really?' said Steve. 'Who else?'

'That female reporter from the *North London Gazette*... Isobelle-somebody-or-other.'

'Did she say why she was interested?'

'No, she didn't - but then I wasn't overly helpful,' replied the nurse, grinning.'

'I'm sensing you're not a fan of hers?'

'You sense right, I'm not! Last year she wrote a piece on this hospital, the nursing staff in particular, questioning our dedication to our patients and to the job. Needless to say it didn't go down too well.'

'Ah, I see,' said Steve.

'Whatever story she's after,' continued the nurse, 'will be at somebody else's cost.'

Steve nodded, thanked her for her help, and left.

His second visit of the morning was to Cutter's flat. He arrived as a gold coloured Saab was being winched onto a tow-truck. He double-parked the pool car, and then got out to watch the operation, his gaze taking in the severity of the damage to the car. Cutter had got off lightly, thought Steve. He noticed the duct taped wing mirror. Something tugged at his memory. He took out his notebook and wrote down the car's registration number.

Steve looked up to the balcony of the first-floor flat, where he saw two workmen fixing sheet timber over a damaged doorway. He studied the height of the balcony, and the distance to the car.

The depth of the footpath was what Steve guessed as standard distance. Even so, it would have taken some effort - or momentum - to clear the footpath and hit the car.

He skipped up the steps. The front door was propped open with a fire extinguisher, and more sheets of timber. He made his way up to the first-floor. The door to Cutter's flat was also wide open. He politely knocked. Realising his arrival would not have been heard over the high pitched wine of power tools, he entered, stopping at a crumpled pizza box and an empty bottle of lager, its spilled contents staining the hallway carpet. He prodded the pizza box with the toe of a highly polished brogue, to reveal its contents - or rather what was left of the box's contents. Curious, he thought, pondering the nutritional value of Cutter's diet, along with his somewhat quirky dining locations.

Steve followed a trail of blood into the lounge. The workmen paused as he entered. He flashed his warrant card, identifying himself as a Detective Constable, and then said, 'I'm looking for the gentleman who lives here. You seen him by any chance?'

They both looked at each other, and then shook their heads. 'Sorry Guv,' said the bigger and older of the two, 'I think he's gone. Done a runner, you might say,' he then added, before turning back to the job in hand.

Steve wondered if they were any good at putting up shelving, but, after taking in the shaven heads, missing teeth, a variety of homemade tattoos showing support for a local lower league football team and the words 'love' and 'hate' across sausage sized fingers on huge fists, he thought better of it.

Looking around the room, he saw a large ornate fireplace, bloody fingerprints smeared across its mantelpiece, as well as the ornamental samurai sword that sat upon it. He crossed to it, pulling out a latex glove from his jacket pocket, which he then put on to prevent fingerprint contamination - even though he thought it unlikely Forensics would be called in to 'dust' the place, because the 'alleged' victim had gone missing, therefore wouldn't be pressing any charges. He gripped the end of the sword's hilt, and then very gently pulled it far enough from its scabbard to inspect the blade. *Christ Almighty!* The ornamental blade had been honed to a razor sharp finish: sharp enough to decapitate.

After wandering around the remaining rooms of the flat, poking into drawers and cupboards and finding nothing of importance, he left, pausing only briefly at the pizza box to once again marvel at Cutter's dietary choice.

Back down in the lobby, Steve found the tenant of the ground-floor flat struggling to move the timber sheets to close the outer door. In her efforts, she hadn't heard Steve approach.

Steve coughed politely, so as not to startle the woman. 'May I help you?' he asked, smiling.

'Oh, yes, please,' she replied, breathlessly surprised.

She was an attractive woman in her early fifties, smartly dressed, and slightly shorter in height than Steve. Her hair was a luxurious chestnut brown that fell to her shoulders, her eyes of a similar colour, her flawless complexion complemented by the minimum of makeup.

Steve effortlessly moved the few sheets of timber, allowing the door to swing shut.

'My knight in shining armour,' she said, smiling at Steve while subconsciously straightening her hair.

'My pleasure, Ma'am,' said Steve, politely returning her smile.

'So polite, too,' she said, as her eyes took in Steve's immaculate dress sense, and boyishly handsome good looks. 'A girl can't be too careful these days... about security, that is,' she said, staring with fascination at Steve's bright blue eyes and long lashes.

'It's all part of the job, Ma'am,' replied Steve, shoving his hands deep into his pockets, while starting to feel slightly uncomfortable under the attractive woman's gaze.

Two perfectly plucked eyebrows shot up in curiosity. '"The job?"'

'I'm a police officer, Ma'am.'

'A police officer! How delightful,' she said, as she idly fingered the gold chain around her neck that disappeared down into her cleavage.

'Detective Constable Steve Marshall, Ma'am.'

'A Detective Constable!' The perfectly plucked eyebrows again shot up. 'But you're so... young.' Steve smiled weakly back, while shoving his hands deeper into his trouser pockets. 'Can I offer you a drink, officer?' she then said, indicating the open door to her flat. 'Tea? Coffee?'

'I'm fine, thank you, Ma'am.'

'Christine. Please call me Christine,' she told him, holding out her hand. Steve responded. She held on to his hand.

Steve coughed, awkwardly, as he managed to retrieve his hand. 'If you don't mind me asking, Ma'am... Christine. Did you see or hear anything last night?'

The attractive fifty-something looked momentarily puzzled, before Steve said, 'Regarding the gentleman from the flat on the first-floor.'

'Oh, him!' she responded, her face darkening with a look of distaste. 'He is certainly no gentleman. He is an offensive little man,' she said.

'Are you aware that the... man in question, met with an 'accident' last night?'

'Yes, it was me who telephoned for the ambulance. Though had I realised it was him, I wouldn't have bothered.'

'So you didn't see or hear anything?' Steve asked again.

'Other than a loud crash, breaking glass, that sort of thing - which I thought was a car accident at first - no, I didn't.'

'You didn't hear any sign of a struggle within the flat itself? A fight, maybe?' he said.

'Since I had my ceilings sound proofed - due to the aforementioned offensive little man and his nocturnal habits - I'm pleased to say I've heard nothing.

Steve nodded. He stared down at the floor, thinking. He noticed what seemed to be a small piece of Anchovy stuck to the toe of his shoe. He fought the urge to bend down and wipe it off. So, I don't suppose you'd know if he had any visitors last night?' he enquired.

'No,' she replied. 'Other than the pizza delivery man, that is.'

Steve looked up, sharply. 'He had a pizza delivered?' Steve had assumed - wrongly, it would seem - that because the pizza and beer were partially consumed, and found in the hallway, Cutter had bought them elsewhere and then brought them home.

'Yes,' said Christine, 'I let him in the front door.'

'Can you describe what he looked like?'

Christine shook her luxurious chestnut brown, head. 'He was wearing a motor bike helmet,' she replied.

'You didn't by any chance see what company he worked for, did you?' She again, shook her head. 'He wasn't wearing one of those jackets that usually bear the name of the pizza company?' he prompted.

'No, sorry. It was a plain leather jacket,' she replied. 'And a bit smelly, too,' she then added, wrinkling her nose at the memory.

Steve gazed at the floor again, and at the offending piece of Anchovy still stuck to his shoe. He hoped it wouldn't leave a permanent mark on the leather.

'Is he still alive?' asked Christine, drawing Steve's attention back to the present.

'Err, yes. Yes he is. Very much so.' Christine look deflated. 'I don't think you'll be seeing him again, though,' he told her. 'It looks like he's packed and left.'

Visibly brightened, Christine said, as her fingers lightly touched Steve's arm, 'Are you sure you wouldn't like a drink? Maybe something a little stronger?'

'Sorry, Ma'am, I'm on duty,' he replied, starting to colour-up.

'Pity,' she said.

CHAPTER 29

The Weasel was a bag of nerves. Ever since Harry Windsor had paid him a visit, he was as jumpy as a scalded cat. The sudden blare of a passing car's horn would have him fumbling and dropping the food he was attempting to serve. He was a mess. He was scared of his own shadow.

He'd just finished serving some hungry construction workers and was in the middle of preparing more burgers, when, sensing another customer, he looked up, only to find there was nobody there. He felt an onrush of fear and anxiety. He cursed himself for his timidity. Get a grip, Jimmy, he silently told himself as he tried to focus on the task in hand.

But he couldn't. His eyes kept flicking upwards, sensing a threat, but seeing none. The Weasel wasn't a hard man like Harry Windsor. He was an inept petty crook with previous convictions: burglary, shoplifting, and handling stolen goods, to name but a few. He'd upset a lot of people over the years, so he relied on his instincts to survive, to get him out of the trouble that his lying, cheating, and underhanded actions often got him into, and, right now, his instinct was telling him he was in danger.

His instinct was correct.

The door behind him, at the rear of his food trailer, was suddenly yanked open, and before he could turn around, a large forearm had wrapped and locked itself around his neck. In desperation and panic, the Weasel's arm shot out, his hand scrabbling and searching for the kitchen knife he'd been using only moments before. As his fingers found and curled around the handle of the long, razor sharp knife, he felt a large hand enclose his, and the knife within it.

Despite all his physical effort, he felt his hand being forced upwards and towards his face, before eventually seeing the knife come into view. In morbid fascination, he watched the juices of a recently cut onion trickle down the blade. He imagined those juices being dark red. He whimpered with fear, and vainly tried to wriggle free from the vice like grip around his neck. But to no avail.

He readied himself for the questions, and the demands, and the threats that would surely come. He knew that whatever answers he gave could very well determine his future well-being. He readied himself to lie, to say whatever it would take to survive. Anything but the truth. Telling the truth would be confirmation of his guilt - whatever that might be.

But when he felt hot breath against his ear, and he heard the question, his determination deserted him. Only the truth could possibly save him. And then he wasn't really sure.

'Tell me about the Eastern Europeans,' said Harry.

The Weasel whimpered again, then pissed his pants.

CHAPTER 30

Steve drove back to the station, returning the car to the pool. As he entered the main reception, the Desk Sergeant informed him the Forensics team was down at Tricky Dicky's premises. He also gave him a handful of telephone message slips, all of them from the reporter, Isobelle Harker.

Sighing, Steve shoved the message slips deep into his pocket, then turned around and headed back out the door to Tricky Dicky's place. He decided to walk. It would only take ten minutes or so, and he couldn't be bothered to sign-out another pool car.

He strode-out along Willesden High Street, taking in its multicultural diversity through the variety of restaurants, shops, and his fellow pedestrians.

Stopping outside one of his favourite shops - a serve-yourself green grocers - he pondered on what to have for dinner that night. Steve loved to cook and, equally, to select the food he intended to cook. After a few minutes of squeezing and sniffing for freshness, he bought two large red peppers and two un-waxed lemons. From a delicatessen two doors further along he then bought some black olives, a jar of capers, mozzarella cheese, and a fresh ciabatta bread loaf. With his goods in a large paper carrier bag - because Steve believed in being environmentally friendly - he continued on to Tricky Dicky's place.

Parked outside the Adult shop was the Scientific Investigation Unit's van, and guarding the entrance door from over inquisitive members of the public, was a bored uniformed constable who Steve didn't recognise. He flashed his ID at the young constable who, after checking it, politely nodded and stepped aside.

Inside the shop, Steve gazed around at the variety of merchandise neatly arranged on the shelving. There was a tall stack of cardboard boxes on the counter next to the cash register. A box lay on the floor, its contents spilled, a variety of sex toys - some of them an eye watering size. Steve figured the box was probably dropped or knocked over in the panic to evacuate the building.

Seeing a door wedged open in the corner of the room, Steve made his way through to the rear of the building, the acrid smell and taste of burnt materials growing stronger in his nose and the back of his throat the further he went. A light was coming from an open door at the far end of the corridor. He stepped through into a medium sized room, eerily lit by portable halogen lights. Steve made the assumption the fire, or the large amount of water used by the fire brigade to extinguish the fire, had fused the electrics.

An area adjacent to the bar had been taped-off to preserve the crime scene, ghostly white suited figures cautiously moving about. Everything was blackened with ash and smoke damage: the ceiling, walls, furniture - everything.

Steve knew the fire brigade had pumped out the excess water prior to the investigation team going in, but there was still enough left for him to squelch through as he approached the taped-off area, while still taking care not to brush against any of the ash covered surfaces. If Steve had been dismayed earlier at the fish oil stain on his expensive leather shoes, he was now mortified. He berated himself for not brining his Wellington boots.

The door to Tricky Dicky's office was gone, leaving only a charred gaping hole. The Forensic Officers were picking their way through what was left of the contents of the office. Just inside the doorway was a blackened shape in what appeared to be the foetal position.

On seeing Steve, one of the Forensic Officers walked over to the tape, nodding a greeting as he removed his mask.

'How's it going?' asked Steve.

The Officer shook his head. 'There's not much left to analyse,' he replied, 'and what we've got left is soaking wet. The fire door did its job. It kept the fire contained long enough for the fire brigade to turn up, but it also kept that poor sod in too,' he said, indicating the blackened form with a nod of his head.

'How do you mean?' asked Steve, frowning.

'While most of the door has gone up in smoke, we still have the mortice lock - it's in the locked position.'

'He was locked in?' said Steve, incredulously.

'The door was locked,' replied the Officer, 'from which side, I can't yet say.'

'And the key?' asked Steve, after a moment's pause.

The Officer shrugged, replaced his mask, and turned back to his work.

'Constable!' came a loud voice from behind Steve, making him jump.

Steve turned to see D.I. Carson approaching, in green Wellington boots, hands stuffed deep into trouser pockets. 'Sir?' said Steve.

Carson stopped next to Steve. He momentarily watched the Forensic Officers at work, all the while jingling the loose change in his trouser pocket. Turning to Steve, he said, 'They got anything yet?'

'Not really, Sir,' replied Steve. 'They think that even if any evidence has managed to survive the fire, it's quite likely to have been destroyed by water or smoke damage.'

They both watched as the Forensic Officers carefully worked around what was left of Tricky Dicky.

'They did say,' said Steve, nodding towards the Forensic Officers, 'that the door was locked at the time of the fire.'

Carson's eyebrows lifted in surprise. 'I guess Tricky finally pissed-off one person too many,' said Carson, with a hint of a smile. 'A fitting end, some might say.'

Steve turned to look at his superior officer. Carson was a man of medium height and in his middle fifties, though looked considerably older. His greying hair was greased back and over his collar; it had probably been a fine looking 'mullet' when Carson was in his prime. His stony face bore the pockmarked scars of teenage acne, and his posture was poor: shoulders hunched, beer belly protruding. This coupled with his choice of suits from the cheaper end of the retail market, gave an overall impression of slovenliness. That impression could not be further from the truth. D.I. Carson was 'old-school', and he was as hard-as-nails. Steve was yet to meet a person who didn't look uncomfortable when talking to Carson. It was the eyes. Carson's eyes were a light hazel brown, and unblinking. He had the gaze of a reptile; the gaze of predator - which could be very useful when interviewing suspected criminals.

He now turned that gaze upon Steve, who immediately started to fidget, and just as he was about to look away, Carson's gaze dropped down to Steve's carrier bag. 'What's in the carrier bag, Constable?' asked Carson, jingling the loose change in his pocket.

'Food, Sir,' replied Steve.

'Food?' said Carson, who hadn't eaten since earlier that morning. 'What kind of food?'

'Err, red peppers, black olives and capers, Sir,' replied Steve, deliberately omitting to mention the more palatable ciabatta and mozzarella, knowing from past experience just where the conversation was going.

D.I. Carson pulled a face that was somewhere between a look of distaste and a sneer, before turning back to the crime scene. 'Let me know when - if - they find any evidence that might indicate who, or what, killed this worthless piece of shit,' he said, turning to leave.

CHAPTER 31

A trail of battered and bruised victims had led Harry to a cosy little pub on the outskirts of Richmond, south west of London, where he had a window seat and was now enjoying a pint. Mollie's car was parked on a meter, which Harry had filled with what seemed to him an extortionate amount of money.

The only information the Weasel had been able to give Harry was meagre, but, coupled with some of his old connections in crime, had been enough to lead him from petty criminal, to pimp, to prostitute, their information bringing him to this part of outer London.

As pleasant as the pint and pub were, this was not where Harry's interest lay. His interest lay in the large detached Edwardian building across the road, a house large enough to make Isobel's father's place look like a weekend retreat. Judging by the number of windows and waste pipes on the front facade, Harry figured it had at one time probably been a hotel. It was now - he'd been reliably informed - an 'exclusive' gentlemen's club. He'd also been informed that the club was owned by a mysterious figure yet run by Eastern Europeans - namely Russians.

The club itself was a legitimate business, but behind the scenes it was a different matter. Crime money was being laundered through the club's bars, restaurant, and licensed gambling facilities. The young women who worked in the club as 'hostesses', were also Eastern Europeans, brought over to the UK on the promise of a better life, the cost of their passage having been paid for them on the condition that they repaid that cost once they'd found employment. On arrival in the UK, however, they'd been presented with a different scenario. A scenario of imprisonment, physical violence, rape, and forced drug taking. Once they'd been mentally broken and addicted to drugs, they were then forced into prostitution and expected to work wherever they were sent across the country.

Harry knew the link between Cutter's claim of having sold Mollie to the Eastern Europeans, and this particular club, was tenuous at most. From what he'd recently learnt, the sex slave trade was rife, and the chance of finding Mollie was slim, but it was all he had.

He took a sip from his pint, and studied the house across the road, brooding over his next move. He was going to have to go in there. The question was: how? Tall, black iron spiked railings ran around the perimeter of the property; the gates were electronic and intercom operated. Harry didn't fancy his chances of scaling the fencing' without being seen or doing himself a serious injury - or both. But then he could hardly just walk up the drive and in through the front door, either. These kinds of clubs didn't just let in any old Tom, Dick, *or* Harry; you had to be rich and connected - and Harry was neither. He also had no doubt they would have security of some kind, probably CCTV, possibly Doormen: hired muscle.

It was mid-afternoon and there were a few large, expensive cars parked on the gravel forecourt. Lunchtime crowd, thought Harry. He watched a silver Daimler pull up to the gates. The electric window came down and arm reached out to press the intercom. A moment later, the gates swung open.

Another twenty minutes passed before he saw a young man and woman walk up to the gates, press the intercom, to then also be let in. He could see, despite their winter coats, they were dressed in 'black and whites': catering uniform. He ruled out trying to sneak in with the staff; he was a stranger, and clearly not dressed for the part. In fact, if he were honest with himself, he was starting to look like a tramp.

Harry had finished his pint, and was at a loss as to what to do, when he saw a Luton van pull up to the gates. The driver's door opened, and the driver jumped down, sauntering over to the intercom. The van had a roller shutter rear door, a Checker Plate step, and a grab-rail fixed either side to aid access to the rear of the van.

Harry made a split second decision. Hastily pulling on his jacket, he left the pub and walked quickly across the road. He now knew how he was going to get in. What he hadn't yet figured out, was how he was going to get out.

Taking hold of a grab-rail, he stepped up onto the Checker Plate step, just as the driver jumped back into his cab, put the van into gear, and drove through the now open gateway and up the drive towards the large house. Not wanting to risk the chance of the driver catching sight of him in his wing mirrors by looking around the back of the van, Harry hung on: waiting, judging the moment.

When he heard and felt the van start to slow, and it'd slowed to a walking pace, he hopped off, quickly disappearing into the shrubbery that bordered the property. Using the borders as cover, he then slowly and silently made his way around to the rear of the house, and in the direction of the disappearing Luton van. After a few minutes, he reached a point from where he could watch the van being unloaded of tinned food and groceries.

Crouched amongst the wet and muddy shrubbery from the recent rains and an agonisingly long forty minutes later the unloading was complete, and with his clipboard duly signed, the driver jumped back into his cab, did a three-point turn, and then drove away. As Harry went to stand, cramp shot up through his legs, causing him to involuntarily cry out.

Lunging for a nearby tree sapling to give him support and to ease the agony of his cramped legs, he quickly looked around, checking to see if anyone had heard him. Nothing.

Despite the autumnal chill, beads of perspiration broke-out on his forehead as he used the sapling to pull himself upright, but in doing so, dislodged a shower of rain drops from its leaves, soaking him further. 'For fuck's sake!' he said, now more wet than dry and covered in mud. Harry wasn't into all this covert crap, he'd much rather go through the front door, all-guns-blazing - metaphorically speaking, of course. Harry was 'old school', he didn't like using knives or guns, just pure physical violence.

When the feeling had almost returned to his legs, he hobbled out of the shrubbery and across the gravelled drive, and to the door the delivery driver had used. It was unlocked. He gently eased it open, listening carefully, all the while anticipating a cry of alarm to ring out. Silence.

He peered inside. A long corridor with a red quarry tiled floor and white painted walls with doors leading off, stretched out ahead of him. He quietly entered, closing the door behind him. Immediately to his right, was a door with a wired glass viewing panel in the upper centre, the muted crash and bang of metal upon metal could be heard from within. The kitchen, he assumed.

As he started to move forward, the overhead lighting flickered into life, causing him to abruptly halt, anticipating company and his discovery.

Nothing. Silence.

He took another few steps. The next overhead light flickered on. Motion sensors, he realised with relief; the lights only came on when there was movement: people about. He noticed the large number of marks on the painted walls and doors along the corridor, suggesting regular traffic passed through. He carried on, wary, before stopping at the first closed door: no glass viewing panel and no signage to indicate what lay behind. He listened for a moment and then eased the door open, the light flickering on to show boxes of groceries and tinned goods. The driver's destination.

The next door along was a cleaner's cupboard.

Harry knew that the chances of finding Mollie in that part of the building were slim, but he believed in being thorough - and he had to start somewhere.

Next door along: locked.

The next door had a 'Private' sign. Also locked.

The next room was different. As the light came on, Harry could see it was carpeted, had a desk, a chair, a desktop computer, filing cabinets, and shelving full of box files. He stepped in. The writing on the spines of the box files, and the stack of invoices and delivery notes on the desk, indicated it was the Catering Manager's office. He wasn't going to find any clues in there, so he turned to leave. As he did so, he noticed a trail of muddy footprints leading into the room. 'Fuck!' he said. He retraced his muddy footprints back to the open doorway. Peering around the door frame, he saw a trail of mud leading back to the outer door. 'Shit!'

It was at that moment when he felt cold metal touch the back of his head. While Harry was anti-gun, he was certainly familiar enough with them to know when one was pressing against his skull.

So much for covert!

And that was his last thought, as he was clubbed across the back of the head, and sent into blackness.

Harry was in trouble. Serious trouble.

The ignorant bliss of unconsciousness prevented him from being aware of just how serious his plight was. But soon enough, he would be. Soon enough, he was going to wake to his worst nightmare, his greatest fear. Soon enough, the panic, the sheer terror, and the thrashing of limbs would set in. Soon, very soon, he was going to scream his lungs out, in the desperate hope that someone, somehow, would save him.

CHAPTER 32

'Tosser!'

Izzy was back behind the wheel, and carving her way through the London traffic. After her fruitless visit to the hospital that morning, in search of Cutter - and still annoyed with the offhanded attitude she'd received from the nurse - she'd spent the remainder of the day in her office. This was for two reasons. The first was to appease her editor, who'd given her a serious telling-off for not delivering the church story in time to go to print, making it perfectly clear that he didn't "give a flying fuck" who she was related to, and if she didn't pull her finger out, she'd be "looking for a new job!"; the other was to go through the laborious task of completing the paperwork for the insurance claim on her car, and to organise a hire car - the cost of which, she'd discovered to her dismay, was not covered by her insurance policy.

As she drove, she found herself reflecting on the conversation she'd just had with her father. How she'd informed him the Saab - which he had bought for her - was now a write-off. Izzy had gone to great lengths to explain to her father that this particular accident had not been her fault, that it had just been "one of those things". Other than asking why she had been at that particular place at that particular time, her father had said very little, which usually meant he was angry and no doubt disappointed with her - again. She had the sneaking suspicion her father had already talked to her editor, and if her editor did follow through with his threat to sack her, her father wouldn't intervene to prevent it.

Well, at least it's a nice hire car, she thought. She had opted for a Smart Car, for no other reason than it looked cute in its black and red livery.

While the hire car didn't have the rumble of power that her beloved Saab's V-6 engine had, it was surprisingly nippy. Or at least it had been; the evening traffic now starting to build was slowing the car to a walking pace.

Izzy checked her wristwatch, and then puffed out her cheeks in a heavy sigh. Having grown impatient with Detective Constable Steve Marshall's lack of response, she had consulted the on-line Electoral Register and located his home address, to which she was now heading.

The traffic lights up ahead changed, allowing half a dozen cars to get through. She moved forward, before yet again grinding to a halt.

Izzy was trying to work out what she was going to say to the policeman, what cover story she should use. As a cutting-edge reporter looking for a story, it wasn't in her nature to be honest and upfront with the people she interviewed. Being honest and upfront sometimes scared people off, or made them clam-up. Izzy had only ever met Steve Marshall on one occasion. What few dealings she'd had with him had been by telephone, and that was usually to try and elicit information on a recently committed crime for a *North London Gazette* news story.

The lights changed, and a few more cars got across the junction. Izzy moved forward a few more car lengths.

She realised that Mollie's parents' house was only a couple of miles away from Steve Marshall's home. She wondered whether to make a detour, to call in and see how Patrick was doing, and to see if maybe he'd heard from Mollie. She then remembered how upset Patrick had been the last time she'd seen him, and the state he was in. She hoped he was okay, and that he hadn't done anything 'stupid'.

She decided she would leave it. Maybe she'd give him a ring tomorrow, when she had more time. She wasn't to know this, and wouldn't find out until much later, but that decision probably saved her life.

Izzy wondered why she was so hung up on finding Mollie. She had yet to hear or see any solid evidence that something had definitely happened to the girl. And as for getting any help from Harry, she hadn't seen him in almost twenty four hours, so she certainly couldn't ask him. As her train of thought moved onto Harry, her feelings and thoughts started to become unsettled. She wondered whether she was really pursuing Harry, rather than Mollie.

The lights changed, and she again moved forward. She was now two car lengths away from the traffic lights. She drummed her fingers on the steering wheel. Her left foot tapped a rhythmic beat on the clutch pedal. The more she thought about Harry, the more unsettled and agitated she became.

A little earlier, she had again called at Harry's house. She'd rung all three doorbells, but, getting no answer, she'd returned to the warmth of her car to wait.

An hour had passed, then two, and just when she'd thought she was going to totally die of boredom - or pee her pants because her bladder was full - she'd seen a young woman in what looked like a nurse's uniform walk up the garden path to Harry's front door. Lucy, Harry's other tenant, she'd guessed, getting out of the car, quickly crossing the road, and trotting up the short garden path just as the young woman found her door keys.

'Excuse me? Hello?' said Izzy.

The young woman, who had one hand on the partially open door while slipping her keys back into her shoulder bag, turned at the sound of Izzy's voice.

'Hi,' Izzy said to the young woman.

The young woman just frowned.

'I'm looking for Harry,' a smiling Izzy then said, hopping from foot-to-foot. 'Is he here?'

The furrows deepened on the young woman's brow. She pulled the door closed with what seemed an unnaturally loud click, before then giving Izzy a long, cool, look.

'Err, I'm a friend of his,' said Izzy, still jigging from foot-to-foot. 'Isobelle Harker - Izzy,' she added, wondering whether to offer her hand, but then deciding against it.

The young woman's eyebrows shot up. 'Ah,' she said, realising. 'The reporter from the *North London Gazette*. You're *that* Isobelle Harker!' she added, smiling - though the smile didn't quite reach up to her eyes.

Izzy started to feel uncomfortable under the steady gaze of the young woman's green eyes. *God, I really hate nurses!* 'It's Lucy, isn't it?' she said, trying to break the ice. 'Have you seen Harry? It's really important I speak to him,' she told Lucy, trying hard not to sound like she was pompous or pleading. 'We are friends, you know,' she then added, failing at both pompous and pleading.

Lucy nodded slowly, her green eyes twinkling, a smile tugging at the corners of her mouth. 'Mm, he has mentioned you.'

'He has?' Izzy replied, a little too quickly and a little too eagerly.

'Mm. But to answer your question, I haven't seen him since last night. If he's not answering the door, I think we can safely say he's not in.'

'Oh...' said Izzy, shifting from foot-to-foot and looking deflated.

'I presume he's got your number?' Lucy politely enquired.

'What?... Oh, yes.'

'Then I'm sure he'll you ring you when he's ready,' Lucy replied, as she turned back to the front door.

'Erm, excuse me?' said Izzy, who was now getting quite desperate. 'Could I possibly use your toilet?' Lucy just rolled her eyes, before taking out her keys, and then turning to unlock the door.

In the hallway, Lucy picked up her mail from a small table, before then starting up the stairs. Izzy paused to look across at the door to Harry's flat, fighting back the urge to dash across the hallway and hammer her fists upon it. Instead, she enviously followed Lucy's shapely calves up the stairs.

When Izzy emerged from the bathroom, the door to Lucy's flat was still standing open, and Lucy was still leaning against the adjacent kitchen door frame, arms folded across ample breasts, an amused smile on her face.

Guessing she wasn't going to be invited to stay for coffee, Izzy hesitated, reluctant to leave. 'Are you sure Harry isn't in his flat, and just not answering the door?' she asked.

'It's possible, though unlikely,' Lucy replied.

'How can you be sure?'

Lucy shrugged. 'I can't. But Harry isn't the kind of guy to hide away. Besides, his mail is still on the table downstairs. But feel free to knock on his door on your way out,' she said, moving towards the flat door. As she did so, Izzy got a quick glimpse into the kitchen, and there, hanging on the back of a kitchen chair, was Harry's leather jacket.

Izzy felt her stomach lurch.

'Was it very late, when you last saw Harry?' she asked Lucy, trying not to sound like a jealous schoolgirl, but failing miserably.

Another sigh, another check of the wristwatch, the lights still on red. The late afternoon was turning into early evening, and the daylight was quickly becoming twilight.

Izzy's shoulder bag was on the passenger seat next to her. She reached in, rummaged around, and then finally found what she was looking for: an opened packet of cigarettes and a disposable gas lighter.

Izzy was a casual smoker. So casual in fact, she couldn't recall how many cigarettes were left in the pack. There was one left. Ignoring the sign on the hire car's dashboard, which clearly stated smoking wasn't allowed in the car, she placed the cigarette into her mouth and struck the lighter, taking three attempts before she managed to produce a flame. She touched it to the tip of the cigarette, drawing deeply, seeing the tip glow red. Just at that moment, the vehicle behind her loudly blasted its horn to tell her the lights had changed to green. Startled, she dropped the cigarette, only for it to land on the carpeting of the passenger side footwell. Fighting against her seatbelt, she desperately scrabbled about trying to locate the cigarette, the smell of singed carpet and the tiny plume of rising smoke, finally helping her to pinpoint the offending article.

Shoving the cigarette into the corner of her mouth, she then crunched the car into gear, hit the button to wind down the side window, floored the accelerator, and then shot forward through a red light, at the same time making eye contact in the rear view mirror with the driver behind and giving him the finger: multitasking at its best.

CHAPTER 33

Harry's return to consciousness was painfully slow, and very confused. He was unable to comprehend where he was, what time of day it was and, more importantly, how long he'd been there. Just how much time had passed? Was he awake or was he dreaming?

He started to lift his head from the cold surface that it rested upon until a sharp bolt of pain shot through his skull, causing him to cry out. He eased his head back down, allowing the pain to reduce to a mere hammering.

Everything was black. Totally, totally, black. No light, nothing. *Am I blind?* And it was cold. So, so, cold. Bone achingly cold. His entire body seemed to be numb.

He tried to move, to wrap his arms around himself and rub some life back into his achingly cold limbs and stop the violent shaking, but he was unable to. What little sense of feeling Harry had left in his body indicated he was lying on the floor, and that he seemed to be wedged tight into a corner, his arms trapped behind him, his knees up towards his chest. He also appeared to be naked.

He tried to blink away the darkness, to focus, but something seemed to be across his eyes. As he scrunched up his face, he also became aware of something across his mouth. Then he realised: there was a cloth bag, a hood maybe, over his head, also heavy duty adhesive tape over his mouth allowing him to breathe through his nose only.

Harry desperately, desperately tried to remember. Where had he been? Who had he spoken to? *Where the fuck was he?*

Nothing. His mind was totally blank. He wasn't even sure if he was who he thought he was, and it seemed the harder he tried to remember, the more his head hurt: so he gave up. He stopped trying to think. He rested his forehead on the floor, to again feel the numbing cold seep through the thin cloth, his resolve and strength draining away as it did so.

With his mouth taped, Harry was breathing hard through his nose. He could smell dirt and traces of paint on the floor. He could also smell stale alcohol... whisky... *the old man!* He could smell his own stale body odour... Izzy... the car...

Cutter! Realising his heightened sense of smell was triggering threads of memory, he desperately tried to grasp one, to hang onto it. Muddy footprints... gun barrel... *Eastern Europeans*...

Harry groaned inwardly, more at his own stupidity than physical pain. He had to make a move. He had to get out of there. He had no doubt that the reason he was unable to move his arms and legs - other than the cold and cramp - was because they were bound with tape.

Naked, blind, and tightly bound, while lying in the corner of a cold stinking room and feeling like an maltreated scrap yard dog, Harry weighed up his options. He figured that if he were to jerk his body upright while pushing hard against the wall that the soles of his feet were pressed against, he would end up in a slouched position, from where he could then shuffle into a sitting position. He also figured that the moment he moved, his cramped body would be wracked with excruciating pain.

He took a number of deep sharp breaths in through his nose to fill his lungs and oxygenate his blood, before then exhaling hard, jerking his body upwards at the same time pushing against the wall.

The muffled cry of agony that shot through his cramped body was suddenly cut short when his head slammed into an overhead steel plate.

He slumped, dazed, but only for a few seconds. Fear and adrenaline raced through his body like express train, kick-starting his senses and sharpening his dulled thoughts, as the realisation and horror of his plight sank in.

He was in a box.

A steel box.

Horrific memories of early childhood, so carefully managed and suppressed, came hurtling back.

Please, God, no! Not this! Please!

Harry fought hard.

He fought hard against the terror that threatened to overwhelm him. He tried to breathe calmly, to focus his mind on anything other than the fact he was locked in a box. He desperately tried to ignore his greatest fear. His only fear.

Claustrophobia.

He failed.

His breathing became erratic. He started to hyperventilate. The strictures of the cold and cramp were quickly forgotten as he fought against his bonds, his body thrashing around the confined space of the box, impervious to the pain he was inflicting upon himself, the scraped skin, and the bruised bones.

He tried to scream for help. But no one heard him.

No one came.

CHAPTER 34

Izzy parked her Smart Car in a parking bay reserved for local residents. As she locked it, she cast an appreciative eye over the top-of-the-range Mercedes sports car parked adjacent. She rang the doorbell to Steve's house long and hard. She waited ten seconds before again pressing the bell. She was about to press it for the third time, when the door suddenly opened.

Still wearing suit trousers, waistcoat, shirt - sleeves rolled up - and tie, stood Detective Constable Steve Marshall, tea towel in one hand, and a frown of annoyance creasing his handsome forehead.

'Hi,' said Izzy, thrusting a bottle of wine - which she'd bought from a supermarket on her way over - out towards Steve.

Moments passed. They continued to stare at each other.

'Izzy,' said Izzy, with her arm out ramrod straight, still clutching the bottle of wine.

Steve's frown deepened.

'Isobelle Harker,' she added, feeling awkward and turning red in the face, 'from the *North London Gazette.*'

Steve's frown quickly disappeared as he realised, then reappeared as he wondered at the purpose of her visit to his home. 'How did you find out where I live?'

'Electoral Role,' replied Izzy, whose arm was beginning ache and waver under the effort.

Steve was still frowning. Then, remembering his manners, he reached out to take the wine. Izzy, taking this as an invitation, breezed past him and into his home, leaving him at the front door holding a tea towel and a bottle of Chablis, with indecision written all over his face.

'Come in,' said Steve, who then had to hurry after her as she disappeared down the hallway, veering off and into the kitchen. When he caught up with her, she was closely inspecting the food produce he'd bought earlier that day, and which was now laid out on the island kitchen unit ready for preparation and cooking.

'You've got an island!' said Izzy, excitedly. 'I've always wanted an island, but my flat's too small,' she added, dumping her shoulder bag and coat on the floor in a corner of the kitchen, to then perch herself on a barstool at the end of the island. 'It's a beautiful kitchen. And so many gadgets,' she said, eyeing the wall mounted TV, coffee machine, and various other top-of-the-range kitchen appliances. 'And it's so *tidy*, too.'

Steve stood and watched her, totally at a loss.

'It's chilled, you know,' she said, beaming at him.

'Sorry?' he replied, blinking.

'The Chablis. It's chilled. It would be a shame for it to get warm.'

Steve glanced down at the bottle of wine in his hand, and then back up at Izzy, his brain proving a little slow in catching up with the whirlwind which had just entered his home. 'Can I get you a drink?' he asked, finally.

'Ooh, that would be lovely,' she replied, as though the thought had never occurred to her. Steve located a glass, filled it, and placed it on a coaster in front of Izzy, who promptly took a large sip and then smacked her lips in pleasure. 'Aren't you having one?'

'I don't drink,' he replied, to which Izzy's eyebrows immediately shot up. 'Well, the odd glass of wine on occasions,' he then added.

Another long awkward moment.

'Mm, something smells good,' said Izzy, finally breaking the silence.

'Oh, yes. Naan bread,' said Steve, remembering.

'I adore naan bread. Especially the flavoured ones. You know, garlic with herbs, or sun-dried tomatoes?' she said, taking another sip of wine, and then tucking her blonde hair behind one ear. 'Out of the packet, into the oven, two mins, done. Delish!'

'Oh, no. It's not out of a packet,' Steve told her, having a quick glance into the oven, 'it's homemade.'

'Fuck-a-duck!' she replied. 'You actually make your own naan bread?'

Steve frowned. He didn't like swearing. And he especially didn't like women swearing. He always felt it was... common. He reached out to replace Izzy's glass back on its coaster, wiping the circles of moisture from the worktop surface as he did so.

Izzy could see that Steve wasn't comfortable. His body language was turning defensive. He clearly didn't like his private space being invaded, and she could see he was close to asking her why she was there. 'So, what are you cooking?' she asked, quickly.

'Well, the dish is called Italian Roast Peppers,' he answered, hovering over the food, hesitating.

'Are you expecting company?' asked Izzy, as the thought finally occurred to her that she might be interrupting something.

'No. Nobody,' he replied, still hesitating.

'Maybe you should wear an apron. You are very smartly dressed.'

Steve nodded, hesitated, and then reached for a bundle of cloth that was scrunched up on the worktop. It was a full-length apron. He shook out the creases, looped it over his head, and then tied it behind his back.

Izzy struggled to suppress a giggle. The reason for Steve's hesitation was because it was one of those joke aprons: printed on the front, from the neck down, was a picture of a woman's body, bare breasted and only wearing black lace panties with stockings and suspenders. 'Nice legs,' she said, struggling not to laugh out loud.

It was Steve's turn to colour-up with embarrassment. 'It was a present,' he managed to say.

'From a girlfriend?' asked Izzy, teasing.

Steve quickly turned to the preparation of the food, explaining to Izzy what he was doing, warming to his theme as he went. 'I put the lightly oiled red peppers into an ovenproof dish, sprinkle over chopped capers, black olives and garlic. Then, grated mozzarella, fresh white breadcrumbs - ciabatta in this instance - a sprinkle of olive oil and white wine -'

'Yes, please,' said Izzy, holding out her empty glass and grinning.'

Steve topped up her glass, ensured it was on its coaster, and then continued. 'I then sprinkle on freshly chopped mint and parsley, season, and then bake in the oven. I usually serve it with either rice, couscous, or maybe orzo pasta, along with a green leaf salad of some kind.'

'Wow, that is amazing!' said Izzy. 'Handsome *and* talented. Would you marry me?'

Steve's head snapped up, to look at Izzy in what she could only describe as shock-horror. 'Joking!' she said, quickly.

'Oh... Of course... Yes,' he said.

'Are you a vegetarian?' asked Izzy. Steve just nodded. 'Me too. And I adore red peppers.'

'Well... there's enough for two...' said Steve, finally.

'Are you sure?'

'Yes. I often do enough to have the following night, or to freeze,' he told her.

With that, Steve put the food in the oven, cleared away the mess he'd made, produced plates and cutlery in preparation of eating at the island, and then decided this was one of those "occasions": he was feeling emotionally fragile.

Steve studied Izzy as he sipped a glass of chilled Chardonnay - Izzy had polished off the Chablis - while she told him about some of her favourite vegetarian restaurants. He wondered at the reason behind her surprise visit. She had been the last person he had expected to see when he'd opened his front door - hence his momentary confusion at not recognising her - until he then remembered he hadn't returned her telephone calls. He also recalled, from previous conversations, that she was headstrong and impetuous, so he assumed her visit to his home was exactly that. She would no doubt, he thought, eventually work her way around to the reason she was there.

After twenty five minutes, Izzy had moved onto the morality of slaughtering animals for their meat - a topic on which she held firm views - and Steve was on his second glass of wine - a rarity for him. It was only when Izzy mentioned a story she had recently written, that Steve took the opportunity to politely, but firmly, interject, and ask her what story she was presently working on.

'It's a historical piece. Have you heard of St Aidan's Church, in Camden?' she asked him. 'I know it sounds boring, but it's not, honestly. It's a little stone church nestled just off the High Street. Most people wouldn't even know it was there, but it's rich in history, and it's really, really old. It's even mentioned in the Doomsday book.'

'Is the gentleman who was admitted to Willesden's A&E last night linked to the piece?'

'Sorry?'

'This morning, at the hospital. You were enquiring after a man called Wayne Salter, also known as Cutter. I was just wondering if he was linked to your church story?'

'Err...'

CHAPTER 35

The steel lid to Harry's prison was unlocked and then thrown open. Harry lay bound and motionless within. A booted foot slammed into the side of the box, creating a deafening boom of reverberating metal, while slightly shifting it on its base.

Harry was still motionless. His panic attack had left his mind and body paralysed and close to unconsciousness. Two pairs of strong hands reached in and dragged him from the box, their owners cursing violently when they realised Harry's bladder had emptied.

Harry's temporary prison was a large lockable tool storage box, designed for use on construction sites. Next to the box were its original contents: an untidy heap of power tools and painting equipment.

The construction site was the gentlemen's club's swimming pool, which was in a building to the rear of the property, and was partway through refurbishment. Around the poolside, scaffolding had been erected to give access for the re-painting of the walls. The swimming pool itself was a twenty five metre pool which had been drained of water. Only one of the powerful ceiling lights was switched on, highlighting a tiled area of the poolside, and leaving the rest of the room in eerie shadow.

The two young men who had pulled Harry from the box - though they had the build and the physique - were not construction workers. Both were shaven headed, and dressed casually in jeans, shirts, and black leather jackets; they were almost clones of each other. Their only distinguishing features were that one wore an eye patch, and the other had both his ears pierced with small diamond stud earrings. These young men were hired help of a different kind; they were hard, they were ruthless, and they were Russian.

Removing the tape from around Harry's ankles, they then half carried, half dragged him across to where a third man waited under the light. This man was in his sixties, smartly dressed in a suit jacket and trousers, open necked shirt, and highly shined black leather shoes. He stood with feet slightly splayed, shoulders squared. One hand held a cigarette, the other was behind his back: confident, calm and strong. He was also Russian.

The two young Russians, 'Eyepatch' and 'Earring', tried to position Harry on his knees in front of the older man, but, due to Harry's weakened state, he kept slumping to the floor. In his native tongue, the older Russian barked an order. Earring hurried off, to then return with a green plastic garden chair and a length of rope he'd found amongst the building contractor's equipment.

They dragged Harry onto the chair, wrapped the rope around him and the chair, before then removing the cloth hood, and roughly ripping the adhesive tape from his face - an action that would normally cause any other person some considerable pain. If the Russians had been hoping for a response from Harry, they were to be disappointed: Harry was oblivious.

The older Russian stepped forward and stared down at Harry, studying him. He reached out a hand and lifted Harry's chin. Harry's vacant eyes stared back at him. From behind his back, the Russian produced a stick-like object, about half a metre in length. He twisted its handle to adjust its setting. It made a faint clicking sound. A ratchet-like sound. He then checked it by holding it mid-air, and pressing a button on the handle, to hear it make a crackling noise, before reaching out to briefly place the tip against Harry's bare chest.

Five hundred thousand volts of electricity shot through Harry's body, making him convulse and writhe.

The Russian checked his watch and waited patiently, as Harry gasped and groaned his way back to full consciousness. 'Good of you to join us,' said the Russian, to Harry, in heavily accented English. 'Now, tell me. Who are you, and what are you doing sneaking around my club?'

Harry stared up at the man standing in front of him, then at Eyepatch and Earring either side, before letting his gaze take in his surroundings, trying to take stock of his situation. He brought his gaze back to the older Russian. Harry wasn't fooled by the calm and placid demeanour; he only had to look into the man's eyes to see that he was cruel and sadistic.

'Are you a thief?' asked the Russian. 'Did you come here to steal from me?'

Harry didn't answer.

The Russian turned to his younger comrades and asked a question in Russian. Eyepatch responded by handing to him Harry's mobile phone, house keys, a car key, and a handful of cash in notes and coins. The Russian looked enquiringly at Eyepatch, who merely shrugged his massive shoulders. The older man put the cash into his pocket, inspected the car key, and then - muttering something in Russian - tossed it back to the younger man, who turned and left.

'You travel light,' said the Russian. 'No identification. Nothing to indicate who you are.'

Harry stared back.

'How about you tell me your name? It would be easier for all of us. Quicker. Less... messy.'

Harry stared back.

Still getting no response, the Russian powered up Harry's mobile phone, with the intention of searching through his contact numbers list, only to discover it was empty. The Russian shook his head. 'Either you are a very careful man, or a very unpopular man. No friends?'

Harry stared back.

The Russian then scrolled through the phone's call register, looking at the recent history of missed, dialled, and received calls. Spotting a regular missed call, he read out the number, which Harry recognised. 'Who is this person that you do not want to speak to?' he asked, as he pressed the dial button and placed the phone to his ear.

Harry's eyes flicked around, searching for a weapon, a means of escape, anything. He saw the open steel box with the power tools piled next to it. His prison he assumed, with a shudder, until his attention was drawn back to the Russian as he realised the telephone call had been answered. He saw the Russian's face register mild surprise, before he finally ended the call without having spoken a word. 'A feisty lady with an expressive vocabulary. Wife? Girlfriend... Harry?' The Russian smiled. 'My name is Victor, Harry. Now that we are on first name terms, why don't you tell me why you are here, huh?' Victor held Harry's gaze, waiting.

Harry stared back. Silent.

Victor lifted the cigarette to his lips, then drew hard, making the tip glow bright red. He inhaled deeply before tilting his head and blowing a stream of smoke upwards. The eyes of Harry and the remaining younger Russian, Earring - who was now standing behind Harry - automatically lifted to follow the mesmerising stream of swirling blue smoke as it curled up towards the overhead light. As they did so, Victor raised and touched the stick to Harry's chest. Again, Harry's body was wracked with convulsions, twisting and jerking, fighting against the ropes that bound him to the chair.

Earring - whose hand was resting on Harry's shoulder - yelped in pain as he received a secondary charge. This brought a smile to Victor's face, as he appreciatively admired the stun-gun. 'Soviet military surplus. Glasnost was good for business,' he said, before instructing Earring to find another chair.

On Earring's return, Victor placed the chair opposite Harry, to then sit astride it, forearms resting across the backrest, cigarette loosely held in one hand, stun-gun dangling from the other. He studied Harry for a moment, before then dropping his cigarette stub onto the floor and casually grinding it out with the heel of his shoe, only to then take a packet of cigarettes from his pocket, and immediately light another. He offered Harry a cigarette. Harry shook his head. 'Sure?' asked Victor. 'It could be your last,' he then added, with a wry smile. Again, Harry shook his head. The Russian shrugged his shoulders as if to say it was Harry's loss.

Victor drew deeply on his cigarette, and then exhaled a plume of smoke. As he did so, both Harry and the younger Russian automatically flinched. 'My business dealings have made me a very rich man, Harry. I have to protect that business, that wealth. And I do. I protect it with a ruthless efficiency. I take whatever steps are necessary. It's not like the 'old days' anymore,' he said. 'Times have changed. So we've had to move with the times. We've had to adapt.'

Victor took a moment to study the tip of the cigarette, and to savour its smoke. 'I do still prefer the old methods, though,' he said, smiling at Harry.

Harry stared back. Watching. Waiting.

Victor then gave Harry an example of how he'd dealt with a recent problem, using the "old methods". He told Harry how he'd discovered one of his men had been stealing money from him: quite a lot, as it turned out. 'He was taken to a derelict warehouse that I own... I own quite a lot of property,' he told Harry, going off on a tangent. 'My accountant advised me it was a good way to invest my 'profits' - and he was right, playing to his strengths. But I digress. My man denied he had stolen from me. He said I was mistaken. I told him I don't make mistakes,' said Victor, with a short bark of a laugh. 'So, he was stripped naked and chained down to the concrete floor, where we left him overnight. When we went back the next morning, we were expecting him to be dead from hypothermia - it *was* the middle of February - but he was still alive, though in a bad way. Ironically, the cold weather had probably prevented him from bleeding to death - the warehouse was infested with rats and they were hungry, you see. Overnight, they had feasted on the 'softer' parts of his body - he certainly wouldn't be fathering any more children...' Victor momentarily paused, a faraway look in his eyes, a smile tugging at the corners of his mouth, before he resumed. 'He told me where my money was. He begged me for forgiveness. And to be taken to a hospital. We left him to the rats, who slowly ate their way through his stomach to feast on his entrails, his screams for mercy echoing off the walls of the warehouse. Nobody heard him. It took him three days to die -'

Victor's attention was drawn by the return of the other young Russian, who approached Victor, whispered into his ear, and then held out a black leather bag. Mollie's bag. Which Harry had left in the glove compartment of Mollie's car. Victor took the bag, handing over the stun-gun in exchange.

After a few minutes of examining the bag's contents, Victor looked up at Harry, his face hard. 'Where did you get the car that you are driving?' Harry just glared back, refusing to answer. Victor shook his head in annoyance. 'Why are you driving Mollie Dolan's car?' he asked, his anger evident.

Harry continued to stare back. Eyes hard. Defiant.

Enraged by Harry's lack of cooperation, Victor abruptly stood, knocking over the plastic chair as he did so, to then hurl the leather bag at Harry, which sailed harmlessly over his head.

Victor looked across to Eyepatch, who was still holding the stun-gun, and gave him a nod of the head. The young Russian touched the stun-gun to Harry's shoulder, holding it there, grinning as he did so.

Victor looked on, and waited. Impatiently.

When Harry had ceased to writhe, Victor got up close, and in Harry's face. 'Who the fuck are you, and what the fuck are you doing here?' he demanded to know.

Harry's body was slumped forward, only the rope prevented him from falling. He slowly and agonisingly raised his head, attempting to focus on Victor's face. Saliva trickled from the corner of his mouth as he struggled to speak. 'Fuck you!' he managed to say, before his head slumped forward again, drained with the effort.

In a rage, Victor kicked out at the upended plastic chair, which bounced off the knees and shins of a barely conscious Harry, before then throwing his arms up in the air in frustration and striding-off, dragging his own mobile phone from his pocket, to then rapidly scroll through his contact numbers, while Eyepatch took the opportunity to give Harry another quick jolt from the stun-gun.

Harry was a mess. He was a physical and mental wreck. And he knew it. He also knew he was in trouble. Deep trouble. His captors were serious players. Harry was no Boy Scout, that was true, but he'd always believed there were ways and means of doing things: the proper way. But these guys had no fear of the law, and no respect for human life, and that made them truly dangerous.

Victor could be seen moving in the shadows at the far end of the room, pacing back and forth, animated in his body language as he continued his telephone call. While Harry and the two young Russians were unable to hear what Victor was saying, it was clear he was having an argument, for the duration of which Eyepatch would give the occasional tap to Harry's shoulder, to send intermittent charges through his body, only stopping when Victor's brisk footsteps and voice grew louder as he approached.

'Wait a minute, wait a minute,' Victor said into his mobile. He walked past Harry, drawing deeply on his cigarette, to then briefly lean-in and study Harry's naked back, before returning to his mobile phone. 'Yes, he does,' he said. A moment passed as he listened, before he again erupted in anger. 'Fuck!' In one swift movement, he disconnected the call, and then violently stubbed out his cigarette on Harry's shoulder blade. 'Put him back in the box,' he ordered the young Russians.

Harry vainly struggled against his captors, wishing himself an early death rather than face going into the box again, until Eyepatch ended Harry's valiant efforts by delivering a charge to the back of his head.

CHAPTER 36

Izzy, for once in her young life, was at a loss for words. How did he know I was at the hospital this morning, she asked herself. *Anyone would think he was a detective.*

She was saved by the sound of her mobile phone ringing. She hopped off the bar stool, retrieved her shoulder bag from the corner of the room, rummaged around in it frantically, before finally locating the ringing mobile.

She looked at the screen and saw Harry's name. Turning to Steve, she said, 'Can I use your bathroom?'

'It's upstairs,' replied Steve. 'If you need to take the call in private, you can use the lounge, you know.'

'Thank you. But I also need to 'pay-a-call',' she said, rushing past him, heading for the stairs. ''Two birds with one stone,'' she said over her shoulder.

Steve shook his head in amazement. *Surely she isn't going to have a telephone conversation while using the toilet, is she?* She was probably taking the call upstairs so there was no possibility of him overhearing her conversation, he told himself, as he turned his attention to the food. *Reporters!*

With the bathroom door firmly shut, Izzy dumped her bag on the floor, and then pressed the button on her phone. 'Harry! Where are you?' she asked, in a hushed tone. 'Harry? Hello? Are you there, Harry?' Izzy listened intently. She thought she could hear faint movement in the background. Other than that, only silence. 'Harry, you shit-head, talk to me!'

The phone went dead. Silence.

'What...' said Izzy, removing the phone for her ear to glare at screen. 'He's done it again. He's cut me off,' she said, immediately calling him back. 'How bloody rude,' she added, as it went straight to answerphone. Harry had switched his phone off. 'HARRY WINDSOR, YOU ARE AN ARSE!' she shouted down the phone. God, she was *so* pissed off with Harry - and, not for the first time, did she wonder why he didn't find her attractive.

Izzy checked herself in the large bathroom mirror. The lipstick she was wearing was a very feminine pale pink colour. She decided it wasn't up to the job. 'Time to go to work, Isobelle,' she told herself, as she rummaged through her bag for an alternative lipstick. She wiped off the pale pink, and replaced it with a vampish blood-red colour.

Before rejoining Steve downstairs, she took the opportunity to quickly check the upstairs rooms. She was impressed by what she saw. And it was *so* clean and tidy. For a fraction of a moment she was having a sense of déjà vu, until she walked into Steve's en-suite bathroom to be impressed by the amount of beauty products in it. She liked a man who made the effort to look after himself.

Back in the kitchen, Steve was serving up the food. 'Everything okay?' he asked Izzy, as she entered.

'Oh, yes. Fine.'

'Only, I thought I heard you shouting.'

'Oh, that. Sorry. It was my editor. We have a love-hate relationship thing,' she said with a shrug, as she hopped back on to the bar stool.

Steve couldn't help but stare at Izzy, still unsure, still uncertain. Then he saw her lipstick. *Wasn't it pale pink when she arrived?* During Izzy's absence, he'd been agonising as to whether or not he should have a third glass of wine. He could feel himself getting light headed, and he really shouldn't be drinking while taking medication.

He topped up Izzy's glass, and then refilled his own. To hell with it, he thought. And - in testament to his new found recklessness - he didn't bother to use a coaster!

CHAPTER 37

Harry was back on the plastic chair, and again it was only the ropes that prevented his cold and weakened body from slumping to the floor. The tape had been removed from his mouth, allowing him to breathe-in fresh clean air, the exhaled vapour clear in the overhead light. After dragging him from his prison and tying him to the chair, the two young Russians had left. Harry was alone.

Or was he? Faint scratching noises could be heard coming from the shadows of the room.

Harry's imprisonment had left him close to breaking point. During his confinement, his emotions had seesawed from rage to despair, and then to thoughts of death: to suicide. His morale could not be lower. In his weakened state, he'd been unable to control his bowels and bladder; he felt degraded. He realised, with horror, he was close to tears. A sob of anguish welled up in his throat. He fought it back. He couldn't let his captors see him like this. This is what they wanted: to break him. He had to be strong. He had to hold it together, he repeatedly told himself.

He tried to take some comfort in how he'd coped while imprisoned. How he'd tried to focus on the positives - if you could call them that. How he'd channelled the pain from the cigarette burn, together with his fear, into anger and the need and desire for revenge.

Many times though, that focus had wavered, slipped, to be replaced with fear and nausea. He'd desperately fought the overwhelming urge to be sick, knowing the consequences would be to choke to death on his own vomit. Then, perversely - such was his state of mind - found himself wishing he hadn't.

He'd also thought about family and friends and the fond memories he had of them, only to sadly realise that the recent ones were few and far between, forcing him to cast his mind further back than he'd anticipated.

He'd thought about Izzy. Her bright blue eyes, freckles, and her big smile, and then found himself wishing he hadn't been so offhanded with her - considering.

He'd thought of the foster brother he hadn't spoken to in recent years.

He'd then thought about his dear, sweet mother. He'd pictured her warm smile, and remembered her loving embrace. Lillian had been more spiritual than religious, believing that when a person died, the human soul lived on in the afterlife with other human souls. Harry was neither religious nor spiritual, but he'd said a prayer to her anyway.

The strange, shuffling, scratching noises again drew Harry's attention. He peered into the gloom. He saw the outline of scaffolding, stepladders, and tins of paint. But nothing moved. At least nothing he could see. Yet, as faint as those sounds were, he was certain someone or something was out there in the shadows, and it was driving him to distraction. His fingertip grip on sanity was slipping, and slipping fast. He found himself wishing his captors would return, just to have company around him, no matter how low that company might be, or what they might do.

Harry then wondered if this was another of Victor's tricks, to break his spirit even further. He thought back to the telephone call Victor had made earlier. He reflected on how angry the Russian had become. Harry felt sure it was Cutter he'd been talking to, which meant Victor now knew who Harry was and why he was there.

This was good news and bad news. The good news was that even if Mollie wasn't at the club, then the Russians certainly *knew* where she was.

Harry tried to reassure himself Mollie would be okay, that she would survive; she looked like a fighter. The bad news, though, was Harry no longer had any doubt that his captors intended to kill him.

Strangely, that thought didn't seem to bother Harry. In fact, it gave him some comfort. Harry had no idea as to how long he'd been held prisoner, it could have been hours, days, maybe even weeks. Either way, at least his time in captivity would not be for much longer. He found himself hoping... no, desperately wishing, that his mother's belief in the spiritual world would be proved correct. That thought brought him a comfort warm enough for him to forget the cold that wracked his body. A small smile tugged at the corners of his mouth as his eyes slowly closed, his pain wracked body beginning to slip away into a deep, deep sleep: to be embraced.

But it wasn't to be. Five hundred thousand volts prevented Harry checking-out before his due time.

'Wondered when you'd be back to finish what you started,' Harry eventually managed to gasp.

As Victor passed Harry, he paused to peer at the cigarette burn on Harry's shoulder. 'That might need a tetanus, Harry,' he said, with the hint of a smile. Then, standing in front of Harry, 'How are you feeling, my friend?'

'What the fuck do you care!' replied Harry.

Victor shrugged. 'Just being polite, Harry.' He extracted a packet of cigarettes from his pocket and lit one.

'Those things will kill you, you know,' said Harry. 'And any time in the next ten minutes would do me fine.'

Ignoring Harry's comment, Victor said, 'So, Mr Harry Windsor, you've come for Mollie Dolan?'

He has been talking to Cutter!

'Why? Is she a friend? Your lover?' continued Victor.

Harry glared back.

Victor drew on his cigarette, and then exhaled, smirking as he did so. 'You came here to rescue her, didn't you Harry?'

Harry said nothing.

'Are you the knight in shining armour, come to rescue the damsel in distress? For love?'

Still, Harry said nothing.

Victor started to laugh. 'No, not love. Money! You're doing this for money, Harry.'

Harry frowned. Something didn't sit right. Had he told Cutter he was supposed to be getting paid for finding Mollie? He tried to recollect their conversation during their fight, but failed.

'Mollie Dolan is here, Harry. I bought her father's debt. She works here as a 'Hostess',' said Victor. 'She pays her taxes and National Insurance. It is legitimate. It is - how you would say - 'above board'. And she has very nice room, here. She is very well looked after. She is not a prisoner, Harry. She can leave whenever she wants. But she won't. Because she loves her father, she has agreed to work off his debt. But,' he said, smiling and gesturing with cigarette in hand, 'even though she is very attractive girl, very talented, and very popular, it will take her a while to repay the debt. A year, maybe two, maybe longer.'

'What you really mean,' said Harry, 'is that she's working here as a prostitute, and she's too afraid to leave, because you've probably threatened to kill her father if she does.'

Victor shrugged his shoulders, noncommittally. 'Semantics, Harry. Semantics.'

'You Fucker!' yelled Harry. 'If I wasn't tied to this chair, I'd rip you to pieces!'

'Maybe. Though I think not,' replied Victor, studying Harry. 'You don't even have the strength to control your own bodily motions,' he cruelly added, reminding Harry of his own physical state and feelings of humiliation. 'Of course, if someone else were to pay the debt, then she could leave immediately...' Victor held Harry's gaze for a moment, before then saying, 'Someone like you, Harry.'

Harry shook his head. 'I haven't got eighty grand.'

'One hundred thousand,' corrected Victor.

'What? The debt is only eighty thousand!' responded Harry, stunned.

'Interest, Harry. Interest. Business is business. I hear you are resourceful man. I'm sure you could find the money, if you had to.' When Harry didn't respond, Victor continued, 'Use some of your old contacts, maybe?'

Still, Harry said nothing. Just shook his head.

Victor looked on. Waited.

When it was apparent that Harry wasn't going to say anything else, Victor looked up, deep into the shadows of the room. He gave a signal. At that, the remaining unlit overhead lighting blazed into life, its glare causing both Victor and Harry to squint until their vision had adjusted. The entire room was now bathed in bright white light, and Harry could now see where he was.

The swimming pool.

He could see the painting contractor's scaffold, various stepladders, tools and dust sheets. As his eyes adjusted, he could see the difference where the new, clean, and pristine coat of paint stopped, and the old and grubby original continued. He saw Earring walking away from a bank of light switches, and back towards the swimming pool. He started to track Earring's direction, only for his attention to be caught, and drawn ahead towards the empty swimming pool.

Only it wasn't empty, and it wasn't water that he was looking at.

The swimming pool walls and floor were tiled in a beautiful Mediterranean-blue mosaic. At each corner, shiny chrome handrailed steps led down into the pool. Harry was poolside of the shallow end, where a depth of one point two metres was picked out in black mosaic on the pool wall. As he looked along its length, he saw the floor gradually fall away to a depth of three metres at the far end; a low springboard diving board; and what had initially caught his attention: tied to the handrail of each set of steps, was a single rope leading down into the pool, and at the end of each of those ropes, was a dog.

Harry didn't know much about dogs and their different breeds, but these two looked to be of the Pit Bull variety. What Harry did know - because it was plainly clear - was that they were strong and powerfully built dogs. And what Harry was almost certain of - judging by their scars - was that they were fighting dogs.

This is what had been making the noises, and now the lights were on and there was human activity, the dogs had suddenly become restless. They skittered about at the bottom of the pool, straining against the ropes that held them, their attention switching between the activity around the pool, and then to each other, and their instinct to fight. What Harry could not figure out, is why the Russians would want to stage a dogfight at this precise moment in time. Maybe torturing the ex-con wasn't the main act, he thought. Maybe I'm just the warm-up gig, before they bring-on the dogs and the heavy wagering that's sure to follow.

Harry was still trying to get his head around what was going on, when Eyepatch came into view, pulling on a length of rope. Harry's gaze followed that length of rope, his brain telling him to expect to see a dog at the other end, only for his eyes to blink a number of times in disbelief, before his brain accepted that he was looking at Patrick Dolan, Mollie's father. Patrick Dolan might not be a dog, but he was certainly being treated like one; the rope looped around his neck, acting as a leash, which Eyepatch took great delight in yanking on. Patrick's hands, like Harry's, were behind his back and bound with tape. And, also like Harry, Patrick was naked.

The big Irishman was now a shadow of the man Harry had first met - a week ago? A month? Harry had lost track of time since he'd been locked in the box. Patrick had clearly lost a considerable amount of weight, his face was florid and red with the physical effort required in keeping up with the young Russian, and there was also evidence of fresh bruising; and judging by his shambolic gait, Harry could also see that he was still hiding his demons in a bottle. It occurred to Harry that he and the man he'd looked upon with such disdain not so long ago had a lot in common.

As Eyepatch approached Victor, Harry said loudly, 'What the fuck is it with you Russians?' Both Victor and Eyepatch turned towards Harry. 'I mean, have you got some kind of homo-erotica-bondage thing going on?' The two Russians stared blankly back. Patrick Dolan just stared - blankly. 'Naked men? Ropes?' Both Russians continued to look blank. 'What I'm saying is,' continued Harry, 'are you a bunch of fuckin' queers?' Harry knew he was being reckless by taunting, deliberately goading, but at that moment he had little or no concern for the outcome.

If the two Russians were not familiar with the term "homo-erotica-bondage", they'd been in the UK long enough to be familiar with the term "queers".

Eyepatch took a step forward, bristling with offended testosterone, nostrils flared, powerful shoulders squared.

Victor, on the other hand, wasn't so easily riled. He offered up a placating hand towards Eyepatch, and a wry smile towards Harry. With a sharp twitch of the head, Victor indicated Eyepatch move away, but the young Russian was clearly pumped and looking for a fight. He took a step towards Harry.

'Come on, you queer Russian wanker! You want some?' shouted Harry, trying to provoke Eyepatch into action while struggling against his bonds.

After a second's hesitation, and another glance at Victor, Eyepatch turned on his heel and strode off towards the edge of the pool, viciously yanking on the rope to drag Patrick along behind him, forcing him to stumble more than once.

Victor went through the motions of lighting yet another cigarette, and then watched intently as Eyepatch removed the rope from around Patrick's neck. Patrick - unresisting, naked and with his hands still bound behind his back - stood by the edge of the swimming pool, shoulders slumped, head bowed: a broken man.

'What are you planning on doing, Victor?' asked Harry, with a sinking feeling in his heart that he already knew the answer.

Victor turned back to Harry, a mild look of surprise on his face, as though he had momentarily forgotten Harry was there. He shrugged his shoulders. 'Business,' he said, simply. 'Tying-up loose ends,' he then added, as if for clarity, before turning his attention back to Patrick, and then Eyepatch, who was watching Victor, waiting.

When Victor finally gave a nod of the head, Eyepatch turned back to Patrick, put the flat of his big palm between the Irishman's shoulder blades, and then gently pushed. Patrick automatically put a foot forward to steady himself, but only found empty space. He half fell, half jumped, into the empty swimming pool, to disappear from Harry's view. He landed badly, going down on one knee, and crying out in pain.

Everybody watched and waited as Patrick struggled back to his feet.

Harry found himself holding his breath.

From his seated position, Harry could only see Patrick from the waist up, who was now standing in profile, and leaning against the side of the swimming pool, favouring his injured leg. Even side-on, Harry could see the pain and confusion etched upon the big man's face. He was totally unaware of his plight, his predicament, or even his whereabouts, and he certainly had no idea what was about to happen next.

Harry watched Victor wave his arm at Earring, who was still waiting at the far end of the pool. He saw Earring untie the rope of the first dog, and then untie the rope that held the second. Struggling to hold the straining dogs, he looked back along the length of the pool, to Victor.

Victor drew on his cigarette, and then exhaled with a sigh, savouring the moment. Then, with a smile of anticipation, he pointed the cigarette towards Earring.

Harry watched in horror and dread, as the two dogs took off at a run along the length of the pool and towards Patrick. Harry saw Patrick's head turn towards the advancing dogs. Had he heard them or sensed them? Harry would never know.

They were on him within seconds. All Harry could see was Patrick's upper body, spasmodically jerking and twitching as the dogs charged and leaped, their bodyweight pounding into him, their powerful jaws locking onto his lower limbs, worrying him like a rag doll, their snarling and growling loud in the cavernous room. Harry saw Patrick's look of confusion change to abject fear. He watched as Patrick opened his mouth.

Harry had never heard anything like it; and he hoped he never would again. The sound that came out of Patrick's mouth, the noise that erupted out from his throat, was an inhuman howl of terror and pain, and mixed with the sounds of savagery, was truly overwhelming.

'For Christ's sake, Victor, at least untie the man's arms. Give him a fighting chance!' Harry shouted.

Victor flicked a glance of annoyance in Harry's direction, before returning his attention back to the swimming pool.

'Patrick, you've got to stay on your feet! You've got to fight back!' screamed Harry. 'Use your feet, Patrick! Kick them! Kick them!'

Harry's words must have gotten through to Patrick.

One of the dogs had its powerful jaws clamped around Patrick's forearm, from where it now hung, it's feet no longer on the ground; the other was locked onto his calf muscle.

Patrick kicked out wildly, at the dog ripping at his leg, for his foot to make a lucky connection with the side of the animal's head, causing it to yelp and release its grip. As a consequence, momentum and loss of balance caused Patrick to stagger backwards, his body slamming against the side of the pool, his bodyweight crushing the dog that hung onto his arm. It fell to the floor, where it lay winded and stunned. Patrick staggered away towards the centre of the pool, all the while, lashing out with his feet at the remaining dog, warily snapping around his heels.

Harry was now able to see the full extent of Patrick's wounds, and the amount of damage that two vicious and powerfully built dogs could do to a man: to human flesh. He stared with revulsion and a morbid fascination, in that such injury could be inflicted upon the human body in such a short space of time - and for that person to still be alive.

What Harry was looking at, was a walking butcher's shop.

Patrick's entire lower body was blood-red. Large chunks of flesh were missing or hanging loose; sinews, tendons, and bone clearly exposed, the trail of blood on the tiled floor, indicating Patrick's weakening and unsteady progress.

The face of the attacking dog was slick with red, also.

'Victor,' shouted Harry. 'If he dies, you've got no leverage!'

Victor continued to watch Patrick, with excitement in his eyes. He ignored Harry.

'If he dies, Victor, what's there to keep the girl here?' yelled Harry, desperately looking for a way. 'What's there to stop Mollie leaving? Walking out?'

'I'm told she has very attractive mother,' said Victor, over his shoulder, without taking his eyes off the ailing and weakening Patrick.

'Patrick,' screamed Harry. 'You've got to run! You've got to get out of there! You've got to run towards me, Patrick, it's too deep at that end! Patrick, you can only get out at this end!'

Patrick was tiring fast, but so was the dog. Harry was amazed Patrick was still on his feet, his loss of blood must be extensive, he thought, and the only thing keeping him going was probably adrenaline, and the alcohol in his body to numb the pain.

'This way, Patrick! Run this way! Run, Patrick, run!'

Patrick took one last swing at the dog, his foot successfully connecting with its shoulder blade. He only managed to temporarily unbalance the dog, but it gave him the head start he needed. He set off at a stumbling run, head down, shoulders forward, building up momentum, heading towards Harry, but with the dog close on his heels.

'Patrick, you can do it! Run! Run Patrick!' called Harry.

As Patrick approached the wall of the shallow end, he launched himself forward, landing face down on the poolside, teetering half in, half out.

Harry instinctively jumped up, but still being tied to the chair, found himself crashing forward onto the floor, and only a short distance from where Patrick lay. 'Patrick,' said Harry, looking into the big Irishman's face, unsure what else to say. He saw Patrick's brow briefly furrow, then saw his eyes widen in recognition, before beginning to crease at the corners, as if in the start of a smile.

But that smile never came. It was replaced with a highly shined black shoe, the sole of which was placed gently and purposely in the centre of Patrick's forehead. A heartbeat later, it gave a slight push, toppling Patrick backwards and into the pool, cracking his head on the hard tiled floor, to leave him stunned and defenceless.

He didn't stand a chance. The remaining dog was on him. It clamped its jaws around his throat, and just as he started to scream, the dog braced its powerful forelegs and worried at the soft exposed flesh, its big, ugly, scarred head thrashing from side to side. Patrick's scream became a strangled gasp, dying completely, as the dog ripped out his throat, and with it, the remaining life from Patrick's body.

And Harry saw it all from where he lay.

With its prey now dead, the dog lost interest, trotting away to lie down in the corner of the pool.

It was now very quiet. A hushed silence.

Earring had walked around the pool to join his comrades. The three of them now stared down into the pool, grinning broadly, thoroughly entertained.

Harry lay still and unmoving on the poolside, and just stared down at Patrick's corpse, watching the blood pool around his body. 'Victor,' he said, quietly, but loud enough to be heard, 'I intend to kill you. I'm going to take your life. And I can assure you, it will be a painful death,' he said, finally, as he continued to watch Patrick, his gaze never wavering.

The confident smile briefly slipped from Victor's face, to return seconds later, but only after he'd touched the stun-gun to the back of Harry's head, sending him back into oblivion.

CHAPTER 38

'Oh... my... God!' said Izzy, dabbing at the corners of her mouth with a napkin. 'That was yum-yum-pig's-bum-sex-in-a-dish-*dee*lish!' she said, before then taking a large gulp of wine.

Steve beamed with pride at Izzy's compliment. An objective observer would probably describe him as "grinning like an idiot". He'd lost track of how much alcohol he'd consumed, and frankly, he couldn't care less. 'So,' he said, grinning broadly, 'why are you really here?'

Izzy's wineglass halted abruptly midway to her mouth, causing a small droplet of wine to fly out and land on the tip of her nose. She levelled her gaze at Steve, and paused for a moment. 'I'll be totally honest with you,' she said, wiping the droplet of wine away. 'I'm undercover. I'm on a big story. A massive story.' She took another sip of her wine, her gaze still holding Steve's. Steve grinned back at her. 'Sex trafficking. Women being forced into prostitution. Here in London,' she told him, waving her wineglass expansively. Both Steve's eyebrows shot up. 'Massive! And I'm going to blow it wide open!' she then said.

'It does happen,' said Steve, nodding his head.

'It does?' said Izzy, suddenly leaning forward. 'Fuck-a-duck!'

Steve's grin disappeared and his eyebrows turned into a frown. 'I thought you said you were undercover?'

Izzy said nothing.

'You weren't being "totally honest" with me, were you?'

After a moment's hesitation, Izzy made the see-saw hand movement that suggested maybe she had, maybe she hadn't.

'Okay,' said Steve, 'so what are you really working on?'

'Well...' said Izzy, hesitating, 'officially, it's a story about a crappy little church in Camden - though I missed the original deadline for that. Unofficially, I'm looking for a missing girl. A student.'

'And there's a story for you, behind this missing girl, I take it?'

'Well...' said Izzy, drawing out her reply, 'hopefully, at some point. I'm actually helping out a friend with my investigative journalistic knowledge,' she said, taking extra care over her pronunciation.

'Who's the friend?' asked Steve.

'I can't reveal my source, sorry.'

'What's your source's interest?'

Izzy said nothing.

'Family member? Friend?'

Izzy smiled back, but still said nothing.

'Okay,' said Steve, with resignation, the smile returning to his face. 'What is it you want from me?'

'Could you make some enquiries? Sort of, unofficially? 'on the quiet'?' she replied, smiling sweetly.

'I'm a policeman,' said Steve, in a mock voice of authority. 'We don't do unofficial, Isobelle.'

'Izzy,' said Izzy, blatantly batting her eyelids.

'Hang on a second,' he said, as he carefully climbed off the bar stool to reach for his police notebook and pen. 'You do know this city has a population of over eight million,' Steve told her. 'People go missing all the time.' He finally found a clean page and readied his pen. 'Has the girl been officially reported as missing?'

Izzy puffed out her cheeks as she gave this some thought. 'I've only met the girl's father, and I think it's unlikely he will have reported it - under the circumstances, that is.'

This last comment drew a curious look from Steve. 'What's the girl's name?'

'Mollie Dolan.'

Steve started to write, but then stopped. He stared at the page, frowning.

'What?' said Izzy, seeing the look on Steve's face.

'She has been reported missing,' replied Steve, trying to remember. 'By her mother.'

'What did she say?' asked Izzy, eagerly.

'Who?'

'Mollie Dolan's mother, of course,' said Izzy, rolling her eyes and giving Steve a mock exasperated look.

'Oh, yes, of course. Uniform took the mother's statement, so I haven't met her. I was looking at the file only this morning.'

'What enquiries have you made so far?'

'Err, none. I didn't quite get around to it,' replied Steve, embarrassed. 'The file said she'd gone missing before - family issues. Spoilt-little-rich-girl, type of thing. You know how it is. Besides, the Post-it note said not to waste too much time on it,' he added, in justification.

Izzy was about to pick him up on the "Spoilt-little-rich-girl" comment, but instead, said, 'Post-it note?' her voice rising slightly.

'My D.I.'s idea of man-management.'

'Not very high-tech,' replied Izzy.

'He's not a very "high-tech" type of guy.'

'Clearly.'

'What were "the circumstances" you were referring to?' asked Steve, remembering.

'Ah, yes,' said Izzy, wondering how much to tell Steve without involving Harry, and without Steve or the police taking full control of the case and shutting Izzy out completely. 'Mollie's father owes money.'

Steve waited. But when Izzy said no more, he said, 'I take it we aren't talking about a High Street bank, here?' Izzy nodded her head. 'And the people the father owes money to have taken the daughter as leverage?'

'Looks that way, though I can't be totally sure.'

Steve looked thoughtful. Then, 'Is Cutter involved in this?'

'Looks that way, though I can't be totally sure,' said Izzy, repeating herself and sounding lame.

'Your "source", your "friend". Do you trust him?' asked Steve.

'With my life,' replied Izzy, immediately, hoping she sounded more confident than she felt, then suddenly realising she'd just confirmed to Steve her friend's gender. Whether that had been his intention or not, he was giving nothing away.

'That's good. Trust is very important,' he said, sombrely.

Izzy watched and waited.

Steve stared down at the almost blank page of his notebook, lost deep in thought. He adjusted the book, aligning it with the edge of the worktop. He seemed to have withdrawn into himself, his carefree mood gone.

'Steve?' prompted Izzy, gently. 'Tell me about the sex trafficking.'

Steve looked up quickly, startled. He shook his head slowly, gesturing with his hands, searching for the words.

Izzy said, 'I recently Googled 'missing women', in the hope of finding a clue on how to go about searching for Mollie. I came across a news article about sex trafficking in Mexico. In a country like that - though I've never been there - I would expect it, because there are lots of poor people there. I mean, it's almost a Third World country, right? But here, in Great Britain, surely not.'

Steve was slowly nodding his head. 'It's happening all over the UK. In most major cities, and even in some of the bigger towns. Women, young women, sometimes girls, are brought over illegally and legally. In both cases it's usually under the promise of a better life. A good job, a nice house or flat, maybe a husband. But when they get here it's a far different reality. The cost of their passage over to the UK is either paid for them, or loaned to them on the understanding they pay the money back once they are in employment, and earning a wage. Some of the women are pressured to repay the money back almost immediately. Often they are threatened with violence against themselves, or their family, back in the girl's native homeland. They nearly always turn to prostitution to pay off their debts.'

'You can't be serious!' said Izzy, appalled. 'Does that happen here, in London?'

'Oh, yes. Absolutely,' he replied. 'But it gets worse. Most of the traffickers aren't prepared to wait for the girl to turn to prostitution. In fact, they never were going to wait. The vast majority of these women, on their arrival in this country, will be taken to a house where they will be held prisoner and forced to take drugs. In time, they become addicts, and to get the drugs they crave, they have to provide sexual services. In this initial stage, the women are often raped. Sometimes gang raped, forced to have sex with multiple men. This is to break their morale, and to increase their need for and dependency on drugs. I believe the process is called 'seasoning'.'

Izzy had both hands held up to her mouth, ashen faced. 'Oh my God,' she whispered.

CHAPTER 39

As Harry regained consciousness, he sensed that something was different. What wasn't different was he still had a pounding headache, and his body felt like a herd of elephants had trampled over it. It took what seemed like a very long minute to realise he was dressed, and slumped across the driver and passenger seat of a car: Mollie Dolan's car. It took an equally long minute for him to ease his pain wracked body into a sitting position, gasping every time he moved his head. Sweating and breathing heavily, he looked out through the windscreen. Other than a few ambient orange streetlights, it was dark and quiet.

Harry had no idea as to where he was.

The car appeared to be parked in a quiet backstreet, behind a warehouse and some retail shops. It certainly wasn't parked across from a gentlemen's club. For a moment, Harry found himself questioning his own sanity. Had he been at the club? Had he been tortured? And had he just witnessed the violent death of Patrick Dolan? Harry knew the answer to the last question, it wasn't something he was likely to forget to soon - if ever. He gave a slight shake of his head to remove the image, but only succeeded in causing himself more pain. He eased his head back onto the headrest and closed his eyes to collect his thoughts. After a moment, he slid his hands into his jacket pockets to check their contents: house keys and mobile phone were both there, his cash was not.

Why have they let me go? He had expected the Russians to kill him, to tie-up yet another "loose end" because he was a potential witness. Not that he would go to the police; it just wasn't the done thing - not his style. Had they let him go for a reason? If so, why? Harry's gut instinct told him that something was wrong.

Very wrong.

The car key wasn't in Harry's pockets. It wasn't in the ignition, either.

If the Russians had gone to the effort of dressing him, returning his possessions - except for his money, the thieving bastards - and putting him in the car with the intention of him leaving, why wouldn't they leave the car key behind?

Harry was having a sense of déjà vu.

His sense of smell was also alerting him. His personal hygiene was not up to its usual standard, he knew that; this was something completely different - yet familiar.

He opened the driver's door, then slowly and painfully eased himself out of the car, which seemed to be sitting a little lower on its suspension than he recalled. He stood for a moment, palms flat on the roof of the car to steady himself, his vision a little blurred. He felt like he was... *drunk!* He tried to remember how many times they'd put the stun-gun to his head. Twice? More? He wondered if those things could cause brain damage.

As he stood there, trying to regain some composure, his eyes travelled along the roof of the car from the front to the back. The car was definitely weighted down at the rear end. Using the car for support, he shuffled his way around to its rear. What immediately caught his eye was the oil leak that was pooling on the road beneath the rear of the car, and this was by no means a small oil leak; the pool was the full width of the car, a considerable amount of oil for a car of its size, especially if it had run all the way from the front of the car to the back. In the orange hue of the streetlight, it was dark, thick, and viscous, as it followed the camber of the road into the gutter.

Easing himself down onto his knees, he peered under the car. The oil was at the rear of the car only, and not the front. Harry had to blink a couple of times to focus. The oil appeared to be dripping from the boot of the car. He dipped a forefinger into the pooling oil, and then held his finger up to the streetlight, rubbing forefinger and thumb together. It looked like oil, it felt like oil. Harry sniffed it; once, then twice. It didn't smell like oil. It smelt like...

Harry suddenly realised what the Russians had done with Patrick's body. He also had a sneaking suspicion as to why they'd let him go.

He hauled himself back to his feet. He had to get out of there, and he had to get out of there quickly - he could already hear the wail of the emergency services sirens in the distance. He took a step, stumbled, and then fell. He struggled back to his feet, set off again, before once more stumbling and falling.

CHAPTER 40

Despite having the hangover from Hell, Steve had still managed to make his early morning start to work, and, as usual for that time of morning, the office was empty, which was a good thing, because - having foregone his expensive and exotic coffee for a bottle of water, an antacid tablet to settle his stomach, and painkillers to ease his headache - Steve was slumped at his desk, forehead resting upon his forearm, and promising himself, *never again.*

Steve's memories of the previous evening were proving to be vague and elusive. He remembered the reporter, Isobelle Harker, turning up unexpectedly. He remembered cooking for her, and something about a missing girl? His next memory was of waking up in the early hours of the morning on his kitchen floor, still fully clothed, and no sign of the reporter.

CHAPTER 41

Izzy was driving to Willesden, also reflecting. As hangovers went, Izzy's wasn't too bad. She had a muzzy head, granted, but it wasn't on a par with her previous episode. Having fallen asleep on her sofa, she, like Steve, had awoken early in the morning, but to the sound of her mobile phone ringing, violently wrenching her from her slumbers. Massaging the crick in her neck, she'd blinked blearily at the screen, only to see Harry's name. Conscious of the last telephone conversation she'd had with Harry - or rather, hadn't - she'd answered it warily. It was the police, and they'd found Harry - or at the very least, a man with his phone - drunk and disorderly and in need of medical attention. The police were trying to locate friends or family to collect him from the station once he'd been discharged. Was she able to take him home?

Izzy wasn't sure whether she should be angry with Harry, or worried about him. She hadn't seen or spoken to him for two days, and the more time that had passed, the more concerned she'd become. But, it would seem, he'd been out getting drunk! Harry was starting to make Jonathan look like a saint.

As she drove, she found herself craving a cigarette. She tutted aloud. She decided Harry's bad-boy-attitude was rubbing off, slowly eroding her clean living lifestyle, and, at this rate, she would end up in rehab.

CHAPTER 42

Steve was still slumped across his desk, patiently waiting for the antacid tablet and painkillers to kick-in, when the office door was thrown open, quickly followed by D.I. Carson bellowing across the room, startling Steve.

'Marshall! Were you sleeping your desk?' said Carson, framed in the doorway.

'No, sir!' Steve replied, jumping up and then wishing he hadn't, as the room started to spin.

Carson frowned, his eyes narrowing as he fixed his gaze on Steve. 'Come with me. We've got a suspect to interview,' he said, before turning and striding off, leaving the door open, and doorway empty.

Steve checked his wristwatch. *Interview?* Who does he want to interview at this time of the morning, he wondered. In fact, what was D.I. Carson even doing in at this time of the morning? He never started early. Steve grabbed his bottled water and set off after his D.I., catching up with him just as he entered the custody suite and was approaching the Desk Sergeant.

'Sergeant,' said Carson.

'Morning, Sir,' said the young Sergeant, looking up from his computer terminal.

'You're holding a murder suspect that we need to interview, Sergeant,' said Carson. The Sergeant frowned, and then checked his computer screen. 'The suspect's name is Harry Windsor,' said Carson, casting a sidelong glance in Steve's direction, and then grinning cruelly at the look of shock on Steve's face.

The Sergeant gave a slight shake of his head. 'No,' he said, simply.

Carson's cruel grin, instantly disappeared as he turned on the Desk Sergeant. 'What do you mean, no?'

The Sergeant gave a slight shrug, as his eyes skimmed across the computer screen. 'Got no one called Harry Windsor, Sir,' he said, nervously. The Desk Sergeant was young, self-assured, and recently promoted but, aware of

Carson's reputation, was feeling less 'self-assured' by the minute.

'Harry Windsor was picked up in the early hours of this morning, in possession of a stolen car that had a dead body in the boot. Now, stop fucking me about, and check again,' said Carson, stabbing his finger towards the computer console.

The young Sergeant was becoming flustered under Carson's scrutiny, and feeling all the more foolish for it. 'I'm sorry, Sir, there's nothing on here to indicate we are holding a murder suspect.'

'Well, just who the fuck have you got banged-up back there?' said Carson, indicating the locked door that led through to the cells.

'Looks like it was quiet night, Sir. Only two occupied. One is Black Alice, a local 'tom' who tried to stab her punter with a stiletto shoe because he refused to pay, the other is a vagrant brought in for 'drunk and disorderly'. According to this, nightshift contacted the Duty Doctor because the vagrant didn't look too good. Looked like he might have been in a fight, or mugged.' From the in-tray on his desk, the Sergeant found the Duty Doctor's written report, and then read out loud, 'Cuts and bruises, recently stitched flesh wound, professionally done but with domestic sewing thread...' The young Sergeant frowned at that, before carrying on, 'Blistering from what appear to be contact burns, disorientation, possibly concussion. Dehydration and traces of alcohol. The Doc dressed the burns, then gave him a tetanus and some anti-inflammatory painkillers. Doc said he'd be okay after some rest. Jesus, he sounds in a bad way. Guess he wasn't drunk after all.'

'What about his possessions?' asked Carson. 'What about ID? Was he carrying any identification?'

The Sergeant turned back to his computer. 'House keys, Nokia 6021 - God, that's old. This guy's certainly no techno-geek,' he said, grinning, as he looked up at the two detectives, before quickly returning his attention to the screen and away from Carson's withering gaze. 'No ID,' confirmed the Sergeant. 'Night shift went through his phone, and then contacted someone to come and pick him up. Says girlfriend, here. Do vagrants have girlfriends?' he asked.

Steve was totally stunned. Had he heard correctly? Had he just heard D.I. Carson say Harry Windsor was a murder suspect? Steve looked at the Desk Sergeant, but his attention was totally focused on the sanctuary of the computerised data, rather than make eye contact with Carson. Steve switched his attention to his superior officer. He could see D.I. Carson was extremely angry. He could see his jaw muscles clenching, his nostrils were flared, and the penetrating stare that was attempting to drill a hole into the top of the Desk Sergeant's head.

Carson, sensing he was being watched, switched his penetrating gaze onto Steve. Normally, Steve would have wilted under such an intense stare and immediately looked away. On this occasion though, he just stared right back. Not from bravado, more from dumb-animal confusion. Carson held Steve's gaze for a moment, before turning back to the Desk Sergeant.

'Sergeant!' said Carson. 'Let's have a look. Let's see who we've got.'

The Sergeant picked up a bunch of keys, and then led the way through to the cells, Carson, then Steve, following. He stopped at a cell door, opened the viewing panel and glanced in, before then stepping back. Carson, hands in pockets, strolled up and peered through. A solitary male figure was sleeping on the bunk, facing the door, bootlaces and belt were missing, a jacket was covering his upper torso in the absence of a blanket, and his lank hair had fallen across his face. Carson narrowed his eyes in concentration as he studied the prone figure, before then tilting his head in an attempt to get a clearer view. He grunted to himself. Then, 'looks like him,' he said. 'Hair's longer. Looks a mess.' Carson sniffed the air. 'Fuckin' stinks, too.' He turned towards Steve. 'Take a look, Constable. Tell me if that's Harry Windsor. If anyone should know, you should,' he added, with a smirk.

'I haven't seen Harry Windsor, since his trial, Sir,' responded Steve, but Carson's glare told him it wasn't open to debate. With his heart in his mouth, Steve tentatively approached the cell door and peered through. The man in the cell was almost unrecognisable. He was a mess, a wreck, a shadow of the man he once was - physical strength, presence, aura, all gone. Steve felt an overwhelming sense of sadness. With a lump in his throat, he turned to the Sergeant. 'Is he okay?' he asked.

'Oh, yeah. He's fine.'

'How do you know?' said Steve, realising he was holding his breath as he waited for the Sergeant's answer.

'When I first came on shift, I checked on our 'residents', as I usually do. Black Alice was snoring her head off, he was awake. I asked him if he wanted a cup of tea. He told me, in no uncertain terms,' here the Sergeant paused for dramatic effect, 'to "fuck off!"''

Steve nodded, and then returned his attention to Harry Windsor. He was wondering who the girlfriend was, when Carson's voice cut across his thoughts.

'Get him out, Sergeant, and put him in interview room number three,' said Carson.

The Sergeant unlocked and then pulled open the door, forcing Steve to take a step backwards. Entering the cell, he nudged Harry awake, gripped his upper arm, and then guided him off the bunk and towards the cell door.

'Sergeant! Aren't you going to cuff this man?' asked Carson, from the doorway.

'Err, I wasn't going to, Sir,' replied the Sergeant.

'This man's a dangerous and violent criminal. He's a villain!' said Carson, involuntary taking a step backwards, his voice starting to rise in pitch.

The Sergeant glanced at the shambling figure in his custody, who looked anything but dangerous or violent. 'I left my handcuffs back on the desk, Sir,' said the Sergeant, turning back to Carson.

'Jesus Christ! Get him into room three,' said Carson, turning on his heel and striding off. 'And get me a PC, to sit-in!' he called over his shoulder, as he left.

The Sergeant mouthed the word 'wanker' to Carson's retreating back, before guiding a bleary eyed Harry Windsor out of the cell and to interview room number three.

Steve followed some distance behind.

Interview room number three was plain yet functional, a small windowless room that contained a table and four chairs, a wall fixed recording machine, and an additional chair close to the door.

Harry was sitting at the table, handcuffed, and hunched over a vending machine cup of tea, given to him by the sympathetic Desk Sergeant, while Steve leant against the wall at the rear of the room, staring at Harry Windsor's back and feeling very uncomfortable; a female PC sat patiently near the door.

It was deathly quiet.

Moments later, the door opened and Carson swaggered into the room, a look of smug satisfaction crossing his face when he saw Harry; this quickly disappeared when he saw the female PC. Stepping back into the corridor he shouted, 'Sergeant? I asked you for a PC! A man, not a woman!' Getting no reply, he stepped back into the room, glaring at a very embarrassed PC, before then warily eyeing up Harry, who was still staring into his cup of tea.

Carson approached the table and eased himself into a chair opposite Harry. He looked over towards Steve, giving him an impatient twitch of the head, indicating he should join him at the table. Steve reluctantly pushed himself off the wall, to take the chair next to Carson.

For a moment there was nothing but silence. Carson was staring at Harry; Steve was fidgeting, looking anywhere but at Harry; the PC was looking bored; Harry was still staring down at his cup.

'Well, well. Harry Windsor. In my nick - again!' beamed Carson. 'How the mighty have fallen, aye, Harry? Have you taken a look at yourself lately, Harry? Because you look - and smell - like a bag of shit!' Smiling broadly, Carson leaned back in his chair, slipped his hands into his pockets, while stretching out his legs, crossing them at the ankle.

Then, as if suddenly remembering, he said, 'Forgive me Harry, where are my manners. I haven't introduced everyone. I'm Detective Inspector Carson. We met a few years ago when you were the Jew's enforcer. I was a Detective Sergeant back then. I nicked you for dealing and possession of drugs. You might remember it?' asked Carson, ruefully, as he rubbed his jaw.

No reaction from Harry.

'The PC next to the door,' said Carson, indicating the PC without turning around, 'I've got no idea who she is, Harry, and frankly I don't care.'

Still no reaction from Harry.

'Now, you must recognise this particular officer,' said Carson, who was thoroughly enjoying himself. 'Detective Constable Marshall.' When Harry still didn't react, Carson continued. 'Detective... Constable... Stephen... Marshall...'

Carson fixed his lizard-like eyes onto Harry's face. Waiting.

Steve stopped fidgeting. He too, stared intently at Harry, and held his breath.

A small frown began to crease Harry's forehead; his eyes blinked. His frown deepened as he stared at the now cold cup of tea, as if seeing it for the first time, before his eyes slowly lifted to meet Carson's gaze. Carson gave Harry the hard stare he was famed for. The stare most men could not hold.

Harry stared back, his eyes empty, no indication of recognition, no indication of emotion, his face blank and expressionless; after a beat, his gaze then slowly moved across to settle on Steve. As much as Steve wanted to look away, to look anywhere but into the eyes of Harry Windsor, he couldn't; he was unable. As Carson watched and waited, eagerly anticipating Harry's reaction, Steve also watched and waited; fearful of Harry's reaction.

As Steve looked into the vacant eyes of the man across the table, wondering what had happened in the intervening years, he thought, for the briefest moment, he saw a tiny light of recognition; the merest flicker. Then it was gone. Had Harry recognised him? Or had he imagined it?

Carson, disgruntled by the lack of confrontation, started his questioning. 'Where were you last night, Harry? What where you up to?' he wanted to know. 'Rumour has it, you retired. I personally find that hard to believe. Hard-core gangland villains like you, Harry, don't retire.' Carson paused, waiting for a response. He didn't get one. Harry continued to blank him.

Carson pressed on. 'Patrol picked you up just after midnight in the Kilburn area. What were you doing there, Harry? Bit of business? Bit of debt collecting?'

Still Harry said nothing.

'Last night - less than a mile away from where you were picked up - a body was found in the boot of a car. The deceased was a local businessman, by the name of Patrick Dolan. His body had been ripped to shreds, his throat torn out. He looked like a fuckin' carcass from a fuckin' abattoir! Word on the street, Harry, is he was in-hock to your employer, Solomon... Oh, sorry, I beg your pardon. Your *ex*-employer,' he then added, pulling his hands from his pockets and holding them up in mock surrender.

Still nothing from Harry.

'Do you want to know what I think?' said Carson, leaning forward and jabbing a finger in Harry's direction, clearly irritated by Harry's lack of response. 'I think you went to collect Solomon's money, and to 'sort out' the big Irishman. To make an example of him.'

Steve was both shocked and stunned. He was shocked at the coincidence: was this the same Patrick Dolan who was the father to Mollie Dolan, the missing student? Was this the father and daughter he'd been discussing with the reporter, Isobelle Harker, only hours earlier? And to hear Harry Windsor was a suspect left him stunned beyond belief. 'Who does the car belong to?' asked Steve, interrupting Carson's ranting at Harry.

'What?' replied Carson.

'The car, Sir,' said Steve. 'The car in which the body was found. Who does it belong to?'

'His daughter, why?'

'Did the vehicle-check, the DVLA, confirm that, Sir?'

'Are you questioning me, Constable?' asked Carson.

Steve hesitated before answering, 'No, Sir. Of course not,' he replied, avoiding Carson's gaze by returning his attention to his fidgeting hands. He thought hard, trying to recall the details of Mollie Dolan's case file. He was almost certain the car Mollie Dolan drove was, in fact, not owned by her; it was a leased car and the lease was in the name of her father, Patrick Dolan.

While Steve was struggling to comprehend what was going on, the enormity and gravity of the situation did not escape him. As his conscious mind struggled with the facts at hand, his subconscious mind was aware of Carson's continuing diatribe against Harry.

'Sir?' said Steve, to Carson. 'Excuse me, Sir?'

'Now what?' said Carson, rounding on Steve.

'I don't think it's appropriate my being here, Sir... being present at this particular interview, I mean,' said Steve, pushing back his chair and beginning to stand.

'Sit down, Constable!' ordered Carson. 'It's not as though you're blood related for Fuck sake. You don't get to choose which villains you can and can't interview. Not in my nick - only I get to do that.'

'Carson!' came an authoritative voice, cutting across Carson's vitriolic flow.

Both Steve and Carson turned towards it.

What Steve had seen in Harry's eyes earlier as the merest flicker of light, was now a raging inferno of anger and hate.

'Anyone ever tell you you're a wanker, Carson?' said Harry. Then, holding his hands up in mock surrender, 'Hang on a minute, I believe I did, the last time we met. When you nicked me and I broke your jaw.'

Harry leaned in towards Carson. Carson leaned back.

'If you're going to charge me, then get on with it and stop fuckin' me about.'

Carson narrowed his eyes at Harry. 'It maybe we can't place you at the scene of the crime when the body was discovered, but I know your being in the area was no coincidence. The forensics guys are going over that car with a fine-tooth comb. I know your prints and DNA are all over that car. It's only a matter of time before we tie you to the crime and the death of Patrick Dolan -'

'Do you know the aforementioned owner of the vehicle we're talking about?' asked Steve directly to Harry, cutting across his superior officer and bringing a scowl to his face. Carson decided to let it go, more interested in Harry's answer.

Harry was studying Steve, curiously.

'Do you know Patrick Dolan's daughter?' continued Steve, who had a hunch there was a connection here somewhere. Sensing he already knew what it was, he just couldn't put his finger on it.

'Yeah, you could say that,' replied Harry.

'Do you know her well?' asked Steve.

Harry paused, and then - thinking of her diary - said, 'I know her intimately.'

'Is there a point to this, Constable?' Carson wanted to know.

'Have you ever driven her car?' Steve continued, ignoring his D.I.

A small smile appeared on Harry's face as he realised. 'Yeah, I drove her car.'

A moment later, so did Carson. 'Fuck!' he said, slamming his open palm down onto the table as he jumped to his feet, sending his chair crashing backwards.

Carson whirled around to face Harry, who had a smile a mile wide across his tired and weary face. Carson's hands where balled into fists, his pockmarked face had turned a deep crimson, his eyeballs bulged in their sockets, and his lips were pulled back, exposing his teeth in a snarl of frustrated rage.

'Easy, Carson,' said Harry, thoroughly enjoying the man's discomfort, 'you might have a coronary - and I'm fucked if *I'm* going to be the one to give you the kiss of life,' he added. Then, 'How about you, officer?' Harry called across to the PC. 'Would you be prepared to give the kiss of life to Detective Inspector Carson, here?' he asked, raising his eyebrows.

The PC, while struggling to suppress a smile, kept a diplomatic silence.

'Are you trying to tell me that you're in a relationship with Mollie Dolan?' said Carson to Harry.

'I didn't say that,' Harry replied.

'What would an attractive young woman like Mollie Dolan see in a washed-up ex-con like you, Windsor?'

'Do you know her, Sir?' asked a surprised Steve, trying to recall if there was a photograph in her case file.

'No,' said Carson, quickly.

Too quickly.

'Let me see if I've got this right,' continued Carson, 'you know Mollie Dolan, you've driven her car, and you're picked up for drunk and disorderly less than a mile away from where her car is parked - in the boot of which is the body of her father. So what are you trying to tell me? It's a coincidence?'

'Depends whether or not you believe in coincidences, Carson,' replied Harry. 'I get the impression you were expecting to find me at the scene of the crime?'

Carson didn't reply.

'How did you know there was a body in the boot of that particular car?' asked Harry.

'A conscientious member of the public thought something was amiss, and phoned it in,' replied Carson.

'A tip-off, you mean?' When Carson didn't respond, Harry continued. 'Now, you see, *that's* what I call a coincidence. That you were hoping to nick me for the second time, based on a tip-off - and which, no doubt, was 'coincidentally' anonymous?'

All eyes turned to Detective Inspector Carson, who appeared to have lost some of his swagger. 'What exactly is that supposed to mean?'

Steve turned to Harry and said, 'Can you prove you know Mollie Dolan?'

Harry shrugged his shoulders. 'I've spent time in her flat... I've met her mother - I don't think she was too keen on me.' Harry gave another shrug.

'You're a lying piece of shit, Harry Windsor. I don't believe a fucking word of it,' said Carson.

'Sir?' said Steve. 'Maybe she's the girlfriend who's on her way here to pick him up?'

This drew a curious frown from Harry, and a strong rebuke from D.I. Carson.

'Don't be fuckin' stupid!'

'But why not, Sir?' asked Steve. 'We know she's gone missing. But, by her mother's own admission, she's gone missing before.'

'I'm telling you, Mollie Dolan is not on her way here,' Carson replied.

'But why not, Sir? What evidence do we have to say otherwise?' persisted Steve.

'Because... just... because -'

There was a knock at the door of the interview room, seconds before it opened, the Desk Sergeant - one hand resting on the door handle, the other gripping the door casing - leaning in. Finding Carson, he said, 'Girlfriend's turned up, Sir,' nodding towards Harry. 'And she's a bit bloody posh. Right, hoity-toity! She's kicking off about illegal detention, human rights, and all that crap. *And,* she claims she's a rep -'

The Desk Sergeant didn't get to finish his sentence, as the door flew open, causing him to stumble forward into the room, a very determined Isobelle Harker, hot on his heels.

'Hey, hey!' said a very flustered Desk Sergeant. 'You can't come in here. This is out of bounds to the general public.' he made a move towards Izzy.

'Lay a finger on me, Sergeant, and you'll be reading about police brutality on the front page of the *North London Gazette - and,* answering to the IPCC!'

The Desk Sergeant stopped in his tracks, unsure.

Izzy quickly scanned the room. Both Steve and the PC had jumped to their feet at Izzy's sudden intrusion. Her eyes paused at the PC before moving on to Steve, where they widened in surprise. 'What are you doing here?' she asked him.

'I work here,' replied Steve, equally surprised.

'Oh... Yes... Of course you do. How silly of me,' she said, making a goofy face.

Izzy then saw Harry. She instinctively took a step forward. 'Harry, how are...' she abruptly halted in both movement and speech, as she took in Harry's state. Her jaw dropped in shock, her hands flew up to her face. 'Christ, Harry. You look awful. You look worse than the last time I saw you. You look shittier than... shit.'

'Excuse me, Ma'am,' said Carson, through gritted teeth, his anger held in check only by his uncertainty about with whom he was dealing. 'As the Sergeant just made perfectly clear, this area is out of bounds to the general public - no matter who they are. This man,' he said, indicating Harry, 'is being interviewed in relation to a suspected murder, and right now you're interfering with a police investigation.'

If Izzy was shocked to hear Harry was a murder suspect, she didn't let it show. She took a step towards Carson, placed her hands on her hips and squared her shoulders, to then study Carson's face intently, pursing her lips as she did so. 'I'm guessing you are Detective Inspector Carson.'

Carson was taken aback. 'Have we met?' he asked, before he could stop himself.

'Possibly... maybe... I'm thinking London Zoo,' replied Izzy, at which Carson frowned. 'The Reptile House,' she then added, as if suddenly remembering.

For a moment, time seemed to stand still. Nobody moved, nobody spoke. It was a tableau in which the silence seemed to stretch for an eternity - until it was shattered by a derisive snort coming from adjacent to the door, where the PC, both hands clamped over her mouth, attempted to quell the laughter that wracked her body.

Steve had visibly paled in anticipation of Carson's reaction.

Carson, torn between how to deal with Izzy and wanting to discipline the PC, angrily pushed stray hair back from his puce coloured face while struggling to find the correct and proper response that wouldn't get him up on a charge of assault.

The Desk Sergeant looked from one person to another, unsure as to what to do.

Harry was still sitting at the table, watching the scene unfold before him. He felt he was at his own private vaudeville show - and there was no disputing who the star act was. Harry allowed himself a small smile: the cavalry had arrived.

'Who are you?' Carson demanded to know, dispensing with formal politeness.

'Isobelle Harker, *North London Gazette*.' Then, 'Senior Crime Reporter,' she added.

Carson's face twitched. He hated reporters even more than he did villains. At least villains' had a code of honour - however skewed it might be. 'And why, exactly, are you here?' he asked her.

'This man,' she said, indicating Harry, 'is helping me with an article I'm writing on London gang crime. How it impacts on society, and how the justice system deals with it.'

Carson, frankly, didn't give a flying fuck what she was writing about or who was helping her, and opened his mouth to tell her so.

'And,' continued Izzy, 'I'm particularly interested in miscarriages of justice.'

Carson closed his mouth.

'You said Harry Windsor was a murder suspect. What evidence do you have to prove that?'

'Yesterday a man was violently murdered, and the suspect was picked up -'

'In that case, he can't have done it.' Izzy told him.

'What!' said Carson. 'Why not?'

'Because he was with me... all day... helping me with the article.'

Carson narrowed his eyes at Izzy. 'All night, as well?'

As Izzy hesitated, a smile started to spread across Carson's face.

'No. Not all night.'

The smile turned into a cruel smirk.

'I dropped him off in Kilburn, just after midnight,' she said, finally.

She saw the look on Carson's face freeze. She shot a quick glance over at Steve, who was staring back at her, frowning; they both knew she'd still been at his flat at that time. She looked back at Carson, whose smile was rapidly disappearing as he recalled that Harry Windsor had been picked up by a passing patrol car just after midnight. Izzy also knew this, but only because she'd managed to elicit the information from the Desk Sergeant, moments ago. The Desk Sergeant, realising he may have provided an alibi to a murder suspect - however unlikely - mumbled his apologies to hastily return to his unmanned desk.

Steve turned to a seething Carson. 'Harry was picked up just after midnight, Sir, so he can't have been responsible,' he said, driving the point home.

Carson threw an angry look at Harry, who merely winked an eye, back at him.

'I swear to God, I'll get you, Windsor. I'll nick you, and bang you up.'

'Why don't you crawl back under your rock, Carson,' replied Harry.

'Get him out of here!' ordered Carson, as he stormed from the room.

On Carson's exit, Izzy turned to Harry, and then Steve. 'Who's died? Who's been murdered?'

Steve glanced across at Harry, and then back to Izzy. 'Patrick Dolan,' he said, simply.

Izzy's eyes widened in horror. She turned to Harry, disbelief and suspicion clouding her face, suspicion gaining ground. Harry met her look, saw the tears beginning to form, to then give a small shake of his head, removing any trace of doubt.

Conscious that Izzy might be curious about the nature and details of Patrick's death, and not wanting to relive it, he decided it was time to leave. He placed the palms of both hands onto the table top, before wearily pushing himself upright to a standing position, wincing as he did so. He shuffled over to stand before them, holding out his manacled hands.

'You okay?' asked Steve, with concern, as he took a key from his pocket to remove the handcuffs.

'Getting old,' replied Harry, rubbing his wrists. He then studied both Izzy and Steve. 'I appreciate what you both did just then. Especially you, Stephen - considering the weight of circumstantial evidence.'

Steve thrust both hands into his trouser pockets, and then looked down at his shoes, shifting uncomfortably from one foot to the other. 'Sometimes you have to do what you believe is the right thing, and not necessarily what you are *led* to believe is the right thing.' He then looked back up at Harry. 'I believe that can apply not only to one's work life, but also social life... and family.'

Harry's gaze - which had followed Steve's, down to the floor - suddenly flicked back up to Steve's face. He studied the younger man's anxious look. Harry's head bobbed slightly in agreement, before saying, 'Hindsight... if only.' Then, with a sad smile and a hint of regret in his eyes, Harry held his hand out to Steve. 'It may be too late for some, but not for others.'

With a smile of relief and an expression that was close to tears, Steve grabbed Harry's hand and shook it vigorously. This brought a grin to Harry's face, and to Izzy's - who never liked to be left out of the loop - a look of confusion.

'Am I missing something here?' she asked.

Both Harry and Steve, looked to each other and then realised.

'You don't know, do you?' said Steve.

'Know what?' replied Izzy, feeling she was the butt of the joke.

'Stephen's my brother,' answered Harry.

Izzy did her goldfish impression, before finally saying in a high-pitched squeak, 'What!... Who?... You two? '

Harry and Steve stared back at her.

Izzy's mouth was moving, but no words were coming out, until, 'Foster brother,' she finally said, correcting him.

Harry paused briefly, a faraway look in his eye, before saying, 'We're family.' Izzy and Steve both looked at him quizzically. Then, before Izzy had chance to question him further, 'Officer?' said Harry, calling over to the PC. 'Would you mind showing me the way out?'

'Wait!' said Izzy, placing her hand against his chest. 'What about Mollie?'

Harry looked deeply troubled as he mulled the question over. Then, finally, 'This is a police matter now.' He looked to Steve, who nodded, then back to Izzy. 'You remember the gentlemen's club your father used to use? Near Richmond? She's there, working as a "hostess" - legitimately, I'm told.' He then turned back to Steve. 'The Russian Mob's involved.

You might want to put a watch on Mollie's mother... Patrick's wife,' he then added, suddenly looking drained. 'I'm tired. I'm going home. Ring me and let me know what happens.' When Izzy reminded him he never answers his phone, he assured her he would. Then, after a nod to the PC, he followed her out through the door, leaving Izzy and Steve staring after him. They watched the door gently close with a soft click.

After a long drawn out moment, Steve turned to Izzy and said, 'Coffee?'

'Cop-shop coffee?' asked Izzy, pulling a face.

'God, no! Deli, a few doors up.'

'Okay,' replied Izzy, relieved.

CHAPTER 43

In the take-away delicatessen, there were three small tables and chairs for those customers wanting to eat-in - only one of which was occupied - along with a narrow wall-fixed countertop that ran partway across a plastered wall, and then across the plate-glass frontage of the shop. This was serviced with high perching stools where Izzy and Steve had opted to sit, both having subconsciously gravitated towards the window seating, feeling more comfortable to be sitting side-by-side, looking out at London life and lost in their own thoughts, rather than sitting opposite and feeling the obligation to make conversation.

Izzy was, at that particular moment, content. She was in one of her favourite places, doing one of her favourite things: in a cafe, in a busy part of London, people watching. And she was sitting in her favourite position: elbows resting on the countertop with a large chocolate sprinkled cappuccino cupped in her hands. As she blew gently onto its surface, her eyes flicked from one point of interest to another.

Steve had an equally large cup of cappuccino, but sprinkled with cinnamon. His gaze too, flicked between watching the hubbub of London daily life, and the act of methodically stirring - counter clockwise - the cinnamon and frothy milk with the wooden stirring stick provided.

Izzy, noticing this, smiled to herself.

'Penny for them?' said Steve.

Izzy looked blank.

'Your thoughts.'

'Oh,' she said, realising. 'I was just thinking about a cappuccino faux pas I once had. I was in a cafe just like this, sitting just like this, and drinking a cappuccino. I was blowing upon it to cool it down, and I guess I must have sighed heavily at the same time, because I blew a dollop of frothy milk clean off the top and onto the window immediately in front of me.' Izzy smiled at the memory. 'I couldn't stop laughing. I laughed so hard I cried.'

'Did you clean it off the glass?' asked Steve.

'No,' said Izzy, still smiling.

Steve frowned.

Izzy returned her gaze to the human traffic outside.

After a moment, 'Carson's a piece-of-work, isn't he?' she said.

Steve nodded.

'Tell me about you and Harry.'

Steve turned back to his untouched coffee and resumed his methodical stirring. 'We're both orphans. Both brought up in Children's Homes and short-term fostering. I was probably more fortunate than Harry. I was only moved a few times before being placed with the woman who was to then raise me as her own - as she did Harry. Lillian was an exceptional woman. She never married and never had - or couldn't have - children of her own. Whether one was because of the other, I don't know. I never asked. I was placed with Lillian first, Harry came a few months later. I think I was unaccepting of Harry at first, in that Lillian's love and attention was now divided between the two of us.' Steve momentarily paused, before then carrying on. 'But you can't help but like Harry. He's a lovable rogue. Having said that, there's a darker side to him. He used to - and still does, as far as I know - become moody and sullen, withdrawing into himself. The local authority moved him many times from Care Home, to foster placement, back to Care Home, unable to find somewhere suitable. I think sometimes he had it pretty rough. In fact, I know he did. I overheard his social worker giving some background on Harry, to Lillian. It was pretty horrific.'

'The scars on his back?' asked Izzy.

'You've seen those?' replied Steve. When he saw Izzy nod, he carried on. 'It used to be that families were paid to foster children. I've no idea if that's still the case, but with an ever increasing number of children without a permanent home, I think the authorities were sometimes not quite so thorough in their selection process of people applying to foster. Anyway, Harry was placed with a family where the husband was a violent alcoholic. Obviously this was not known at first. As punishment, the husband used to thrash Harry with a length of bamboo stick, and then lock him in a small dark cupboard under the stairs. That's the reason he's claustrophobic.'

'He's claustrophobic?' responded Izzy, surprised.

'Very.'

Izzy found herself thinking back to an earlier conversation she'd had with Harry. She'd asked him what it had been like being in prison. He had replied, "Cramped."

'With the start in life that he had, I guess it's hardly a surprise he took the path that he did.'

'Yet, your start in life wasn't much different,' said Izzy. 'In fact, strikingly similar. But you took the opposite path. You took the path of good. The right path. You're a policeman, a Detective Constable, a pillar of the community. You couldn't possibly get any more opposite than that. Than an illiterate villain who does his talking with his fists.'

'True,' conceded Steve. 'But Harry and I are two very different people. Though having said that, there are a few similarities... But I guess that's probably down to nurture,' he added, with a shrug of indifference. 'There's no denying Harry can look after himself. He's very capable. He protected me from school bullies on more than one occasion. And I'll always be eternally grateful for that. And while he might not have had an expansive education, he's certainly not illiterate. In fact, if you knew his IQ level, you would be surprised.'

'How high?' asked Izzy.

'You'll have to ask him yourself. It's not something he likes to talk about.'

'Give me a clue,' she said.

'I can guarantee you, it's higher than both mine and yours.'

'You don't know my IQ level,' replied Izzy.

'I don't need to,' said Steve. 'Anyway, I don't think Harry's choice of path was entirely of his own making. It could be said he had some help. Was coerced, if you like.'

'In what way?' asked Izzy, eager to know.

'Lillian was an actor. Her fellow actors and colleagues would often visit the house, to say hello or maybe run through their lines. They were an eclectic mix of personalities. It was always a busy household. Then there was the tall, elegant, and dignified gentleman who would occasionally call. Whom I, as a child, assumed was part of Lillian's acting fraternity.'

'Solomon!' said Izzy.

Steve raised his eyebrows, and then nodded his head. 'Yes, Solomon.'

Izzy beamed back, pleased he was impressed.

'Henry Solomon. An accountant, a small-time crook, and soon-to-become one of the biggest gangland crime boss's London has ever seen - with Harry's help.' Steve briefly paused in the stirring of his coffee, and then continued. 'Harry got himself expelled from school for attacking two other boys. Lillian was deeply upset, because Harry had been doing well at his studies, 'knuckling down' as they say. It may have been a coincidence, but Henry Solomon turned up not long after Harry had been escorted home by the school's headmaster. Personally, I think Lillian rang him. Why, I have no idea. But it wasn't long after that, that Harry started working for some of Solomon's legitimate businesses. I guess the rest is history.

'Do you think he was guilty of the drug offences he was jailed for?' asked Izzy.

'I've asked myself that question many, many times. Solomon and Harry were old-fashioned villains. They weren't into drugs. So I was surprised when drugs were found in Harry's car.' Steve sighed heavily. 'It was myself and D.I. Carson who arrested Harry. Back then, Carson was a Detective Sergeant, and I was a uniformed officer. Why he took me along, I don't know. There were two other Uniforms, waiting outside as back-up. He could have taken one of them.'

'Maybe he thought your being there would make the arrest a smoother transition,' said Izzy.

Steve gave a snort of derision. 'I think it more likely it appealed to his twisted sense of humour. In the months leading up to Harry's arrest, he'd vacated his rented flat and moved back into Lillian's home to care for her. Lillian it seems, had had lung cancer quite some time and managed to hide it well. She was diagnosed as terminal... Anyway, after searching Harry's car, Carson arrested him at Lillian's bedside.' Steve swallowed hard, and then carried on. 'It was not one of my finest moments. Certainly not one I'm proud of. In fact, the only man who kept his dignity was Harry. The three of us exited the house, that's when Harry made me promise Lillian would be looked after. I of course agreed.'

Steve abandoned his methodical stirring of his cold coffee, to look up and gaze out of the window. It had begun to rain. He watched the droplets of water run down the glass, chasing each other. Izzy watched and waited. Then, when he didn't look like he was going to continue, she asked, 'What happened next?'

Steve blinked two or three times, returning to the present. 'That's when Harry head-butted me in the face, breaking my nose - for the second time - and gave Carson a left hook, breaking his jaw.'

'Ah, the "mitigating circumstances",' said Izzy, remembering.

Steve continued. 'Harry then stood back, raised his hands, and allowed the Uniforms to take him in.' He pushed his untouched cappuccino away from him. 'Lillian died while Harry was on remand. He attended her funeral in handcuffs. He was sent for trial a few weeks later, and subsequently jailed for three years. D.S. Carson and I were promoted on the strength of Harry's conviction. And ever since then, Harry has carried the guilt that he wasn't there for Lillian in her last moments, and that his arrest may have speeded-up her passing. He may well be right. Up until today, Harry and I haven't seen or spoken to each other since his trial...'

Izzy could see Steve was struggling with his emotions. She laid a hand on his forearm, and squeezed gently.

Steve then said to Izzy, 'I aspire to be what Harry could quite easily be. Harry aspires to be anything other than Harry. As a kid, he was my hero,' he said, quietly. Then, almost in a whisper, 'Guess he still is...'

'Do you think Harry had anything to do with Patrick's death?' asked Izzy.

'In what way? Responsible? Capable?'

Izzy stared back, noncommittal.

'Harry's a hard man. I'd say he's capable of most things.'

'You said yourself, Harry very rarely starts a fight.'

'Let us hope so,' replied Steve.

'I believe in him,' said Izzy.

'Maybe you know him better than I do.'

'Woman's intuition,' said Izzy. 'A bit like you aren't what you appear to be.'

Steve shifted, uncomfortable.

'So, Stephen,' continued Izzy, 'what are we going to do about Mollie? How do we go about getting her out of that club?'

'We?' replied Steve, surprised.

'Yes, we! We can't just leave her there, for God's sake. If "hostess" means what I think it means, then Christ knows what acts of sexual depravity they are forcing her to carry out, just to pay off her father's debts,' she said, becoming more and more animated. 'I mean, it could be whips, chains and ropes. Bondage!... S&M! -'

'We don't know that, exactly. We have to look at the known facts. Weigh-up the available evidence.'

'Okay,' said Izzy, 'what are the facts? What is the evidence?'

Steve took out his notebook and pen, and then paused to gather his thoughts. 'Mollie Dolan has been reported missing. That's a fact. But it's not the first time. The first time she went missing was over a family dispute, confirmed when she was finally found. That's a fact. Also, we only have Harry's word that Mollie's at this so-called gentlemen's club -' Steve quickly raised his hand when he saw Izzy on the verge of interrupting him. 'I'm not disputing what Harry said. What I'm saying is, does he know for a fact she's there? Did he see her? By his own admission, his information she's "working legitimately" is second-hand. That is a fact as we know it, but not evidence. Would you not agree?' he asked Izzy, reviewing what he'd written so far.

'Okay. Yes, I would,' said Izzy, reluctantly, before reaching across to relieve Steve of his notebook and pen.

'Patrick Dolan is in debt,' she said, writing. 'Threats have been made against his family -'

'Both of which may be fact,' said Steve, 'but solid evidence?'

Izzy looked at Steve, coolly, before continuing to write. 'Patrick Dolan found dead! Fact *and* solid evidence!' she said, with an exclamation mark flourish, for emphasis.

'Fair point,' replied Steve. Then, after a pause, 'Have you ever been to this club?'

'Once. A charity function a few years ago.'

'What's it like?'

'Affluent. High-brow,' said Izzy, pulling a face. 'Can't say I saw any prostitutes or Russian gangsters, though,' she admitted.

'To go in officially, we're going to need a search warrant. And I'm afraid there is nowhere near enough evidence to obtain a warrant,' said Steve.

'But we've got to try, surely?' said Izzy.

After a moment's hesitation, Steve put his hand into his jacket pocket and dug out his mobile phone. He made a call to D.I. Carson. Izzy heard Steve request a search warrant, and then outline on what evidence it was based, realising just how flimsy the evidence was. Steve listened, for what seemed to Izzy, quite a long time, before acknowledging his D.I.'s opinion, and then disconnecting.

Steve stared at the blank screen of his mobile phone, a puzzled look on his face.

'Well?' said Izzy, already knowing what the answer was going to be.

'Not enough evidence,' he replied. Then, seeing Izzy's face drop, 'He did say he would discuss it with the Super, though - the Superintendent, that is.'

'Well, that's something, isn't it?' she said.

Steve shrugged, his puzzled look, deepening. 'It's weird. He seemed so... reasonable about it. I don't think I've ever known D.I. Carson being reasonable,' he said.

'If he speaks to the Superintendent, how long before we know?'

'Hours... Days... Weeks... Never! There's no way the Super will apply for a warrant on a rich man's club without cast-iron evidence. It's just not going to happen.'

They both stared morosely out at the rain.

'Right, then,' said Izzy, 'in that case we move to plan B. If that fails, plan C, and then finally plan D.'

Steve looked at Izzy with some trepidation. He knew he was about to get sucked in. He knew the best thing he could do, would be to climb off his stool, and leave. And he certainly knew he shouldn't ask what plan B was. So he didn't. But, being too polite to walk away, and too much of a gentleman to ignore Isobelle's comment, he instead found himself asking what plan D was.

'Plan D,' replied Izzy, 'is when we give up the cause, go to a bar, and then get shit-faced,' she said, smiling demurely.

Once again, Steve found himself musing over Isobelle Harker's eloquence.

CHAPTER 44

Harry had opted to walk the few miles from the police station to his flat. While he didn't have any money to pay for bus or taxi fare, he could have quite easily made a phone call and called in a favour for a lift home. But the real truth of the matter was he wanted to be alone with his thoughts, to try and make sense of recent events. The nature of Patrick's death still haunted him, and after his imprisonment, being outside in wide open spaces in the fresh air - such as it was in London - was a relief.

As he strode along, he realised he had no idea what day it was, or how long he'd been kept prisoner back at the club. Pausing at a street vendor's news stand to check the day and date on the front pages, he was shocked to discover it was only yesterday that he'd been taken prisoner and tortured. It seemed to Harry as though the ordeal had lasted much longer. He also realised it was almost two weeks since Mollie was first thought to have gone missing, and a week since he'd started his search.

Let the police do the rest, he thought.

At his local convenience store, Harry had talked the proprietor into allowing him some credit to stock up on some of the basics: bread, butter, milk, baked beans, bottled water and a newspaper - and cigarettes.

Tired and weary, Harry was now back home, in his flat. The doors were locked, the blinds were pulled, and for the first time since it was fitted, he was attempting to prepare some food in his kitchen.

Harry had always eaten out; he never cooked - didn't really know how to cook. But at that particular moment in time, he couldn't face people, didn't want to talk to anyone, so he decided to eat in. He was attempting beans on toast. After burning the toast for the third time, as he struggled to master the multi-function electronic display of the built-in oven grill, he gave up, and had baked beans on thickly buttered bread instead. But to Harry, who hadn't eaten a proper meal for almost two days, it was a meal fit for a king. After he'd finished, he dumped the pots and pans into the sink, grabbed a large bottle of mineral water, and then trudged off in the direction of his bedroom. There, he stripped off, leaving his clothes where they fell, and wearily slipped in between the sheets, instantly falling into a deep and tormented sleep.

CHAPTER 45

The blare of a car horn was left trailing in their wake as Izzy and Steve battled their way through the London evening traffic in Izzy's hire car. Izzy was driving.

Try as hard as he might to appear calm and collected, Steve was a bag of nerves; the knuckles on the hand that gripped the door handle had turned white, and his right foot repeatedly pressed down on an imaginary brake pedal. 'Couldn't you have hired a slightly bigger, more solid type of car?' he said to Izzy, feeling extremely vulnerable to a potential crash, physical harm, and decapitation.

'Don't you like it?' she asked, taking her eyes off the road for far longer than Steve was comfortable with. 'I think it's quite cute - and they're extremely nippy,' she then added unnecessarily, as she switched lanes three times over a distance of less than a hundred metres, before slowing to join a queue of traffic for a roundabout up ahead.

She turned to Steve. 'You look good in a tux,' she said, admiring his evening wear. 'Is it rented?'

'Certainly not,' replied Steve, desperately trying to focus on his breathing and prevent a full-blown panic attack. 'Waxman Brothers, Bethnal Green. Made-to-measure.'

'It fits you well... in all the right places,' she said, as she put the car into gear and eased forwards.

Steve flicked her a sideways glance, looking for meaning, but Izzy's eyes were on the traffic ahead, as she once again put the car into gear, eased forward, and then braked.

Steve returned his gaze out through the windscreen.

'Do I look okay?' she asked him.

'Very nice,' said Steve, still looking ahead.

Izzy had opted for a formfitting black trouser suit. The trousers were a slim fit, emphasising her long shapely legs and accentuating the roundness of her buttocks; the jacket was a collarless box type, finishing short of her midriff, a single button holding it closed. Underneath, she wore a cream satin camisole-type top - no bra *again* - complemented by a pearl choker and a cream clutch purse. She wore her hair up in a topknot. The charity function at the gentlemen's club hadn't stated evening wear, but past experience told Izzy it would be quite formal. Her choice of attire had been more from a practical point of view rather than style.

'I really don't think this is a good idea, you know,' said Steve.

'What's not a good idea?' she said, turning back to him.

'Tonight,' he replied. 'Anything we find will not be admissible as evidence without a warrant.

As Izzy reached the roundabout, she tapped on the brakes, glanced to her right, and then stamped on the accelerator, shooting across and around.

'We have an official invite - or rather the *Gazette* does, and we are attending on its behalf - and it's a worthwhile charity.'

'Who's the charity?' asked Steve.

'Err... that's not important. The important thing is, we are quite innocently attending, and if by any chance we 'stumble' across anything that may be 'helpful' in the future...' Izzy then gave Steve an exaggerated wink of the eye, before saying, 'Covert.' Then, as an afterthought, she said, 'Do you think Harry should be here, too?'

Steve shook his head. 'D.I. Carson is looking for an excuse to 'throw the book at him', as they say - and probably at me, too.'

'You worry too much,' said Izzy.

'That's what my therapist says,' replied Steve, more to himself.

'You've got a therapist?'

Steve risked releasing his grip on the door handle to check his watch. 'We're going to be late,' he told her, 'and I hate being late.'

'Fuck-a-duck!' said Izzy, amazed that Steve had a therapist, before flooring the accelerator and jumping a red light.

'Fuck!' said Steve, simply, stamping on the brake.

CHAPTER 46

Harry's return to waking consciousness was, at first, agonisingly slow. His unconscious mind slumbered peacefully in a deep, dark, womblike sanctuary until the razor sharp talons of consciousness hooked themselves in to his unconscious mind, and drew him upwards to the surface of harsh reality. Though his mind refused to relinquish the warmth and safety of oblivion, it was a losing battle. Upwards and onwards his mind rose, through a morass of old thoughts and old images, up through new ones struggling to form, picking up speed and accelerating through the light spectrum. Going from the safety of darkness, through the uncertain greys, accelerating towards the harsh reality of daylight, and with it, the unknown, the unsuspecting, the dangers, the fears, the threats: *all* unwelcoming.

Harry opened his eyes. It was dark. He blinked a few times, trying to focus. It was still dark. For a brief moment, he had an unsettling sense of déjà vu, a sense of panic, he couldn't quite place. He turned his head; the digital display on his bedside alarm clock read six in the evening. He was in his own bed, he was in his own flat, and he knew his name was Harry Windsor. Other than that, everything else was a blank.

He pulled back the duvet, swung his long legs out, and then eased himself into a sitting position on the edge of the bed. He rested his forearms on his knees for a moment, head dropped, hair hanging down, while he waited for consciousness and memory to fully return. He wondered whether he'd been drinking heavily, out on a bender, maybe. He didn't feel like he was hung-over, in fact, physically, he felt quite good. If only he could wake up.

He reached out for the bedside lamp, fumbled, and then switched it on, blinking at the sudden harsh light. He attempted to massage some life back into his face, to wipe the remnants of sleep from his eyes, only to be surprised by the length of stubble on his face. It must have been quite a bender, he thought to himself, as he pushed his hair back from off his face, only to catch sight of the soiled clothing, unceremoniously dumped on the bedroom floor.

The memories came flooding back like a tidal wave, like a tsunami threatening to overwhelm him: images of blood, ripped flesh, and the pleading eyes of a dying man. He fought to quell the panic that rose within him, feeling the room start to tilt, and forcing him to grip the edge of the bed to steady himself. He took a deep breath then slowly exhaled, then repeated the process, drawing in fresh air, feeling his rapidly beating heart start to slow.

He sat for a moment to collect his thoughts, a sheen of cold sweat covering his naked body, before finally standing and pulling on a full-length bathrobe, tying and knotting it at the waist.

Harry opened the front door to his flat, peered out into the lobby, and for a moment listened intently, still not in the mood for conversation or company. Seeing the coast was clear, he retrieved his pile of mail and morning newspapers from the table, to then retreat back into his flat.

He dumped the pile onto his kitchen table, and then sat down to sift through it. He was surprised to see there were two early morning newspapers in the pile; Thursday and Friday's. Harry frowned. The newspaper he'd brought into the flat on his return from the police station was also still on the kitchen table; it was dated Wednesday.

Surely I haven't been asleep for two days, he thought, as he looked out through the French doors and to the small garden beyond, dimly lit from the overspill of the kitchen light.

He switched on the wall mounted television, to then select a twenty four hour news channel. It was indeed Friday. His mobile phone was also on the kitchen table. He glanced at the screen: no missed calls. He clearly remembered asking Steve and Izzy to let him know about Mollie.

Harry dialled Izzy's mobile; it went straight to voicemail. He then dialled the number for the *North London Gazette*, even though he suspected it was unlikely she would be there at that time of night on a Friday. He was informed Izzy was on annual leave that day. Harry then - reluctantly, because he hated anything to do with the old bill - phoned Willesden nick, only to be told the same thing: that D.C. Marshall was on leave. *What the fuck was going on? And what the fuck were they doing about Mollie?* He tossed his phone down onto the table, disgusted. Surely, he asked himself, Stephen was doing something about getting Mollie out of that club?

On reflection - after he'd calmed down - Stephen was the one person who could be relied upon to do the right thing. Providing it was within the law, that is. But Harry still had the hump. He was also starving hungry. Having finally mastered the new grill's multi-function display, he then cooked himself beans on toast, with a side order of eight slices of heavily buttered toast. This cooking malarkey is a piece of cake, he thought, and then wished he'd been adventurous enough to have bought fresh eggs and bacon to have done a fry-up.

After his meal, he enjoyed a large mug of tea, content to watch the news, until it started to repeat itself. Only then did his concentration start to wander, his gaze turning more to the garden outside, rather than the television. He picked up the TV remote and pressed the standby button. For a while he sat in complete silence, staring out at his small courtyard garden, his gaze repeatedly returning to the stone feature, buried beneath which was the urn that contained his mother's ashes.

Harry knew, with a heavy heart, that he'd got some thinking to do. A decision had to be made. With that, he went in search of a bottle of whisky, a glass, and his recently purchased - yet still unopened - packet of cigarettes. Tightening the belt to his bathrobe while slipping on a pair of Rigger work boots, he then stepped outside into the garden. It was a cold and crisp November evening, with the night sky clear of cloud cover, reducing the light pollution and allowing a handful of stars to shine through. There might be a frost tonight, he thought, as he gazed up at the London night-time sky.

Once seated on the garden bench with his bathrobe pulled tight against the chill, a glass of whisky in one hand and an unlit cigarette in the other, he then took a large swallow of his drink, feeling the burn as it trickled down his throat, and the satisfaction of its warmth spreading throughout his body. Turning his attention to the Greek urn, he said, quietly, 'Hello, mother. How are you?' He always asked his mother how she was, which was stupid really, considering she was dead. But Harry felt it was only polite and courteous to do so. And, while Harry wasn't a religious man, he liked to believe there was something after this mortal life. What? He really didn't know. He just didn't want to believe the end was a pile of ash, or rotting flesh and decaying bones.

For a moment, he paused, as he wondered what to say, where to start. He found himself reflecting on how tired and weary he often felt - physically and mentally. He told his mother how he wasn't getting any younger, and didn't seem to be able to take the knocks as easily; how he felt the pain more, and how the bruises seem to take longer to fade. He told her how difficult he found it going straight, trying to do the right thing, and that staying on the straight and narrow was like having one hand tied behind your back; that it wasn't a perfect world in that the injustices far outweighed the justices; that playing by the rules, being on the side of right, was not the winning side.

As Harry quietly told his mother of his struggle, of his anguish, he realised he'd developed a conscience, that he cared. *Christ, when the fuck did that happen?* What he also realised - and found more unsettling - was that he felt vulnerable, even - God forbid - scared.

Harry then wondered when he'd become afraid. Was it his recent ordeal? No, before that. Was it when he was a child and would be beaten? No, he'd stopped being afraid of that sort of pain after the first few beatings. No, it was when he was arrested at his mother's bedside, when he realised he would not be there for her in her last moments.

Harry's mind drifted back. He was in Lillian's study. The room was softly lit by an old-fashioned standard lamp that stood in the corner, a tall, elegantly hand carved piece of wood, topped with a parchment-like shade that depicted an image of a street scene from Tudor times, its light spilling downwards over an old leather Chesterfield armchair in which Harry was comfortably sitting reading a book which he had selected from Lillian's large collection. On one side of Harry was the fireplace in which a fire had been lit, the coals radiating a physical and visually comforting warmth. On the other side was a large imposing hospital bed, in which lay the gaunt and fragile sleeping form of Harry's foster mother, Lillian.

As Lillian's health had rapidly deteriorated, and the extent of the cancer had become clear, and with pain management being the only option left open, Harry had had Lillian brought home from the hospital, hiring professional carers to administer to her needs: preparing her food, monitoring and controlling her medication, and tending to her personal hygiene; all of this, twenty four hours a day, seven days a week.

The only sounds in the room to be heard were the gentle hiss and crackle of the fire, the rhythmic tick-tock of a grandfather clock, and the intermittent sound of pages being turned, until a soft, yet polite tap was to be heard at the study door. Harry quietly stood, crossed the room, and then opened the door to one of Lillian's carers, who smiled politely as she silently handed Harry a bowl of food, before turning to leave. Easing the door closed, Harry returned to Lillian's bedside, where he gently roused her from sleep.

'Hello, Henry,' said Lillian, softly.

'Hello, Lillian,' replied Harry.

'How are you?' she asked.

'I'm fine. You?'

Lillian smiled weakly. 'The usual. Tired.'

'Hungry?' Harry asked her.

Lillian gave the merest of shrugs. Her body had become so weak, her digestive system was unable to cope with solid food, so what little she was inclined or able to eat would first have to be cooked, and then blended to a puree. Harry had also consulted a top nutritionist on the best possible diet for Lillian, to ensure she got the minerals, vitamins and nutrients that were vital to help keep her strength up, not that it would make any difference in the long-run; Harry just wasn't prepared to give up and accept the inevitable outcome.

After electronically raising the bed head to a comfortable angle, and then checking the temperature of the bowl's content, Harry proceeded to gently and patiently feed Lillian small but manageable amounts of the prepared food. He always took his time, he never rushed; just the effort of swallowing the food left Lillian drained and exhausted. Harry preferred to be the one to give Lillian her meals. He felt it was one of the few things he was able to do for her, that didn't require medical qualification, or the loss of her dignity - and dignity was about all she had left.

He spent a lot of time in that armchair, watching over the woman who'd raised him, sometimes reading to her when she was awake, often sleeping in it when she wasn't.

'How's the food?' he asked her, making conversation. Lillian pulled a face. 'It'll help,' he told her.

'Silly boy,' said Lillian, with a sad smile.

Harry shifted, uncomfortable.

'How was your day?' she asked, changing the subject.

'The usual,' Harry replied, shrugging his shoulders. 'Ran an errand for Mr Solomon.'

'And how does he feel about you spending so much time here, rather than you... working?'

Harry again, merely shrugged.

After a moment, Lillian asked, 'What kind of errand?'

While Harry had never been totally candid with Lillian about the full nature of his employment and what it was exactly that he did for Mr Solomon, she had never asked and as he had always hoped she never would, he didn't want to enlighten her. He certainly didn't want her to know the truth, because he knew she would be disappointed in him. The "errand" he'd just referred to had been a long-term outstanding debt that Mr Solomon had asked Harry to collect for him by using his 'skills' in persuading the debtor to see the error of his ways, which Harry had duly done as, in turn, did the debtor.

The debtor was a used car salesman based in Kilburn, which is where Harry had found him at his half empty car lot, sitting in a squalid Portakabin that served as an office. Harry guessed the car salesman to be in his early sixties, and judging by the accent, originally from South East London; he was a big-old-lump, with an attitude to match. Also in the Portakabin was probably the biggest black man Harry had ever seen, who said nothing, just glared at Harry, giving him the eye: hired muscle.

The car salesman had been full of excuses. He was also not happy with Mr Solomon's interest rates. He said he couldn't pay. Didn't want to pay. In fact, had no intention of paying, he finally decided, flicking a glance across at the big black man for support. Harry told the car salesman that Mr Solomon didn't like people who took the piss, or showed him disrespect. Harry then told the car salesman, that due to personal reasons, family reasons, he really wasn't in a good frame of mind for any aggravation.

The car salesman's response wasn't favourable.

It was at this point that Harry had used his skills of persuasion - on both men. Once he'd finished, he'd taken what money was in the petty cash box, and every set of car keys to the cars parked on the lot, with the intention of sending a crew back for them later.

Harry didn't want to contemplate what Lillian would think if she knew the debtor had been hospitalised, as he looked up to meet her cool gaze, trying to find the right words.

'I've known Henry Solomon for a very long time,' she told him, 'and I'm aware of his business interests, legitimate and...' She paused, partly through reluctance to voice the word aloud, and partly to catch her breath.

Harry offered her a glass of water with a straw, from which she took a few sips. Not for the first time, did he find himself musing at the nature of the friendship between his foster mother and Mr Solomon. Over the years, Henry Solomon's visits to Lillian's home had only been occasional, and in more recent times, rarer still.

'As you know, I never had children of my own. Wasn't able to. So I never experienced the joy in hearing the word mother,' she said, smiling wistfully. 'I was always conscious that you and Stephen had not had what could be called the best start in life. When you came to me I so very much wanted to make you happy. To see you happy. To try and make up for all of life's hurts. I was conscious you had both spent time in Children's Homes, and I didn't want the two of you to go from one strict regime to another. I wanted you to experience the joy in playing as children should.

To enjoy what few remaining years of childhood were left to you, before entering into adulthood, and becoming individuals in your own right.' Lillian paused for a moment, closing her eyes, and to catch her breath. When they fluttered open, Harry offered some more water, which she gratefully took before continuing. 'It was my dearest wish that, despite your troubled formative years, you would both turn out to be fine young men. Moral and upstanding. Knowing right from wrong. But, more than anything else, being happy and content.' Lillian's gaze drifted from Harry to the open fire, her tired eyes taking on a faraway look before finally saying, 'I have to confess, the role of being a parent was... daunting. I was unprepared. I'm not sure whether or not I made a good job of it, of being a moth... a foster mother.

'You did a great job,' said Harry, reassuringly. 'Nobody could have done better. We're both happy and content, and we both know what's right and what's wrong. Stephen took the path of right. I... well,' he said, with a wry smile, before offering some more food and leaving the sentence incomplete.

When Lillian had had enough, Harry offered her some more water, and then, with a tenderness only ever witnessed by Lillian and her carers, took a napkin and gently dabbed her mouth, before then ensuring that her covers were straight, and she was comfortable.

'What are you reading?' she asked, seeing a book resting on the arm of the chair.

'Macbeth,' he replied, picking up the book.

'Ah, the 'Scottish play',' she said, referring to the play by the name used by many in the theatrical world, rather than its original name, which was said to bring bad luck if uttered aloud. 'One of Shakespeare's finest, and shortest, plays. Read to me,' she said to Harry, with a tired smile.

So Harry read to her. He read it aloud, and in the manner intended - in iambic pentameter, breathing life into the words, and bringing an expression of contentment to Lillian's face. Every now and again Harry would look up to check on her.

After a while, seeing that she was tiring, Harry stopped. 'Do you need to rest?' he asked, gently.

'Some might say, Henry, that you, Macbeth, and the play have some similar traits. In that you are at war with yourself,' she teased, smiling. 'My prince amongst thieves.'

Harry merely raised an eyebrow, and smiled back. He watched Lillian turn away, her eyes slowly close, and the smile slip from her face. His gaze shifted to see the barely noticeable, but reassuring, rise and fall of the duvet. He sat and watched her for a while. Then, just when he thought she'd slipped into sleep, she spoke.

'There is something you ought to know... have a right to know... about your employer. About Henry Solomon.' Lillian opened her eyes and turned back to Harry. 'Firstly, you must be very careful -'

Harry frowned, opening his mouth to speak, until Lillian, with the slightest shake of her head, and a feebly raised hand, stopped him. Instead, he leant forward to gently take her skeletal hand in his, painfully reminded of her frailty, and waited while she gathered her thoughts.

'I have often struggled with my conscience on this... whether I should tell you... whether I have the right to tell you,' she said, looking into his eyes with what Harry could only describe as a look of despair and sadness.

With a heavy heart, he waited.

'Henry, you are -'

The sound of the front doorbell shattered the tranquil peace, cutting Lillian short. Harry's smile faded as he glanced up at the grandfather clock, and the late hour. In the hallway, the footsteps of the carer could be heard, followed by the sound of the front door being opened, the murmur of voices, and then the door being closed, followed by more footsteps.

Harry watched the door handle of the study door, turn and then open. There in the doorway, in uniform and looking very ill at ease, stood Stephen. 'I don't believe I heard you knock, Stephen,' said Harry, in a low voice. 'You also appear to be in uniform.'

Stephen shifted from one foot to the other, appearing reluctant to enter the room, a decision that was made for him by the impatience of the man waiting behind, as he roughly brushed past and around the young constable, forcing him to step meekly to one side. The man with the sneer on his pockmarked face - who was not in uniform - introduced himself as Detective Sergeant Carson. He then, without a trace of sincerity, apologised for the lateness of the hour and wished Lillian a speedy recovery, before turning to Harry, and informing him he was being arrested for possession of drugs with intent to supply.

The stunned silence that followed seemed loud and long.

Harry just stared at Carson, a part of him wanting to believe it was a wind-up, but knowing it wasn't; he only had to look at Carson's cruel grin to see that it wasn't. He looked back towards Stephen, who was doing his best to look anywhere but in Harry and Lillian's direction. 'Stephen,' said Harry, 'is this true?' Stephen glanced at Harry, nodded his head briefly, and then dropped his gaze, shamefaced, towards his feet.

Harry - who'd barely moved since the unexpected arrival of their visitors - felt Lillian grip his hand with a fierceness and strength that belied her frailty. Her grasp had also reminded Harry of where he was - in the presence of a dying woman. His shock and surprise were quickly replaced by anger. At that moment he could quite easily have killed Carson. But that was not the place, was not the time.

Fighting to control his fury, he informed Detective Sergeant Carson that he would be allowed to put the handcuffs on him, but only outside of that room. After only a moment's hesitation, and seeing the fierce expression in Harry's eyes, Carson agreed.

Harry gently squeezed then kissed the back of Lillian's hand, before getting to his feet, to then lean over and quietly tell her it was all a big misunderstanding, promising he'd be back to finish reading the Scottish play to her. He looked into her smiling face, into the kindly eyes that were now filling with tears, and struggled to quell the fear that he was abandoning her at her time of greatest need - and that it might also be the last time he'd see her.

He kissed her on the forehead, told her he loved her, and called her mother for the first, and what was to be the last, time. He then left the house and was - eventually - arrested in the front garden.

Harry's thoughts returned to cold harsh reality. Pulling his bathrobe tighter, he took a long, hard, swallow of his barely touched whisky. He wondered what it was his mother had been about to tell him.

He would never know.

He thought about the guilt he'd carried since her death. Guilt which had, at times, weighed so heavy it threatened to overwhelm him: guilt for not being there when she needed him.

Harry's thoughts then turned to Patrick. Should he have done more? Could he have done more? Again, he would never really know.

He thought of Mollie. He thought about what she might be doing at that very moment. About the *things* she might be doing at that very moment.

He then thought about justice and injustice. About right and wrong. About righting a wrong.

He took a sip of whisky. After a moment, he reached into the pocket of his bathrobe for a disposable lighter, and with a glance at the Greek urn and a mumbled apology, followed by a promise to quit again tomorrow, he then lit the cigarette he'd been holding. He still hadn't, to that day, finished reading Macbeth. He tried to recall the storyline. He seemed to think that betrayal was one of its themes.

A decision had been made. Time to make a phone call. A phone call that would change his life.

CHAPTER 47

With the main car park full, Izzy was forced to drive around to the overspill car park at the rear of the property, much to her annoyance, because this would mean having to walk all the way back around to the front of the building, she thought, as she parked nose-in towards the shrubbery.

Steve and Izzy were cordially greeted by the maitre d', and a waitress with a tray of fluted glasses filled with champagne. Steve took one, knocked it back, and then took another. On seeing Izzy's raised eyebrows and surprised look, 'To steady the nerves,' he said, simply. Then added, 'It was a... long journey,'

First impressions of the club's main reception area were of imposing architectural grandeur. The room was large, the ceiling high, with its plaster cornice and rose both deep and intricate. The few doors leading off were wide and heavy with architrave to match, the skirting boards high and solid. Dado rail divided heavily embossed wallpaper of two different yet traditional designs; the carpet was thick and luxurious and similar in style. The value of the room's fixtures and fittings was clearly reflected in their quality.

Steve looked around the room. He noted the tall, broad shouldered men in tight fitting tuxedos, who stood impassive and expressionless before the doors that were for club members only and the wide stairway that led to the upper floors, their passive demeanour betrayed only by their shifting eyes as they monitored the non-club members: the guests of the hosting charity.

Steve and Izzy were shown through to a large function room that was filled with tables laid in preparation for the evening's meal, and adorned with party decorations, balloons and banners; the room was a hive of activity. Waiting-on staff busily scurried amongst the smartly dressed and elegantly turned out guests, some of whom were seated at their tables, some mingling and making idle chatter prior to the commencement of the eagerly anticipated meal.

CHAPTER 48

Harry negotiated the powerful sports car through the streets of London with the skill and ability of a professional driver, using the clutch and the gears to slow and to accelerate, only occasionally using the brake. The car, which he'd borrowed, was in immaculate condition, the luxury interior pristine. This was due to infrequent use and regular valeting, which, judging by the faint aroma of cleaning fluid, had been done recently. Harry wasn't surprised; it was typical - and he wouldn't have expected any less. What was also typical was the choice of radio station, which sprang to life as the ignition was turned: jazz.

Harry was enjoying himself. And he had to admit, he missed having a car. He used public transport for two reasons: one was financial, allowing him to focus all his resources on the flat conversions; the other - and probably the real reason - was to distance himself from the trappings of his former life, of which, at one time, he'd had many. Maybe once the flats are finished and things have settled down, he mused, until a thought crossed his mind: Would I be able to finish the flats? With a heavy heart, he thought back to the decision he'd made and the subsequent phone calls. *Have I made a pact with the devil?* He tried to convince himself he'd done the right thing. The only thing.

After Harry had made his telephone call, he'd gone through to his bedroom, pressing the play button on his compact music system as he passed, to hear Radio Three playing the melodic sounds of baroque music, only to stop abruptly when he caught sight of himself in the full-length mirror fixed to the wardrobes. He stood for a moment, staring.

At first, he didn't recognise the hollow-eyed man with the haunted look that stared back at him. The man with the beginnings of a beard, long, lank, matted hair, and pale skin with dark circles around the eyes. A man was who was wearing Harry's bathrobe. The man then shrugged-off the bathrobe, letting it drop to the floor, allowing Harry to see the old scars, but also the new, slowly fading and beginning to heal. He saw the tired posture of a man who was exactly what he appeared to be: a man very close to the edge, a man who was a shadow of his former self and on the brink of a breakdown. Harry was disgusted with the man. Disgusted that he'd allowed himself to become weak. Harry then asked the man what'd happened to his 'bottle', his self respect.

Harry and the man stared each other out.

Harry won.

Harry watched the man reach into a bedside cabinet, take out some electrical hair clippers, then proceed to carefully trim off his lank and matted hair, leaving a new close-cropped hairstyle. He then went into the bathroom where he meticulously shaved off the beard, before then stepping into a scalding hot shower, to wash away the dirt, the grime, and to mercilessly scrub away the guilt and self loathing. After that, he turned the temperature down to what felt like Arctic sub-zero, bringing forth chest shuddering gasps of breath, as his heart and blood circulation were kick-started into skin tingling overdrive, to complete the cleansing process.

Harry stepped out from the shower, feeling refreshed - reborn, almost.

Returning to the bedroom, he switched off the radio's soothing music, and put a CD on, an old favourite he hadn't played in a long time. He selected a track, cranked up the volume, and then with a smile, pressed play. GUNS N' ROSES, 'Welcome to the jungle', blasted out of the speakers.

Harry decided to forego his usual attire of jeans and tee-shirts for something more appropriate; more formal. He opened up the part of the wardrobe he hadn't opened for a long time. The part that held his suits. His 'work' suits. He looked over the row of cellophane wrapped garments, and then chose a black, single-breasted, lightweight two-piece. It wasn't really suitable for the time of year and weather, but he wanted something that didn't restrict his movement, his reflexes and reactions. He also chose a plain white shirt and a narrow black tie. Harry liked the funereal look. He found it ironic.

He then checked himself in the mirror: clean-shaven, hair neatly cropped close to the skull, and smartly 'suited and booted'; shoulders squared, posture straight: looking good and feeling good. He pulled on a black three-quarter length overcoat, turned the collar up against the cold, but didn't button the front. Then, after searching through a drawer of 'accessories', he pulled on a thin pair of black leather kid-gloves, and after checking his appearance once more, he left the house.

The night air was cool and the sky still clear as he made the five minute walk to the Kings Arms, striding-out with a spring in his step and a smile on his face, a vague, yet familiar feeling stirring within him, a good feeling.

The creak of the un-oiled hinges on the heavy oak-type door noisily announced his arrival when he stepped in. As he adjusted his collar and removed his gloves, he glanced around, only to have an overpowering sense of déjà vu. Other than the middle-aged bloke playing the fruit machine in the corner, the pub was exactly as it was the last time he'd been there: Barman polishing glasses, two Underground workers at the end of the bar and an elderly couple playing dominoes. Exactly the same that is, as when he'd last entered, not when he'd left: his assailants' on the floor, their girlfriends' wailing hysterical.

Strolling to the bar, he saw and sensed the looks of confusion. As he passed the elderly couple, recognition crossed the old lady's face. Smiling, she reached out and touched his arm as he passed. Harry also received and returned a nod of acknowledgement from the Underground workers.

The Barman looked up, paused, and then frowned, before recognition crossed his face, also. 'Usual?' he said to Harry, picking up a pint glass.

'No. Whisky. Equal measure of water, one ice cube.' The water was Harry's token gesture to sobriety.

'You look... different,' the Barman said, as he changed the glass and poured Harry's drink. Harry simply nodded his thanks and paid for his drink, before then asking the Barman to order him a mini-cab, as he placed the change into the charity box that was fixed to the end of the bar.

While waiting for his cab to arrive, he stood at the bar, one foot on the brass foot rail, one hand resting on the bar, the other cupping his drink, lost in thought. There had been no mention of what had happened the last time he'd been there.

When the creak of the door interrupted Harry's thoughts, he - as did the other patrons - turned to look. A wall of sound preceded the group of five young people who entered: three guys, a blonde and a brunette. They were halfway to the bar when the short guy leading the group came to an abrupt halt, causing his friends to bump into the back of him, complaining loudly as they did so. Shorty stared intently at the man standing at the bar, a confused look upon his face. Harry, whose glass had been halfway to his mouth when they'd entered, held Shorty's gaze for a moment, before then winking an eye at him and knocking back the last of his drink. He then gently placed the empty glass onto the bar top, before slowly turning to face the group, all of whom were now focused on the tall, well-dressed stranger who was slowly and carefully pulling on a pair of black leather gloves. Shorty's eyes flew wide, as his confusion disappeared as quickly as it had arrived.

As recognition and comprehension became apparent, they quietly and slowly backed-up towards the door, quickening their pace as they neared, jostling in the open doorway to be the first out.

An audible sigh of relief was to be heard, followed shortly after by the toot of mini-cab horn.

The mini-cab driver recognised both Harry and his destination address. Some years before it would seem - on Mr Solomon's instruction - Harry had intervened on behalf of the driver's employer, who was being heavily leaned-on to pay protection money to a West London gang who was trying to increase the size of its manor by encroaching on Mr Solomon's. Harry had shown them the error of their ways and the employer had been eternally grateful; he still had to pay the protection money, but to Mr Solomon, and at a more reasonable rate.

The cabbie - like most cabbies the world over - was not short of an opinion, and talked through the entire journey.

Harry just gazed out of the window, lost in thought, occasionally grunting an answer in response to a question. The cabbie, having heard that Harry no longer worked for Mr Solomon, innocently asked if they were still close. Harry again merely grunted, noncommittal.

As they pulled up outside the old man's home, the cabbie commented that Mr Solomon had been a fool to let Harry go from his employ, and an even bigger fool to replace Harry with that psycho, Cutter, before then asking Harry to pass on his regards to Mr Solomon. There was a time Harry would not have tolerated such disrespect of his now former employer, but the man's words had left him with a sense of unease - as did the word 'former'.

Harry instructed the cabbie to wait for him, before then walking up the familiar path to the old man's house, a path he'd walked up only a week previously, yet it seemed like a lifetime ago.

The front door, as usual, wasn't locked, and the hallway was dark, lit only by the overspill of light from the open study door at the far end. As he approached the light, he was met midway by a large dark shape that moved with purpose, stealth, and a snuffling wet nose.

The old man was sitting at his desk, a ledger opened, but talking on the telephone. Harry only overheard part of the conversation *'...he's an asset, and an investment...'* before the old man caught sight of him, ending the call, to then come from behind his desk and greet him warmly. He commented that Harry looked well, but he also looked... different. The old man paused, as if remembering, before then telling Harry he looked like his old self.

The old man looked different too: he looked happy. And well he might, thought Harry; he's got what he wanted. *He's got me back in his employ.*

After offering Harry a whisky - which he declined - the old man invited him to sit by the fire and to talk. Harry politely declined that too, saying he had business to take care of; maybe later. The old man acknowledged the polite prompt by opening his safe, removing a bulky leather document case, then re-locking the safe, before handing the case to Harry, who opened it up to inspect its contents: one hundred thousand pounds in bundles of fifty pound notes. That was the price for Mollie's freedom. The irony was not lost on Harry that it was also the cost of his; the old man having agreed to lend Harry the money - at a very generous interest free rate of credit - providing Harry returned to his employ.

Leaving the old man's house with the means to Mollie's freedom, Harry then instructed the cabbie to his next destination: to pick up a car.

CHAPTER 49

After what seemed to be an inordinately long period of fixed smiles, handshakes and mundane conversation, Izzy decided enough was enough, and turned on her heels to head back towards the main reception.

'Isobelle?' called Steve. 'Where are you going?' he asked, when he finally caught up with her back in the main reception area.

'Well,' she replied, 'I was going to go upstairs, where the 'business' is 'conducted', and do what any good reporter would do - and what comes naturally to most women - which is to snoop!' Seeing a look of scepticism cross Steve's face, she then added, 'And, we might see Mollie. Maybe we can talk her into leaving with us.'

'Depends how much fear she's living under. How scared she is,' said Steve.

'Do you think she knows about her father?' asked Izzy.

'Hard to say. If they have told her, and that her mother might be next, it could make their hold over her stronger. Then again, the shock could send her over the edge.' Steve looked around the reception area, taking-in the muscled tuxedos. He shook his head. 'If this club is being used as a 'front' for organised crime, then the real evidence, the solid evidence, will be away from the general public. It will be figuratively speaking - and possibly even literally - at the back.'

Izzy frowned.

Steve inclined his head, indicating for Izzy to follow.

Hooking her arm through his, they then exited the main entrance, and casually made their way around the side of the building and back towards where they were parked: at the service entrance.

Izzy and Steve entered through the service door, pausing warily as the overhead lighting flickered into life. 'Motion sensor lighting,' said Steve. 'Very clever. Very economic.'

'As in energy saving, you mean?' whispered Izzy. When Steve simply nodded, she continued, 'Are you trying to tell me we are dealing with... *green gangsters?* Fuck-a-duck! What is the world coming to,' she said, loudly.

The sudden crash and bang of metal upon metal made them both jump, until they realised it was the sound of the kitchen in full flow, no doubt preparing and cooking the food for the charity event.

Gripping Steve's elbow, Izzy said, 'I'm not sure about this, now.'

Steve turned, and seeing doubt in her eyes, said, 'It'll be fine. We just need to look like we belong. That we're meant to be here.' He gave her a reassuring smile. 'Maybe, if I drape a tea towel over my arm, I can pretend to be a waiter.'

At that, the kitchen door flew back, crashing against the wall, and a large shiny wheeled box came hurtling towards them, closely followed by a heavily perspiring kitchen porter, both of which passed Steve and Izzy at speed and without the merest glance or interest, intent on delivering the hot food up to the function room.

Izzy and Steve watched him go, and then breathed a sigh of relief.

Cautiously, they made their way along the corridor, opening doors and looking into rooms where possible. At a door marked 'Private', Steve listened closely, before gently turning the handle and pushing the door open. A light flickered on to reveal a medium sized, window-less room: an office. They quickly entered, closing the door behind them.

The room contained two desks with chairs and desktop computers, filing cabinets, shelving with various types of boxed files, and a couple of worn armchairs.

Seeing that the desk along the back wall had a computer with a large plasma screen, and that it was switched on, Steve pulled up a chair and sat down. The screen was split into individual squares - smaller frames - all showing a different image and all numbered. 'CCTV,' he said, over his shoulder, to Izzy. As he peered closer, he saw a number of images: the grounds of the club, the main entrance, the front car park, and also the overspill car park at the rear - also the service entrance, he realised, saying a silent prayer that nobody had been monitoring the computer to witness their arrival. At the bottom of the screen were two arrows, left and right, and a row of icons. Reaching for the computer's mouse, he then clicked onto the right hand arrow, which took him to a second screen of multiple images. These were of the interior ground floor, covering the club members' restaurant, the three bars, the function room where the charity event was being held, the main reception area where guests were still being greeted, and a variety of other elegant rooms. Steve moved the cursor to the image showing the main reception area, then double-clicked, enlarging the small image to full-screen. Moving the cursor down to the row of icons - one of which appeared to be for sound, another for record capability - he double clicked on the sound icon, conversation between the guests and the staff that were greeting them clearly audible.

Izzy had seated herself at the other desk. After the finding the desk drawers locked, she had turned her attention to the desk top. Other than the computer, the desk top had an empty in-tray, a telephone, and a half filled cup of cold disgusting looking coffee.

She stared at the dark screen of the computer, where she could see her outline faintly reflected. It's bound to be password protected, she thought, it hardly seems worth the effort; until she caught sight of the small red light on the bottom corner of the monitor. The power to the monitor hadn't been switched off. *Not so green after all, hey Ivan?* Then, *what's the possibility?...* She reached for the mouse, and the second she touched it, the screen sprang to life. *Yes!*

Her euphoria though, was short lived. On the screen was an Excel monetary spreadsheet. Izzy inwardly groaned, finances never had been her forte. She squinted at the screen, forcing herself to read the information in the hope of gleaning a clue, of finding some evidence.

She could feel a migraine coming on.

Steve, not seeing anything of interest or out of the ordinary on his monitor, clicked on the arrow again to reveal a third screen of images. He wondered just how many cameras they had around the property. These new images were not of the outside, nor of the ground floor, they appeared to be of the upper floors, of the corridors leading to the bedrooms and, as Steve stared hard at the screen, the bedrooms themselves!

In at least half a dozen of the bedrooms, Steve could see that the lights were on. He could also see people having, or about have, sex, and all were beautiful young women with middle to old-aged men. Peering at an individual frame, Steve could see a man lying full-length on a bed, hands clasped behind the back his head, and completely naked. He appeared to be waiting. He also appeared to be well-endowed. Steve clicked to full-screen to get a better look. Just as he did so, the emergence of a figure to the left of the frame drew his attention. The full-screen shot showed a woman emerging from what Steve assumed was an en-suite bathroom. The woman was blonde and large breasted. She was also naked. Steve stared intently as the young woman climbed onto the bed to lie next to the man, before then taking his penis in her hand and working him up to an erection. He certainly is well-endowed, thought Steve.

'Found anything?' asked Izzy, cutting through Steve's thoughts.

'Err...' stammered Steve, quickly clicking back to the previous screen, 'no. Just checking the CCTV,' he managed to say, feeling guilty and disgusted with himself. Disgusted because of his voyeurism, and guilty at his feelings of arousal. 'How about you?' he said, turning.

Izzy puffed out her cheeks. 'Not sure. I'm looking at what appears to be an Excel credit and debit spreadsheet, lots of names with corresponding payments either to or from. No indication as to the reason for those payments.'

'Is there a consistency? A pattern, if you like, to the debits and credits?' Steve asked.

'The only "pattern" I can possibly see, would be the names and the amounts. There are a lot of Anglo-Saxon sounding names, paying infrequent, yet reasonably large amounts. Thousands of pounds in some cases. Then there are a few Anglo-Saxon sounding names who receive regular yet smaller amounts. And then we have a few Russian, or Eastern European sounding names, who, it would appear, receive hundreds of thousands of pounds. What for, I have no idea.'

Steve glanced at his watch, conscious of how long they'd been there. 'Does the file have a name at the top of the screen? It should show a filename. What's the file called?'

Izzy's eyes flicked up to the top of the computer screen. She shrugged her shoulders. 'Looks like it's in Russian,' she replied.

'What about the tabs of the individual worksheets along the bottom of the screen?'

Izzy shook her head. 'The same. Russian.' At Steve's lack of response, Izzy looked up from the screen to see him deep in thought. 'You don't speak Russian, then?' she asked him.

'Nyet,' he replied after a moment, when he realised Izzy had spoken to him.

'Ho, Ho, very droll,' said Izzy, rolling her eyes. Then, 'It could be bulk orders for goods, for all we know, anything from toilet rolls to trifles.'

'Or they could be blackmail payments,' said Steve, softly.

'Blackmail? What makes you say that?' asked Izzy, suddenly curious.

'What about other files?' said Steve, keen to steer Izzy away from the subject rather than explain - or show - his reasoning. 'There must be other files on there?'

'Already tried, they're password protected.'

Steve frowned. 'All of them?' Izzy nodded. 'So how did you get into that one?'

'It was already open,' she replied. 'I guess the last user forgot to close it down.'

'That seems a bit careless,' said Steve, still frowning, his frown then deepening further as he watched Izzy take a small silver USB stick out of her purse and insert it into the computer. 'What are you doing?'

'I know a man who speaks Russian,' she replied, simply.

'But without a warrant, that's illegal,' said Steve.

'So arrest me,' she said, as she started copying the spreadsheet to the memory stick. As she moved the mouse across the desk to reposition the cursor, her hand bumped the coffee cup. She instinctively released her grip on the mouse to grasp the cup and move it to a safe distance, but as she did so, she froze, her eyes locked on to the half drunk cup of coffee.

'Steve?' she said, her voice wavering a little. 'The coffee cup!'

Steve glanced at the cup in Izzy's hand. 'It looks disgusting. Probably instant. I wouldn't drink it if I were you,' he said, with forced levity.

'It's warm,' said Izzy, her eyes still locked on.

'I still wouldn't drink it,' he said, again.

'It's *very* warm.'

Their eyes met, both realising: maybe the last user hadn't been so careless after all.

'Oh, dear,' said Izzy.

'Oh, bollocks,' said Steve.

CHAPTER 50

Harry was feeling good. He could feel a sense of excitement. He felt what he could only describe as 'alive', for the first time in years. As he turned the sports car onto the A406, he pulled the GUNS N' ROSES CD from the inside pocket of his overcoat and slipped it into the CD player. He skipped through 'Knockin' on Heaven's door' and 'Sympathy for the Devil', before finally selecting a track, cranking up the volume and then pressing the play button.

He floored the accelerator, feeling the car leap forward in response to 'Paradise City', his smile turning into a broad grin and then into a soft laugh as he hurtled along the A406

Harry pulled into the overspill car park. Seeing an available space adjacent to a Smart Car, he then reversed in - should that he need to make a quick exit. He then walked around to the front of the building, intent, on this occasion, to use the main entrance and enter the club with at least some dignity.

In the main reception he was greeted by a buzz of excitement, closely followed by the maitre d', and a waitress offering him a glass of champagne.

He declined the champagne, quietly informing the maitre d' that he wasn't there for the party, he was there to see Victor and he was expected.

The maitre d' politely invited Harry to follow him, leading him away from the party and the noisy crowd. They walked along a wide hallway, thickly carpeted and ornately decorated, past a busy restaurant; then through a bar area that hummed with conversation between its affluent male patrons, and the few young and stunningly attractive hostesses who were flitting among the club members, ensuring their needs were being met.

The maitre d' finally brought Harry to a room that had an open fire and a variety of armchairs; a quiet and comfortable room, the silence broken only by the murmurings of conversation. Harry looked around to see only a handful of patrons, all male, and all of an age and apparent distinction. This room was reserved for the rich and the connected: the elite.

Harry was led across to the far corner of the room, where two large wingback chairs were separated by a low table. In one chair was Eyepatch, a cruel smirk on his face as he watched Harry approach. In the other was Victor, who was reading the *Financial Times*, which he lowered as they neared. Victor turned to Eyepatch and inclined his head, indicating he give up his seat to Harry. Eyepatch slowly stood to his full height, in no rush, and all the while holding Harry's gaze with an amused look.

Harry figured the man standing at arm's length before him had probably got three inches in height and twenty pounds in weight over him. He returned the big man's stare, coolly, calmly, and unwavering. For a brief moment, Harry thought he saw uncertainty and doubt, until the sound of Victor's voice, issuing an order to the maitre d', broke the spell. As Eyepatch moved a discreet distance to another chair, his gaze still fixed on Harry, Harry gave him a wink of the eye, just to wind him up.

Victor invited Harry to sit.

Placing the leather case on the floor next to the vacant chair, Harry removed his gloves and coat, to then sit, just as the maitre d' returned bearing a tray. He placed a tall glass of clear liquid and ice on the table close to Victor - Harry assumed it was vodka, with Victor being Russian - followed by a shorter glass containing what looked to be whisky with a single ice cube. Harry wondered if it was a coincidence or a lucky guess. The maitre d' then handed both Victor and Harry a slim metal tube, each containing a good quality cigar.

Harry watched as Victor removed his cigar from its casing, briefly examined it to appreciate its quality, before then lighting it and puffing it into life.

'You look different,' said Victor, finally.

Harry merely shrugged, saying nothing.

Victor took another draw on his cigar, blowing smoke towards the ceiling.

Harry idly wondered whether the smoking ban included private clubs.

'These are good cigars, you should try one,' said Victor, indicating the metal tube still held within Harry's hand.

'I'm trying to cut down. I'll save it for a special occasion,' he replied, slipping it into his jacket pocket.

'Health is important,' said Victor, nodding. 'I smoke too much, I know that. It'll probably be the death of me -'

'Victor,' said Harry, quietly interrupting, 'I didn't come here for sociable conversation, and I really don't give a flying-fuck about your health, either. Where's the girl?'

Victor levelled his gaze at Harry, searched his expression, and saw only resolve. He gave a slight nod of the head in acceptance, before looking across to Eyepatch.

Harry watched the big Russian leave the room.

Victor took a sip of his drink, then replaced it on the table. After a moment he said, 'What happened the other day, in our leisure facilities, was purely business. A necessity. I'm sure a man like you can understand that?'

Harry studied the man sitting across from him. If he was remorseful, he didn't look or sound it. 'How's the refurbishment coming along?' he asked, drily.

'Slightly behind schedule. We had to get a specialised cleaning company in,' he admitted.

They sat for a moment. Not speaking. Waiting.

'What will you do with the girl?' asked Victor, conversationally.

'I think that's my business, and doesn't really concern you anymore.'

Victor smiled as he said, 'I'll be sorry to see her go. She was one of my favourites. She was... inventive. As well as being a valuable asset and investment, she -' Victor's smile slipped, to then be replaced with a frown, as he reached into his pocket to pull out a softly vibrating mobile phone. His frown deepened as he glanced at the caller ID, before placing the phone to his ear and listening intently, responding quietly, yet urgently, in Russian. While Victor took the call, Harry found his memory strings being tugged, but couldn't work out why.

When Victor ended the call and turned back, Harry could see the smile was a little too forced. The phone call had not been good news. 'Problem?' asked Harry. Whatever Victor's response was going to be, Harry didn't get to hear it, because at that moment, Mollie walked in, leaving Eyepatch waiting near the door.

All heads turned to watch the beautiful, dark haired young woman make her way across the room. Victor stood as she approached; Harry reached down for the leather case and then did likewise. As she neared, Harry could see that the photograph Patrick had given to him did not do her justice. Her hair was long, luxurious, and jet black, the colour of her eyes only a shade lighter. In the photograph, she hadn't been wearing makeup; tonight, she was. When she reached Victor, she courteously greeted him with an extended hand and a smile. Harry, studying her closely, noticed the warmth of her smile did not stretch as far as her tired eyes, nor did the heavily applied makeup completely cover the dark circles beneath.

Victor gallantly kissed the back of the young woman's hand, before introducing her to Harry. Harry extended his hand: her grip was firm but cool to the touch, her fingers delicate. Keeping his voice low, Victor explained to Mollie that Harry was her new 'benefactor', that he now held her contract of employment, that she was now his responsibility.

As Harry listened to Victor's 'spin', on Mollie's situation, he watched her face. He saw her smile falter. He saw doubt and confusion as she tried to translate Victor's words into reality. He saw Mollie look from him to Victor, then back again.

Still holding the girl's hand, Harry searched for the right words. 'I'm here on behalf of your father, Patrick,' he said, finally. At the mention of her father's name, he felt her grip tighten. He also saw her eyes widen in surprise at what he was certain was hope. Finally, uttering the words he'd silently promised to Patrick, Harry said, 'It's time to go home,

Mollie.' Mollie opened her mouth to speak, but no words came out. Her hand flew to her mouth, her eyelids fluttered, fighting emotion, failing. Harry watched a single tear track down her face.

Still smiling like the genial host, Victor turned to Harry. 'You have something for me?'

Harry handed him the leather case, which Victor tucked under his arm.

'Aren't you going to count it?' asked Harry.

Victor shook his head. 'No need.'

'Why? Because I have an honest face?' replied Harry.

Victor simply smiled. 'You'll have to excuse me, I have other business to take care of. I'm sure you can find your own way out.' With that, he walked away, Eyepatch close behind.

Harry watched Victor and his henchman leave, with a sense of suspicion, anger, and unfinished business. Turning his attention to Mollie, he found her staring up at him, her face betraying a mixture of emotions.

'I don't understand,' she said, in a soft wavering voice that revealed a faint trace of Irish lilt. 'I can go home? I mean, how? How did my father get the money? They told me he didn't have it. That I had to pay off his debt. They told me they would hurt my parents if I didn't,' she said to Harry, her big beautiful eyes filling with tears, her face creasing with anguish, her hands fluttering like small birds as she looked around, her panic building. 'Please tell me they're okay?' she asked Harry. 'My father?' Gently taking Mollie by the shoulders, Harry opened his mouth to speak. 'My mother?' she then said. Harry looked away, unable to meet her eyes, unable to find the words. 'It's my mother, isn't it? They've hurt my mother!' she said, interpreting Harry's hesitation as such. 'Please tell me they haven't hurt her?' she implored, as grief overcame her and her knees buckled.

Tightening his grip to prevent her from collapsing, Harry said, 'Your mother is safe and well. You'll see her soon. It's time to go home, Mollie.' With that, Harry scooped up his coat, and with a supportive arm around Mollie's waist, ushered her from the room, giving her no time to think or to ask questions. Now was not the time for her to hear the truth about her father.

Instead of leaving by the main entrance, and walking around to the overspill car park at the rear, Harry opted for a shortcut. Following his instinct, they made their way along carpeted hallways towards the rear of the building and the kitchen, the steady flow of waiters and kitchen porters indicating they were heading in the right direction.

They eventually came to the long corridor with the red quarry tiled floor and the white painted walls which led to the kitchen and the service entrance that Harry had entered by on his first visit. As they started along the corridor, he noticed a sign on the wall, indicating the direction to the gymnasium and the swimming pool. He struggled to suppress the memories and the anger that flared within him.

They passed a number of closed doors: the catering manager's office, the door marked 'Private', the cleaner's cupboard, the dry stores cupboard and on towards the sounds of a busy kitchen, and the exit. Harry was keen to leave the building as quickly as possible. Not just for Mollie's sake, but for the memories it held - and the fact that he didn't trust Victor.

They reached the service door. Harry pushed hard, throwing the door wide open, onto the darkened car park and the sense of imminent release, of freedom. He stepped to the side, allowing the cool evening air in, and for Mollie to exit. He started to follow, but then instinctively stopped. He hesitated for the briefest moment, before turning to look back. What he saw was what he'd seen on his first visit: a long corridor; a long, empty corridor, with an unreadable sign at the far end.

He was about to turn away, when movement caught his eye; four people passing the end of the corridor before disappearing from view. Four people who he instantly recognised: Earring, leading the way, closely followed by Stephen, then Izzy, with Eyepatch bringing up the rear. Four people heading in the direction of the gymnasium... and the swimming pool.

Harry's vision was blurred with the effort of concentration. He blinked hard, trying to focus. The corridor was empty. Had he just seen what he thought he'd seen? Or did he imagine it? With all that'd happened in the last two weeks, Harry had, on more than one occasion, found himself doubting what was real and what was not. *Why were Stephen and Izzy at the club?* Harry didn't suspect Stephen was there on official business, not dressed in a tuxedo and with a civilian in tow - and a reporter, at that. What he was sure of was that it was bound to be trouble.

A voice cut through his thoughts, drawing his attention. He turned to see an anxious looking Mollie, staring at him, her arms wrapped around her upper body to ward off the evening's chill. After removing his leather gloves and car key from his coat pockets, he then draped it over Mollie's shoulders, turning up the collar and pulling it close. 'Mollie, there's something I need to do before we can leave. It won't take long, I promise. Then I'll take you home, okay?' She responded with a tentative nod of the head, and even managed a tiny smile.

Harry pointed the electronic key fob across the car park to where he'd left the car, and then pressed a button. When a clunk was heard and the car's hazard lights had flashed on to indicate the car was unlocked, Harry gently pushed Mollie in its direction, again promising he wouldn't be long. He watched her walk across the car park and climb into the car, before turning to re-enter the club.

CHAPTER 51

Eyepatch paced back and forth, the electric stun-gun swinging in his hand, impatient. He momentarily paused to check his wristwatch in the singularly lit overhead light, before recommencing his pacing, the stun-gun now rhythmically tapping the side of his leg. Where the hell was Victor, he wondered. Until this unforeseen "business" had arisen, Eyepatch had been on a promise with Irana, one of the hostesses, and at this rate he wasn't going to make it. Victor didn't allow the hired help to fraternise with the girls unless they were prepared to pay for it, but the young Russian had never paid for sex in his entire life, and he certainly wasn't going to start now. What Victor didn't know wouldn't hurt him.

A noise from the far side of the swimming pool drew his attention. He peered into the darkness, the powerful overhead light restricting his range of vision. He called out, demanding a response from his comrade, who he'd sent to adjust the lights and tend to the dogs. The useless fat bastard has probably fallen over, he told himself, not getting an answer.

Turning his back on the gloom, he looked down at the two inert and hooded figures bound to the plastic chairs, and wondered at the Victor's constant need for dramatics.

He circled the chairs, the stun-gun twitching impatiently, as he came to a halt behind the seated figures. He looked down at the hands of the policeman. They were crossed and bound at the wrists with duct tape. He could see a reddening of the skin where the tape was biting into the policeman's exposed flesh.

Reaching out, he gently pressed the tip of the gun against Steve's wrist. He watched with sadistic pleasure as Steve's body bucked and writhed against his bonds, fighting to escape from the point of pain, his cries of protest muffled. Laughing softly, Eyepatch applied the gun a second and then a third time for good measure. Only when the convulsions had finished coursing through Steve's body, and he was slumped forward, hooded head hung low and barely conscious, only then did the Russian tire of his victim, to then move on to the next.

Looming over Izzy, Eyepatch looked down on the hood that covered her head, remembering the faint sprinkling of freckles on her clear complexion, and the big blue eyes that had stared back at him in fear and anger, as he'd taped her mouth and bound her to the chair, but not before she'd lashed out with her foot, catching him in the groin, both surprising and yet arousing him with her fighting spirit. Once each foot had been secured to a chair leg, he'd taken the opportunity to run his hands over her shapely trousered legs and up to her crotch, where his thick fingers had roughly rubbed at her through the cloth that covered her modesty, taking great delight at the look of disgust in her eyes, before then placing the hood over her pretty head. He wondered whether Victor intended to feed the female reporter to the dogs, along with the policeman: probably. It just seemed such a waste. Maybe Victor would let him fuck the bitch, first, he hoped: probably not.

As he reached over Izzy's shoulder to undo the single button that held her jacket, she flinched at his unexpected touch and the anticipation of unknown harm. The jacket fell open to reveal a cream satin camisole that shimmered in the light as her body trembled.

Eyepatch checked his watch once again, to then look up and out into the gloom, only to be greeted by the sounds of scrabbling.

Placing the stun-gun on a section of scaffolding, he returned his attention to Izzy. Carefully taking the edges of her jacket in his large hands, he gently, almost ritually, peeled it open and back to expose her shoulders, his fingers lightly tracing the line of her collarbone, marvelling at her young, flawless skin.

Izzy flinched yet again at his touch.

Eyepatch's rough hands slid down, catching the delicate fabric, to cover and then grasp Izzy's breasts. He squeezed hard, his thumbs tracking back and forth over her hardening nipples. His breath caught in his throat as he became aroused to the point where it was painful, his hardness pressing against the nape of Izzy's neck as he leaned over her. He could feel the blood coursing through him, and with it, a desperate urge that needed to be satisfied.

Izzy was terrified. She had never been so frightened in all her life. These guys weren't messing about. They were playing for real. When the huge bald man with the earrings had opened the office door, he had - after his initial surprise at finding them there - calmly taken a mobile phone from his pocket to then make a brief call. At that point, Izzy thought the worst that might happen would be that they would get roughed up a bit, before being thrown out of the club for snooping. That was until the second large bald man with the eye patch and the cruel grin had turned up. That was when Izzy knew they were in serious trouble.

Izzy was suffering from sensory deprivation. The hood over her head was thick and heavy, making it stiflingly hot and difficult to breathe, and as well as blocking out the light completely, it also muffled sound to an almost inaudible level: though not inaudible enough to block out Steve's cries of pain as they tortured him. And torture was exactly what it was. She didn't need to see it to know that. As hard as she tried, she could not block out the images of what they might do to her. At the very least, they would probably rape her, at worst, they would kill her. She just wanted to cry. The grip on her breasts was hard and bruising. She felt a sob welling up in her throat, but swallowed it down. She promised herself that if she were to survive this, she would try to be a better person: a good employee, a dutiful daughter.

Releasing his grip on Izzy's breasts, Eyepatch stepped around and in front of her, to then plant a foot either side and straddle her chair. Slowly and methodically he undid the belt to his jeans, followed by the zip, to then ease down both his jeans and underwear, allowing his penis to spring out. He was well-endowed and proud of it. He always enjoyed the look of fear and excitement on a woman's face when she saw his size for the first time, and he was particularly looking forward to seeing the reaction in the big blue eyes of this feisty young woman.

Taking his rigid cock in his right hand, he stroked himself, feeling a slight bruising from where the girl had caught him with her foot. Maybe he should make her kiss it better, he thought, with a smile. Enjoying the anticipation of what was to come, he reached out and grasped the cloth hood to remove it, but then hesitated when the thought that the bitch might bite him crossed his mind, until he remembered the stun-gun and its persuasive powers.

With his smile turning to a broad grin, confident that the gun would teach the girl some manners, he released his grip on the hood, to then turn and reach out for it.

But it wasn't there.

With his cock still in his right hand, his left arm still outstretched and with a look of confusion and bewilderment upon his face, Eyepatch stood frozen, unmoving; questioning his own sanity and memory. That was until a faint sound caught his attention, breaking the spell. The faint sound of a click. The faint sound of a repeated click. A ratchet type of sound.

As he frantically searched the gloom, trying to pinpoint the source of the sound, he felt a brief and unpleasant sensation: unpleasant because it was the sensation of fear, brief because he wouldn't have to experience it for too long.

A black tubular shape shot out of the darkness, lunging towards his head. Torn between pulling up his jeans to allow himself greater mobility and defending himself from attack, the big Russian hesitated before finally throwing his hands up to protect himself.

He hesitated too long.

He felt the tip of the stun-gun being brutally rammed up against his remaining eye, the agonizing pain from its impact becoming seemingly paltry the moment Harry pressed the button and five hundred thousand volts burnt out his cornea and part of his brain.

Izzy had felt her tormentor move from behind her to stand somewhere in front, where, she couldn't be sure, but guessed he was still close. She held her breath: body taut with tension and fear, ears straining until he suddenly moved, making body contact and causing Izzy to cry out in response.

For a heartbeat moment, nothing happened. She sensed he was facing towards her and she sensed she knew the reason why, just as she'd sensed an urgency as his large rough hands had moved over her body; she knew he was aroused.

When she heard the muffled yet unmistakable sound of a zipper, she knew what he intended to do, and she felt sick to her stomach at the thought of it. She felt a hand on the cloth that covered her head. She braced herself for what was about to happen, unsure what to do. Should she fight? Should she comply? She had to survive.

She felt sick.

But then something happened. She sensed a change. The hood stayed on and her tormentor's hand moved away. He was completely still. Unmoving. If his legs had not been making bodily contact, she would not have known he was there. Then, as she heard what sounded like a muffled cry of pain, she felt the man standing before her violently move, stumbling as though in a hurry, body contact completely broken.

Silence.

She sat still, straining to hear. Waiting.

Nothing.

Was this a trick, she wondered. Had he gone away? Was this just another way to torment her? She couldn't hear a thing. She couldn't sense anything - or anyone. She wondered how Steve was and if he was okay. She had the awful feeling they'd killed him. She felt a huge wave of remorse. She felt responsible for involving him in this foolish and now fatal escapade.

She felt a pair of hands touch hers. She gasped. She heard a faint 'snick', sound. She went rigid with fear.

He'd come back.

Yet the touch felt different, as the tape that bound her wrists was being cut. It felt gentle, almost caring. She then felt the same gentle hands carefully cutting through the tape that bound her ankles.

Her bonds had been cut. She was free.

Or was she?

She held her breath, her body still taut with tension.

And still she waited.

In one quick and fluid movement, the cloth hood was whipped off, the overhead light suddenly blindingly bright, forcing her to clamp her eyes tightly shut. Just as she did so, the 'gentle' hands ripped off the tape that covered her mouth, causing her to squeal in pain and raise her hands instinctively towards her face, using them, now in absence of the hood, to shield her eyes. She blinked rapidly, eyes stinging with tears, unable to focus on the dark shadow that towered over her, before it moved to crouch over another figure, slumped on a chair a few feet away: Steve.

She saw the crouching figure release Steve from his bonds, saw it check on his physical condition, and then - with their heads close, their foreheads almost touching -talk to Steve in a low and compassionate tone - to which she was sure she heard Steve respond - before standing and turning back to her.

Izzy was still sitting and still squinting through spread fingers, as the back-lit shadowy figure moved towards her. Something tugged at her memory. Something seemed familiar.

She tentatively rose, taking a hesitant step backwards, unsure. From a standing position she found the angle and intensity of the overhead light eased considerably, and her vision start to return.

The tall shadowy figure started to take form. It was a man with close cropped hair, and who appeared to be smartly dressed. She still couldn't quite make out the facial features. She watched him take another step towards her. Instead of retreating, she stood her ground, frowning as she did so and blinking hard, trying to focus.

Something familiar... confident... swagger...

Izzy could see facial features starting to become clear. The first was a lazy grin. A big lazy grin. 'Oh-me-God!' she exclaimed, her hands flying to her mouth, her eyes going wide, beginning to fill with tears. 'Harry? Is that you?'

'In the flesh,' he said.

Without warning, Izzy threw herself at him, locking her arms tightly around his neck, and then burying her face deep into his shoulder.

Harry felt her body heave under the muffled sobs. He felt the tears of relief on his neck. He wrapped his arms tightly around her. She felt good. 'Missed me?' he said, quietly into her ear.

Izzy's response was a muffled, 'Fuck, yeah!'

After a moment, she stepped back, self-conscious, wiping away her tears with the back of her hand, smearing her mascara. Her vision fully restored, she looked Harry up and down, taking in the well fitting suit and the new haircut - and the leather gloves. 'You look... *hot!* ...different,' she said, finally.

'It has been said,' he replied.

'You look... like Jason Statham.'

Both Harry's eyebrows shot up. 'I think I can live with that,' he said.

A polite cough caught their attention. Steve was now standing, but leaning heavily on the back of his chair for support. Seeing him, Izzy hurried over to embrace him in a concerned, sisterly-type hug.

'How are you feeling?' said Harry to Steve, joining them.

'A little unsteady,' replied an ashen looking Steve. 'What did they do to me?'

'Electric stun-gun,' replied Harry. 'You were lucky. They had it on a low setting. They were only toying with you. They were probably saving you for the final act. The grand finale.'

'Which would be what?' asked Steve, with a look of puzzlement.

With half a glance over his shoulder in the direction of the swimming pool, Harry replied, 'Feeding time.'

Izzy started to speak, 'Feeding -'

'You both have to leave, and you have to leave now,' interrupted Harry. 'All the players aren't here yet, and the final act has yet to be performed. It's better if neither of you are here when it is.' Harry looked into their faces. He saw doubt and he saw resistance. Turning to Steve, he said, 'You're not here in an official capacity, are you? You haven't got a warrant, have you, Steve?'

Steve shook his head, reluctantly. 'No. We're here unofficially. It was my idea,' he said, briefly flicking a glance at Izzy before carrying on. 'The funny thing is though, Harry, neither of us is carrying ID, just in case we did get caught, yet they seemed to know who we were.'

There was no doubt in Harry's mind as to whose idea it had been to visit the club, but now was not the time for blame. 'There's a lot going on here. A lot has already gone on. And there's more yet to happen. Believe me, you do not want to get involved. This could ruin your careers. You're best off out of it. I'll deal with this. I've got nothing to lose.'

When Izzy opened her mouth to protest, Harry shook his head. Both Steve and Izzy could see that Harry's mind was made up.

'I want you both to leave, and I want you to leave now,' he continued. Then, to their surprise, 'Mollie's waiting in the overspill car park. Take her home.' Turning to Steve, 'She doesn't know about her father, yet.'

Steve nodded, understanding and accepting.

Harry then reached behind and under his jacket to the small of his back, to withdraw a cream clutch purse from the waistband of his trousers. Passing it to Izzy, he said, 'I'm guessing this is yours. I got it off a fat bloke with a Russian accent.'

Izzy quickly dug into it, before triumphantly bringing out the memory stick which she then held aloft. 'Evidence!' Then, seeing the look on Steve's face, she added, 'Okay, I'll send it in as an anonymous tip-off.' Steve nodded. 'Oh,' she then said, remembering. 'I did a Land Registry Search on this club before we came here. I know who owns it,' she told them, looking at Harry, while avoiding Steve's curious gaze, whom she'd 'neglected' to tell. Harry looked back, waiting. 'Henry Solomon,' she said, and when Harry simply nodded, 'You knew?' was her response.

'Let's say, I'm not surprised.'

'Oh,' said Izzy, again, having another thought. 'I'm driving a Smart Car.' When both Steve and Harry looked at her blankly, she continued, 'It's a two-seater.'

'Black and red?' asked Harry. When Izzy nodded, surprised, Harry said, 'We'll swap. You take mine. Mollie's already sitting in it.'

'You've got a car?' said Steve, a little surprised. 'I thought you'd given up on those kinds of trappings?'

'Err, sort of,' said Harry, while searching his pocket for the car key, before then holding it out towards Steve.

Izzy handed Harry the key to her hired Smart Car, and then reached to take the other key from Harry's hand. 'I think, under the circumstances,' she said, looking at Steve, who still leaning on the back of the chair, 'it would be better if I were to drive.'

'Noo!' said Steve, shooting out a hand with surprising speed, to then snatch the key from Harry. 'I'm sure I'll be fine.'

'Actually,' said Harry, 'I think Steve might be more comfortable with this vehicle than you, Izzy.'

Izzy, who was clearly disgruntled, pouted - purely for effect - and then said, 'How will we recognise your car?'

'Well, it's parked next to your Smart Car, and, hopefully, Mollie's still sitting in it.' Casting a sidelong glance in Steve's direction, he then added, 'I wouldn't worry though, you won't have a problem recognising it.'

'Harry?' said Steve, staring with a look of puzzlement at the key within his hand. 'This key?'

'Yes, Steve?' replied Harry, blankly.

'It looks like mine.'

'Yes, Steve.'

'The key to my Mercedes.'

'Yes, Steve.'

'My top-of-the-range Mercedes convertible sports car, which is my pride and joy, and a very rarely driven - except for special occasions.'

'Yes, Steve.'

'You went to my house and stole my car?' said Steve.

'Borrowed. And it's a very nice drive, too,' replied Harry, struggling to suppress a grin.

'How did you get past my state-of-the-art alarm system to get the key?'

'Ah, yes,' said Harry, looking suitably embarrassed as he gripped both Steve and Izzy's arms, gently ushering them towards the exit. 'You may have to get someone to take a look at that. I'm more than happy to pay for the damage.' As Steve opened his mouth to protest, Harry pulled up short. Still gripping Steve's upper arm, and now with serious expression upon his face, Harry said, 'Steve, when this is all over, we need to talk. There are things you need to know about... family stuff.' Steve studied Harry's face. Seeing the seriousness, he simply nodded in acknowledgement. 'Now, you really do need to get out of here,' said Harry, pushing them away.

Steve turned to leave.

Izzy hesitated.

'Harry,' she said, looking up at him, 'can *we* meet up after this is over? Maybe have a drink? Get something to eat?'

Harry looked down, to see hope in her big blue eyes. She really was an attractive and vivacious young woman. 'Yeah, that'd be good. I'd like that,' he said, with an affectionate smile, watching her face light up in response. 'Maybe go to that pub opposite your place again?' Izzy nodded enthusiastically. 'Then maybe get a Donner kebab... with chilli sauce, garlic sauce... oh, and not forgetting the sliced gherkin.' Harry watched her look of delight change to mild confusion, then recollection, and then finally to realisation, her eyes flying wide, her mouth dropping open. With that, Harry gave her his big lazy grin and a wink of the eye, before turning to disappear into the gloom.

Izzy watched Harry disappear into the shadows. She was, for once in her life, speechless. Had Harry just said what she thought he'd said? Did it mean what she thought it meant? She suddenly felt giddy with excitement, like a lovestruck teenager. She almost giggled, if it hadn't been for Steve turning back to grab her arm and drag her away in the opposite direction.

Harry heard them moving off, away towards the exit to the car park, and safety. He then remembered he'd left his GUNS N' ROSES, CD in the car's player - with the volume still set at full blast.

He smiled.

He heard a muffled curse as Izzy and Steve almost fell over Eyepatch's unconscious body.

'Holy shit!'

Probably Izzy, thought Harry.

'HOLY SHIT! Is that real? This guy must be deformed!'

Definitely Izzy, thought Harry, his smile broadening.

CHAPTER 52

Victor was in a good mood. In fact he was in an exceptionally good mood, and with some impending "business" to take care of, that mood was likely to improve even more. The reason for Victor's good mood was an unexpected encounter he'd just had with one of the club's members, an opinionated and garrulous old fool who - having spent quite some time in the Private Members' bar - had seen fit to tell Victor how to run his own club. The club member, who was also a Sitting Member of Parliament, had expressed his "disquiet" over the "unsettling presence" of Victor's "body guards".

Being the silent partner of the club had been a good investment for Victor in that it was a healthy and legitimate business. Its greatest value, however, was in how he used it to legitimise his other businesses - namely, laundering their proceeds. This was the only reason he tolerated the buffoons and idiots who used the club, that and the fact that some of them occasionally became useful, even profitable, as the offended club member had just discovered.

Aware that other club members were watching on, Victor had given the offended member a fixed smile, apologised profusely on behalf of his men, and promised to address the matter. He'd then invited the offended member to his private study for a glass of port, which the member had quickly and greedily accepted.

Victor had been the genial host. He'd poured the man a glass of good quality port, and then told him he had something he might find of interest. With that, he'd turned a television on and then slipped a DVD into its player. The offended member had looked on with curiosity, to then almost choke on his port when images of himself and two of the club's hostesses appeared on the screen. There could be no disputing the hostesses were ensuring the club member's 'needs' were being 'met', but what they were offering was not canapés and champagne, but a service of a far more intimate nature: a service that pushed the boundaries of decency, could be questionable in the eyes of the law, and was likely to be wholly unacceptable to the club member's family, colleagues and constituents.

Victor had watched the old fool visibly pale, seen perspiration break out on the man's forehead and then watched his breathing becoming more laboured as the panic had set in. He'd been saving this particular club member for a rainy day, but never mind - it'd been worth it.

Victor had informed the Right Honourable Member he could keep the DVD; he had plenty more. He'd also told the Right Honourable Member, that he would be in touch to discuss a donation towards the restoration fund for the swimming pool, and, as one of his constituents, he also had some questions on the government's policies for border control and immigration that he might like to put to the House for debate. With that, Victor had told the club member to help himself to more port if he wished, then left to attend to other business, reminding himself to send one of his men back to check the old fool hadn't died of a heart attack. He also hoped his men hadn't grown impatient and started attending to "business" without him.

As soon as the Victor went through the door that led to the swimming pool, he knew something was wrong. There was a noise - a noise which grew louder as he approached the pool. The noise was the sound of fighting.

He passed through the circle of light, past the two inert and hooded figures bound to the plastic chairs, to then stop at the edge of the pool.

He looked down at the source of the noise to see that both dogs had been released from their tethers and were now attacking each other. For a moment, Victor watched with rapt attention, both fascinated by the dogs' pure viciousness and ability to ignore pain as they ripped at each other, yet angered that his two prized and very expensive fighting dogs had somehow got free, and that neither of his men where anywhere to be seen.

He looked up and out into the darkness, straining to see into the furthest corners of the large room, to impatiently call out the names of his men. Other than the dogs fighting, the only other sound he heard was the echo of his own voice.

Turning, he took a few steps back towards the prisoners and repeat the process in the opposite direction - to look and to call out.

Nothing.

Jacket tails pushed back by both hands on hips and cursing loudly in Russian, Victor took another step forward, stopping suddenly at the feel of something underfoot. Something soft and wet, and yet something that felt like it had crunched.

He reached down to pick up the small object, an object slightly smaller than the palm of his hand in which it now lay. He held it up to the light to study it. It was dark, wet and sticky, made darker still by the artificial lighting. Victor's first thought was that it was autumn leaf mulch, brought in on the boots of the building contractors, until the light caught on something embedded within the mulch. He peered closer at what appeared to be a small speck of glass. A small speck of glass attached to a tiny stick of yellow metal.

It was a diamond studded earring... and it was still attached to its owner's ear.

Victor instinctively looked down to where he'd found it. A few inches away, lay another. His eyes then followed the trail of dark viscous spots that grew in size and number, to become one large pool beneath and around the chair of one of the prisoners.

Victor quickly looked up and around, checking.

Nothing.

Then, with the severed ear still sitting in his palm, he took a step forward to reach out and slowly draw the hood from the prisoner. What he saw sitting before him, was one of his men, Duct tape across his mouth, eyes partially closed and glazed, raw, ragged flesh, slowly weeping and congealing blood where his ears had once been; semiconscious. Victor tossed the severed ear onto the floor, then used the cloth hood to carefully wipe the blood from his hand, before dropping it into the lap of the bleeding man and turning to the second hooded prisoner, his expression resigned and accepting: knowing.

Through his life, Victor had seen and dealt enough pain and misery to the human body, to make him - or so he thought

- immune, but his breath caught in his throat at what he saw. The man who stared back at him was not the man he once knew. He was not the strong, ruthless and faithful lieutenant who had served him so well in recent years. The man sitting before him was a husk, a shell, a zombie. The eye that stared back at him was the eye of a monster. The skin around the socket was blistered and burnt, the white of the eye a deep crimson red from burst blood vessels and capillaries, the centre now opaque. The eye was staring, but unseeing. The young Russian's mouth was agape, saliva trickling from its corner, mucus from his nose. He was conscious but unaware.

For the briefest of moments, Victor surprised himself by feeling a sense of sadness, but just as he started to analyse why he should feel that way, his sense of smell set off the alarm bells to his highly tuned survival instinct.

His head snapped up, eyes quickly scanning. At the same time he took a step back, slipped a hand inside his jacket, to then pull out an automatic handgun. He sniffed the air. He could smell smoke. Cigar smoke. A good quality cigar smoke. 'Harry?' he called out. 'Harry?' He paused, waiting. 'I know it's you, Harry.' Victor's head moved slowly from side to side, eyes narrowed, looking for movement, ears straining to hear over the noise of the dogs that were still fighting in the pool behind him. 'They warned me about you, Harry. They told me to be careful, and not to underestimate you.'

He waited, his breathing seeming loud in his ears, until he heard a noise over to his left, his head turning quickly, his grip tightening on the gun. He looked, and he listened. Still nothing.

Starting to feel uneasy, he turned back to face front, only to see Harry standing behind his two men, relaxed, at ease, and with the twitch of an amused smile on his face. In one leather gloved hand, he held the stun-gun, in the other, a smouldering cigar.

Surprised, Victor visibly flinched, then silently cursed himself for showing fear, knowing that Harry had seen it.

'Hello, Victor,' said Harry, his smile broadening at Victor's reaction while taking a small step forward, to then watch Victor take a small step back.

'Why are you here, Harry?' said Victor, eyes narrowed. 'Did you forget something?' he added, sarcastically. Harry returned Victor's stare, while savouring the cigar. 'We had a deal, Harry. What happened? You come to take your money back?' he asked, arms wide, gun still in hand. 'I thought you had honour, Harry? I thought you followed the villain's code?'

'I do, Victor,' replied Harry, peering closely at Eyepatch and Earring with morbid curiosity. 'I also have principles. You don't hurt women or involve family,' he said, as he inspected the end of the stun-gun while taking another casual step forward, matched again by Victor's casual step backward. 'I also don't like people taking liberties,' he added, as he touched the tip of the gun against the side of Eyepatch's face.

Both Harry and Victor looked on as the big Russian's body shuddered while the gun's charge surged through him, eliciting no response other than an increased flow of mucus and saliva on the man's blank features.

Looking a little disappointed at his victim's lack of reaction, Harry turned his attention back to Victor.

'Careful, Harry,' said Victor.

With weariness in his voice, Harry said, 'Maybe I'm getting soft in my old age. Maybe it is time for a change.' For a moment, Harry was lost in thought, staring at Victor, but not really seeing him, gently drawing on the cigar. Then his eyes blinked, refocused, back to the present. 'Maybe it's time for some debts to be repaid. To be honoured... Vengeance to be taken, justice to be meted out,' he said, taking a longer step forward.

Victor raised his gun to point at Harry's midriff. 'This is not how it was supposed to happen, Harry,' said Victor, shaking his head with regret.

'Nice cigar, by the way,' said Harry.

'I thought you said you were saving it for a special occasion,' responded Victor, automatically.

'I have,' replied Harry, with a broad smile that reached up to his eyes.

'Drop the stun-gun, Harry,' said Victor, features hardening, grip tightening on his own gun.

With a look, and a shrug of indifference, Harry tossed the electric stun-gun away, for it to disappear into the darkness with a clatter. 'Not really my style, anyway,' he said to Victor, while watching him carefully.

'Don't get any ideas, Harry. I will shoot you. You know that.'

Harry gave another shrug. The stakes had changed. The balance of power had shifted. Despite Victor holding the gun, Harry had now become the predator, Victor the prey: and they both knew it. But Harry knew the outcome was going to depend on who had more 'bottle'.

'I hear you are a good boxer, Harry. A very good boxer.' Then, with a less than confident smile, 'Can you out-box a bullet, Harry? Are you that good?'

Harry estimated the distance between him and Victor was about two metres.

'Distance is too great, Harry,' said Victor, as if reading Harry's mind. 'Judging by your height, I'd say you have a long reach. But not long enough,' he added, his smile growing in confidence.

'You seem to know a lot about me, Victor.'

'"Know your enemy", isn't that what they say, Harry?'

'"Know thy self, know thy enemy. A thousand battles, a thousand victories". Sun Tzu, an ancient Chinese military general, strategist and philosopher, believed to be the author of *The Art of War*.'

'I'm impressed,' said Victor. 'They didn't tell me you were intelligent as well as dangerous.'

Harry shrugged. 'I read a lot.' Then, 'Who's "they", Victor? You keep saying, "they".'

With a knowing smile and a gentle shake of his head, Victor slipped his freehand into his jacket pocket, to then pull out a packet of cigarettes. Harry watched carefully as the Russian gangster deftly flipped the top, shook one loose, to then raise the packet to his lips and draw it free. He then returned the packet to his pocket, at the same time taking out an expensive Zippo-type lighter, which he struck once, twice, three times, but to no avail. Gripping the cigarette between middle and forefinger, he removed it from his mouth and waved it at Harry, shaking his head more vigorously.

'Nyet! No! Go home, Harry, while you still can. While you're still able,' replied Victor.

Harry's head dropped, his shoulders slumped, expression resigned. 'This battle may be won, Victor, but the war is not yet over,' said Harry.

Victor waved a hand dismissively, replaced the cigarette back into his mouth, and again struck the lighter. Still to no avail.

Harry looked up, watched Victor grow more frustrated before angrily tossing the lighter into the darkness.

Harry checked his own cigar was still alight, before extending his arm and offering it to Victor, taking a step forward as he did so, only for Victor to jerk his gun back up, barrel steady.

Harry stopped dead mid stride, upper body leaning slightly forward. Victor and Harry held each other's gaze.

Seconds passed, the tension high.

When the shot didn't come, Harry slowly straightened. Then, equally slowly, reached into his own jacket pocket, to withdraw a cheap gas lighter which he then showed to Victor.

Victor nodded, twitching his fingers impatiently, indicating Harry throw it over to him. 'Gently, Harry,' he warned, cigarette dangling from the corner of his mouth.

Harry still had one leg forward of the other, but, instead of stepping back, he gently eased his weight from his front foot to his back foot, while still holding Victor's gaze, before turning his attention to the lighter, flicking it into life a couple of times, as if checking it still worked. 'There's an ancient Italian fighter I know of, who also is considered an expert tactician - at least that's what he tells me. Unlike me, however, he's not an exponent of "girly boxing",' said Harry, switching his attention back to Victor.

With a heavy and irritable sigh, Victor asked the question that was expected of him. 'And what exactly, is "girly boxing"?'

Harry gave him a small knowing smile as he raised the lighter, indicating he was about to throw it, while tensing his trailing leg at the same time. 'I was hoping you'd ask me that. It's what you could call a style of fighting,' he replied, as he gently threw the lighter towards Victor.

Victor watched the lighter sail through the air towards him, his free hand reaching out to catch it.

As Harry started to push down, preparing to shift his balance, he said, 'It's a style of fighting that can out-box a bullet, Victor...'

The lighter flew a little high and a little to Victor's right, forcing him to stretch to catch it. As he did so, he realised he'd been tricked.

Harry watched the Russian reach for the lighter, his body turning slightly as he did so, the gun moving away. Executing a skip-in sidekick, Harry launched himself forward, covering the intervening distance in a fraction of a second, his knee snapping up to waist height, before then shooting his leg out horizontally, his foot slamming into the centre of Victor's chest.

The momentum lifted Victor off his feet and propelled him backwards, towards the swimming pool, at the same time as the gun went off, the bullet displacing the air close to Harry's head, the deafening explosion echoing around the room, briefly silencing the fighting dogs, and leaving an agonisingly painful ringing sound in Harry's ears.

The two dogs - though bloodied and weary from fighting each other - were on Victor in seconds, dragging him around the pool like a rag doll, quickly shredding cloth and exposing soft skin, to then rip chunks of flesh from his body.

Harry stood by the edge of the pool, looking down dispassionately, immune to the inhuman howls of pain. 'Purely business, Victor, purely business,' he said, quietly. Then, as an afterthought and with considerably less eloquence, 'Oh, and fuck you too, Victor. I guess smoking did kill you in the end after all,' he said, tossing the cigar in after him.

CHAPTER 53

Harry walked the familiar path for the second time that evening. As usual the front door wasn't locked. Unusually though, it wasn't closed either, but slightly ajar. Harry slipped into the darkened hallway, easing the door shut, to then stand and listen. There was the overspill of light at the far end of the hall, and other than the faint trace of murmured conversation, the house was quiet - and there was no sign of the dog.

A dark figure stood hunched over the freestanding safe, his back to the study door. A figure whose hands frantically scrabbled and clawed at the safe's locked door, angrily cursing and swearing, yet in hushed reverent tones, subconsciously respectful of the peace and tranquillity of the room, the gentle tick of the grandfather clock, the crackle of the embers in the fire... the faint wheeze of laboured breath.

A coloured spectrum of yellow, black, and purple bruising surrounded Cutter's glassy eyed stare, maniacal in his efforts. A film of sweat coated his forehead, to periodically trickle down his swollen, yet slowly healing, broken nose. In his hands - one with surgical tape and splints holding broken fingers, the other, bloodied and crudely bandaged with a quality silk neckerchief - was a large, old-fashioned, wood handled, slot-headed screwdriver, which he'd found on the premises. He was attempting to insert the flat blade of the screwdriver into the narrow gap between the metal door and frame, but the blade was slightly too thick. Cutter's frustration increased as he struggled time and time again to get purchase, but time and time again the screwdriver would suddenly and violently slip, veering off to gouge yet another groove into the painted metal surface, sending Cutter off balance and angering him even further.

Solomon was still behind his desk, still in his chair, not by choice but bound by tape. His mouth and nose had been bloodied by Cutter's fist, waistcoat and shirt, ripped apart with no regard for decency or quality of cloth, white cotton vest sliced clean down the front by Cutter's sheaf knife, now laid upon the antique desk and also bloodied - though not by Solomon or Cutter. Livid red, blistered burn marks, interspersed with blobs of molten candle wax, contrasted with the pallor of the old man's parchment-like skin, the instruments of his suffering lying not too far away. A large ornate candle lay on its side upon the desk top, it's flame burning vertically upwards, spreading a pool of molten wax. A fire hearth poker protruded from the embers of the fire, it's tip a glowing red.

The big German Shepherd dog lay near the open doorway, it's eyes heavy, appearing to be close to sleep, which it was, the pool of blood that spread from beneath its body slowly growing.

'I will get what I deserve, old man, even if I have torture you to death, you old fucker,' said Cutter, as he rammed the tip of the screwdriver once again into the safe, and wrenched back hard. 'You owe me. I did the shit jobs. I cleaned up after you. I did the work your bastard son wouldn't do,' he said, jerking on the old screwdriver, only for the wood handle to split in half, and the exposed pointed metal tang to dig deep into the bite wound on his injured hand. 'What has Harry got that I don't?' he screamed in agony, throwing the split wood to one side, tone no longer hushed or reverent.

'It's time to move on. Henry's come back. Come home,' said Solomon, between laboured breaths. 'And you've become a liability.'

'I want what's coming to me! I want what's due!' raged Cutter, lashing out with his foot, to kick at the steel door again and again. 'Where's the fuckin' key, old man?'

The safe, like its owner, was old and made to last. It wasn't giving up its contents to brute force, any more than the strength of will that burned in the old man's eyes could be dampened. Solomon weakly shook his head, saying, 'Whatever you do, Harry will avenge me. Family always sticks together.'

'Does Harry know the truth? All of it? Does he know you betrayed him?' asked Cutter. 'Does he know you framed him? If he did, he'd kill you himself,' he said. 'You showed him no respect. No honour. You know Harry lives by the old code. Personally, I think Harry Windsor is a wanker, but I got respect for him.'

'Harry sees the big picture,' said the old man, gently nodding his head. 'Family is everything. Harry will understand...'

Solomon's voice tailed off, and Cutter froze as a faint noise reached both their ears, a faint noise that sounded like the whine of an animal: the whine of a dog - the whine of a dog pleased to see someone.

Cutter - whose back was still to the study door - was rooted to the spot, his body taut like a coiled spring, feeling vulnerable, his mind racing, his senses heightened.

He sensed danger.

He listened. He listened hard, ears desperately straining for the slightest sound. But all he heard was the gentle tick of the grandfather clock, the crackle of the embers in the fire, and the faint wheeze of laboured breath.

His eyes flicked to the left. He saw Solomon, still bound to his chair, looking towards the study door, a smile upon his face. On the desk in front of the old man lay his sheaf knife. In the fire, the poker was glowing red. Both were out of arm's reach.

Breathing in deeply, Cutter tightened his grip on the broken screwdriver, body tensing. *Surprise is the key!*

From his crouched position over the safe, he started to quickly turn, rise, and then launch himself at the approaching danger all in one fluid movement, breath exploding from his body as he did so, while whipping the screwdriver up and over his head, to then bring it slashing downwards.

A faint 'snick', sound was heard.

As Cutter turned and leapt, screwdriver swinging in an arc towards his silent and unknown attacker, he realised he'd made a mistake. He'd misjudged. He'd misjudged his own timing and that of his attacker, who'd already crossed the room and was almost upon him.

Cutter's momentum came to an abrupt halt, like hitting a wall. A wall named Harry.

He dropped the screwdriver.

Harry had read Cutter's body language. He'd seen him tense up, preparing to attack. So Harry had attacked first, timing and delivering his blow with maximum effect, his fist slamming into Cutter's oncoming body, into his chest, driving the breath from his lungs and leave him gasping for air. As his knees buckled and he began to sag, Harry's free hand gripped him by the back of the neck, drawing him in close to support his weight, intimate like a lover's embrace, his ragged and desperate breath loud in Harry's ear.

The pain to Cutter's chest was excruciating. The power of Harry's punch, combined with his own forward momentum, had left him breathless and weak. The bruising felt like it stretched deep inside his chest, every fought-for breath causing a stab of pain. 'Harry, you're a wanker and you punch like a girl,' gasped Cutter, as he struggled to stand.

'Knock-knock-knockin' on heaven's door,' sang Harry, quietly into Cutter's ear. 'I always preferred the Bob Dylan version myself. How about you?' he asked.

Cutter feebly attempted to break free from Harry's embrace, but seemed unable. He looked down to see that Harry's gloved fist was still pressed up against his chest, and, bizarrely, it felt like he was anchored to it.

'Wayne, you finally got what you deserve. What was coming to you. And it's certainly been long overdue,' said Harry, uncurling his fist, to then take a step back.

Cutter stood, swaying, still unsteady on his feet. He looked down at where Harry's fist had been only seconds before. He frowned in puzzlement and confusion, struggling to comprehend. He tentatively reached up to touch the bone handle that appeared to be horizontally glued to his chest, jolts of excruciating pain shooting through his body as he did so. He looked up at Harry with disbelief on his face, finally realising. 'You fuckin' stabbed me!' he gasped. Harry stared back, expressionless. 'You fuckin' stabbed me... with a fuckin' knife!' he said, again, shaking his head in bewilderment. 'You don't use knives!'

Harry shrugged. 'Guess I've fallen in with the wrong crowd,' he said, simply.

With that, Cutter's legs gave way and he crumpled to the floor, slumping backwards to end up leaning against the door of the safe. Looking down at the flick knife embedded in his chest, he again shook his head in disbelief, before then looking over at Solomon, who gazed smugly back. Turning back to Harry, he said, 'Don't trust that old fucker, Harry, he'll do you over. He set you up, Harry. One of his bent coppers planted the drugs in your car. That old fucker,' Cutter tried to raise his hand and point at Solomon, but didn't have the strength, 'is the reason you got banged up, Harry.'

'I heard,' replied Harry, looking over towards the old man, who smiled back benignly.

'He also ordered the hit on the big Irishman, and tried to frame you for that too,' said Cutter, his voice getting weaker.

'No, Cutter,' replied Harry, a darkness crossing his face. 'That was you, and only you.'

'No,' he whispered, his chin now resting on his chest, his eyes closed. 'It's in there... all of it... the truth,' he finally managed to say, the slightest twitch of the head, indicating the safe.

Cutter fell silent.

Harry looked down at Cutter's body for a long thoughtful moment. When he returned his attention back to Solomon, he found the old man watching him carefully, the smile gone, uncertainty in his eyes. Harry studied the old man before then saying, 'What's in the safe?'

The old man noisily cleared his throat before answering. 'Henry... Harry, you know Cutter cannot be trusted. He's a compulsive liar and would say anything to save his own skin,' said the old man, softly, reassuringly. 'He's not like you, Harry. He has no loyalty to anyone other than himself.'

Harry approached the old man, and the nearby fireplace, to stand and gaze down into the dying embers of the fire. 'So, you didn't set me up, then? It wasn't because of you that I got banged up?' he said, over his shoulder. 'Cutter did say I should "look closer to home". I thought he was referring to Stephen.'

'Harry, would you be so kind as to cut me free, please? These bonds are quite uncomfortable, and I really could do with a strong drink,' said Henry Solomon, with a strained smile.

But instead of releasing the old man, Harry reached down to extract the poker from the hot embers. Straightening, he then studied its glowing red-hot tip. 'What's in the safe?' he asked again. When Solomon didn't answer, Harry turned. The old man still looked uncertain, his eyes questioning, waiting.

Harry replaced the cooling poker back onto the hook of its companion set. He then reached across the desk, not for Cutter's knife, but for the roll of the remaining tape. He picked it up, snuffing out the burning candle as he did so, and then moved away.

'Harry?' said Solomon, puzzled.

Harry removed the neckerchief that bound Cutter's hand, before then approaching the injured dog. He quickly located the single knife wound, high up on the dog's chest, delivered by Cutter, as the dog had leapt up in defence of his master.

Wadding the piece of cloth, Harry then pressed it against the animal's wound, using the tape to tightly bind it into place to and staunch the flow of blood, all the while talking to the dog in a low reassuring tone.

From his chair, the old man scrutinised Harry's every move, to then give a sharp intake of breath when he saw Harry part the animal's thick long coat and withdraw a shiny silver key that had been clipped to the dog's collar.

As Harry approached the safe, the old man said, 'How did you know?'

'As you said yourself, other than you, I'm the only other person the dog ever trusted, and I've petted him often enough over the years to have discovered your secret key long ago,' replied Harry.

With the toe of his shoe, Harry pushed Cutter's dead body to one side, to then kneel, unlock and open the safe, revealing its contents. For a moment, Harry was like a statue, unmoving, staring into the safe. Solomon watched and waited, the look of uncertainty now replaced with the look of fear.

Harry reached into the safe. The first item he removed was a black leather case. A quick check of its contents confirmed what Harry had expected: bundles of fifty pound notes, yet considerably less than there had been earlier in the evening. If Harry had to make an educated guess, he figured about eighty thousand less.

At this discovery, Harry's shoulders slumped, his face taking on a look of reluctant resignation.

The old man looked on, barely daring to breathe.

Harry placed the leather case on top of the safe, to then continue his search. He withdrew a handful of papers. He flicked through a few, not really sure what he was looking for, and now, if he were honest, not really caring. Two items caught his eye: an official document, and a small notebook. The document was a lease, the name on it interested him enough to slip it in to his inside jacket pocket; the notebook was filled with names and what appeared to be payments. Harry recognised a few of the names as past and present members of the Queen's Constabulary. The presence of one name, a not so long ago promoted D.S., brought a satisfied smile to his face. The absence of another pleased him more.

As he stood, notebook in hand, he heard what he thought was the old man sighing with relief. 'I'm sorry, Harry. I'm sorry I deceived you. You didn't deserve it. But what I did was for your own good. You were making a big mistake, Harry. I had to put that mistake right.'

Harry studied the old man as he spoke. Listened to what he had to say, and how he said it. He sensed the old man was uneasy, nervous. Something wasn't right.

Harry turned his attention back to the safe and its contents.

'Harry, please. Untie me,' urged the old man.

Harry reached in and brought out another bundle of papers. He soon found what he was looking for, what the old man didn't want him to find, hoped and prayed he wouldn't find.

An envelope.

The name and address on the envelope was in shaky, yet beautifully hand written script. Within the envelope was an equally beautifully written letter. Harry instantly recognised the handwriting: it was Lillian's, his mother's. He also had no difficulty recognising the name and address. It was addressed to him... and it had been opened.

Harry skimmed through the letter before carefully folding and replacing it in its envelope, to then also slip it into his jacket pocket.

Harry couldn't quite take in what he'd just read. It contents were brief and vague, almost cryptic. It was dated after his arrest, when his mother's illness would have been at its worst and her strength at its lowest, so it would have taken some effort to write. It had left him bewildered, his emotions in conflict: relief, sadness, anger. Relief that his mother had always believed he was innocent of the crime he'd been jailed for and that she knew with whom the blame lay: his father. *His father?* She had always wanted to tell Harry and Stephen about their parentage, but didn't know how, and the longer she had left it, the harder it had become. She asked for his forgiveness, expressed her love for him and Stephen, and how she hoped they would go on to lead happy and contented lives. She had signed-off the letter, *your loving mother*.

The sadness Harry felt was that his mother wasn't there in person to be able to tell him.

The anger was towards the man sitting not too far away, for having the letter, reading the letter but, more importantly, depriving Harry of peace of mind, of closure.

Harry returned the remaining papers to the safe. He then stood and approached Solomon, his face a mask of stone. To Harry, the old man suddenly looked frail, no longer invincible, and there were tears in his eyes. Harry wasn't sure if they were from fear or regret. 'Why?' he asked, simply.

'I was afraid. Afraid you would leave my employ. We make a good team. I had to take steps. It's not too late, Henry. We can again be a force to be reckoned with. With you at my side, we can dominate London gangland. We can be as strong as the Krays ever were.' The old man looked at Harry, held his gaze, his tired and rheumy eyes imploring. Harry looked away, back to the cooling embers of the fire. Partly because he was afraid he would be drawn back under the old man's spell, but largely because something was tugging at his memory and he couldn't recall what. Something else in the letter...

Father!

Harry's head snapped around, startling the old man. 'The letter mentions my father...' At this, the life seemed to drain from Solomon's body. His shoulders slumped, his head dropped, shaking from side to side in denial. 'You know, don't you? Tell me,' said Harry.

'Henry, please,' replied the old man, indicating his bonds.

'Tell me!' shouted Harry, his anger and frustration taking both him and Solomon by surprise, the old man flinching, eyes flying wide. Harry stepped back, a sense of guilt at a moment's disrespect. 'Tell me,' he said, again, this time quieter but firm.

Solomon stared at Harry, mouth open, blinking, until finally realising, accepting. He seemed to take a breath, and then a second, steadying himself. Then, 'On your birth certificate is the name, Henry James Windsor. Windsor was your birth mother's maiden name. Henry James are also my forenames...' The old man paused.

Harry stared back blankly. His brain seemed to have stopped working. The old man was trying to tell him something, but his head was full of confusion. He couldn't make the connection.

Solomon could see that Harry wasn't making the connection. 'I gave you the name of Henry,' he said, simply.

Harry continued to look blank. The grandfather clock continued to tick, and the old man continued to wait.

Harry was speechless. He was stunned at what he'd just been told. He felt as though his whole world had imploded. That the ground beneath his feet had disappeared. He tried to speak, but no words would come out. He blinked rapidly in an effort to focus, to make sense of what the old man had said. He felt like he'd been hit by an emotional juggernaut.

The old man went on to explain how he'd met Harry's birth mother. How they'd had a brief affair - he was married at the time - she'd then fallen pregnant and intended to keep the baby. Sadly she'd died in labour. He explained that after Harry was named, he was then placed in an orphanage because it was the best thing for everyone. He also told Harry how, a few years later, Lillian had become his mistress. How she'd asked him, begged him, to leave his wife - which he wasn't prepared to do. How she was desperate to have children. How he'd asked and then arranged for Lillian to foster two boys, and how Lillian had then pleaded with him not to involve the boys in his way of life. 'I wanted to tell you. Tried to tell you -'

'Stephen's my... brother?' said Harry, his emotions in conflict and awe at this sudden new-found-family news.

'Half-brother,' Solomon replied. Then, seeing a flare of annoyance in Harry's eyes, '*We* are family, Henry, and family should stick together.'

'And does that include Stephen?'

The old man looked at Harry, and then shook his head. 'I don't think Stephen will fit in with our plans, do you?'

'You're right,' said Harry. 'Family is important. Family should stick together. And will do from now on,' to which the old man smiled. 'And you are also right in that Stephen won't fit... and neither will I.'

'Henry?'

'You have no morals, you have no principles, and you have no respect. You have nothing but greed and the need to manipulate. No more. You're on your own, old man,' said Harry, placing the notebook with names and payments on the desk, open.

An invitation.

'What are you doing, Henry?' asked Solomon.

'I'm going to do something I thought I'd never do. I'm going to phone the police,' he replied, with a smile, as he turned away. Approaching the German Shepherd, he then gently picked the dog up in his arms, and then, with a little difficulty, managed to grasp the leather case from the top of the safe.

'Henry... Harry, you can't leave me this - tied up! The police...'

'You'll be okay. Just lie, you're good at that.'

With that, Harry turned and left the house for what he sincerely hoped would be the very last time.

After adjusting the passenger seat of Izzy's hired Smart Car to accommodate the injured dog, Harry then made a quick and anonymous phone call to the police, from a nearby phone box. Climbing into the car, he looked at the dog and said,

'Hang in there, boy, I know someone who can fix you,' as he turned the key in the car's ignition, the dog watching him with trusting eyes. On hearing the engine start, he then added, 'Cleaning this car of your blood, however, is going to take a serious amount of fixing. In fact, it's probably going to cost Izzy her deposit.' He smiled. 'At least it'll cover the fact she's been smoking in here,' he said, sniffing the air. Turning back to the dog, 'After we get you fixed, I've got a play I need to finish reading to someone special. You're welcome to listen in.'

He then turned on the car radio, tuning it in to a rock station in time to hear GUNS N' ROSES version of 'Sympathy for the Devil'.

A big lazy grin spread across Harry's face.

HARRY'S REVENGE

When an old friend is brutally murdered, Harry is left devastated, angry, and wanting *revenge...*

Harry's Revenge is Andy's follow-up novel to *Harry's Justice* and is due to be released sometime early 2020. If you would like notification of its release date, just go to andywiseman-author.com for an update or to pre-order your signed copy.

ABOUT THE AUTHOR

Andy Wiseman is an 'indie author', which means he relies on social media, word of mouth and readers' reviews to sell his books. This also means it takes time to build a following and become an established name. Until then, Andy continues to work a part-time job while working his way towards becoming a full-time author.

Harry's Justice - which has received critical acclaim - is Andy's debut novel. If you've enjoyed reading it, then help him realise his dream of becoming a full-time author by posting a review on the sites below. A few words are all that is needed.

andywiseman-author.com

Facebook